Welcome to Boston . . .

It was a crude drawing of a house with a sharply pitched roof. At the apex of the roof was a wind vane in the distinctive shape of a rooster. Beneath it, in the attic of the house, was a woman hanging from a rope. Her head was twisted at a grotesque angle by the coil around her throat. Limp arms hung at her sides, her tongue hung out of a gaping mouth, and her dead eyes were rolled back in her head. I read the caption. The name Shepard, scrawled below, had been crossed out and replaced with my name—Shanahan.

"It's a message."

I jumped, startled by the sound of the voice. JoAnn stood behind me.

I said, "What are you talking about?"

"I didn't get it until you showed up." She said, "They must have found out you were coming in tonight."

"Who?"

The union. The boys downstairs are telling you that you may think you're in charge of this place, but you're not. And if you try to be"—she pointed at the drawing—"you're going to end up just like the last one."

"Ellen Shepard killed herself," I said.

"Yeah, right." She gave me a sour smile as she turned to leave. "Welcome to Boston."

HARD LANDING

LYNNE HEITMAN

AN ONYX BOOK

ONYX
Published by New American Library, a division of
Penguin Putnam Inc., 375 Hudson Street,
New York, New York 10014, U.S.A.
Penguin Books Ltd, 27 Wrights Lane,
London W8 5TZ, England
Penguin Books Australia Ltd, Ringwood,
Victoria, Australia
Penguin Books Canada Ltd, 10 Alcorn Avenue,
Toronto, Ontario, Canada M4V 3B2
Penguin Books (N.Z.) Ltd, 182–190 Wairau Road,
Auckland 10, New Zealand

Penguin Books Ltd, Registered Offices:
Harmondsworth, Middlesex, England

First published by Onyx, an imprint of New American Library,
a division of Penguin Putnam Inc.

Advanced Reading Copy Printing April 2001

First Printing, April 2001
10 9 8 7 6 5 4 3

Prologue

Angelo rolled over, reached across his wife, and tried to catch the phone before it rang again. He grabbed the receiver and held it before answering, listening for the sound of her rhythmic breathing that told him she was still asleep.

"Yeah?"

"Angie, get your ass out of bed. You gotta do something for me."

He recognized the voice immediately, but didn't like the tone. "Who's this?"

"Stop screwing around, Angie."

He switched the phone to his other ear and lowered his voice. "What the hell you doin' calling over here this time of the night? You're gonna wake up Theresa."

"I need you to find Petey."

"You gotta be kiddin' me." He twisted around to see the clock radio on his side of the bed. Without his glasses, it took a serious squint to turn the blurry red glow into individual digits. Twelve-twenty, for God's sake, twelve-twenty in the friggin' morning. "I got an early shift and it's raining like a sonofabitch out there. Find him yourself."

"I'm working here, Angie. I can't leave the airport."

"Never stopped you before. Call me tomorrow."

"Don't hang up on me, damn you."

The receiver was halfway to the cradle and Angelo could still hear the yelling. *"Don't you fucking hang up on me!"* But that wasn't what kept him hanging on. *"You owe me. Do you hear me? More than this, you owe me."* It was the desperation—panic even. In the thirty years he'd known him, Big Pete Dwyer had never even come close to losing control.

Angelo pulled the receiver back. With his hand cupped over the mouthpiece, he could smell the strong scent of his wife on it—the thick, sweet fragrance of her night cream mixed with the faintly medicinal smell that seemed to be everywhere in their home these days. "What the hell's the matter with you?"

"If you never do nothing else for me, Angie, you gotta do this thing for me tonight."

The old bedsprings groaned as Theresa turned. When he felt her hand on his knee, he reached down and held it between both of his, trying to warm fingers that were always so cold lately. She was awake now anyhow. "I'm listening."

"He's probably in one of those joints in Chelsea or Revere. There's gonna be some guys out looking for him. I want you to find him first."

"Are you talkin' about cops? Because I ain't gonna—"

"No. Not cops. I can't talk right now."

Big Pete had to raise his voice to be heard, and for the first time Angelo noticed the background noise. Men were shouting, work boots were scraping the gritty linoleum floor, and doors were opening and slamming shut. "What's going on over there?"

"Just do what I tell you."

"What do you want I should do with him? Bring him over to you?"

"Fuck, no. Angie, you're not getting this. Find Petey and stash him somewhere until I finish my shift. Keep him away from the airport, and don't let no one get to him before I do. No one. Do you hear?"

The line went dead. Angelo held the receiver

against his chest until Theresa took it from his hand and hung it up. "What time is it?" she murmured.

"It's twelve-thirty, baby. I gotta go out for a little while."

"Who was that?"

"Big Pete needs me to find his kid."

"Again?"

"Yeah, but this time there's something hinky about it. Something's going on."

"Mmmmm . . ."

He leaned down and kissed his wife on the cheek. "Go back to sleep, babe. I'm gonna take the phone off the hook so nobody bothers you."

The big V-8 engine in Angelo's old Cadillac made the bench seat rumble. He sat with his boot on the brake, shaking the rain out of his hair and waiting for the defroster to kick in. With fingers as cold and stiff as his wife's had been, he tapped the finicky dome light, trying to make it come on. Where the hell were his gloves, anyway, and what was that garbage on the radio? Damn kids with their rap music, if you could even call it music. He punched a button and let the tuner scan for his big band station while he searched his pockets for gloves.

"*. . . with friends and family on that flight are advised to go to the Nor'easter Airlines terminal at Logan Airport, where representatives—*"

Angelo froze. What the hell . . . ? He wanted to turn up the volume, but couldn't get his hand out of his pocket. His heart started to pound as he tried to shake loose and listen at the same time.

"*Again, if you've just joined us, we're receiving word—*"

The scanner kicked in and the rage-filled rant of a midnight radio call-in host poured out. Angelo yanked his hand free, leaned down and, god*dammi*t, cracked his forehead on the steering wheel. Still squeezing the glove in his fist, he jabbed at the tuner buttons until the solemn tones of the newscaster emerged again from the static.

". . . we know so far is that Nor'easter Airlines Flight 1704, a commuter aircraft carrying nineteen passengers and two crew members, has crashed tonight just outside of Baltimore."

Angelo put both hands on the steering wheel to keep them from shaking.

"That flight did depart Logan Airport earlier this evening. The information we have at this hour is that there are no survivors, but again, that report is unconfirmed."

The bulletin repeated as Angelo reached up and used the sleeve of his jacket to wipe the condensation from the windshield. He peered through the streaked glass and up into the black sky. There was nothing to see but a cold, spiteful rain still coming down. But he felt it. He felt the dying aircraft falling to the earth, falling through the roof of the old Cadillac. He felt it falling straight down on him.

Goddamn you, Big Pete. Goddamn you.

Chapter One

When the seat belt sign went out, I was the first one down the jetbridge. My legs wobbled, my muscles ached, and my feet felt like sausages stuffed into leather pumps that had been the right size when we'd boarded six hours earlier. All I wanted to do was get off the airplane, check into my hotel, sink into a hot bath, and forget the five hours in the air, the half hour in a holding pattern, and the interminable twenty-five minutes we'd spent delayed on the ground because, the captain had assured us, our gate was occupied.

The captain had told an airline fib.

When I'd looked out my window and down at the ramp, I'd seen no wingman on my side of the plane, which meant we hadn't been waiting for a gate, we'd been waiting for a ground crew to marshal us in. Hard to imagine. It's not as if we'd shown up unexpectedly. The crew that finally did saunter out was one man short and out of uniform. I made a mental note.

At the bottom of the bridge, the door to the departure lounge was closed. I grabbed the knob and could have sworn it was vibrating. I turned the knob, pushed against the door—and it slammed back in my face. Odd. Behind me, fellow passengers from the flight stomped down the jetbridge and stood, cell phones and carry-ons in hand, blinking at me. I gave it another shot, this time putting my shoulder into it, and pushed through the obstruction, which, to my embarrassment, turned out to be a family of four—mother, father, and two small children. They'd been pinned there by a teeming mob, the size and scope of which became clear when the door swung wide, and the rumble I'd heard became a full-fledged roar.

There must have been a thousand people smashed into the departure lounge, at least twice the number that would be comfortable in that space. Judging by their faces and the combustible atmosphere, they were all supposed to be somewhere besides Logan Airport in Boston. It was Ellis Island in reverse—people trying to get out, not in.

The gate agent who had met our flight was past me before I knew it.

"Excuse me," I said, but my voice evaporated into the crowd noise. I tried again.

"Baggage claim is that way, ma'am." Without bothering to look at me, the agent pointed down the concourse, turned, and vanished into a wall of winter coats.

I stood and watched the current of deplaning passengers flow through the crowd and out to baggage claim, quiet hotel rooms, and hot baths. Technically, I could have joined them. I was anonymous in Boston, and my assignment didn't officially begin until the next day. But in the end, I did as I always did. I worked my way over to one of the check-in podiums, stowed my coat and bag in a closet, clipped on my Majestic Airlines ID, and went to work.

I spotted a senior ticket agent shuttling through the crowd from gate to gate, moving with as much authority as circumstances would allow. When I caught up with her, she was conferring with a young blonde agent at one of the podiums.

"You'll have to wait your turn," she snapped before I ever opened my mouth. "There's a line."

If there was a line at this podium, it was cleverly

disguised as an angry throng. I slipped around the counter and stood next to her. "I'm not a passenger. I'm the new general manager."

She checked my badge, eyes dark with suspicion, thinking perhaps I was an imposter volunteering to be in charge of this mess.

"I'm Alex Shanahan. I came in on the Denver flight."

"The *new* GM? That didn't take long."

"What's the problem here?"

"You name it, we've got it, but basically we're off schedule. Nothing's left on time for the past two hours. In fact, nothing's left at all."

I read her name tag. "JoAnn, maybe I can help. If I could—"

"Are you *deaf*? Or are you *stupid*?"

We both turned to look across the podium at a man who was wearing an Italian suit with a silk tie that probably cost more than my entire outfit. As he berated the younger agent, she stared down at her keyboard, eyes in the locked position.

"Do you *know* how many miles I fly on this airline every year?" He pointed his phone at her and her chin started to quiver. "I *will* not sit in coach, I *will* sit in first class, and you *will* find me a seat if you have to buy someone else off this *goddamn airplane*."

Even in a lounge filled with angry people, this guy was drawing attention. I leaned across the podium so he could hear me. "Can I help you, sir?"

"Who the hell are you?"

I took him aside and listened to his patronizing rant, maintaining eye contact and nodding sympathetically so that he could see my deep concern. When he was finally out of steam, I explained that the situation was extreme and that we might not get him up front this time. I asked him to please be patient and work with us. Then I promised to send him two complimentary upgrades. Frequent fliers respond to free upgrades the way trained seals respond to raw fish. It took a promise of five upgrades, but eventually, with one more parting shot about our "towering display of incompetence," he took my card and my apology and faded away.

I found JoAnn heading for another podium. "At least give me the number to Operations," I said, tagging after her. "I can call the agent there."

She scribbled the number on the back of a ticket envelope and handed it to me. I used my own cell phone and dialed.

"Operations-this-is-Kevin-hold-please." Kevin's Irish accent seemed far too gentle for the situation. When he came back, I told him what I needed.

"Have you talked to Danny about this?"

I plugged a finger in my non-phone ear and turned my back to the crowd. "If he's not standing there with you, Danny's too far away to be in charge right now. I need help now, Kevin. If you can't help me, someone's going to get killed up here."

There was a brief pause, then, "Go ahead."

I spoke to Kevin for five minutes, taking notes, asking questions, and getting advice. When I hung up, the noise, much like the frustration level, was on the rise and JoAnn was contemplating a call to the state troopers. I couldn't see how a couple of big guys with guns and jackboots would calm the waters, so I asked her to wait. I found a functioning microphone, pressed the button, and took a deep breath.

"I'm Alex Shanahan, the general manager for Majestic here at Logan."

The buzz grew louder.

I kicked off my shoes, climbed on top of the podium, and repeated my introduction. When people could see *and* hear me, it made all the difference.

"Ladies and gentlemen, I apologize for the inconvenience of this evening's operation. I know you're uncomfortable and you've had a hard time getting information, so that's where we're going to start. Is anyone out there booked on Flight 497 to Washington, D.C.?" A few hands shot up hopefully. Others followed more hesitantly.

"Your flight was scheduled to depart at 5:15. The aircraft just came in, and the passengers from Chicago are deplaning as I speak at Gate"—I checked my notes—"Forty-four." Heads popped up here and there as people stretched to see the gate. "We can either clean the cabin, or we can get you on board and out of town. How many of you want to leave now?" I had to smile as every hand in the place went up.

"I'm with you, people, but right now I'm asking the passengers booked to D.C. Be prepared, ladies and gentlemen, that the cabin will not be as clean as you're accustomed to on Majestic, but you'll be gone and we'll still be here." As I continued, flight by flight, the noise began to recede, the agents worked the queues, and some semblance of order began to emerge.

Four hours later, at almost ten o'clock, the last passenger boarded. I closed the door and pulled the jetbridge. The agents had either gone to punch out or to other parts of the operation, leaving the boarding lounge as littered and deserted as Times Square on New Year's Day. I was hungry, I was exhausted, I was wired, and I hadn't felt this good in almost eighteen months, not since I'd left the field. There is nothing like an epic operating crisis to get the adrenaline surging.

I went to the closet to retrieve my coat and bag, and in my hyped-up state nearly missed what was tacked to the inside of the closet door. It had been crazy when I'd first opened this door, but even so I would have noticed a sheet of notebook-size paper at eye level—especially this one. I took it down and stared at it. It was a crude drawing of a house with a sharply pitched roof. At the apex of the roof was a wind vane resembling a rooster. Inside the house in the attic, a woman hung from a rope, her head twisted to a grotesque angle by the coil around her throat. Limp arms dangled at her sides, her tongue hung out of a gaping mouth, and her eyes, dead eyes, had rolled back in her head. My adrenaline surge receded and I felt a thickening in my chest as I read the caption. The name Shepard, scrawled below, had been crossed out and replaced with my name—Shanahan.

"It's a message."

I jumped, startled by the sound of the voice, loud and abrupt in the now-deserted terminal. JoAnn stood behind me, arms crossed, dark eyes fixed on the drawing in my hand. "That's part of the message, and tonight's operation was the rest of it."

"What are you talking about?"

"I didn't get it until you showed up," she said, "but now it makes sense. They must have found out you were coming in tonight."

"Who?"

"The union. The boys downstairs are telling you that you may think you're in charge of this place, but you're not. And if you try to be"—she pointed to the drawing in my hand—"You're going to end up just like the last one."

"Ellen Shepard killed herself," I said.

"Yeah, right." She gave me a sour smile as she turned to walk away. "Welcome to Boston."

Chapter Two

"I can see the fucking aircraft from my office, Roger. It's sitting on the apron waiting for a gate. Send someone out there, they can hand the goddamned thing through the cockpit window."

The voice emanated from behind one of two closed doors. It was lean, tough, and rapid-fire, with a boxer's rhythm of quick cuts and clean jabs. I couldn't place the accent exactly, but Brooklyn was a good guess. Whoever it was, he was in early. I'd wanted to be the first one to the office on my first day.

"Roger, listen to me. *Would you listen to me?* We can't wait one more minute. The hospital's been on call for this thing for hours. For all I know, they already got the guy cut open."

The second office, I assumed, had belonged to my predecessor and would now be mine. I tried the knob. Locked. With nothing else to do, I checked out my new reception area. It was a typical back office operation for an airline, a neglected pocket of past history filled with forty-year-old furniture built to last twenty. This one had the extra-added features of being small and cramped. There was a gunmetal gray desk—unoccupied—that held a phone, a ten-key adding machine, a well-used ashtray, and an answering machine, of all things. Behind the desk on the floor was a computer. I could have written WASH ME in the dust on the monitor. The copy machine was ancient, the file cabinets were unlabeled, and the burnt orange chairs and low table that made up the seating area cried out for shag carpet. The whole office was light-years away from the smooth teakwood desks, sleek leather chairs, and turbocharged computers at headquarters in Denver.

I was so glad to be back in the field.

"I'm trying to tell you," thundered The Voice, "you don't *need* a gate for this. There's gotta be somebody around. *Jesus Christ,* Roger, I gotta do *everything* myself?"

The phone slammed, the door flew open, and he was past me, his voice trailing him down the corridor along with echoes of his hurried footsteps. "I'll be with you in a minute. I just gotta go . . . do . . ." And he was gone. I looked into the office he'd just vacated. Sitting quietly in a side chair was an uncommonly spindly young man, probably early twenties, with wavy blond hair, a pale complexion, and long legs covered with white cotton long johns. He wore a tight lime green bicycle shirt that emphasized his narrowness, and a pair of baggy shorts over the long underwear. A praying mantis in Birkenstocks. "Oh, hey," he said when he saw me.

"How are you?" is what I said, when "Who are you" would have worked much better.

"Kidney."

"What?"

"I'm waiting for the kidney," he said. "It was supposed to come in early this morning, but someone at the airlines screwed up. It just got here. I think the dude's going to get it himself."

Something clicked and the alternative dress made sense. "You're a courier."

He nodded. "Working for the hospital."

"Was that Dan Fallacaro?"

"That's what he told me." Something out on the ramp drew his attention. "There he is, man. Cool."

He unfolded himself from the chair and stepped over to the side wall of the office, which was a floor-to-ceiling window onto our ramp operation. Sure enough, the figure that had just about plowed me under was now sprinting across the concrete through the rain toward a B737 idling on the tarmac. He had on a company-issued heavy winter coat, but no hood or hat, and he carried a lightweight ladder. The courier and I stood side by side in the window watching as Dan Fallacaro climbed the ladder, banged on the cockpit window with his fist, then waited, soaked to the bone, to receive a small cooler about the size of a six-pack. He cradled it under his arm as he stepped down and collected his ladder. When he turned to jog, gently, back to the terminal, I saw that he hadn't even taken time to zip his jacket.

"Awesome," said the courier. "I didn't know you could do that."

"Some people wouldn't do that."

The courier checked his watch. Thinking about that fragile cargo, I had to ask, "Are you a bicycle courier?"

"In Boston? You think I'm crazy? I've got a Ford Explorer. See ya."

While I waited for Dan to reappear, I went back to the reception area. When the phone on the reception desk rang, I grabbed it. "Majestic Airlines."

"Hey, Molly . . ." It was a man's voice, strained, barely audible over the muffled whine of jet engines and the sound of other men's voices. "Molly, give Danny a message for me, wouldya?"

"This is not—"

"I can't hear you, Molly. It's crazy down here. Just tell him I got his package on board. I handed it to the captain myself. Make sure you tell him that part, that nobody else saw it."

"Who is this?"

"Who the hell do you think? This is Norm. And

tell him I put her name on the manifest, but not the Form 12A, like he said. He'll know."

Norm signed off, assuming to the end that he'd been speaking to Molly.

The heavy door on the concourse opened and shut, those same hurried footsteps approached, and he was there. Dan Fallacaro in the flesh, out of breath, and *sans* cooler.

"Nice save," I said. "I'd hate to be responsible for the loss of a vital organ on my first day."

"Thanks." He peeled off the wet winter coat. Underneath, his sleeves were rolled up, his tie was at half-mast, and the front of his shirt was damp. It clung to his body, accentuating a chassis that was wiry, built for speed. From what I'd seen, his metabolism was too fast to sustain any spare fat.

"I'm Alex Shanahan," I said, extending my hand.

"I know who you are. I work for you." He wiped a wet palm on his suit pants and gave me a damp, perfunctory handshake. "Dan Fallacaro. How you doing?" Even though he looked past me, not at me, I could still see that he had interesting eyes, the kind that gray-eyed people like me always coveted. They were green, a mossy green that ran to dark brown around the edges of the irises. His phone rang and he shot past me into his office.

I waited at a polite distance until the call ended, then waited a while longer until it was clear he wasn't coming back and he wasn't going to invite me in. I moved just inside his doorway and found him sitting at his desk, drying his face and hands with a paper towel. If he felt any excitement about my arrival, he managed to keep it in check.

"What's the story with the kidney?" I asked.

"It got here late."

"How'd that happen?"

"Somebody in Chicago put it on the wrong flight. Had to be rerouted."

"You didn't have enough gates?"

"Nope."

"Because you're off schedule?"

"Yep."

"How come?"

"Winter."

"Uh-huh. Why'd you have to go get it yourself?"

He unfurled another towel from the roll on his desk and snapped it off. "Because Roger Shit-for-Brains is on in Operations this morning, I can't find my shift supervisor, and even if I could, no one would do what he says." He bent down to wipe off his shoes.

"By any chance, is Norm your shift supervisor?"

He popped up. "Did he call?"

"Just now," I said. "He gave—"

Dan grabbed the phone . . .

"He gave me a message for you."

. . . slammed the receiver to his ear . . .

"Do you want the message?"

. . . started to dial . . .

"The package you asked him to take care of is onboard."

. . . and stopped. "He told you that?"

"He said he put the name on the manifest but left it off the 12A. He handled it personally and no one else saw it."

He hung up the phone slowly, as if relinquishing the receiver would be a sign that he believed me, a sign of good faith he wasn't ready to offer. With one hand he tossed the wet paper towel into the metal trash can, where it landed with a thud. With the other he pulled a comb from his drawer and dragged it haphazardly through his thick, damp hair. "Molly can get you settled in." He raised his voice, *"Mol, you out there?"*

If Molly was within a hundred yards, she would have heard him, but there was no response.

"For chrissakes, Molly, I saw you come in."

A woman's voice floated in. "I told you before, Danny, I wasn't going to answer when you bellowed."

Satisfied, he stood up and began gathering himself to leave. "She can get you set up," he said, grabbing a clipboard and keys from his desk. I could have been the droopy potted plant in the corner for all that I was registering with him.

"We need to talk about last night," I said as he walked out the door.

"What about last night?" he snapped, executing a crisp about-face.

"Since you weren't around and I was, maybe I can brief you."

He folded his arms across the clipboard and held it flat against his chest. "The shift supervisor wasn't answering his radio," he began, accepting the unspoken challenge, "and the cabin service crew chief was AWOL along with everyone else on his crew. No one was cleaning the cabins. The flight attendants wouldn't take the airplanes because they were dirty, and they wouldn't clean 'em themselves because it's not in their contract. The agents were trying to do quick pickups onboard just to get them turned when they should have been working the queues." His words came so fast he sounded like a machine gun. "Chicago was socked in. Miami took a mechanical, and there was only one functioning microphone which you used to make announcements while standing on top of the podium at Gate Forty-two."

"You didn't mention that I was barefoot."

"It's not because I didn't know." He had enough self-control not to actually sneer, but he couldn't do much about his brittle tone.

"And you didn't mention the hundreds of inconvenienced passengers, all of whom were jammed into the departure lounge screaming for blood. I thought we were going to have to offer up one of the agents as a human sacrifice."

His grip on the clipboard tightened. "What's your point?"

"My point is that the operation last night was a complete disaster, and there was some indication that it was all orchestrated for my benefit—some kind of 'Welcome to Boston' message from the union."

"Who told you that?"

"It doesn't matter. I'm now in charge of this place, you are my second in command, and I think we should talk about this. I want to understand what's going on."

"Last night is handled."

"What's handled?"

"I spoke to the shift supervisor about not answering his radio. As far as the crew chief on cabins, I've got a disciplinary hearing scheduled for Thursday. He was off the field. I know he was, everybody knows he was, but no one's going to speak up, much less give a statement, so I'll put another reprimand in his file, the union will grieve it, and you'll take it out. End of story."

"Is that how things work around here, or are you making a prediction about me?"

"I need to get to work," he said. "Is there anything else?"

"Could we . . . do you mind if we sit down for a minute? I'm having a hard time talking to the back of your head."

His jaw worked back and forth, his green eyes clouded over, and his deep sigh would have been a loud groan if he'd have given it voice. But he moved back behind his desk, immediately found a pencil, and proceeded to drum it against the arm of his chair.

I closed the door and settled into the seat across

from him. "Dan, are you this rude, abrupt, and patronizing with everyone? Or is this behavior a reaction to me specifically? Or maybe you're unhappy with someone else, Roger-Shit-for-Brains, for example, and taking it out on me." I thought of another option. "Or maybe you're just an asshole."

His reaction was so typically male it was hard not to smile. He looked stunned, flabbergasted, as if my annoyance was totally unprovoked. Who, me?

"Why would I be mad at you? I don't even know you."

"Exactly my point. Most people have to get to know me before they truly dislike me."

He stared for a few seconds, then laid the pencil on his desk, and rubbed his eyes with the heels of his hands. When he was done, I noticed for the first time how thoroughly exhausted he looked. His eyeballs seemed to have sunk deeper into their sockets, his face was drawn, and his cheeks were hollowed out as if he hadn't had a hot meal or a good night's sleep in a week.

That's when I got it.

"You're upset about the ashes, aren't you?" He fixed those dark green eyes on me in a tired but riveting gaze. "The ones Norm handled for you."

"Goddamn him—" He was up on his feet and ready to go after Norm, and I knew I was right.

"Norm didn't tell me."

"Then who did?"

"I figured it out myself. Form 12A is a notification of human remains onboard. He said he put the box in the cockpit and not in the belly, so I have to assume the remains weren't in a coffin. And since your boss hung herself last week—"

"Last Monday. She died last Monday night."

"So another reason you might be this angry and upset is that you and Ellen Shepard were friends and

I've walked in on a particularly difficult time because today is the day you're shipping her ashes home."

He sank back into his chair, dropped his head back, and closed his eyes. He looked as if he never wanted to get up again.

"Why all the mystery? Why not put her name on the manifest?"

"Because I didn't want the scumbags downstairs stubbing out cigarettes in her ashes."

"Tell me you're exaggerating."

"We're talking about the same guys who screwed over almost a thousand passengers last night just to send a 'fuck you' message."

I sat back in my chair, and felt my excitement about the new job and being back in the field drain away.

"I should have been here," he said, his head still back, eyes glued to the ceiling. "But I had to—I just should have been here."

He didn't actually say it, but that sounded as close to an apology as I was going to get. "I'm sorry about Ellen, Dan."

"Did you know her?"

"No."

His head popped up. "Then why would you be sorry?"

"Because you knew her."

This time when he bolted up, I couldn't have stopped him if I'd tackled him.

"Debrief is at 0900 sharp," he said, throwing the door open. "It's your meeting if you want it."

I sat and listened one more time to the sound of his footsteps fading down the long corridor. The door to the concourse opened and closed, and I knew he was gone. Eventually, I pulled myself up and went out to meet my new assistant.

"Don't take it personally," she said when she saw me. "He's that way with everyone."

Molly had a flop of dark curls on her head, big brown eyes, and full red lips that occupied half her face. Her olive complexion suggested Hispanic blood, or maybe Portuguese, this being Massachusetts. She was probably in her late fifties, but her dainty stature made her seem younger. She was thin, almost bird-like, but judging from the hard lines around her eyes and the way she'd spoken to Dan, she was more of a crow than a sparrow. At least she had a voice like one.

She squinted at me. "You're the new GM."

"And you're Molly."

"Danny's been a little upset these past few days."

"Judging from my first"—I checked my watch—"fifteen hours in this operation, he's got good reason."

She leaned back in her chair, crossed her legs, and took a long, deep sideways drag on a skinny cigarette, all the time looking me up and down like girls do in junior high when they're trying to decide who to be seen with in the school cafeteria. She might not have been inside a junior high school for over thirty years, but she still had the attitude.

"So they sent us another woman," she said, eyebrows raised.

"Apparently."

With a swish of nylon on nylon she rose from the chair and sidled around to my side of her desk. It's possible I'd passed muster, but more likely she couldn't resist a golden opportunity to dish.

"He found her, you know."

"Who?"

"Ellen."

"Dan found Ellen's body?"

"When she didn't come in that morning, he's the one who drove up to her house. She was in the attic." Molly reached around to the ashtray on the desk behind her and did a quick flick. "When he found her, she'd been hanging there all night."

I reached up instinctively and put a hand on my own throat, which was tightening at the thought of what a body looks like after hanging by the neck for that long. With my thumb, I could feel my own blood pumping through a thick vein. "It must have been horrible for him. Were they friends?"

She nodded as she exhaled. "He won't talk about it, but, yeah, he hasn't been the same since. Like I said, we don't take it personally." She reached behind the desk again and opened a drawer, this time coming back with a big, heavy ring chock full of keys. "I'll let you into your office."

She went to the door, and I stood back and watched her struggle with the lock.

"How's everyone else around here taking it?" I asked. "What's the mood?"

"Mixed. People who liked her are upset. People who didn't are glad she's gone. It's that simple. More people liked her than didn't, but the ones that didn't hated her so much, it made up for all the rest."

"Mostly guys down on the ramp, I hear. Not the agents."

She nodded. "You showing up the way you did last night and doing what you did, that's given them all something else to talk about. Everyone's waiting to see what you're like, what you're going to do about Little Pete." The lock was not releasing and she was getting frustrated.

"Who's Little Pete and why is he 'Little'?"

"Pete Dwyer Jr. He's the missing crew chief, the one who caused all that trouble last night. Most of it, anyway. Everyone calls him Little Pete because his pop works here, too. Big Pete runs the union."

"I thought Victor Venora was president of the local."

"Titles don't mean much here. And they have nothing to do with who's got the real power."

"And who would that—"

With a final, forceful twist, the door popped open. *"Cripes!"* Molly jerked her hand away as if it had been caught in a mousetrap. "I broke a nail. Damn that lock." She took the mound of keys, marched back to her desk, presumably for emergency repairs, and called back over her shoulder, "Go in. I'll be with you in a minute."

The door swung open easily at my touch. The office was slightly larger than Dan's. Instead of one floor-to-ceiling window on the ramp-side wall, it had two that came together at the corner. Unlike Dan's office, the blinds were closed, filtering out all but a few slats of daylight that fell across the floor like bright ribbons. The air smelled closed-in, faintly musty. In the middle of the space, dominating in every way, was a massive, ornate wooden desk. Its vast work surface was covered with a thick slice of glass. Underneath was a large, carved logo for . . . *Nor'easter* Airlines?

"Some desk, huh?" Molly leaned against the door-jamb with a new cigarette.

"It looks out of place," I said, walking over to open the blinds.

"It belonged to the president of our airline."

"Our airline" was how former Nor'easter employees always referred to their old company, which had teetered at the precipice of bankruptcy until Bill Scanlon, the chairman and CEO of Majestic, *our* airline, had sailed in and saved the day. As a result, Scanlon was revered by most Nor'easterners. It was the rest of us Majestic plebeians they resented.

I didn't tell her that no one at Majestic headquarters would have been caught dead with a desk like that. It didn't match the corporate ambiance, which was simple, spare, and, above all, featureless.

When I pulled the blinds, the sun splashed in on a linoleum floor that was wax-yellow and dirty. The corner where I was standing was covered with a strange white residue, almost like chalk dust. It reminded me of rat poison. The morning light brought grandeur to the old desk, showing polish and detail I hadn't noticed. I also hadn't noticed the single palm print now clearly visible in the dust that coated the glass top.

"Has anyone been in here since Ellen died?"

"Danny and I were both in here looking through her Rolodex for someone to contact. Turns out an aunt in California was her closest living kin. If you need anything, it's probably in there"—she pointed with her cigarette at the desk—"supplies and all. Ellen was pretty organized that way." She turned to go and caught herself. "Oh, I should warn you, don't keep anything important in there. It doesn't lock anymore."

"Is it broken?"

"You could say that." She moved into the office and perched on the arm of one of the side chairs.

I walked around to the working side of the desk. The handsome wood facings of the drawers were scarred and scratched around the small locks, and the top edges were splintered and broken where someone had pried them open. I put my finger into a sad, gaping hole where one of the locks was missing altogether. "What happened here?"

"The union."

"The union broke into this desk? Why?"

"Just to prove they could."

That was a comforting thought. I stood up and looked at her. "What did Ellen do that had them so upset?"

"Well, let's see. She was a woman, she was from Majestic, and she wanted them to work for their wages instead of sitting around on their butts all day. That's three strikes."

I slipped the hangman's drawing out of my briefcase. I felt a tingling in my neck when I looked at it.

I handed her the page. "Have you ever seen this before?"

"Not that version. Where did you get it?"

"Someone left it for me last night as some kind of a message."

She shook her head. "That didn't take long. I guess they figure they'll start early with you, keep you on the defensive from the start."

"It means they knew I was coming in on that flight."

"No doubt."

"And they saw where I'd put my bags, which wouldn't have been easy in all that chaos. Someone was watching me."

She shot a stream of smoke straight up, and handed the drawing back. "They're always watching."

I followed the smoke as it drifted up to the ceiling. This was apparently old hat to Molly, but I found it hard not to feel just a little shaken up by a drawing of a woman hanged by the neck with my name on it.

Molly stood to go.

"Did someone steal her pictures, too?" I asked.

She looked where I was looking, at the bare walls. "This office is exactly the way she left it," she said. "She never hung any pictures."

"How long was she here?"

"Almost thirteen months."

The walls were painted an uncertain beige, and had scars left over from previous administrations, where nails and picture hangers had been torn out. I walked over and touched a big gouge in the Sheetrock where the chalky center was pushing through.

"She didn't leave much behind, did she?"

Chapter Three

Molly was putting the call on hold just as I walked through the door.

"How was your first debrief?"

"Long."

"You've got a call on line one," she said, "and it must be important because he never waits on hold and he never calls this early."

I checked my watch. It was ten o'clock in the morning. "Who is it?"

"Your boss."

"Uh-oh." The quick flash of nerves was like a caffeine rush. "Where's he calling from?"

"He's in his office in D.C."

She said something else, but I didn't hear what because I was already at my desk, bent over the notes I'd made from debrief, cramming for whatever question Lenny might think to ask about last night's operation. Someone I admired and deeply respected once told me that the best opportunities to make a good impression come from disaster—from how well you handle it. Last night certainly qualified as a disaster, and I was about to test that theory on my new boss.

After a quick moment to gather my thoughts, I made myself sit down, then picked up the receiver. "Good morning, Lenny. How are you?" Jeez, I sounded like such a stiff.

"Very well, Alex. And how you doin' this morning?" His deliberate Louisiana drawl sounded as if it were floating up from the bottom of a trash can, and I knew he had me on the speaker phone. I hated speaker phones. You could be talking to a crowd the size of Yankee Stadium and never know it.

"I'm well, Lenny, thank you."

"Can we talk about a few things this morning?"

"Of course." I heard the whisper of pages turning and imagined him leafing through his tour reports, zeroing in on Boston's, and reading with widening eyes about the debacle from last night. But I was ready, poised to jump on whatever he chose to ask.

"So . . ."

I waited, muscles tensed.

". . . when did you get in?"

"Last night."

"Good trip out?"

"Uh, yes. The trip was fine."

"Glad to hear it."

The pages continued to turn. I inched a little farther out on the edge of my seat, straining to hear, waiting for the real questions to start. And waiting. And . . . and . . . I couldn't wait. "Lenny, we had a few problems in the operation last night. I don't know if you saw the tour report, but—"

"Was it anything you couldn't handle?"

"No, we handled it. It was—"

"Good. Listen, I need to ask you to do something for me."

Not exactly the grilling I'd anticipated. The paper rustled again and this time the sound was more distinct, a slow, lazy arc that I recognized. Lenny wasn't leafing through tour reports. He was reading a newspaper. I eased back in my chair and relaxed. No pop quiz today. Disappointing, in a way. "What can I do to help?"

After a short pause I heard a click, and I knew he'd

taken me off the speaker phone. "You've got a ramper up there, an Angelo DiBiasi. Have you heard this story?" Without the squawk box his voice had an instantly intimate quality. The rest of the world was shut out. Only I could hear what he was saying.

"No, I haven't heard the story."

A group of ticket agents, talking and laughing, burst into the reception area and greeted Molly. I rolled my chair backward across the floor until I could reach the door and launch it shut.

Lenny was still talking. "He's one of the night crawlers, works midnights. I knew him when I was there. You knew I used to work in Boston, right? Before I came to D.C.?"

"I did." He'd mentioned it no less than six times during my interview.

"Anyway, old Angie's gotten himself into a little trouble."

"What did he do?"

"Damned if I can tell. He may have been in the wrong place at the wrong time regarding a cargo shipment"—which meant he was stealing—"but I feel bad about terminating a guy with over forty years in, I don't care what he did."

Forty years? I was used to stations out West, where twenty years was a lot of seniority. "What's his status?"

"Fallacaro fired him, he filed for arbitration, and now he's waiting for his hearing. But Angie's not a bad guy. You have far worse up there, and the thing is, his wife is sick. He's sixty-three years old. It could take up to a year to get his case heard, and I'd prefer not to put the two of them through it."

The group outside was getting louder, and I had to pay close attention. I could hear what he was saying, but what I needed to know was what he wasn't saying, and I had the sense that there was a lot. "If Angelo's on to arbitration, that means Ellen denied his grievance."

"Yes. Yes, she did and I can understand why. Ellen needed to establish herself as the authority there. But you don't have that situation. You've got much more field experience than she did, and now that you're sitting in the general manager's chair, it's perfectly legitimate for you to overturn the firing. As you know, I can't get involved until after arbitration."

When I didn't respond, I felt Lenny trying to read my silence. He wanted me to simply agree to do what he'd asked, but it was hard when I didn't know the players. Overturning a firing was a big deal. It would send a strong message about me to all of the people who worked in the station. I wanted to make sure it was a message I wanted to send.

"You still there, Alex?"

"Sorry, Lenny. I'm still here."

"Have you had a chance to hook up with Victor Venora?"

"He's on my list, but I haven't gotten to him yet."

"Here's an idea for you," he offered, his tone brightening considerably. He was taking a new tack. "You set a meeting with Victor, a president-of-the-local-GM-get-acquainted sit-down, and the first thing you do before he even opens his big mouth is tell him you're bringing Angie back. Start right in with a gesture of goodwill to the union. You'll knock his socks off."

I swiveled in my chair so that I could see out the window, looking for breathing room. Lenny was closing me in. I tried to decide if I was being crafty and shrewd or obstinate and stubborn. Sometimes they felt the same to me. What I knew was that he wanted me to commit to a deal without even knowing what this guy Angelo did and he wanted me to do it without making him ask explicitly, in which case it would for-

ever be my idea. It didn't sound that risky and I had
no reason to distrust Lenny, but I'd also been burned
by bosses in the past for agreeing to far less.

I had to go with crafty and shrewd.

"Lenny, stealing is automatic grounds for termination, and—"

"I never said he was stealing."

No, he hadn't. But he'd just given me the way out.
"You're absolutely right. You didn't say that, and it's
clear that I need to gather some facts so that I'm more
prepared to discuss this with you. I hope you don't
mind if I take a day or so to do a little research. I'd
like to talk to Dan, since he's the one who fired him."

We either had a pregnant pause or he was still reading the newspaper and checking out the sale at Bar-
ney's. I waited through his long exhale, and I could
feel the test of wills making the phone line stiffen. I
started to worry. This was my new boss, after all.

"I apologize, Alex."

"Excuse me?"

"I really do. Now that I think about it, I see that
I'm putting you in a tough spot. I know you have to
get your feet on the ground, and I know what a tough
bunch you've got up there. I'm just trying to give you
some ideas because I want you to do well, that's all.
Take your time, gather some facts, and see if you
don't agree with me on this Angelo situation. But
whatever you decide, it's your call."

I was feeling less crafty by the second. How hard
would it be to do what I was asked for once in my life?
"I'll look into it right away," I said, and I meant it.

He hung up, leaving me squarely on the side of
obstinate and stubborn.

The crowd of agents was gone when I opened the
door. I signaled to Molly, who was just finishing a
phone call, then went back to my desk and waited.

When she came in, she was reattaching an enormous clip earring to her phone ear.

"What's up?" she asked.

"What did Angelo DiBiasi do?"

"He stole a thirty-six-inch color TV set. Tried to, anyway."

My heart began to sink. "There's no chance of a mix-up or misunderstanding? No question about what happened?" *No possible grounds for overturning his termination?*

"The only question is how Angie could be so stupid. Danny caught him loading it into his car. He fired him on the spot because it was theft and theft—"

"—is automatic grounds for dismissal. I know. What's wrong with his wife?"

"Breast cancer. She had it once, and now she's got it again." Molly turned glum. "Poor Theresa," she sighed. "Seems like she's been sick forever."

My heart went right ahead and sank.

Chapter Four

The afternoon shift had already begun by the time I finally made my way downstairs to meet Kevin, the operations agent who had been so helpful the night before. Compared to the bright, soaring spaces reserved for paying customers, little attention is paid to employee-only areas at an airport. For the most part, the spaces down below were rabbit warrens, and this one was no exception. Graffiti covered the walls, trash overflowed the bins, and flattened cigarette butts littered the concrete floor. A door left open somewhere let in a cold draft that carried the smell of jet fumes in to mingle with the bitter aroma of burned coffee.

Kevin was on the other side of a door with a window labeled OPERATIONS. He stared at his monitor, with a phone balanced on one shoulder and a radio clutched in his other hand. He looked as capable and businesslike as he had sounded. When I saw that he probably had a few years in, I wasn't surprised. The Operations function is Darwinian—survival of the calmest.

When he heard me come in, he nodded in my direction and kept talking into the radio. "We need to hold that gate open for the DC-10. It's on final."

I couldn't make out the response, but whoever was talking sounded confused. Kevin wasn't. "Because it's the only gate I've got left that will take a 'ten. Everything else is narrow-body only."

While I waited, I reacquainted myself with an Ops office. This one, rectangular and about ten paces long, had what they all had—weather machines, printers of every kind, monitors, radios, phones, and file cabinets. It also had a bank of seven closed-circuit TV monitors. According to the labels, there was one camera for each of the six gates, Forty through Forty-five, and one for Forty-six—a slab of bare concrete used for the commuter operation, which was ground-loaded, no jetbridge. On the wall was a picture of our leader, the Chairman and CEO of Majestic Airlines. It was a black-and-white head shot that wouldn't have been out of place if this were 1961 and it was hanging next to an eight-by-ten glossy of John F. Kennedy. He stared out at me, and I stared back, knowing how insulted the great Bill Scanlon would be to hang in such a cheap plastic frame. I tried not to linger over the photo, to look away, to move on. But I hadn't been able to move on for the better part of the last year.

Normally, the only thing that makes the end of a relationship bearable is that many of the painful reminders of the person you are trying to stop loving can be removed from your life. You can throw away pictures, burn letters, and give all those books he gave you to the used bookstore. But as long as I worked for this airline, Bill Scanlon would always be gazing down from the wall in some office, reminding me of the way he used to look at me. Or I would come across his signature on a memo and remember the way his hand used to feel resting lightly on my hip. His imprint on this company—indeed, on the entire industry—was so broad and deep, I would never really get away from him. After all, he was, according to *BusinessWeek,* "The Man Who Saved the Airlines." Looking at the image of his face, I felt what I had felt almost from the first day without him in my life. I missed him.

Kevin finished his call and stood to greet me, bending slightly at the waist and extending his hand in a gesture that felt oddly formal given the setting. "Welcome to Boston, Miss Shanahan. Kevin Corrigan, at your service."

I shook his hand. "Call me Alex."

"Thank you, I shall with pleasure." The glint in his clear blue eyes suggested a wry intelligence, and the Irish accent I'd heard over the radio was even more charming in person.

"You saved the operation last night, Kevin. But don't tell anyone because I'm getting all the credit."

"As well you should." He sat back in his chair and swung around to face his computer, raising his voice to accommodate for having his back to me. "It's good of you to come down. Usually I toil in complete obscurity, unless someone wants to yell or complain. In that case," he chuckled, "I'm far too accessible. How are you settling in?"

"Good. I'm over at the Harborside Hyatt until I get a chance to look for a place."

"Doesn't sound too homey."

"Based on what I saw last night, I need to be close to the airport for a while. I'm hoping that was the worst of it, that it can only get better."

"Not necessarily, but that's why you're here, isn't it?" He swung around and grinned at me, eyebrows dancing. "After all, you did ask for this assignment."

"How did you know that?"

"Everyone knows. In fact"—he reached over to rip something off the printer—"everyone knows everything about you."

My neck stiffened as I thought about the hangman's drawing in the closet last night. I didn't think I wanted everyone to know everything about me, particularly where I was at all times, but I was hoping that's not what Kevin meant. "I'd be really embarrassed if everyone knew my shoe size."

"Shall I give you the rundown?"

I rested my hips against the long work counter that served as his desk. "Give it to me straight."

"You've been with the company fourteen years, all on the Majestic side. You started out as an airport agent and worked your way up from there. You've lived and worked in a dozen different cities. Somewhere along the way you managed an MBA by going to night school. You've spent the past eighteen months at headquarters getting staff experience. That done, you're on a fast track to VP, maybe even to be the first woman vice president in the field."

I secretly loved hearing that last part. "You should write my résumés. Who's the detective?"

"There are no secrets here. One day someone knows. Before long everyone knows, and then it's as if we've always known."

"So I'm finding out." I pulled down a clipboard hanging on a nail and checked out the tour report. I hadn't seen a tour report in the entire eighteen months I'd been in headquarters, so now I was taking every chance to look at one, to remind myself that I was back in the field, and every time I did, it gave me a little boost. It was like hearing a favorite old song that comes on the radio after a long absence and being reminded of how much you liked it. This evening looked more promising than last—skies were clear, at least for now, all equipment was in service, and no crew chiefs were on the sick list. I hung the clipboard back on its nail and drifted back over to the window, a chest-high rectangle that ran the length of the office.

Directly outside, two rampers were loading bags onto a belt loader and up into the belly of the aircraft. Their movements were slow, disinterested. Not far away was a cluster of carts and tractors painted in Majestic's deep purple colors. Paint was peeling, windows were cracked, and parking was confused and disorderly. In the distance, Delta's operation gleamed. Even from where I stood, their safety markings and guidelines in reflective white and yellow paint were bright and visible. Every piece of equipment was in its proper place, and everyone was in uniform. I turned back into the office. "What's going on around here, Kevin?"

"I beg your pardon?"

"Crew chiefs are walking off their shifts, Dan Fallacaro looks as if he's just stepped out of his own grave—"

"Don't blame Danny. He's a good man and it's not his fault. He's the best operating man around."

"I'd like to think so, but to put it kindly, he's been a little hard to pin down. Everyone is whispering, no one is doing any work, this place is a mess, and no one here seems to notice."

"No one does notice. We're all accustomed to it."

"Are you saying this is normal?" I walked around so that I could see his face because it looked as if . . . he *was*. He was smiling. "Did I say something funny?"

He glanced up from his screen. "Oh, no, I'm sorry. It's just that you sound like all the rest when they first get here. People who come into this operation from the outside are always shocked and amazed. Don't worry, it will wear off."

"I don't want it to wear off. I'd rather fix the problems." Jeez, was I really that pompous and self-important? "All I'm saying is—"

"I know what you're saying. What Ellen found out and what you will, too, is that nobody wants this place fixed or else it would have been done a long time ago. The game is rigged."

"I don't believe that."

"You will."

"Maybe it was true during the Nor'easter years, but the merger makes it a new game with new rules."

"That's what Ellen thought, too," he said.

"Maybe Ellen Shepard wasn't the right person for the job. The field is a whole different story than staff, and she had no operating experience. Everyone in the field wondered how she even got this job. And we all resented her for getting it, at least until she killed herself."

"It would be nice to think that, wouldn't it? That she succumbed to the pressures of the job?"

"I've heard that the pressures were pretty intense."

"No doubt about that. I came to work one day and the freight house was on fire. A week later, all of the computer monitors in the supply room were smashed to smithereens. One night a full twenty-five percent of the entire midnight shift called in sick. And you couldn't keep track of all the stuff that was stolen off this field. Worse than that, she was getting phone calls at home, threats and warnings of a personal nature." He shook his head. "Terrible stuff. Very sad if you liked the woman, which I did." The phone rang and he paused before picking it up. "Ellen Shepard wasn't under pressure, she was under siege."

I'd stared out the window long enough, so this time I checked out the bulletin board. Most of what was up there was old enough to have turned yellow and curled at the edges. Kevin finished his call.

"All this harassment," I said, "was because she was trying to change around a few shifts and cut overtime?"

"Ellen Shepard is not dead because she tried to cut overtime, and it's not because of any personal problems she may have been having. That's just the convenient party line. Her problems were all right down here on the ramp. One of them in particular just got the better of her that night, that's all."

"Which one?"

"Can't say."

"Why not?"

"I keep my beliefs to myself," he said. "That's the secret to my longevity."

"Don't tell me you're one of the conspiracy theorists."

His expression didn't change.

"That is an absurd rumor," I said, with a little more passion than necessary. "The police ruled Ellen's death a suicide. And besides, if Ellen was murdered by one of her employees, what possible motive would the company have to cover it up?"

"I've been at Logan a long time," he said, "long enough to know that every rumor has some seed of truth, no matter how small."

There was just enough calm rationalism in his tone to unnerve me. If I believed he knew how to optimize gates and which aircraft to dispatch and when, why wouldn't I believe him about this? "You're really starting to disturb me, Kevin."

"You should be disturbed." He stood up, walked over to the closed door, and mashed his cheek against the glass window, peering first to the left and then to the right. He came back to me and whispered in a tone that was urgent and serious. "This is not a safe place, especially for a woman, and if no one told you that, they should have." The twinkle had gone out of his eye. "Don't try to take on the union. Don't try to be a hero, and don't expect to make your career in this place. Just put in your time and get out in one piece. That's the best advice I can give you."

Then he turned around and went back to work as if the conversation had never happened.

I went to the window and watched the rampers working their flight. The sky, still clear, was already darkening in the early winter afternoon. I saw more winter gear on the ramp. Heavier coats. Gloves. It was getting colder, and I wrapped my arms tightly around me to keep from shivering. Low clouds were gathering in the western sky and I wondered, if I were outside, could I smell snow coming?

Chapter Five

Dan was already working when I arrived the next morning. I stood in the back of the ticketing lobby and watched through the crowd of passengers as he checked bags and issued boarding passes. He was doing it just right, moving them through like cattle at auction, but somehow making each cow feel special, as if they were the only one in the chute.

When I moved behind the counter, I spotted Dan's briefcase on the floor along with a pile that turned out to be his overcoat and suit jacket. He hadn't made it to his office yet.

"Anything I can do to help here?" I asked.

"I think we've got it covered," he said, poking at his keyboard with two fingers.

"I'm on my way to the office. Do you want me to take your coat and jacket?"

"They've been in worse places." He beckoned the woman who was next in line.

"Okay." All I could do was try. "When you're finished here, I'd like to talk to you about a few things. How much longer do you think you'll be?"

He stepped up into the bag well and gauged the length of his line. "Fifteen minutes."

I checked his line, too, and it looked like a good thirty minutes to me. "When you're finished, meet me down on the concourse for coffee," I said. "I'll buy."

Dan greeted his next passenger while I walked

down the length of the counter, greeting the morning shift as I went, trying to tie names to faces and get to know my new employees.

Forty-five minutes later, Dan was sitting across the table from me at the Dunkin' Donuts, turning a black cup of coffee blond with five packets of sugar and two plastic tubs of cream.

"You should take up smoking," I said. "It would be better for you."

"We're all going to die sometime." As he took a sip, his eyes scanned the concourse like radar for any problem that might need his immediate attention. His plan seemed to be to give everyone and everything except me his close attention.

"I want to know what's going on around here."

"Say again?"

"I think you heard me."

"I heard you, but I have no idea what you're referring to."

"You do know, and this thing you're doing right now, this deflecting, it's annoying as hell. It'd be easier if you would just answer the question."

He chewed on the plastic stirrer and, in his own good time, turned slightly in his chair, enough that I could claim a small measure of progress.

"I spent time yesterday talking to some of my new employees," I said, leaning closer so that I wouldn't have to raise my voice. "Half of them believe that Ellen Shepard was murdered by someone who works downstairs on the ramp. Almost all of them think that you've gone off the deep end since her suicide."

"What's that supposed to mean?"

"That you're out of touch, disappearing, not answering your beeper. They can't find you when they need you. Last night's a good example."

He started to get agitated, but then clamped down as if he didn't want me to see his reaction. As far as

I could tell, he didn't want me to know anything about him. "People are going to think what they're going to think," he said coolly, "and no one needs to worry about me."

"All right. Let's not worry about you. Let's talk about the operation. This whole place is paralyzed by rumors about Ellen Shepard, and almost no one believes she killed herself."

His eyes narrowed. "And why do you think that is?"

"Because no one is talking to them. No one is giving them the facts and answering their questions. In the absence of the truth, they're going to think the worst."

"And you know what the truth is?"

"I know the police investigated, ruled the death a suicide, and closed their investigation. I know she was found hanging in her home, and I know that you're the one who found her after she'd been there all night. I also know that she was your friend."

He was angled back, still chewing on the stirrer. He was wearing an enigmatic little smile and shaking his head, the message being that I would never get it.

"If there's more to it, why don't you tell me?"

"You want to know the rest of it?" The smile faded. "Ellen died a week ago. Since then not one representative of Majestic Airlines outside of this station has done one thing to pay their respects. No flowers, no phone calls, no letters or cards. Not from Lenny or goddamned Bill Scanlon. Just a whole bunch of cover-their-ass questions." He almost knocked over his coffee and made a great save before slumping back in his chair. "The first thing we heard from outside the station was you showing up from headquarters to take her place."

"I'm not from headquarters. I've spent eighteen months there out of fourteen years. I've got as much field experience as you do."

"Whatever."

"Is that what's going on here? Do you resent me because you think you should have gotten this job?"

"I wouldn't take the job if they begged me."

"Is it because I came from staff?" That was my last guess. I wasn't going to play twenty questions trying to figure out what his problem was.

"All I know is you're on the fast track," he said, "and I'm going to be in Boston forever. So it doesn't matter to me. You understand?"

"No."

"You can take all the credit when things go well, you can blame me when they go wrong. I don't care about my career. I don't care about getting promoted. What I do care about is being left alone to do my job the way I need to. Just because I'm not out where people can see me all the time doesn't mean I'm not doing my job. And the next time you want to know something about me, ask me and not my employees."

Dan's name boomed from the loudspeakers. Before they could even finish paging him, he was on his feet gathering up all the dead sugar packets and heading for the trash.

"Dan, if you walk away from me like you did yesterday, it's going to make me angry, which might not make any difference to you, but it will ruin my entire day because I'm going to have to spend it trying to figure out how to deal with you." He stood with the trash in one hand, his cup in the other, staring down the concourse toward the gates. "I don't want to *deal* with you." I said, backing off a little, "I want to *work* with you."

He tapped his chair a few times with his free hand. He didn't sit down, but neither did he walk away.

"Losing a friend in the way that you did has got to be tough. If there is anything I can do to make it easier for you, I will do it."

"I'll deal with it."

"Fine. While you're dealing with it, think about this. Do you want to work with me? If you don't, we'll discuss alternatives."

His hand grew still on the back of the chair. "I'm not leaving here."

"That's not what I asked you to think about. Do you want to work next to me? That's the question and I want a definitive answer."

"I'm not leaving Boston," he said flatly, then stalked over to toss his garbage. He came back and said it again, just in case it wasn't clear. "There's no way I'm leaving Boston. And if you and this fucking company try to get rid of me the way you did Ellen, I'm going to blow the whistle on what's going on around here, so help me God."

He turned quickly and he was gone. He must have spotted the confused elderly woman as we were talking because he went straight for her. He read her boarding pass, offered his arm, and helped her to her gate. Then without looking back, he melted into the river of passengers, gliding smoothly through the crowd, weaving in and out until I couldn't see him anymore.

He'd disappeared on me again, leaving me to sort through a whole bunch of responses I never had a chance to give, and one big question. What exactly *was* going on around here?

Chapter Six

Molly was long gone by the time I made it back to my office, and Dan had been cagey enough to get through the rest of the day yesterday and all day today without bumping into me once. There had been Dan-sightings all over the airport, but I never managed to catch up with him. I sat down at my desk to try to find the bottom of my in-box.

I dispensed with the mail from headquarters—the usual warnings, threats, and recriminations disguised as reports, memos, and statistics—putting it aside to ignore later. I reviewed the station performance report from Dan, which said we were over budget and under-performing. No kidding. And I drafted a perfunctory response to a perfunctory question from Lenny asking why that was. Most of what was left was from the suspense file, things that Ellen Shepard had reviewed and filed for later handling. Many of the documents had her handwritten notes in the margins. Her hand-writing was careful, neat, and very controlled. You could have used it to teach cursive writing to school-children. Halfway through the stack, I began to get a sense of her, to hear her voice. She spoke a language we shared, the language of work.

You could tell by her questions that she was new to an operation. She had lots of them—questions about the equipment, manning, about why we do things the way we do, about people who worked for her and how much things cost and why. Her inexperience showed, but so did her doggedness. When she hadn't gotten a thorough answer, she'd simply asked again. And judging from her correspondence with the union, she didn't back down. She may have been a staff person and she may have taken a good field assignment away from someone more qualified—say, for instance, me. But I had to admit that she had worked hard. She had tried.

When I finally hit the bottom of the stack, I had one item left that I didn't know what to do with. It was an invoice from a company called Crescent Security. It had no notes, no questions, nothing to indicate why it was there and what I should do with it. So I did what I usually did in those situations—suspense it for a few days and deal with it later. With that taken care of, I sat back in my chair and stared straight ahead. It had already been dark for several hours, and the windows had turned into imperfect mirrors, reflecting back to me a picture of institutional emptiness—and there I was in the middle of it. As I sat and stared at my reflection, which was particularly chalky in the hard-edged, artificial glare of the fluorescent lights, I wondered, vaguely, what other people like me were doing tonight. I wondered if Ellen had ever looked at herself like this and wondered the same thing.

It occurred to me that if I couldn't see out because of the light, then anyone on the ramp could look up and see in. From down there my office must have looked like a display case in the Museum of Natural History. I went over to close the blinds and took a quick peek outside. I was relieved to see the operation humming along. Tugs were rumbling back and forth, tractors were pushing airplanes off the gates, and crews were loading boxes and bags and trays of mail into the bellies of large aircraft. A line of snow show-

ers had passed us by to the south, bringing in its wake
slightly warmer air that hung in a dense, wet fog that
diffused the light on the ground and softened the
scene. If Monet had painted our ramp, it would have
looked like this.

It was time to go home—or at least back to my
hotel. I did a quick search of the desk, thinking maybe
I would find the file on Angelo DiBiasi so I could
keep my promise to Lenny. I hadn't had a chance to
ask Disappearing Dan about the case, and at the rate
I was going, it would be another week before I was
ready to make a decision. I found a drawer filled with
hanging files, each with a color-coded tab labeled in
Ellen's handwriting. I riffled through the neat rows
and found nothing on Angelo. I tried the middle
drawer. Nothing there except company phone books,
a bound copy of the union contract, a few office supplies, and a pocket version of the OAG. The Official
Airline Guide was a typical airline employee accouter-
ment, a schedule for all airlines to all cities. Ellen's
was more current than mine, so I threw mine out and
tossed hers into my briefcase. When I did, something
slipped out from between the pulpy pages. It was a
United Airlines frequent flier card—and it was issued
in Ellen's name.

What was she doing with this? Only real passengers
had these. The only point in having one was to earn
free air travel, and we already had that. And to earn
miles you had to, God forbid, pay for your ticket.
Airline employees would do almost anything before
they did that. I thumbed through the guide to see if
Ellen had been gracious enough to highlight a destination or turn any corners down. I should have known
better. I was willing to bet that Ellen had been a book-
mark kind of a girl—no turned-down pages allowed.
The guide had neither, but on the back of the card
was the phone number for customer services. If

United was like our airline, I could call their electronic system and get the last five segments she'd flown, a very helpful feature if you've forgotten where you've been.

I dialed the number and connected. The electronic gatekeeper asked for the account number, which I punched in straight from the card. The second request was a stumper. I needed Ellen's zip code. The airport zip code didn't work, which meant she must have used her home address on the account.

I hung up and went to look for it in Molly's Rolodex. I hadn't realized how quiet it was in the office until the phone rang in the deep silence and nearly launched me out of my shoes. As I answered the phone, I felt guilty, as if I'd tripped an alarm with my snooping. "Majestic Airlines."

"The Marblehead police are trying to get in touch with you." It was Kevin on the other end and he didn't bother to say hello.

"Why?"

"They're holding Danny."

"For what?"

"I'm not sure, but they want you to go and pick him up. Do you want the cop's name and number?"

I took down the information as well as directions on how to get to Marblehead. It was about thirty-five minutes up the coast from the airport.

"I've got another call," he said. "Do you need anything else?"

"No. *Wait* . . . What's in Marblehead?"

"Ellen Shepard's house."

The buzzer was loud in the quiet lobby. When it stopped, the door to the back offices opened, and Detective Pohan leaned out to greet me, keeping one foot back to prop open the door. He was in his late forties with a slight build, baleful brown eyes, and a droopy mustache that was as thick as the hair on his head was thin. "You got here quick. I appreciate that. You want to come on back?"

I followed him down a long, narrow aisle that ran between a row of offices to the right and a cluster of odd-sized cubicles to the left. I noticed there wasn't a whole lot of activity. Maybe the Marblehead detective squad didn't have much call for a night shift.

The last office in the row was a conference room. The door was closed, but I could see Dan through the window, sitting alone at a table. All eight fingers and both thumbs were drumming the tabletop. I couldn't see it, but I would have bet that his knees were bouncing like a couple of pistons.

Pohan reached for a file from his desk. "Ellen Shepard's landlord says Majestic Airlines is handling the affairs of the deceased."

"We are?"

"We've been instructed to call this fellow in Washington if we had any problems." He held the file open, inviting me to read the name he was pointing out. "Here, I don't have my glasses on. What is that? Castle? Castner?"

"Caseaux," I said, emphasizing the last syllable the way Lenny did. "Leonard Caseaux. I work for him."

Pohan nodded in Dan's direction. "This one asked us to call you first."

"He did?" I checked again to see if this was the right guy. What was bad enough that Dan had felt a need to call me, of all people? "Why is he here, Detective?"

"He was caught breaking into Ellen Shepard's house."

"Breaking in?"

"It's the second time. The first time the landlord saw him trying to climb through a window. This time he got all the way through, but he set off the burglar alarm."

I looked at Dan through the window. He'd grown still and was staring down at the table like a wind-up toy that had wound down. He looked sad. "Do you mind if I talk to him?"

"Go ahead. He's not in custody or anything."

Pohan opened the door and followed me through. Dan popped up immediately and stood with his hands in his pockets. "I'm sorry about this," he said, trying to look at me as he spoke, but mostly maintaining eye contact with the floor. His cockiness was all gone. It was hard to be angry with him when he looked like a guilty puppy about to be smacked with a rolled-up newspaper.

"Why were you crawling through Ellen's window?"

"To get into the house."

"For what possible reason?"

His eyes cut over to Pohan. From the way they looked at each other, I knew Dan and the detective had covered this ground before. Pohan checked his watch, dropped the file on the table, and sighed deeply. "Why don't we sit down?"

When we were all settled, Pohan took charge. Nodding in Dan's direction, he said, "You can ask him, but my guess is he's looking for whatever we missed that will prove that Ellen Shephard was murdered."

The hair on the back of my neck stood up. Rumors were one thing, but hearing the word "murdered" uttered by an official detective in these official circumstances gave it more weight than I would have liked. "Is there reason to believe she was?"

"None."

I turned to Dan. "What makes you believe Ellen was murdered?"

"Because I know she didn't kill herself."

Pohan leaned forward, elbows on the table, hands clasped together. "Mr. Fallacaro, I know Miss Shepard was a friend of yours, and I know you think we didn't do all we could, but we can't change the facts of this case."

I could almost see Dan's blood pressure rising, so I went for a diversion. "For my benefit, Detective, could you outline the facts of the case?"

Pohan leaned back in his chair and reached up to stroke his mustache in what seemed to be an old habit. He let his attention linger on Dan for another moment, then opened the file.

"There was no evidence of forced entry. According to you, Mr. Fallacaro, the dead bolt was locked when you got there. You used the landlord's key to get in."

He paused for confirmation, got none.

"All windows and doors were secured. No evidence of a struggle. According to the autopsy, the only signs of trauma were in the neck area around the rope. No blows to the head. Landlord identified the rope. Said it had been in the attic of the house for several years, so no one brought it in with them. She was on prescribed medication for chronic depression—"

"She was taking antidepressants?" I asked.

"Yes."

I looked at Dan, but it was impossible to tell if he had known that already. If he hadn't, he was hiding it well.

"We found an empty bottle of wine in the house. From her blood alcohol, it looks like she drank the whole thing herself that night. Drugs, alcohol, depression . . ." His voice trailed off as he closed the file and spread his hands over it. "This thing was ruled a suicide from the get-go, and we have found nothing to indicate that she was murdered."

Dan's chair squealed lightly as he sat back from the table. "She never would have killed herself," he said, "but if she did, she would have left a note."

"That's not always the case. You might be surprised to know that most suicide victims don't leave notes."

Pohan's patience impressed me. Dealing with angry and grieving survivors must be part of his job, the same as dealing with irate passengers was part of mine. I'd rather have mine.

Dan was shaking his head, looking as if he'd never, ever be convinced. Pohan was the more rational of the two men, but Dan's the one I had to work with.

"Detective, I didn't know Ellen, but from what I've seen, she was meticulous. If she took the time and effort to hang herself, which is not an impulsive act, wouldn't you think she would have included a note in her planning?"

He leaned back in his chair. "She was thirty-five years old and unmarried. She had no family. By all accounts, she wasn't seeing anyone. Who would she leave a note for?"

Dan's response was volcanic. "She had friends. People cared about her."

Pohan raised his hands as if to still the waters. "I'm sure she did. It's clear that you cared about her. All I'm saying is maybe she didn't know that. Maybe that's all part of the explanation for why she did it."

It was hard to argue a point like that. I watched Dan as he rocked back and forth in his squeaky chair. Pohan watched us both. "This isn't the cleanest way to close this thing out," he said. "Lots of unanswered questions, I know, but that's what happens in suicides. Unfortunately, I've seen it over and over. I'm sorry."

No one said anything and Pohan discreetly checked his watch, probably thinking there wasn't much else to say. When we didn't make any move to leave, he smiled sheepishly. "Listen, I'd offer you some coffee or something, but I've got to pick up my kid. Hockey practice."

"Of course," I said. Then I looked at Dan, slouched down in his chair, defeated. "Detective, I know you have instructions to call Mr. Caseaux, but do you think this time you'd be comfortable letting me handle things?"

His face scrunched up under the big mustache, and I knew I was asking him to do something he didn't want to do. "I said I'd call you first, but I never said I wouldn't call Caseaux. We have pretty specific instructions."

"I know you do. How about if I promise this won't happen again? I'll give you my personal guarantee."

I don't know if it was my sincere request or the fact that he was late for hockey practice, but he agreed.

"Thank you," I said. "Just one more thing. Is Ellen's house still considered a crime scene? Is that part of the problem with Dan being there?"

"No. We've finished our investigation, but Mr. Fallacaro has no authorization to be in the house, and if he doesn't stay out, he's going to get shot. The landlord lives across the street, and the old guy watches his property like a hawk. He usually takes his shotgun when he goes over to check on the place."

"All right."

When I stood up, they did, too. Dan was out the door in a flash. Pohan paused to give me a business card.

"Detective, thanks so much for your help. I—we really . . ."

When I turned to find Dan, he was already down the corridor getting himself buzzed out the door.

Pohan watched him go, shaking his head in a way that seemed almost mournful. "There's one thing you learn pretty quick in this line of work," he said. "Things aren't always as they seem. But then, sometimes they're exactly as they seem."

Chapter Seven

Even though it was almost nine o'clock at night, Sal's Diner was filled with the aroma of a greasy griddle, and I knew my nice wool coat was going to carry the scent of frying bacon right out the door with me and into next week.

Dan was hunched forward with his fingers woven around his cup, staring into his coffee. "Why'd you'd come?" he asked.

"Because of our close personal relationship."

He dipped his head even more, almost hiding the brief flush of embarrassment that colored his face. "I know, I know. I haven't been much help—"

"You've been a complete asshole."

He accepted the rebuke without comment. It felt so good, I threw in another one for good measure. "I understand that you lost a friend, and I can even understand why you might resent me, but you never even gave me a chance."

"What was I supposed to think? Here you are this big-time fast-track superstar hand-picked by Scanlon to come in here and *handle* things for the company. I figured it was your job to shut me down or report back on what I was doing."

"You thought I was brought in here by no less than the chairman of the company to keep an eye on *you*?" I wasn't mad at him anymore because he'd called me a superstar. "You must be pretty important. Either that, or I'm not."

"That's not . . . I didn't mean . . ." When he finally raised his eyes, I smiled to let him know I was teasing him. He sat back, exhaled deeply, and seemed to relax for the first time all evening. He draped his arm across the back of the booth and pulled one leg up next to him on the bench seat. The waitress took the move as a cue to come over, top off his coffee, and leave the check. When he reached over and pulled it to his side of the table, I figured we'd turned a corner.

"Why don't you just tell me what's going on with you, Dan?"

"I know what everyone thinks," he said. "I know what the police are saying, and I know you believe them. But there is no way Ellen Shepard killed herself. No fucking way. She was murdered."

His tone was even, he held steady eye contact, and he was completely calm for the first time since I'd met him. There was no question in my mind that he believed what he was saying. "Who do you think killed her?"

"Little Pete Dwyer."

"The missing crew chief from Sunday night?"

"Right."

"Why him?"

He shrugged vaguely and stared up at the ceiling. "I hear things."

"You're going to have to do better than that, Dan. Don't treat me like a fool."

He knocked back the rest of his coffee, and the knee started going again as he regarded me. I waited.

"Okay," he said finally. "I've got nothing hard. Just a lot of suspicious stuff, people talking, things Ellen was doing lately that I didn't get."

"Like what?"

"In the last few weeks before she died, she was

doing a heavy-duty research job on Little Pete Dwyer. She was asking a bunch of questions, reading his personnel file, looking at all his performance reviews."

"She could have been looking for a way to deal with the guy. I've done that, especially with a hard case, trying to figure out why they are the way they are."

"You don't need to do research to know why this guy's a shithead. It's because of the old man, Shithead Sr. They're two of a kind. And anyway, it doesn't explain why she had me staking him out."

"Staking him out? You mean, sitting in a car in the shadows, drinking bad coffee, and waiting for him to show up so you can, what . . . *tail* him?"

"Yeah."

I looked for the ironic smile, a sign that he was kidding, exaggerating at least. He was perfectly serious. "You guys were in your own B-movie. What did you find out?"

"We found out Angelo DiBiasi's got balls bigger than his brains. Poor bastard. Talk about being in the wrong place at the wrong time. I'm sitting in the truck down by the freight house waiting for Little Pete to show up, and Angie rolls by a in a tug dragging a TV set on a dolly. I caught up with him just as he was loading it into his car."

"What happened with Little Pete?"

"Busting Angie basically blew my cover."

"And you never found out why Ellen was after him?"

He shook his head. "I assumed she got a tip from her snitch."

"Snitch?"

"She had a snitch down on the ramp, a guy who used to tip her off."

Of course she did. "Why don't you just ask the snitch what it was about?"

"I don't know who the guy is. She kept it a secret to protect him." He must have noticed a hint of skepticism in my expression. "I know this doesn't make much sense," he said, "but it will. Ellen always made sense. I just don't have all the pieces yet."

"What reason would Little Pete have to kill Ellen?"

"I think it must have been for the package."

I stared at him.

"Oh, yeah. I didn't tell you this. One night I was at the airport later than usual, and Ellen comes into her office. She picks up the phone and starts talking to someone about something that's in this package. Then my phone rings, I answer it, and that's it. She knows I'm there. She gets up and closes the door, so that's all I got."

"How could you fail to mention that little detail?"

"Because so much stuff has been happening around here that I sometimes can't keep it all straight. And you're the first person I've been able to talk to about it. I figure he killed her for the package."

"You don't know that." We were jumping to some very large conclusions here with very few facts, something that was against my religion. "What could have been in this package?"

"I don't know. Could be she found out about one of Little Pete's scams, or the old man's. She could have had enough to fire their asses."

"He would have killed her to keep his job?" I tried not to sound as alarmed as I felt, but between this discussion and the one with Kevin, I felt my management prerogatives becoming more and more limited.

"She may have uncovered something that would put them both in jail. That would be enough to send Little Pete over the edge. He's not exactly the most stable guy to begin with."

"Is that where you've been disappearing to at night? To stake out Little Pete?"

"I've been trying to keep an eye on him, but it's

impossible with just me. Near as I can figure, he's been AWOL four times since she died."

"Four times in nine days. When does he work?"

"He doesn't. That's what you saw on Sunday night. But his pop always covers for him, and none of his union brothers are going to rat him out." Dan was concentrating hard on one of the sugar packets left over from his coffee. He was folding it smaller and smaller until it was the size of a toothpick. "Where do you think he goes when he disappears like that?"

"To a bar," I guessed, "or home to sleep. Maybe to a girlfriend's house."

"He comes up here to Marblehead."

"Do you know that for sure?"

"One night I followed him halfway up here, but he must have spotted me because he turned around and went to a bar in Chelsea. Then tonight I find out the old guy, the landlord, he's been complaining to the police about someone coming in and out of Ellen's house in the middle of the night."

"That would be you, wouldn't it?"

"No. The cops assumed it was me but it wasn't, because if I could walk in the front door, why would I be climbing through the friggin' window?"

I had to think about that. Dan used a logic that was uniquely his own. "That would say that Little Pete has the security code and a key to the house. Why would that be?"

"The guy who killed her had the code—the code and the key. You heard what Pohan said. No forced entry."

I was beginning to understand his logic. It was circular. "Dan, that's not the only thing he said. What about the antidepressants and the alcohol? Did you know about any of that?"

"Yeah. No. I mean, antidepressants keep you *from* being depressed, right? *Anti*depressants. So if she was taking them, she wasn't depressed. And she wasn't a boozer. A drink of wine every now and then, but I never saw her drunk." He knew he was stretching, and he knew I knew. But he was so certain and he was trying so hard to convince me—it didn't hurt to listen and besides, I had no place else to be but my hotel room by myself.

"If he killed her," I said, "I wouldn't expect him to come back to the house, the proverbial scene of the crime."

"He's looking for the package. That's why I've been trying to get in the house, to find it."

"So your theory is that he killed her for this package, but he's still looking for it."

"Right. She probably hid it somewhere."

I thought about the splintered desk in my office. "Are you sure it's in the house?"

"Without a doubt. She never left anything important at the airport."

Thinking of the desk reminded me of Ellen's frequent flier card. "Do you know why Ellen would be flying full-fare on United?"

He shook his head. "Ellen never traveled anywhere. And even if she did, there's no way she'd pay for a ticket. Nobody in the business does that."

The card was stiff in the pocket of my skirt. I could feel it. And I could feel myself getting sucked right off that slick, vinyl banquette and into the Ellen Shepard affair. I knew if I showed that card to Dan, that was exactly what would happen. But I couldn't very well sit on it when he was struggling so hard to make sense of her death. Besides, I had to admit to at least a little curiosity. I dug it out and laid it on the table in front of him.

"What is this?" He had a hard time picking the flat card off the table. Finally, he slipped it off the edge and into the palm of his hand.

"Ellen had a frequent-flier account at United."

"That doesn't make any sense." He looked up at me. "You know what I think this is?" He put the card back on the table and then picked it right up again. "She was probably earning miles with her credit card or phone calls or some shit like that. I even saw on TV the other day where you can earn miles for buying hair plugs."

"I doubt she was doing *that*."

"What I'm saying is this by itself doesn't mean she was buying airline tickets."

"If you know Ellen's home zip code, we can figure that out right now." I reached over the table and turned the card in his hand so he was looking at the back. "There's a customer service phone number."

"I don't know what it is up here. Oh-two-something . . . *wait*." He dropped the card and pulled something that looked like tissue paper from his breast pocket. "Have you got a cell phone?"

I pulled my phone from the pocket of my bacon-scented coat.

"The cops wrote me a ticket for being at the house. It's got the address and the zip. Ready?"

He read me the number and I dialed in again. When I got to the request for the zip code, I punched in the number he gave me, and I was in. Dan watched closely as I went through the menu. The first option gave me her total miles. Eighteen thousand. She had definitely used this account. I punched the selection for the last five segments traveled and signaled Dan for a pen, which he produced immediately. As the computer reeled off the destinations, I jotted the city codes down on my napkin. Dan's eyes grew wider with each one—DEN, SFO, ORD, IAD, and MIA. Next to each city code I wrote the date of travel.

As I punched off and tucked the cell phone away, he grabbed the napkin. "We have service to San Francisco and Chicago and Washington Dulles. We fly non-stop to Miami and, for God's sake, the company's headquartered in Denver. What the hell was she thinking paying for travel?"

"Given that you never even knew she was gone, I'd say she was doing it to hide her trips. If she'd flown on Majestic, people at the station could have tracked her through the system, right? They'd have known where she was going."

"Hell, they'd know what seat she was sitting in and what drink she ordered. People in this station are worse than the CIA that way." He picked up the card again and tapped it on his index finger. "Can I keep this? I want to call my buddy over at United. He can get me all the activity on the account. Maybe we can figure out what she was doing."

The waitress came around for the third time, and for the third time we told her we didn't need anything else. This time she loitered long enough that Dan pulled out a few bills and paid the check. I noticed he'd left her a generous tip. We in the service business appreciate each other.

Dan sat in the passenger seat as we cruised down mainstreet Marblehead in my rented Camry. Every once in a while he'd let out a big sigh and shift around, as if the seatbelt was just too constraining. We were on our way to Ellen's house, where he could pick up his car.

I tapped the steering wheel with my two gloved index fingers, trying to find the best way to ask the question. "Dan, why do you think Ellen was being so secretive?"

"What do you mean?"

What I meant and didn't know how to ask was why *she* didn't clue him in if they were such great friends. Why the secret travel? Why not include him on the snitch, or whatever was going on with Little Pete? "Don't take this the wrong way, but you seem so determined, obsessed even with finding out what happened to her. You're obviously very loyal to her, to her memory." I was trying to watch the road and check his reaction at the same time, but he was staring out the window and I couldn't see his face. "If she was involved in something that pertained to the station and its employees, why didn't she include you more than she did?"

He continued to stare out the window, leaving me to wonder if I'd overstepped the bounds of our tenuous new friendship. I rolled up to a stop sign and sat with my foot on the brake.

"Dan?"

The bright neon tubing in the window of a corner yogurt shop cast an eerie pink glow into the car, illuminating his profile when he turned to look straight ahead. "Did you ever hear of a guy named Ron Zanetakis?"

"Ramp supervisor at Kennedy?"

"Newark. I worked for him when I was a ramper down there. When I was getting ready to leave to come up here for my first management job, he gave me this little speech, like he was my old man or something. He told me how to be a good manager."

A honk from behind reminded me that I was still standing at the stop sign. I moved ahead. "Which is how?"

"Never walk past the closed door."

"What does that mean?"

"Manager's walking through the operation and comes across a door that's supposed to be open, but it's closed. He puts his ear to the door and hears something going on in there. Nobody knows he's at the door, and the easiest thing in the world would be to walk away. But the good ones, they will always go through the door. If it's locked, they'll bust it down. They're not afraid to know what's going on. Ellen never walked past. She was never afraid here, which is why I can't believe she'd kill herself over a few threatening phone calls. And she always backed me. Maybe she didn't always tell me what she was doing, but one thing I knew is when I went through the door, she'd be right behind me. Turn here," he said, almost after it was too late, "go five streets and hang a left. Her house is down at the end on the right."

When I made the first turn, I stole a glance. Dan was staring straight ahead through the windshield, but didn't appear to be looking at anything. He didn't even seem to be in the car with me. "That meant a lot to you, Ellen backing you up?"

"It may not sound like much, but in a place like Logan, it's important. To me, anyway." His voice drifted off and he went back to whatever place he'd been in.

I began to count streets. Ellen's street was a black-top road. The only sound in the car was the wheels popping as we rolled over random bits of gravel, and I wondered if it had sounded this way the morning he had come to find her.

A low-slung black coupe parked under a single street lamp was the only car on the dead-end street. I assumed it was Dan's and pulled in behind. The clock on the dashboard showed eleven minutes after ten. The house was up on a slope and I was too low down to see it, so I stared straight ahead, just as Dan did. But I was looking at a thick stand of great old trees, winter bare in the intermittent moonlight.

"I was thinking, Dan, if you wanted to get into the house, why wouldn't we get permission and use the front door?"

"Can't. Lenny got himself put in charge by the aunt

in California, and he's keeping the place locked up tight. No one gets in unless he says so."

It was hard to tell if he was exaggerating. Dan had his own way of presenting the facts. If it was true, it seemed pretty odd to me. "He's probably trying to be nice and help her out. Maybe this aunt is old. Maybe she doesn't travel. Have you asked him? You could even offer to help."

"I'm not one of Lenny's favorite people. In fact, I'm on his permanent shit list."

I looked at him and I knew, just knew, that every question was going to raise ten more.

"It's a long story," he said, reading my mind. Then he turned in his seat to face me, and I could have sworn I saw a lightbulb over his head. "But I bet he'd let *you* in."

"Dan—"

"You could offer to help get things organized up here. He'd probably tell the landlord it's okay and—"

"Dan."

"What?"

"I'm not sure how involved in this I want to get. I'm already enough of an outsider around here, and the job itself is going to be as much as I can handle. And if Lenny finds out what happened tonight, I won't be one of his favorite people either."

He slumped back in his seat, the lightbulb clearly extinguished. "What you're saying is it would be a bad career move to find out that someone in the company murdered Ellen."

"That's not what I said, and it's not fair." Although he did make a good point. Not that I had to protect my career at all costs. But I also didn't want to throw it away trying to prove that a woman was murdered by an employee of Majestic Airlines if she really did kill herself.

"You're right." He popped open the car door. "That

•

was a cheap shot. But maybe you could just think about it." He stepped out, then leaned over and poked his head back in. "Thanks for coming up tonight. I really didn't think you'd do it."

"Call me impulsive."

"Impulsive, my ass," he laughed. "You may have surprised me, but I don't get the feeling you surprise yourself much."

I smiled because he had me and we both knew it. "I don't know why I came up. I don't know why I'm interested in this whole thing. I'm still working that out. But the thing with Lenny, I will think about it."

"See you tomorrow, boss."

After he'd turned his car around and was moving down the street toward the highway, I did a U-turn, intending to follow. But with the car facing the opposite direction, I had a full view of Ellen's house. It was built on a rise, gray clapboard with black shutters bracketing its many windows. I wondered if Ellen's walls inside were bare. As I thought about it, I started to understand why the ones in her office might have been. Photos, posters, and paintings. Prizes, awards, and certificates. Each would have revealed a piece of her—where she'd been, who she'd loved, what she'd accomplished. Even what she'd dreamed about. I was beginning to understand what Kevin meant when he'd said there were no secrets at Logan. In such a place, it was no longer a mystery to me why Ellen Shepard would want to keep some part of herself to herself.

I took one last look, leaning into the dashboard so I could follow the line of the pitched roof all the way up to the point. My stomach did a little shimmy when I saw what was up there and realized why I recognized it. It was the rooster wind vane, the same one that was on the mystery drawing. Whoever had drawn that sickening picture had been to Ellen's house.

Chapter Eight

The last cherry tomato in my salad was rolling around in the bottom of the bowl, slick with salad dressing and eluding the dull prongs of my little plastic fork. No one was watching, so I plucked it out, dropped my head back, and plopped it into my mouth. At least I thought no one had been watching. I looked up to find my office filling up with men in deep purple Majestic ramp uniforms.

"Can I help you gentlemen?" I asked, dumping the plastic salad bowl into the garbage. It had felt like more, but it turned out to be only four guys. Even so, as I watched them mill about my office, I began to appreciate for the first time the value of having a desk the size of an aircraft carrier. It gave me the opportunity to peer steely-eyed across its vast, cherry-stained horizon at people who barged in unannounced, uninvited, and apparently unencumbered by any respect for my authority.

"We're here for the meetin'."

The man who'd spoken was fifty-ish with a pinkie ring and hair too young for his face. It was jet black and worn in a minor pompadour.

"I don't remember calling a meeting," I said, "and I don't know who you are."

"I'm president of Local 412 of the International Brotherhood of Groundworkers. This here's my Business Council, and we come for Little Pete's hearing."

The youngest of the four men was posed against the wall, staring vacantly out the window and looking like an underwear model. No one had mentioned that Little Pete was not little at all, and not just because he was well over six feet tall. He had a thickly sculpted, lovingly maintained bodybuilder's physique, which was shown to good effect by the shrink-wrap fit of his uniform shirt. He was an intimidating presence, more so when I thought about Dan's belief, Dan's *fervent* belief, that this man had killed Ellen. When he glanced over at me and we locked eyes, my mouth went dry.

The other three men were smaller, older, and resoundingly ordinary by comparison. I addressed myself to The Pompadour. "You're Victor Venora."

He neither confirmed nor denied, simply gestured to his right, "George Tutun, secretary," and to his left, "Peter Dwyer Sr. He's the vice president. Like I said, we're here for the meetin'."

I stole a quick look at the senior Dwyer, the man Dan had referred to as "Shithead Sr." Just as Little Pete wasn't little, Big Pete wasn't big. "If I'm not mistaken, Victor, Dan's the one who's chairing the hearing for Pete Jr."

"He ain't around."

I checked the clock on my desk, a more discreet gesture than looking at my wristwatch, although why I cared about being polite, I couldn't say. "Perhaps because you're three hours early. That meeting is set for four o'clock."

"This time worked out better for us."

"I see." Ambush. Instead of sending one steward with Little Pete, which would have been routine for a disciplinary discussion, all the elected officials of the Boston local of the IBG had shown up. To up the ante, one of the council members was Little Pete's father. Either they'd had success in the past with such brute-force tactics, or they took me for a spineless moron.

"Well, I'm delighted to meet you, all of you. If you'll excuse me . . ." I moved out from behind my desk, stepped between Victor and Big Pete, and poked my head out to find Molly, who was just coming back from lunch. "Molly, would you beep Dan and ask him to come to my office?"

"He's with the Port Authority," she said, peeking around me to see who was there. "You want me to interrupt?"

"Please. When he gets here, ask him to come in, but first tell him his four o'clock meeting arrived early."

"So that's what's going on," she said, shaking her headful of heavy brown curls. "Don't let them rattle you. They do this all the time." Which meant they didn't necessarily believe I was a spineless moron, but they were there to find out.

The humidity level in the small office was on the rise as I closed the door and settled back in. All the warm bodies were throwing off heat. They'd also brought with them the earthy smell of men standing around indoors while dressed to work outdoors. I didn't mind. It reminded me they were on my turf.

Victor was droning on as if we were still in mid-conversation. ". . . unless you want we should wait for Danny . . ."

"Why would I want that?"

"Maybe you'd want to let him handle things from here on out."

My audience was watching, even Little Pete, waiting to see if I would scurry to safety through the escape hatch Victor had just opened. Somewhere in the back of my brain, Kevin's warning was rattling around. "Don't take on the union," he'd said. I looked at the elected officials of the IBG standing in front of me and considered his advice. For about half a second.

"Dan will be joining us shortly, and if you'd like to wait for him, I'd certainly respect that. Otherwise, I'm ready to proceed. Pete Jr."—I gestured to the chair across the desk from me—"would you mind sitting here?" He began to stir himself as I surveyed the others. "Which one of you is his steward?"

"Big Pete." Victor apparently spoke for everyone today.

"Okay. Not to be rude, but why are the rest of you here? I only ask because I'd like to know if things work differently in Boston than everywhere else in the system."

"We just thought this being your first disciplinary hearing and all—"

"This is not my first disciplinary hearing, but if you want to stay, you're welcome."

They looked at each other, but no one left, so I began. Pete Jr. was now sitting in front of me, making his chair look small and picking at a scab on his forearm. The expression on his face was lazy and dull, and I almost wondered if there was anyone home in there.

"Where were you between five and nine p.m. on Sunday?"

"Working my shift," he mumbled.

"Why couldn't anyone raise you on the radio?"

"I don't know."

"He didn't have a radio," said Victor helpfully. "That's on account of you people not buyin' enough."

I ignored Victor and concentrated on Little Pete. He somehow managed to look hard and coddled at the same time. He wore his dark hair in what I think they call a fade—longer on top and buzzed short on the sides. Something like you might see on a quasi-skinhead. But he also had curving lips that seemed frozen into a pampered sneer. When Victor spoke for him, he'd look down and pick at the crease in his pants or the arm of the chair. But when I spoke to him, he'd look straight at me, and behind that bored, dullard expression his eyes would be on fire, as if the very sight of me set him off. There was creepiness behind those eyes, residue from some long-smoldering resentment that couldn't have anything to do with me, but felt as if it had everything to do with me. It was unsettling.

"Even without a radio," I said, "if you were working your shift, then you can explain to me what happened that night and why your crew was not around to clean the cabins."

"He don't know nothing about that," Victor said, louder this time.

"You'd have to be comatose not to have noticed those problems. Either that or absent altogether, and I'm not talking to you, Victor."

I looked up at him and knew immediately that I had made a mistake. Victor was breathing faster, his cheeks puffed out, and his voice rumbled up from someplace way down low. "We *ain't* got enough manpower. We *aint* got enough equipment. We *can't* spend no overtime. *How do you people expect us to do our jobs?*"

Manpower shortage. Jeez. The oldest, most tired argument in the industrialized world. "First of all, stop yelling at me. Second, the afternoon shift may or may not be understaffed," I said evenly, "I don't know. It has nothing to do with the fact that Pete Jr. as crew chief did not answer his radio all night. He wasn't in his assigned work area, nor was any member of his crew." It was an attempt to bring the discussion back to where it belonged, but the guy who was supposed to be the subject of the meeting had found another blemish to inspect, this one on his elbow. I stared at him, feeling frustrated and trying not to show it.

"Petey"—the elder Dwyer smacked his son on the back of his head with his glove—"sit up, boy. Show some respect."

I was regarding Pete Sr. in a whole new light when Victor erupted again. "You got guys running *all* over the ramp *trying* to keep up. Someone's gonna get *hurt* out there, and it'll be on *management's head*." He took a quick breath, "On top of that, you got Danny Fallacaro sneaking around all hours of the night spying on your own workers. Spying on good men trying to do an honest day's work. George, what do they call that . . . that thing they did to Angelo?"

"Entrapment."

Holy cow. George could speak after all. "What's wrong with a manager visiting one of his shifts?" I asked. "That's his prerogative."

"That's not what he's doing. He's—"

Victor stopped. Pete Sr. had laid a discreet hand on his arm. "You're absolutely correct, miss. Danny's got a right to go anywhere in the operation at any time. Just as you would. The thing is," he paused for a pained smile, "an unexpected visit kinda sets the guys off. Makes everybody nervous. Makes 'em feel like they're doing something wrong even when they're not."

"That ain't the thing, Pete."

"Shut up, Victor." Big Pete's voice was low and calm and raspy, and it cut through Victor's blustering like a scythe through tall grass. "Do you mind if I sit?" he asked me, making it clear that the real meeting was about to begin.

"Not at all."

Without having to be told, Little Pete sprang up like a jack-in-the-box, leaving the chair vacant for his father. I was now staring across the desk at Big Pete. He had his son's square face and hair the color of my mother's silver when it hadn't been polished for a while. Between gray and brown, the color of tarnish, and it looked as if he cut it himself. Maybe without a mirror. His skin was weathered but reasonably unlined for a man who had spent much of his life on the ramp. Being out in the elements worked on people differently. Usually it aged them, but with this man it seemed to have worked in the opposite way, wearing away all but the hardest bedrock of bone, muscle, and gristle.

"The problem I see," he began, "is the men are starting to feel nervous. And when the men get nervous, there's no telling what they'll do. The whole situation becomes"—he tilted his head one way, then the other as if the right word would shake out—"unpredictable."

There were lots of people in the office, but Pete's manner, his tone of voice, the way he looked at me, excluded everyone but the two of us.

"Unpredictable?"

"Look at it this way." He tapped my desk lightly with his index finger. "Boston's a high-profile city, high visibility—especially after what's just happened. You got a lot of people watching you. What I'm sayin', if things go good, all credit to you. If things go wrong, well . . ." He sat back, resting his hands lightly on the arms of the chair. "There's been some sat in your chair who didn't deal so good with that kind of pressure. But then, they didn't have your experience, neither."

Pete Sr.'s eyes were an interesting shade of gray, an anti-color. They were cunning and observant and, I was sure now, conveying a message only I was meant to receive. Little Pete was all heat, but I understood now that I had far more to worry about from his father, who was ice cold. And at that moment, delivering a big fat threat.

"It's like this thing with Angelo," he said. "You know about Angelo, right?"

"I know what I need to know about Angelo."

"The thing of it is, Angie's got forty-two years in—"

"Forty-one."

He smiled graciously. "I stand corrected, but can

you imagine that? One night he's working his shift, doing his job, and he gets scooped up in some kind of a sting operation and fired over what amounts to some misunderstanding."

"Which part was the misunderstanding? The part where he took a TV out of the freight house or the part where he was loading it into his car?"

Pete was unfazed. "If he's left alone, you don't know but that misunderstanding coulda been cleared up to everyone's satisfaction without no one losing his job. That's what the union's for. But that's not my point. What the men out there are thinking is what kind of a place we got here when management sneaks around in the middle of the night laying traps for us? I don't think that's how you want to handle things."

"How would I want to handle things?"

"First off, we can forget about this manpower problem for now. We'll work with what we got. Then maybe, as a goodwill gesture to the men on the ramp, you could see your way clear to bringin' Angie back to finish out his forty-second—excuse me, forty-first year. And one more thing . . . Danny Fallacaro starts going home to bed at night."

I leaned back in my chair and tried to figure out how that deal was good for me. Then I tried to figure out how we'd arrived at the point of talking about a deal for Angelo instead of reviewing Little Pete's lousy performance. It had happened when Big Pete had taken over the negotiation, and when had this become a negotiation, anyway? I scanned their faces. They were all watching me, but Big Pete was the only one who gave me the feeling he could read my thoughts.

"Let me see if I can understand what's going on here," I said. "You show up in my office uninvited at a time when you know Dan is somewhere else." I nodded toward Victor. "Bad Cop here sets the table

by making a demand for additional manning, something you know you're not going to get. Then you,
Good Cop, graciously withdraw the request if I agree,
as a 'goodwill gesture,' to bring back Angelo the thief,
and by the way, keep Dan off the midnight shift. And
nowhere in there is any acknowledgement of the fact
that Pete Jr. spent most of his shift Sunday night
somewhere else besides the airport."

He smiled, letting me know that I had nailed the
situation, and he didn't much care.

"The problem I'm having is, I don't see your leverage," I said, "unless you're implying that a certain
element of disruption will occur in the operation if
you don't get what you want."

By the time I was finished, the room had fallen
completely silent. No coughing or shuffling or sniffing.
I could smell the pungent vinegar dressing floating up
from the salad plate in the bottom of the garbage. Big
Pete was squinting out the window. "I didn't say nothing like that."

"Good, because I'm not prepared to simply bring
Angelo DiBiasi back on payroll because you threatened me." Given what had just transpired, I was inclined to never bring him back, no matter what Lenny
wanted.

Big Pete was wistful. "If that's what you gotta
do . . ."

"As for Dan, I've been here three days, he's been
here three years. You can see how it would be difficult
for me to question his judgment. That being said,
there is something I want."

Big Pete turned away from the window suddenly
very interested.

"I want the jokes about Ellen Shepard's death to
stop. I want every cartoon, every drawing, and every
sick reference to disappear from the field. Forever. If

that could happen, then maybe Dan and I would both sleep better at night."

"And he'd be sleeping at home?"

"Yes."

"That can be arranged. But I really think you should reconsider on Angelo. It would mean a lot to me personally."

"And I think you should consider that leaving the field in the middle of a shift is as much grounds for termination as stealing a television." I glanced over at Little Pete, who was studying his thumbnail, and I was almost relieved when he didn't look up. I turned back to his father. "Let's call that friendly reminder my goodwill gesture."

Big Pete heaved a great, doleful sigh. When he stood, I noticed he was less than six feet tall, much less physically imposing than his son, but still a man who commanded all the attention in the room when he wanted to. When he started to move, so did everyone else. Before he walked out, he leaned across my desk, offering one hand and putting the other palm down on the glass. It made me think of the palm print I'd seen there on my first day. When I took his hand, it felt cold. "Welcome to Boston, miss. Working with you is going to be a real pleasure."

After they'd left, I stood for a long time with my arms wrapped around me. I couldn't tell which had given me the chill, Big Pete's cold hand or his gray eyes, which seemed even colder. I looked down at the palm print he'd left on my desk. Then I leaned over and, using the sleeve of my blouse, wiped every last trace of it away.

Chapter Nine

"I can't believe the balls on those scumbags, showing up like that." Dan slid down into the chair where first Little and then Big Pete had sat earlier in the day and started drumming the armrests with his fingertips. He'd called in just as the hearing had broken up. Once he'd heard that he'd missed all the fun, he'd spent most of the afternoon in the operation. "What else did they want?"

"Two things. For me to bring Angelo back and for you to stop your nightly surveillance."

"What did you tell them?"

"That I wouldn't bring Angelo back—not yet, anyway—and that you would stick to the day shift from now on."

"Why'd you make that deal?"

"Because I wanted to show the union I'd work with them, which I'm willing to do up to a point. Besides, I don't think we gave up much. It's dangerous for you to be lurking around the airport in the middle of the night, and you weren't finding anything anyway."

He was wounded—his finger tapping ceased—but it passed quickly. He started again almost immediately.

"Why is everyone so hot for me to bring Angelo back? He seems pretty small-time to me."

"Who's everyone?"

"Lenny wants me to deal him back. Now these guys are trying to turn the screws. The more people try to make me do it, the less I want to, and I don't even know the guy."

"Lenny's just a lazy bastard trying to make nice with his buddies in the union. Big Pete's trying to show you and everyone else that he's in charge. As far as anybody else, Angie's been around forever. Everybody knows him and his wife, knows she's been real sick. He's got these baby grandsons. They're twins and they're so cute, these kids. A lot of us went to their christening last year."

"You sound sympathetic."

He shifted his weight and started bouncing one knee in rhythm with the tapping. "I got no problem with what happened to Angelo. To me, stealing is stealing. By the same token, the thing you've got to understand is the guy's been doing it for years, ever since he's been on midnights, anyway. Dickie Flynn and Lenny before him, they knew what he was up to, but they couldn't be bothered."

The sharp vinegar flavor from the garbage still hung in the air. I joined Dan on the other side of the desk, taking the second guest chair and getting some distance from the smell. "Dickie Flynn was the guy Ellen replaced?"

"Yeah. He was the last Nor'easter GM."

"Did you work for him?"

"He had my job when I first got here from Newark, and I worked for him as a ramp supervisor. Dickie worked for Lenny, who was still the GM. Once the Majestic deal closed, Lenny moved up to vice president and down to D.C. Dickie and I both got bumped up."

"What was he like?"

"Dickie? A walking disaster. The guy was in the bag ninety-eight percent of the time. It's a miracle the place was still standing after he left."

"And Lenny put up with that?"

"Molly and I covered for him. She ran the admin stuff and I ran the operation. Besides, Lenny never saw the worst of it. It wasn't until after he left for D.C. that the hard boozing started."

"He had to have known."

Dan shrugged. "I never try to figure out what Lenny knows."

"What happened to Dickie?"

"His wife left him, took the kids, he lost all his money. Same things that happen to a lot of people in life, only he couldn't handle it. Started hitting the bottle."

"No, I meant why did he leave the company."

"Poor bastard got stomach cancer and died about six months ago."

"That's sad."

"A goddamned waste is what it was. I never met a better operations man than Dickie Flynn when he was sober. What I know about the operations function I learned from Dickie."

"Was he as good as Kevin?"

"Better. Dickie started out as an operations agent, then he went to the ramp and then freight. I think he also did a stint on the passenger side." He shook his head. "What a waste. The guy was a mess right up until the day he died."

"What about Lenny? Did you ever work for him?"

"Not directly."

"Why did you say the other night that he doesn't like you?"

"Because he doesn't. What do you want to do about Angelo?"

I laughed. "If you don't want to tell me, why don't you just say so?"

"It's not that. It's a long and boring story and not all that important and I'm tired."

"All right, let's talk about Angelo. He's sixty-three

years old with a sick wife and forty-one years of service to the company. With a story like that, no arbitration panel is going to let a termination stand. Lenny wants me to bring him back, so I should do it before the panel does it and takes the credit. I score points with my boss and the union."

"You're probably right."

"Then why don't I want to do it?"

"Because you're stubborn."

"Are you sure he's harmless?" I asked.

"He's harmless."

"And you don't have a problem with it?"

"Not me, boss."

"All right."

"So you want me to bring him back?"

"All right means I'll think about it some more."

Dan laughed at me, then segued into a big yawn, which made me yawn and reminded me of just how long this day had been. I stood up to stretch. "Let me ask you something else. If Ellen did find something out about Little Pete, does it stand to reason Big Pete would be involved?"

"Little Pete wouldn't know what shirt to put on in the morning if it wasn't for his old man."

"That's what I thought. I was speculating on how things might be different around here if we could blow both Petes out the door. Victor is incredibly annoying, but I'd still prefer dealing with him over Big Pete. And I can't think of one good reason to have Little Pete around. He's scary."

"I told you."

I went over to the window and shifted the angle of the blinds so that it would be harder to see inside the office, if anyone had been so inclined. It was already dark again. I hadn't left the airport once in daylight. Come to think of it, it was dark in the morning when I came in. I was beginning to feel like a vampire. "Do you have any idea what Ellen may have had on father and son?"

"Drugs."

"Really?"

"I was thinking last night after I got home how out of the blue one day, for no reason, she starts asking me a bunch of questions about the Beeches."

"The Beechcraft? The commuter?"

"Yeah. Those little mosquitoes we fly down to D.C. three times a day. Our last flight of the day connects to the Caribbean."

"Southbound is the wrong way for drug trafficking."

"It connects on the inbound, too. Her questions were all about the cargo compartments, capacity, loading procedures. I think she was trying to figure how much extra weight they could take. Maybe where you could hide a package. She also asked me for a copy of the operating procedures for the ramp."

"Wait a second . . ." I went to the overhead cabinet of my credenza and opened it. "She had her own procedures manual. It's right here. Why would she want yours?"

Dan came around the desk and pointed at the logo emblazoned across the manual. "Those are Majestic's procedures."

"Not surprising, considering we are Majestic Airlines."

"We weren't always, not here in Boston, anyway. She wanted my old Nor'easter manual. I gave it to her and now it's gone."

"That's very odd." I slid the manual back onto the shelf. "You haven't been Nor'easter for over two years."

He went back to his seat while I turned around, opened the file drawer in my desk, and thumbed through the plastic tabs. "Something was in here the other night having to do with Nor'easter . . . here it is." When I reached down and pulled it up, all I had was an empty hanging file with a label. The Nor'easter/Majestic Merger file was missing. It was the only one that was. I showed Dan the empty file.

"Could mean nothing," I said.

"Nothing around here means nothing."

I left the file on my desk as a reminder to ask Molly about it. "I don't know about the merger or the Beechcraft or the procedures manual. What I do know is that you could go to jail for running drugs, to say nothing of losing your job."

I smiled at Dan and he smiled back. "I like the way you think, Shanahan."

"Are you free tomorrow night?"

"Friday night? Are you asking me out on a date, boss?"

"I got a call this afternoon from Human Resources in Denver. Ellen's Aunt Jo in California was named as beneficiary in Ellen's life insurance policy, and they were missing some information. Lenny wasn't around, so they called me and I in turn offered to contact Aunt Jo for them. Jo Shepard is her name. She's the older sister of Ellen's late father. Did you ever talk to her?"

"No."

"How did you know where to send the ashes?"

"Lenny left me a message. He's been dealing with her from the start."

"Yeah, from what I gather, Aunt Jo is older and doesn't travel much. When Lenny called to inform her about Ellen, he offered the company's assistance in handling her affairs. Selling her car, getting rid of the furniture, paying final bills. She took him up on his offer, had a power of attorney prepared and sent to him."

He slumped back in his chair and groaned. "We'll never get into that house."

"Not so. She's overnighting a copy to me. It should be here tomorrow."

The spark came back into his eyes. You could even have called it a gleam. "Are you shitting me?"

"I explained to her who I was. I told her who you were and that we were here in Boston and we wanted to help, too. I figured it was worth a shot. She was more than happy to have all the help she could get, and since the power of attorney designates 'authorized representatives of Majestic Airlines' as her proxy, it will work for us, too."

Dan was shaking his head, taking it all in. "Jesus Christ, Shanahan, I can't believe you did that. You're all right, I don't care what anyone says."

"I hope Lenny feels the same way when he finds out."

"Who cares what Lenny thinks? Better to ask forgiveness than permission. That's what I always say."

"I care what Lenny thinks, and look how well it's worked for you."

He bounced out of the chair and headed for the door, looking as if he had things to do and places to go.

"I've already talked to Pohan," I said, calling after him. He stopped just outside the door. "You call the landlord. We'll need to get a key. And see if he knows how to change the code on the burglar alarm. If he doesn't, call the security company. If you can get that done tomorrow, we can go tomorrow night—that is, if you're free."

I could have seen his ear-to-ear grin in the dark. "I'll clear my calendar."

Chapter Ten

The sound of the car doors slamming cracked so sharply in the sleepy neighborhood, I halfway expected the neighbors to come out on their porches to see about the disturbance. While Dan went to get the key from the landlord, I stood by his car and stared up at the house. No one had closed the curtains in Ellen's house or drawn the blinds, leaving the windows black, unblinking, the interior exposed to anyone who dared to approach. I had agreed to this search—I had made this search possible—but now that I was here, it seemed like a better idea in concept than in practice.

Dan arrived and handed me the key. There was no ring, no rabbit's foot, nothing but a slim, bright sliver that disappeared into the palm of my gloved hand.

"Let's go, boss. I'm freezin' my ass off out here."

"Aren't you . . ." I couldn't find the right word because I knew he wasn't afraid. A feeble gust of wind came up, sending long-dead leaves scuttling over the blacktop. "Aren't you even a little uneasy about going in there?"

"No. Why?"

I looked up again at the forbidding structure. "I don't know. I just think—"

"Shanahan, you're thinking too much. Follow me." And he was off. When I caught up, he was waiting for me on the porch. While he held open the aluminum screen door, I used the light from the street to find the dead bolt. It was dim, but I could still see that the cylinder was as shiny as a new quarter.

"New locks?"

He nodded. "She's the one who put in the security system, too. The landlord wouldn't pay for it."

I took off my glove and touched the lock face. It felt cold. "Something must have scared her."

The dead bolt slid back easily, and the same key worked in the knob. A piercing tone from the security system greeted us. I knew that it was just a reminder to disengage the alarm. Even so, it felt like one last warning from the house, one last chance to turn back. Dan slipped past me and, reading from a minuscule scrap of paper, punched a six-digit code into the keypad on the wall. The buzzer fell silent, leaving the house so still I almost wanted the noise back.

"I'm going to start in the basement," Dan said, already halfway to the back of the house.

"We need to reset this alarm," I called, making sure he could hear me. "Wasn't that the whole point of getting a new code?"

"Oh, yeah." He came back, referred again to his cheat sheet, and punched in a different string of numbers. "There you go, all safe and sound."

He was gone before I could respond. The air in the house was frigid. It felt dense and tasted stale, as if a damp breeze had drifted in from the ocean some time ago and never found a way out. And there was an odor. Faint. Sweet. From the body? How would I know? I didn't know what a dead body smelled like.

I shot the dead bolt, turning the interior knob on the shiny new lock Ellen had installed. She'd felt the presence of danger, taken reasonable precautions to keep it outside her door. But she had not been safe. If she had killed herself, then the real threat had been inside the house, inside with her. On the other hand, if she hadn't killed herself—I wrapped my coat a little tighter—then it was really dumb for us to be in here.

The rooms were slightly dilapidated, showing the house's age, but the residue of grander times lingered. Chandeliers hung from high ceilings, although some of the bulbs were out. The decor, at least the part Ellen had contributed, was impeccable—simple, spare pieces placed in sometimes surprising but always perfect relation to one another. And unlike those of her office, the walls were not bare. They were hung with paintings and prints that were contemporary and seemed to be carefully selected. Edward Hopper had been a favorite, with his haunting images of urban isolation and people staring into the middle distance, into their own desolation.

As I moved from room to room, I looked for evidence that intruders had been there. I saw no drawers open, no seat cushions askance. Still, I had an odd feeling that Dan was right, that the soul of the house had been disturbed, that Ellen's sanctuary had been violated in some way.

I had the same feeling upstairs, standing at the foot of her bed, staring at the brocade comforter and the elegant pile of matching pillows. I hadn't made my bed once since I'd moved out of my mother's house. I didn't see the point. Ellen had made her bed either the morning of the day she'd died, or—this was a really strange notion—would she have taken time to make it before she'd gone upstairs to kill herself?

The rest of the bedroom was predictably uncluttered, as was her bathroom, but when I opened her bedroom closet, I was stunned—and then I laughed out loud. I had finally found something about this woman that was authentic and unguarded and completely, delightfully out of control. Her walk-in closet was a riot. It wasn't messy as much as . . . relaxed. Especially compared to the rest of the house. It was as if her compulsion to shop had fought a battle with her obsession for order. Order never had a chance. Hanging racks to the left and right were crammed with silk blouses and little sweaters and wool suits and linen slacks and one linen blazer that I found particularly swanky. Her shoes had completely overwhelmed the handy shoe shelf and escaped to the floor.

It took a long time to search the closet—she'd owned a lot of handbags that I had to go through—and when I was finished, I didn't want to leave. For one thing, it was warmer in there. But mostly, standing in that closet I recognized Ellen as a real person, a person who had an obvious weakness for natural fibers and good leather pumps. I could have gone shopping with this woman, and we would have had a good time.

I was turning to leave when a single sheet of lined paper tacked to the inside of the closet door caught my attention. It had dates and distances and entries penciled in Ellen's hand, and when I looked around on the floor, I had to smile. There were two pairs of well-worn, mud-covered running shoes, the expensive kind, lined up right next to her trendy little flats. Ellen had been a runner, too. I did what all runners do—immediately checked her distances against mine. I might not have had her discipline—she ran more often than I did and on a schedule as rigid as everything else about her life—but I had endurance. I ran farther.

Something creaked in the ceiling directly above my head, something loud. Dan was supposed to be in the basement, but . . . there it was again. Loud, groaning footsteps. Definitely footsteps. I was on the second floor and the noise was coming from overhead, so either Dan wasn't in the basement anymore, or—I flinched at the sound of a muffled thud—someone was in the attic.

I stepped quietly into the hallway. A door was ajar, framed by a light from behind. Through the opening

I could see the wooden steps inside that climbed, I assumed, to the attic.

More footsteps and then another loud crash. I held very still and listened, feeling every footstep in my chest as if it were my own ribs creaking under the weight rather than the dry hardwood planks overhead.

"Is that you, Dan?"

The second thud had a different quality, more like a deliberate kick, followed by "JesusChristsonova*bitch*. Yes, it's me."

I let out the deep breath I hadn't even known I'd been holding, climbed the steep stairs, and emerged through a planked floor into the attic. It smelled of mothballs and lumber, and my eyes were drawn immediately to the apex of that familiar pitched roof where I knew Ellen had hung from a rope until Dan had come to find her.

He was sitting on a trunk rubbing his shin. He must have left his coat and tie somewhere. His collar was unbuttoned and I could see the band of his cotton T-shirt. It was warmer in the attic than any other part of the house, except for Ellen's closet maybe, but still cold. I picked my way over to where he was sitting, careful not to step off the planks.

He looked up at me. "What do you think 'fish' means?"

"Is this a trick question?"

"Look at this." He handed me a page from a desk calendar for Monday, December 22, 1997, with the handwritten notation that said FISH 1016.96A.

"Fish? I have no idea. Was this in her office?"

"On the floor behind the desk."

"On the floor? Where's the rest of the calendar?"

"Gone. So's the tape from her answering machine."

"Which one? Inbound or outbound?"

"They're both gone."

"Wow," I said, "that sounds kind of . . . not random. As if whoever took them knew her and had talked to her on the phone. That wouldn't be Little Pete, would it?"

"It could have been if he was calling in threats to her."

"I guess you're right. The rest of the house doesn't look as if it's been searched. If someone's been in here, they were looking for something specific and they knew where to look." I tapped the calendar page with a fingernail as I tried to think about what we hadn't found. "Did you find any computer diskettes? Or maybe an organizer? Did she carry a briefcase?"

"There's no organizer or disks. Her briefcase is downstairs, but there's nothing in it but work stuff."

"What about her car?"

"It's in the garage. I checked it a few days ago. There's nothing in it."

I looked at the note again. Fish. What could that possibly have to do with anything? He waved me off when I tried to give it back to him. "You keep it. I'll just lose it."

I stuck the calendar page into the pocket of my coat and sat next to him on the trunk. "You have no idea what they might be looking for?"

"Not a clue."

The space was large for an attic. Several matching footlockers were randomly scattered around the floor, as was some old furniture, too tacky to have been Ellen's. For an attic the place was clean, but still not the image I would want to take to my grave. Several cardboard boxes were stacked neatly to one side. "Have you checked these boxes?"

"No. That's why I came up here. Want to take a look?"

We went through the boxes and lockers. Each one had a colored tag, the kind the movers use for inventory, and it made me think about my own moving boxes, which had tags on top of tags. We found nothing that you wouldn't expect to find in the attic—Christmas ornaments and old tax records and boxes of books and clothes. The most intriguing box was labeled PERSONAL MEMENTOS. I wanted to sit in the attic, take some time, and go through it piece by piece, but for reasons other than what we'd come for. I wanted to find out about Ellen.

When we were finished, Dan and I sat on a couple of the lockers and looked at each other. Illuminated by the bare bulb from the ceiling, his face was all pale angles and deep hollows.

"She didn't have any shoes on."

"What?"

"The rope was over that high beam there." He pointed up into the apex of the roof. "One end of it, anyway. The other end was knotted around that stud. The cops think she climbed up on this and kicked it over." He went over to one of the lockers and nudged it with his toe. "She was wearing some kind of a jogging suit thing, but nothing on her feet. They were white. That's what I saw first when I came up the stairs. Her feet were totally white and . . . I don't know . . . like wax or something. It's funny because it was pretty dark up here, but there was light coming from somewhere." He checked around the attic, finding a window at the far end covered with wooden slats, like blinds closed halfway. "Through there, I guess. She was facing me. Hanging, but perfectly still, which was weird. And her eyes . . . I thought your eyes closed when you died." He bowed his head, and when he raised it again, the light over his head showed every line in his face. "When I think about that day, I still think about her feet. I'd never seen her bare feet."

He found the trunk again, sat down, and put his face down in his hands. "I'm so tired tonight."

I didn't know what to say, so I said nothing. I

thought about what it must have been like for him standing by himself in the attic, looking at her that way. I wondered how something like that changes you. As I watched him rubbing his eyes, I found myself wishing I had known him before he had seen her that way.

"Did you see any mail when you were downstairs?" He'd summoned the energy to stand up.

"No, come to think of it. But I wasn't looking."

"I'm going down to see if I can find it."

"I'll be right down. I'm going to turn off the lights first." And I wanted something from her closet. I didn't know why, but I wanted her running log. As Dan clopped loudly down the wooden stairs, I took one last look around the attic and the personal mementos box caught my eye again. It had neat handles cut into the sides, and when I picked it up, it wasn't heavy. I decided to take it also because it didn't belong in the place where she'd died.

I carried the box and the running log to the bottom of the staircase and went back up to get the lights. Dan had not only left every light burning in every room he'd searched, he'd also left a couple of drawers open in Ellen's desk along with the cassette door on the answering machine. Dan was right. Both of the tapes were missing. I had closed everything up and reached over to turn off the desk lamp when I noticed the red light on the fax machine. It was out of paper. According to the message window, there was a fax stored in memory. I knew Ellen would have paper nearby, and it didn't take long to find it. I dropped it in the tray and waited. After a few beeps, the machine sprang to life, sucked one of the pages into the feeder, and started to turn it around, spitting it out, bit by tiny bit. With a surge of nervous anticipation I plucked it out. A second one started right behind it.

It was written in cutout letters like a ransom note.

It wasn't addressed to me. It wasn't meant for me, but it still made me shaky enough that I had to sit down. It said, "Ellen Shepard is proof that dogs fuck monkeys." I sat in her chair and stared at it. It had to be from someone at the airport, from one of her employees, and how sick was that? Having to show up at work every day knowing that you might be glancing at or talking to or brushing past the person who wrote this? Thinking about harassment in the abstract was one thing. Holding it in your hands was another.

Probably because I knew what was coming, the second one seemed to take even longer. This one was handwritten, the message scrawled diagonally. "Mind your own business, cunt."

And they kept coming, one after another, each more crude and disgusting than the last. As they rolled off, I checked the time and date stamps and the return fax number. They'd all been sent in the middle of the night from the fax machine in the admin office—my office. But at least they were old. At least there wasn't someone at the other end right this minute feeding the stuff in as fast as I could pull it off. Real-time torment—that was a thought that made my stomach lurch, and it occurred to me that maybe she had left the paper tray empty for a reason.

The last one to roll off was another one-liner, this one typed. "Regular place, regular time on Tuesday" was all it said. There was no name and no signature. According to the time stamp it had been sent at 2307 hours on Saturday, January 3—two days before she died—from a Sir Speedy in someplace called Nahant. It was from the snitch. Had to be. I put it in the pile, turned off the light, and was into the hallway when I heard it. It was so sudden and unexpected in the mostly dark, empty house that it was like an electric shock to my heart. It took a moment for me to calm down and realize that it was only the sound of the phone ringing. Ellen's phone. It was a perfectly ordinary, everyday sound and it scared me stiff. That it rang only once and stopped was even more chilling. Right behind it came the sound of the fax machine powering up again in the dark office. It was a sound that was so common, so mundane, and it was one of the most frightening things I'd ever heard.

I called for Dan. No answer. He could have been anywhere in the huge old house. The fax began to print and my pulse rate began to climb. I called again and then realized that even if he came, he wasn't going to do anything for me that I couldn't do for myself, right? It was just a fax machine, for God's sake.

I turned on the light and went back into the office, creeping up to the machine as if it was a rattlesnake. The page scrolled out slowly, leaving me to read it one word at a time. "We're" . . . the machine seemed louder than before . . . "watch" . . . and slower . . . "ing" . . . and it took everything I had not to just rip it out before it was finished . . . "We're watching you" is what it said and below that the number 1018.

At first I couldn't move, then I couldn't move fast enough. I was out of there, banging off the hallway walls and down that grand staircase. I'm not sure my feet even touched the ground. I tried the front door. Locked. Trapped. Then I remembered the dead bolt . . .

Dan, just coming up from the basement, took one look at my face. "What happened?"

"I just got . . . there's this message." I started to show him, but there wasn't time. "We have to go. Right *now*."

"All right. Just let me reset the alarm."

I had a hard time threading the key into the lock, and then again on the other side. When we were in the car, I showed him the last fax that had rolled off. He held it up to the light of the street lamp. "What's this number, this 1018?"

I cringed to even think about it. "It's my hotel room."

"Those bastards," he said. "I swear I'm gonna kill someone before this is over."

"*Who* exactly? What *bastards*? Who would know we were here unless they followed us? They could be watching right now."

"Let them watch." He started the engine, but paused to turn on the dome light and look at the fax more closely. "It came from the airport. Fucking Big Pete. It's starting all over again."

I reached up and turned off the light.

"Calm down, Shanahan."

"Why?"

"They're just trying to scare you."

"Mission accomplished. Let's get out of here, Dan. Right now."

As he pulled away from the curb and drove down the quiet street, I peered into every parked car, checked for movement behind every swaying tree. I wasn't sure I'd ever feel safe again.

"You might want to do one thing," he said, after we'd gone a few blocks in silence.

"What?"

"Change hotel rooms."

"Hotel rooms? I might want to change cities."

Chapter Eleven

When I arrived at the airport Monday morning, Molly was already bent over her desk in the quiet office, lost in deep concentration.

"You're in early," I said.

Her head snapped up as she swung around in her squealing chair. I flinched and, trying not to spill my tea, dropped my keys.

"Ohmygod . . . don't sneak up on me like that."

"I'm sorry. I wasn't aware I was sneaking." I reached down for the keys. "What are you doing here? It's not even seven o'clock."

Hand to her chest, she drew a couple of theatrical breaths. "It's time for invoices. I save them up and do them once a month. And I'm going to need signatures, so don't go too far. Here"—she handed me my morning mail—"this should keep you busy."

"Yes, ma'am. Come in when you're ready." As she turned back to her work, I unlocked the door and fled to the sanctity of my own office, where I could continue to unravel in private.

I was still unhinged from Friday night. I was supposed to have spent the weekend apartment hunting. Instead, I'd holed up in my hotel room eating room-service food and watching pay-per-view movies. The only times I'd gone out were to run, and every time I had, I'd looked over my shoulder at least once and resented it.

With my coat off, my tea in hand, and the mail in front of me, I tried to go through my morning routine. But the normal routine did not include standing up to adjust the blinds three times, or rearranging the chairs in front of my desk, or straightening all the pencils in my drawer. It seemed that Ellen had already done that, anyway.

After not having looked all weekend, I finally gave in and pulled the faxes out of my briefcase. Nothing about them had changed since Friday, and they were just as offensive in the light of day. I still felt that scraping in the pit of my stomach when I looked at them, but I couldn't stop looking at them. Molly arrived, giving me a good reason to put them aside. Facedown.

She pushed through the door with a heavy ledger, an accordion file, and a large-key calculator, all of which she arranged methodically on her side of my desk.

"All you need is a green eyeshade," I said.

"Never mind what I need. I've got a system, and it's worked fine for some twenty-two years. The bills get paid on time, we don't pay them twice, and the auditors are happy."

"Before we start, I have a question for you," I said. "Do you know where I can rent a VCR for my hotel room?"

"Are we boring you already?"

"I've watched every pay-per-view movie offered this month, some twice. I need something fresh."

"I'll see what I can do. One of the agents' husbands repairs TVs. I'll bet I can get you a deal."

"I'll bet you can."

She handed me a ticket envelope. "Sign this first."

I opened it and looked inside, trying to decipher her loopy handwriting. "What's this?"

"It's a pass."

"I know it's a pass," I said, signing. "But who is Our Lady of the Airwaves? Patron saint of radio broadcasts? Sister Mary Megahertz?"

"Air*ways*," she said, snatching it back, "not waves. It's the chapel here at the airport. They have an auction every year and we always donate a pass."

"Ah." Ellen's frequent-flier travel popped into my mind. "Did you ever request any passes for Ellen on United?"

"I never requested any passes for her, period. She spent all her time here at the airport. Weekends, too."

"So you didn't know she was buying tickets on United."

"She was most certainly not doing that. I would have known."

She gave me the first invoice. One hundred and fifty thousand dollars for three hundred barrels of deicing fluid, a reminder that I was in a true cold-weather station for the first time in my career. "How many of these will I sign this winter?"

"Could be two, could be ten. Depends on the weather."

"That narrows it down." I signed and passed it back. "I found a frequent-flier card in the desk: Ellen flew at least five times on United that we know about. Dan's finding out if there were more."

She handed me the next invoice without a word. It was to reimburse a passenger whose coat had caught in the conveyor belt at the security checkpoint, and it was almost a hundred bucks.

"This is pretty expensive dry cleaning," I said.

"It was a suede coat."

"Was the belt malfunctioning?"

"No. In fact, the checkpoint supervisor thinks the passenger might have done it on purpose trying to get a new coat."

I signed it and handed it back. "Wouldn't be the first time. What about Ellen's travel?"

"I'll believe it when I see it. You'll have to prove it to me."

"All right. Dan's got the card. He can prove it to you."

The next invoice was for ticket stock, and the one after that for snow plowing in the employee parking lot. I signed them all. "Molly?"

"Ummmm . . ." She was busy shuffling papers.

"I found something in Ellen's suspense file the other night, and I don't know what to do with it. It was a copy of an old invoice from 1992. It had no notes or instructions. Any idea why she may have had it?"

"Let me see it."

The mystery invoice from Crescent had popped out of suspense and was in my in-box again. I dug it out and gave it to her. "Did she ask you to pull it for her?"

"No. Means nothing to me."

"Do you know the company?"

"Sure. Crescent Security. They've done some work for us, nickel-and-dime stuff like background checks, but I haven't heard anything about them for a few years. Do you want me to do anything with it?"

"Stick it back in follow-up for next week. If nothing comes up by then, toss it."

"One more." The last invoice she gave me covered the cost of a new windshield for one of the tugs on the ramp. It was attached to a requisition, which had been approved by Ellen.

I read the explanation. "Wear and tear?"

"With a baseball bat. The boys on the ramp were upset about the last bid." She started to collect her files, then glanced over matter-of-factly. "So, what did you two find up in Marblehead? Anything?"

"What?"

"You and Danny were up there on Friday, weren't you?"

"How did you know that?"

"Everyone in the station knew."

Catching my reaction, she stopped sorting the files. "Oh, please. It's not like you can sneak around. You have four hundred people working for you, and every single one feels entitled to know what you're up to at all times, especially if it has to do with Ellen."

I turned the faxes over and slid them across the desk to her, keeping the one from the snitch and the one to me aside. "I found these."

She paged through the stack, no more affected than if she had been flipping through wallpaper samples.

"These are nothing," she said with a dry chuckle. "You should see what they wrote about her in the bellies of airplanes."

"Is this amusing?"

She shifted all the way back in her chair, looking more surprised than angry. But then her neck stiffened, and so did her backbone. "What do you want me to say? Yes, it's horrible. And yes, it offends me. But it doesn't surprise me. You work around here long enough and you get used to it. That's the way it is."

"This is *not* nothing." I snatched the faxes from the desk and held them up, surprised at my own angry reaction. But I couldn't help it. It was all starting to get to me. "How can anyone ever get used to this?"

Her trademark red lips seemed to grow more vibrant. Then I realized it was really her face growing more pale. "I don't believe I like your tone."

She stood up and huffed out, leaving all her files on my desk and me staring at the spot in the chair where she had just been. The lemon had been floating in my tea too long, and it tasted bitter when I drew one last sip. I slammed the cup into the trash, then sat by myself and tried to figure out whom exactly I was mad at.

"Molly?"

She must not have gone far because she was back instantly, standing in the doorway, hands on her hips.

"I'm sorry, Molly, that was uncalled for."

"Why are you yelling at me?" she demanded. "Why are you yelling at all?"

"Come back in and I'll show you."

"Can I bring my cigarettes?"

"Yes."

When she was good and ready, she strolled back in and sat down, closing the door behind her. In my entire career with Majestic, I'd never spent so much time with the door closed. I pulled the "We're watching you" fax out and showed it to her. "This came to me Friday night at Ellen's house. I was standing right there and the thing just rolled off." I pointed at the number. "That's my hotel room." Remembering the sound of the machine in that silent house set off a shiver. "It scared the shit out of me."

She shook her head and resumed her seen-it-all attitude, sticking a cigarette between her lips and talking around it. "I've got to admit, that would be upsetting, but it doesn't mean someone followed you. I told you, all the agents at the counter were chattering like magpies about how you and Danny were going up to Marblehead to find Ellen's 'murderer.' " She rolled her eyes as she fired up.

"How do people know these things?"

"As far as the hotel room, that's easy. Someone probably knows someone who knows someone at the Hyatt. Otherwise, they eavesdrop. They read the mail when it comes in. They listen in on phone conversations. They have friends and cousins and brothers and sisters who work around town. They compare notes and put two and two together. That's why we always close the door."

I thought back to last week. The door had indeed been open when Dan and I talked about getting the power of attorney and going up to Marblehead.

Molly was perched on the edge of her chair watching me, her small, manicured hands dangling off the ends of the armrests. "Molly, do you believe Ellen was murdered?"

She shook her head. "It makes for good gossip, but it just doesn't fit with the facts. I'm sorry."

I wasn't, and for the first time since I'd gone to Ellen's house, my shoulders came down from around my ears. "Help me understand what's going on around here."

She nodded as she drew deeply on the cigarette, letting her eyes close and leaving a bright red ring around the white filter. "About three months ago Ellen changed the manning on the ramp. There's nothing wrong with what she did. In fact, it was probably overdue. But bottom line, it made for fewer full-time union jobs and a lot of favorite shifts being moved or going away. She also cut the overtime, which to some was worth as much as their salary. And, she cracked down on sick-time abuse, vandalism, theft and pilferage."

"In other words, she was doing her job."

"If this were anyplace but Boston, I'd agree with you." She spoke with great patience and tolerance, making the most of her role as station historian. "But here you have to take history into consideration, and management has a history of looking at these problems with a wink. Either that or a blind eye. When Lenny ran the place, he winked a lot. Dickie Flynn was blind. Blind drunk."

"And Ellen was neither one."

"That is a true statement."

"Dan told me about Dickie."

"What did he tell you?"

"That his wife and kids left him and he went into the tank."

"He would say that." She took a drag and stared out the window for a long time, lost in her own thoughts. "Like oil and water, those two. Danny always resented covering for Dickie, and Dickie was usually threatening to fire Danny for one reason or another. As if he could. The place would have run into the ground without Danny."

"Dickie wasn't an alcoholic?"

"He was, but Dickie was a sweet man who got lost somewhere along the way. Something happened to him, I don't know what, but it wasn't because his wife left him. Twyla and the girls adored him. She never would have left him if not for the drinking."

"What about Lenny? What kind of manager was he?"

"A deal maker. Lenny's a very charming guy when he wants to be, but truth be told, he only cares about making the numbers and getting promoted. You'll get along fine with him if you just make the numbers. That's where Ellen got into trouble."

"How?"

"Coming over from Majestic and being young and a woman and from staff, she was trying to prove herself. I think she tried too hard, went at it too fast, and tried to change everything at once. You have to work slowly around here, especially with the union."

"Is that when the abuse started?"

"At first the union did like they always do when they get threatened. Slowed down the operation, delayed flights, set fire to the place. Equipment started disappearing or going out of service, and they wouldn't come to Ellen's meetings. The usual stuff."

"*That's* the usual stuff?"

She shrugged. Smoke drifted through her lips as she nodded toward the slightly crumpled faxes on my desk. "But then these type messages started showing up, and I felt like something changed. They were, like you say, more personal. And she started getting them at home. As far as I know, the union has never taken their grievances into a manager's home. On the other hand, they never had to work for a woman before, either. Maybe that's what really set them off."

"When did things start to get personal?"

"Two, maybe three weeks ago. Around the time she found the dead rat in her mailbox.

"A dead rat?"

"Yeah, it was disgusting. Head was crushed, all stiff and dried out."

"How do you know?"

"She took a picture."

"That's certainly presence of mind."

"She wanted to have proof. I think that's when she changed her locks and, if you ask me, that was the beginning of the end. Ellen was always so put together. You know what I mean? The hair, the nails, the clothes. But after that it was almost like she didn't care. She put in more and more hours at the airport, most of the time in her office with the door shut. I think she was afraid to go home. I'm pretty sure she was losing weight."

"Tell me about her last day."

"She was here in her office by herself all morning with the door shut. She took a few calls, but mostly I think she was calling out. About one o'clock I saw the light on her line go off, the door opened, and she came out. She was trying to hide it, but her nose was all red and she had sunglasses on. She told me she wasn't feeling well, packed up, and went home. I never saw her again."

"You have no idea what happened?"

"No. And usually I know everything. Whatever it was, she kept the secret well."

"I wonder if she confided in anyone. You don't know who she was talking to right before she left that day?"

"No. She was answering her own phone. I do have a log of all her phone messages, if you think that would help." She went out to her desk, this time taking her invoices with her. When she came back, she had yet another of her ledgers, which she opened on my desk in front of me. It was a single-spaced listing of callers, dates, and times of messages Molly had taken for Ellen.

"Are you keeping tabs on me, too?"

She turned to a page with my name across the top. Listed were all the messages I'd received since I'd been there.

"Dickie used to accuse me of not giving him messages," she said, "like he could even remember anything that happened from one day to the next. That's when I started keeping track. It really comes in handy sometimes."

I studied the pages, several pages with Molly looking over my shoulder. "These non-Majestic people, do you know who they were to Ellen?"

"When someone calls, I ask what's it about. If they say, I write it down on the message. I don't log that part, but I can remember most of them. Like this one"—her bracelets rattled in my ear as she reached across to point out an entry—"this was the woman who used to cut her hair. Here's a call from her aunt on Ellen's birthday. It was the only message I ever took from her. This woman here, I remember she wouldn't say what she wanted and she never left her phone number. Said it was personal."

"Julia Milholland. Sounds very old Boston. She called three times in one week?"

"She was trying to set up some kind of an appointment with Ellen."

I pulled out a pad, copied down Julia Milholland's name, and checked out the rest of the list. "Matt Levesque. I know him. He's a manager in the Finance department. We've done work together."

"He was usually returning Ellen's calls. I think she worked with him on the merger. And he's a director now, not a manager."

"Ellen worked on the merger?"

"She came here from that assignment, some kind of a task force."

I opened the drawer and pulled out the empty hanging file labeled NOR'EASTER/MAJESTIC MERGER. "Do you happen to know where this file is?"

"I don't know where it is now, but she had it on her desk a couple of weeks ago."

I copied down Matt's number. "I think it's time I called my old pal Matt and congratulated him on his promotion."

Chapter Twelve

"I've got Lenny on line one," Molly called from her desk, "and Matt Levesque on line two. Matt says he's only going to be in for a few more minutes."

I checked the time. It wasn't even six o'clock in Boston, which meant it was still early in Denver. "Tell Matt I have to talk to my boss and it'll be maybe ten minutes. Ask him to please wait."

I took a moment to review my list. I'd been keeping track of things to tell Lenny, or things he might ask me. There was the freight forwarder who'd had his shipment of live lobsters stolen out of our freight house for the third time in a month. There was the ever escalating incidence of sick time and corresponding overtime on the ramp. There was the FAA inspector who we'd caught trying to sneak a handgun through our checkpoint—a surprise inspection we'd passed. And there was Angelo. His was the first name on the list and the only one I'd done nothing about. I knew I'd end up bringing him back, but so far I hadn't been able to pull the trigger. Dan was probably right, I was just being stubborn. I picked up. "I know why you're calling, Lenny."

"You do?" He had me on the box again.

"I've been a little slow in following up on Angelo, but I'm going to get to it this week and I'll make a decision. You have my commitment."

"That's good, Alex. It's not why I was calling, but

it's good to know you haven't forgotten my request. Hold on for me, would you?"

I slumped down in my chair and eavesdropped as he signed something for his secretary and asked her to send it out right away. I should have known better than to open with a mea culpa. It set exactly the wrong tone and who knows? He may have gone through the entire phone call and never raised the issue. Damn.

"I see we think alike, Alex." Lenny was back.

"In what way?"

"I just got off the phone with Jo Shepard out in California."

Uh-oh.

"She tells me you two had a nice chat."

I slumped down in the chair even more. I was close to horizontal, and the Angelo issue was starting to look more and more workable. At least with Angelo, my sin was in having done nothing. I couldn't make the same claim with Aunt Jo. I almost blurted out my second mea culpa, but decided to wait for his reaction first. "I spoke to her last week." I said. "Human Resources called from Denver and needed some information."

"Why didn't you tell me that you and Ellen knew each other?"

"We didn't. Did Jo Shepard tell you that we did?"

"No. But I surmised that the two of you must have been friends. Otherwise, why would you be interested in gaining access to her house?"

"Well, it wasn't that so much as I thought I could help her with Ellen's personal effects. There doesn't seem to be anyone else."

"Is that why you went up there on Friday? To help with her effects?"

I squeezed my eyes shut. Did everyone know everything that I did? I might as well post a daily schedule. This was getting out of hand. I didn't want to be lying to my boss. "No. No, that's not why I went up there, Lenny. The truth is that Dan has a theory—"

"That Ellen was murdered by the union in Boston. And he wants to get into her house to find the proof. Am I close?"

"You're right on target." I should have guessed that he would have known.

"Alex, listen to me. You should have called me before doing something like that . . . and I suppose I should have warned you about Fallacaro."

"What about him?"

"He's bad news, Alex. He's already ruined a couple of careers, including his own. And he didn't do Ellen any favors. He's always got his own agenda working, and I'm sure he does here, too."

I sat up straight. "What do you mean by that?"

"He's the one who encouraged Ellen to take such a hard line with the union. She got caught in the cross fire. Now he blames himself, and his way of dealing with it is to deny the obvious, to insist that she was murdered." Lenny's Southern accent grew deeper and richer as his frustration grew. I'd promised myself when I'd called Aunt Jo not to regret it later, not to do that to myself. Fat chance. As I listened to Lenny, I felt the guilt like a clinging vine growing around that defiant resolve and squeezing the life out of it.

Lenny was still going. "And I'll tell you something else. He's destructive. This ridiculous story is destructive for the airline, and as the Majestic Airlines representative in Boston, Alex, it's your job to make sure that a damaging and false story like that doesn't get out of hand. I don't want to see myself on *Sixty Minutes*. Do you?"

"Of course not, but this doesn't seem like Mike Wallace territory to me."

"No? Think about it. Five years ago you had the female ramp supervisor at Northwest who was murdered at Logan. Now here's another young woman dead at Logan, this time with Majestic. She was young, single, not that experienced, working in a tough place with a tough union. Majestic is high-profile, Bill Scanlon is high-profile, and she picked a strange way to die. You could spin an interesting tale."

That was true, but . . . "You make it sound as if the company is trying to hide something."

"No. No matter what Dan Fallacaro says, Ellen killed herself. If we did anything wrong, it was in not getting her out of there before it was too late." He paused for a long time, and when he spoke again, his voice was softer, with more rounded corners than sharp edges. "That was my fault. I should have seen how overwhelmed she was." He picked up the receiver. "Alex, I'm not going to make the same mistakes again. It's my job to keep you focused on the right things, and that's all I'm trying to do. Pay attention to the airport and what needs to get done there. Get the numbers up and don't get distracted. I'll hold Scanlon off until you can get things under control there."

"*Scan*lon?" My heart did a double clutch.

"Boston has been receiving what you might call unusual interest from the chairman." He stretched out the middle 'u'—un-yooo-su-al. "I've had calls from him almost every day since you've arrived."

"About what?"

"About the problems in your station. I know you've only been there a week, but he's not interested in excuses. I can only do so much before he loses patience with the both of us."

Lenny had no idea how hollow his threat was. I wasn't afraid of Bill. But I also didn't want him interested in my operation. I stood up, paced over to the window, turned around, paced back, sat down, and stood up again. I didn't want to see him; I didn't want to talk to him on the phone; even talking about him touched on a nerve that was still painfully exposed. Moving to Boston had been a way to put distance between us, and he had promised to honor that decision. I could only hope that in spite of any problems I was having here or what Lenny might say, he would keep his promise.

"Do you understand?" Lenny asked me.

"I understand."

"I appreciate your commitment on Angelo," he said, "and I'd like to ask for another. My plan is to send someone up there from my Human Resources staff here in D.C. to handle Ellen's personal effects, someone who has some training in this area. For my peace of mind, can you promise me that you will work on the problems at the airport until I can free someone up?"

"Yes, I can do that."

"That means you will stay out of Ellen's house?"

I really had no good reason not to make him that promise. "I'll stay out."

"Do I have your word?"

"You have my word."

"Good. Now, all you have to do is ask and I'll take care of Fallacaro for you. You can bring in your own guy—or gal."

I didn't think I knew any "gals." "Take care of him how?"

"I'll make him a ramp supervisor in the farthest place I can find from New Jersey."

"Do you mean Boston?"

"I mean New Jersey. Newark. If he gives you any more trouble, tell him that. And call me when you've come to a decision about Angelo."

"I will."

When I hung up, Molly was in the doorway with

her coat on. "Matt's calling back. He got tired of waiting and hung up."

I checked my second line, unaware that it had
even rung.

"And I'm going home. Don't forget that tomorrow
is Tuesday and you've got your staff meeting."

"Thanks, Molly. Have a good evening."

I punched up Matt's call. He'd been promoted since
the last I'd seen him, so instead of a manager's cubicle
in the midst of the hoi polloi, he'd be in a big window
office sitting in a high-backed swivel chair behind his
turbo desk.

"Have you got your feet up on the desk, Matt?"

"That's what it's for, isn't it?"

"And I'll bet you haven't looked at the mountains
for a week." Matt had a magnificent view from his
side of the building. I'd spent most of my time in
headquarters gazing out the window at the canvas
peaks of Denver International Airport and in the
background, the real thing—the majestic peaks of the
great Rocky Mountains.

"We're much too busy to appreciate the natural
beauty of our surroundings. I hear it's more exciting
where you are. What's it like out there?"

"It's like an airport, Matt." I checked the view out
my window, where I could see a line of purple tails
with Majestic logos, one on every gate. "We have airplanes here and passengers and cargo. You should
come out sometime and see what kind of business
you're in."

"No time for that." I heard the clacking of his computer keys, and I knew he was checking e-mail. "I'm
talking about all the rumors. Word here is everyone
in Boston thinks someone murdered Ellen Shepard.
Don't you feel weird? I feel weird, but you're sitting
in her chair."

"What happened to her is not contagious, Matt, and

I like to think of it as my chair now." I touched the armrest, felt the rough, nubby weave that wore like iron. This chair was probably going to survive the next twelve general managers. "I feel sad about what happened to Ellen, not weird. She was more than a rumor. You know that. You worked with her."

"That was two years ago," he said. "She wasn't suicidal when I knew her."

"I'm not sure she would have announced it, particularly to a sensitive guy like you. How did she sound when you talked to her last week?"

"How'd you know I talked to her?"

"You left a trail of phone messages. What did she want?"

"She had some questions about an old Finance project. I don't think it would pertain to anything you're doing now."

His voice was taking on that arch, staffy quality that really got under my skin. It was a good thing I'd known him since he was a baby analyst. "Matt, if you don't want to tell me what she wanted, say so, but don't give me that secret Finance handshake bullshit."

The clacking keys went silent. "Why do you need to know? Are you thinking she was murdered?"

"I've got some problem employees here, and I think Ellen was building a case to get rid of at least one of them. If she was, I'd like to finish what she was doing."

"Hold on." I heard him get up and close his office door. "That's not why she called," he said when he was back, "but I'll tell you anyway. She was looking for an old schedule, something from our task force days."

"The Nor'easter Acquisition Task Force?"

"Yeah. We worked on it together. She wanted the schedule of purchase price adjustments."

I opened a drawer, found a pad of paper, and started taking notes. "What's a purchase price adjustment?"

"Adjustments to the price Majestic paid to buy Nor'easter."

"What's special about them?"

"Nothing. They're just expenses that are incurred as part of the deal, so they get charged against the purchase price instead of normal operations. That's why you keep them separate."

"What are some examples?"

"Lawyers. You have to have lawyers to negotiate and draft documents for the transaction, and they charge a fee for that. Accountants, consultants, anyone we hire for due diligence. We wouldn't purchase their services if we weren't doing the deal, so their fee gets charged to the deal."

"That doesn't sound particularly relevant to the ramp in Boston."

"I told you."

"There's a schedule of these charges?"

"Yeah. Ellen maintained it when she was on the task force. She didn't have a copy of it anymore, so she called me."

"What does it look like?"

"It's nothing but a spreadsheet. Down one side you've got the payee and the nature of the expense if it's not obvious. Down the other you've got the dollar amount."

"Why would she be interested in something like that two years after the fact?"

"I haven't got a clue."

"You don't know, or you're not telling me?"

"She wouldn't say. I told her where to find it and that was it."

"Which is where?

"Archives. All the merger files have been archived for about a year now."

"Can you send a copy of that schedule to me?"

"I'd have to sign it out, and I don't think I want my name on anything having to do with Ellen Shepard. That whole subject is taboo around here right now. We're not even supposed to be thinking about it, much less talking about it. I could get into trouble."

"Come on, Matt. How many times did I bail you out in the past? Don't you remember that time when you were working on that appropriations request for San Francisco and you needed that information right away and I was the one who went back out to the airport that night to get it—"

He groaned. "Look, I don't know what you're doing up there, but if I get you this thing, you have to keep my name out of it."

"Your sterling reputation is safe with me."

My second line lit up and flashed several times before I remembered Molly wasn't out there to pick it up. Then my beeper went off. I checked the number.

"There's something going on here, Matt. Operations is beeping me. Would you just send a copy of everything Ellen asked for?"

"Yep. But we never had this conversation."

"If you say so, Matt."

Kevin was talking the instant I punched the second line. "You'd better get down here," he said. "We've got a problem."

Chapter Thirteen

I walked down the corridor past the door labeled MEN'S LOCKER ROOM. The second door had no designation, just two flat globs of hardened putty where the ready room sign might have been at one time. I could hear masculine voices inside.

For as many years as I'd worked in the field, it still wasn't easy for me to walk into a ready room. Some airports were better than others, but for the most part, the ramp was dominated by men and the ready room was where they congregated to do what men in packs do. I took a moment to gather myself, then pushed through the door.

There were eight guys in there, all in various stages of readiness—eating, reading the newspaper, playing cards. One was sleeping. All conversation ceased abruptly with my arrival, leaving an old color TV set to provide the soundtrack. I felt as if I was trespassing in the boys' secret clubhouse.

"Gentlemen," I said, concentrating on keeping my voice strong and steady, which wasn't easy, the way they were staring. "I haven't had a chance to meet most of you. I'm Alex Shanahan, the new general manager, and I'm looking for the assignment crew chief."

Most of them went back to what they'd been doing. A few stared with a bored expression that was probably reserved just for management. Since it was an evening shift, most of the men were on the younger side, some just out of high school. They had that pale, hardened look of kids who had grown up in the dark spaces of big cities. I had no friends in this room.

I was really wishing I'd worn a skirt with pockets because I couldn't decide what to do with my hands. That I was even aware of my hands was a bad sign. "Let me ask you again—"

"He ain't here." The voice floated up from the other side of a La-Z-Boy recliner.

I walked around and found a man with a dark, curly beard, a bald head, and a prodigious belly. He seemed right at home reclining in front of a TV.

"Do you know where he is?"

"Could be anywhere."

"I guess that means he could be in here."

"He's not in here."

He tapped his fingers on the cracked Naugahyde armrest. I searched the concrete walls. "Why isn't the assignment sheet for this shift posted?"

The response came from behind me, and it was a voice I recognized. "Because everybody on my shift knows their job." Big Pete leaned against the wall next to what appeared to be an inside entrance to the men's locker room. He must have just come in, because if he'd been back there the whole time, I would have felt his presence.

"Someone *doesn't* know their job," I said. "We have a Majestic Express flight that's been in for twenty minutes. No one met the trip, the bags are still onboard, and the passengers are down in claim waiting."

"There's no one in here who's on the clock," he said without even so much as a perfunctory check around the room. "One of us goes out there, you're going to pay double-time. Your shift supervisor would know that. Or Danny."

Dan was at a meeting off the field, and my shift

supervisor was stuck with a customer down at the freight house—probably the forwarder with the lobsters, or without the lobsters, as the case may be—but I saw no reason to explain all that. "I think you and I can resolve this."

"We could," he said, "but as you can see, I'm not on the clock yet." He was dressed in street clothes and completely relaxed, a man in full command of his environment. We were on his turf now.

"If the contract says double-time, then I'll pay double-time. And I will also take the name of the ramper who didn't cover the flight."

Out of the corner of my eye, I saw a man at the far end of the room stand and pull on his jacket. "I'm on the clock." he said. "I'll work it."

I turned to look at him. He was probably in his early forties, with the sturdy legs and all-over thickness that develop naturally from a lifetime of hard physical labor. His manner was brusque—rough even—but there was gentleness in his face that had somehow managed to survive even in this unforgiving place.

"Johnny, you're not on the clock." Pete stared at him, firing a couple of poison darts intended to shut him down. It probably worked on everyone else.

"I am on the clock." Johnny's manner toward Big Pete was polite and entirely dismissive. "You don't have to pay double-time," he said to me. "I'll work it myself."

"That's against procedures, Johnny. The union ain't responsible if you get hurt."

The big man turned and faced Big Pete, his massive arms stacked like firewood across his chest. "The union ain't responsible for my safety," he said, "and thank God for that."

Pete turned and crossed his arms also. Now the two

men were face-to-face. "You pay dues like everyone else here, John."

"That don't make you my representative, Peter."

Someone had killed the volume on the TV, so the only sound came from a guy sitting at a wooden table munching potato chips. Another had stopped in the middle of tying his shoe and was still bent over his knee, watching the drama unfold. John wasn't moving a muscle, and Big Pete was no longer leaning against the wall. The way they looked at each other made it clear that whatever was between these two had not started that day, and wasn't going to end there.

Big Pete, as calculating as a cockroach, must have figured the same thing because with a slight nod of his head and a fleeting smile he deffused the tension. The moment passed and everyone resumed normal activities. Without another word, John was out the door, pulling his hood over his head. I watched through the window as he lumbered across the ramp, climbed into a tug, and drove away.

There was a swinging door where Big Pete had been standing. I made a management decision not to follow him into the men's locker room. Instead, I walked out of the boys' clubhouse and went to see Kevin, as much to see his friendly face as anything else.

"Who is this guy John or Johnny?" I asked when the Operations office had cleared out and Kevin and I were the only ones left in the room.

"Mr. John McTavish, one of your better employees." He turned his chair around and stretched his legs straight out. "He and his brother both. Between the two of them they do the work of six men."

"I don't know about his brother, but John doesn't seem to be afraid of Big Pete."

"Johnny's not afraid of much. Did they go at it, those two?"

"There was some testosterone present."

"Not surprising. There's bad blood there. They were on opposite sides of a contract vote a few years back. Johnny Mac for, and the Dwyers against. It was bitter."

"What contract vote?"

"The IBG vote. It was on the last Nor'easter contract proposal, the one just before the merger. And a seminal moment it was in the long and lively history of this grand operation. For the IBG, too, you could say. It split the Brotherhood right down the middle."

I smiled. I did enjoy Kevin's hyperbole. "A labor contract that was a seminal moment? Do tell."

"Three years ago when the IBG contract came up for negotiation, Nor'easter was in dire straits, as I'm sure you're aware. The company made a proposal to the union asking for what amounted to a laundry list of concessions and give-backs. When the proposal came up for a vote, some of the brothers took one side, the rest took the other."

"I'm guessing Big Pete Dwyer would be a hard-liner."

"Right you are. No concessions to management, ever, no matter what. Johnny McTavish was on the other side. His feeling was, if they didn't help bail the company out, there would be no more company. And he was right. The contract lost by the slimmest of margins, and that's the reason Nor'easter is gone today, may she rest in peace."

"At least you guys didn't go bankrupt."

"Tell that to the four thousand people Majestic laid off. That was over two years ago, and most of us still haven't gotten over the shock."

"It doesn't appear that John and Big Pete have buried the hatchet, either."

"No. I don't think they ever will. Dwyers and McTavishes, they are cut from different cloth."

From my vantage point at the window, I could see

John unloading the bags from the stranded Majestic Express. "How is it no one showed up to work this flight?"

"The kid who usually works it called in sick. That's what I was told."

"Okay, but any one of forty or fifty rampers on shift could have covered."

"Sure, they could have, the problem being, in this station most rampers won't work the Express."

"What does that mean? We have seven Expresses every day. You're saying they refuse to work them at all?"

"It's not the Express so much as they won't work prop jets. Won't go near 'em, especially the senior men. Usually the junior guy on shift gets stuck with the trip."

"Okay, I give up. Why won't they work the props?"

"It's because of the crash."

"What cra—" I stopped for a moment. "The Baltimore crash?"

He nodded. "Nor'easter Express flight 1704. Went down on approach just outside of Baltimore, which is why most people remember it that way. What they don't remember is that the flight originated in Boston."

"Which means it was loaded here."

"Precisely. Rampers are a superstitious lot. And it's not just them. You won't find many in this station that will talk about The Incident. Bad luck. That's how we refer to it, 'The Incident,' just so you'll know."

"When was that? Ninety-four? Ninety-five?"

"Twenty-two hundred hours on the evening of March 15, 1995. Easy to remember."

"The Ides of March," I said. "Not to be indelicate or disrespectful in any way because I know it must have been extremely difficult for everyone here, but that was years ago. You're not even the same airline, and furthermore, if I remember right, the cause of that crash was pilot error. It had nothing to do with the ground operation."

"Ah, but that's the nature of superstition, isn't it? It's neither rational nor reasonable."

"Is it possible this superstition can be explained by the fact that rampers simply don't like to work these little airplanes because they're a pain in the ass to load?"

His coy smile said it all.

I reached up to rub my temples because my head was throbbing, and as soon as I realized that, it occurred to me my legs were aching, and when I noticed that, I couldn't help but feel the stiffness in my neck. I'd been in this station nine days, and every day had been longer than the one before.

"Kevin, I came into this job under the impression that I was supposed to be in charge of this operation at Logan. How come I can't find anything that I'm in charge of?"

He laughed. "We do have a unique way of doing things here. It takes a little getting used to."

"Has anyone ever tried to take action with the union on this issue?" Just contemplating the idea made me want to go to the hotel, get in bed, and pull the covers over my head. But that was probably just what they wanted.

"It's so ingrained now, most of the boys would rather lose their job than work a prop. You'd have to fire them all."

Big Pete was making his way across the ramp, in uniform now and apparently on the clock.

"I don't think so," I said. "You'd just have to fire the right one."

Chapter Fourteen

According to Ellen's running log, the Esplanade along the Charles River had been one of her favorite haunts. It was in the heart of the city, nowhere near Marblehead, yet she'd gone back to it over and over. I understood why when I tried it myself. With the skyline of Boston to the south, Cambridge to the north, and the Charles in between, there was something dazzling to gaze at from every angle, especially on a night like this when the clear winter air brought the lights of the city so close.

It felt good to run, to be outside and not cooped up in my hotel room watching videos. I'd made a decision not to feel threatened every minute of every day, to take charge of my life again, and it felt good.

I'd left my cell phone in the car, which didn't help much when my beeper went off somewhere around the Harvard Bridge. I had to run around Cambridge until I found a pay phone. The number on the beeper wasn't one I recognized, and when I dialed, it didn't even ring once.

"Shanahan?"

"Dan?"

"I've been beeping you for twenty minutes."

"Twenty minutes, huh?" It was ten minutes, at most.

"What's that noise?" he asked. "Where are you?"

"I'm out running. Is this your car phone number?"

"Yeah. I'm on my way to the airport. If we get cut off, it's because I'm in the tunnel."

"Why don't you tell me why you called *before* you go into the tunnel?"

"There was a fight tonight at the airport. Two rampers got into it. They called me about a half hour ago from the hospital."

"Who's hurt and how bad?"

"It was Little Pete Dwyer and Terry McTavish. Little Pete's at the hospital. Cuts and lacerations. I don't know about Terry."

"Is Terry McTavish John's brother?"

"Yep."

"That's a coincidence."

"That two guys with the same name are brothers?"

"No, no. We had a stare-down last night between John McTavish and Big Pete. It was when you were at that sales meeting."

"Shocked the shit out of me," he said. "Terry's not a guy who causes trouble."

"Do you know what the fight was about?"

"No idea. I'm on my way in to do the investigation."

"Do you want help? I can be there in an hour."

"No. I want you to hear the grievance, so you need to stay out of the action. That way it never has to go out of the station."

"You don't want it to go to Lenny."

"When Lenny hears our grievances, he always finds for the union. Or he makes some deal. There's nothing they can do bad enough that Lenny won't cut a deal and bring 'em back to work."

"That sounds like an exaggeration."

"You can check the record."

"All right. What time is it? I don't have a watch on."

"It's just after nine." The connection was starting to break up. "What are you doing out so late?"

"Call me when you're finished and give me the details," I said, ignoring the question. He sounded like my mother.

"You gonna be at the hotel?"

Before I could answer, the line went dead. He must have gone into the tunnel.

A United B767 under tow crept along the outer taxiway toward the maintenance hangar. I could see it from my hotel window. Except for anti-collision lights, the aircraft was dark, all engines off. Moving like that through the night, it looked like a submarine running in deep water.

It had been almost three hours since Dan had called about the fight. I imagined him down there, interviewing closed-mouth rampers, trying to conduct an investigation, trying to figure out who had done what to whom. It was hard waiting. I could have beeped him, but I knew he'd call when he had something.

The Celtics were on TV keeping me company. Listening with one ear, I knew it was late in the campaign and the Celts were out on the West Coast getting clobbered by Golden State, of all teams. I came away from the window, stood in the light of the TV, and stared blankly. Someone in the hometown team's shamrock green uniform had just been called for goaltending. I started to turn it off, but then sat on the bed instead and watched.

My father had loved basketball. And football. And baseball most of all. His hometown Cubs were his favorite, but he'd watch any team. He'd sit by the hour in front of the TV, which is what he used to do instead of engaging with the rest of the world, including my brothers, my sister, and me. I started sitting and watching with him, and pretty soon he started teaching me all the rules, all the teams, and all the players. I was a good student. He'd quiz me, and when I knew one he didn't expect, his face would light up and he'd be so proud. And when he'd fall asleep, I'd still be watching, trying to learn more names, to memorize more stats so that when he woke up, I could make his face light up again. I began to love the thing he loved, which was as close as I ever got to him.

The Warriors were on a 12–0 run, and there didn't seem to be much hope. Besides, I'd lost the thread. I didn't know any of these players. I reached up with the remote and clicked it off.

For a while I sat on the bed and stared at the phone. Eventually, I was staring not at the phone but into the corner of my room where I'd left Ellen's box of personal momentos. I hadn't touched it since the night we'd bolted from her house. I'd started to a couple of times—Dan asked about it almost once a day—but over the weekend I hadn't wanted to be reminded. After Lenny's call on Monday, I wasn't sure I wanted to open it up at all. I knew that if I did, I'd find out all kinds of details about Ellen, the odd and unique ones that would turn her into a person to me. If I opened that box, Ellen would come out and sit in the room next to me and talk to me and I'd get to know her and pretty soon I wouldn't be able to put her back.

I stared at the phone a little longer. Stood up. Paced around. Wished I had brought work home with me. The second time I looked at the box, it was already too late. I went to the corner, picked it up, and hoisted it onto the bed. Before opening it, I laid my hand over it, palm flat, pausing for a moment before disturbing the contents. Then I lifted the lid and began.

Dan had tossed in the mail he'd found at the house, and it was right on top. It was a large stack until I took out all the coupon flyers and catalogues. What was left was a couple of bills and a plain postcard.

Not much different from my own mail. According to her bills, Ellen had paid a fortune to heat that big house, and she was a frequent purchaser of cable pay-per-view movies, the single woman's best friend. At the Marblehead Athletic Club she'd charged the same bagel and cream cheese at the juice bar three days a week, every week, in December. Four times in the month, once a week on Mondays, she'd been charged fifty dollars for something coded PT, which I took to mean personal trainer. I started to put it back into the envelope when I noticed the date of her last session—January 5. It was the day she died. Seemed strange to work out, then go home and hang yourself. A phone number was provided on the invoice. I put it aside to call sometime when it wasn't the middle of the night.

The last item, the postcard, had looked like junk mail because of the computer-generated address label, but the single line of type across the back identified it as something far more interesting. "Have been unable to contact you by phone," it read. "Please call me." And it was signed by none other than Julia Milholland, the mystery woman with the old-Boston name. Whoever she was, she was persistent. And discreet. Not only had she never left a clue in her multiple phone messages, the front of the card was blank. No title, affiliation, or company name, but there was a return address on Charles Street. I put it with the health club invoice.

The rest of the box was filled with Ellen's ubiquitous hanging files with colored labels, which is not how I stored anything personal. I thought the one labeled LETTERS was promising, but I didn't get too far into the newsy notes from Aunt Jo and chatty letters from high school and college chums before realizing that what I needed was a box of letters *from* Ellen.

She'd kept a stack of photo ID's, mostly from school, work, and health clubs. I remembered seeing

Ellen at a few company functions and meetings. I knew what she had looked like, but this was the first time I'd seen a picture of her. She had chin-length red hair and hazel eyes. She had high cheekbones that came down to a rather square jaw. She wasn't pretty in the classic fashion model sense, but she was attractive in an unusual way. She didn't smile much, it seemed, at least not in the photos. I lined them up in chronological order and watched her age all the way up to the last one taken in Boston. The first was a Florida State driver's license issued on her sixteenth birthday. I stared at it for a long time before I was satisfied there was nothing in her smile, nothing in her eyes to portend a life already almost half over.

If people can be defined by the things they keep and the things they let drift away, for Ellen, so specific in everything she did, it would be particularly true. Nothing was in that box that hadn't meant something to her. What surprised me was that they meant something to me, too. Mass cards for the deceased, some with the last name Shepard, reminded me of a worn leather box my mother had kept in the basement, filled with old family photos, black-and-white, stiff with age. It reminded me of a picture I'd found in that box of my mother on her graduation day from a Catholic grade school in St. Louis. She was squinting into the camera, wearing a shy smile. It was the first time I'd ever seen my mother as a girl. I stared at that picture forever. She'd looked hopeful, something I'd never seen in her in real life. It was the first time I'd understood that she had been young once, that she had lived a life before me, one that didn't include me.

Ellen's rosary was in a velvet pouch with a First Holy Communion label stitched in gold. I hadn't thrown mine away, but I hadn't kept it, either. I didn't know what had happened to it. This one was tiny and delicate, made for eight-year-old hands with mother of pearl beads and a simple gold crucifix. I hadn't held a rosary in so long, I'd forgotten what it felt like.

Her birth certificate was there from a hospital in Dade County, Florida. When I pulled out an unlabeled file in the back, a news clip fell onto the cotton sheets. When I turned it over, I was confused for a moment because the woman staring back from the brittle, yellowed newsprint could have been a seamless addition to the chronology of Ellen's ID photos. It could have been Ellen in middle age. But it was a photo of her mother, and this was her obituary.

Anna Bache Shepard had died when she was forty-eight years old. She'd been survived by Joseph T. Shepard, her husband of nineteen years, and her fourteen-year-old daughter, Ellen. Services were held at Christ the King Catholic Church in Miami Shores. I read the clipping a second time, wondering why she'd died so young, but there was no cause given. I understood why after I'd read the only other document in the file, her death certificate. Ellen's mother had committed suicide. She'd hanged herself.

Chapter Fifteen

The phone finally rang—at 5:14 A.M. At some point during the night, very late, I'd leaned against the headboard, put my head back to rest, and fallen into a dreamless sleep. When I opened my eyes, the lights were still on, the contents of Ellen's box were spread across my bed, and Anna Bache Shepard's death certificate was still in my hand.

"You weren't sleeping, were you, Shanahan?" Dan used his louder-than-normal car phone voice, and the line crackled.

"Are you on your way home?" I swung my feet to the floor and stood up to stretch, my spine popping in three places. My left arm was asleep, dead weight hanging from my shoulder. It began to tingle as I shook it.

"I'm just pulling into the parking lot of your hotel. I'll meet you downstairs in two minutes."

We made a good pair, the two of us, waiting in the lobby for the coffee shop to open. Dan sat forward on a low couch, knees bumping the faux-marble table that held his notes. His soft, faded jeans somehow stayed up without the benefit of a belt. His white cotton dress shirt was open at the collar and filled with those tiny wrinkles you get from wearing your clothes around the clock. He had the same wrinkles under his eyes.

"Like I told you last night," he said, "it was Little

Pete Dwyer and Terry McTavish beating the crap out of each other. Both of them got hurt, and neither one will say what happened." He glanced up and caught me stifling a yawn. "Shanahan, if I'm the one who was up all night, how come you look like shit?"

"I was with you in spirit," I said, remembering the puffy-eyed, slack-haired visage in my bathroom mirror this morning. I'd been tempted to wear my sweatshirt with the hood up, drawstring pulled tight. Instead, I'd put my hair in a ponytail, washed my face, and declared myself presentable. "How bad were the injuries?"

"Terry's got a big bruise on the side of his head and a broken hand. From what I hear, Little Pete's got stitches over one eye, but I never saw him. My dumbfuck shift supervisor took his statement, drove him to the hospital, and let him go home from there. Lazy bastard. He didn't even do a substance test."

"Fighting isn't necessarily enough for probable cause."

"He could have used aggression for probable cause. That's what I did for Terry. I had him pee in the bottle when I took him to the hospital to get his hand set. I can tell you right now, though, it's going to come back clean. Terry McTavish is a Boy Scout."

"What do their statements say?"

"Little Pete claims self-defense all the way." He leafed through his file, found the page he wanted, and pulled it out. "Says he was walking across the ramp when Terry jumped him from behind and threw him to the ground. That's it. Except for the fact that he's a lying sack of shit."

"What's Terry's story?"

"He doesn't have a story. I spent all night trying to crack him. All I could get him to say was he had a good reason to do what he did, and he shouldn't lose his job over it."

"No witnesses?"

"None that are talking."

"Do you think—" I stopped and glanced around the lobby. The desk clerk was in the back, and the lone bellman was across the floor out of earshot. Still, I lowered my voice. "Maybe this has something to do with your drug-smuggling theory. Terry could have stumbled into something, and now he's afraid to say what."

"I don't think so. I've been asking around, some of my off-the-record sources. The ones who will say anything swear there's nothing like that going on at Logan at the moment. I don't know if that's the truth, or if it's because Little Pete is involved, but I'm getting nothing on drugs. Dead battery."

"What does your gut tell you about last night?" I was learning that Dan was always in close communication with his gut.

"I think Little Pete was drunk last night, and whatever happened came out of that."

"Drunk during his shift?"

"It wouldn't be the first time."

"Little Pete's a drunk?"

"I thought you knew," he said.

"How would I know that?"

"It's common knowledge."

"Not to someone who's been here two weeks."

He shrugged. "Sorry, boss."

I had a bad feeling, the shaking, rolling, want-to-throw-up seasick feeling I always got when I heard about airport employees drinking on the job. I could just see Little Pete Dwyer careening around the ramp devoid of motor skills, around *airplanes,* in a forklift or a loader. God forbid he should smack into an engine or punch through a fuselage. God help us all if he did it and never told anyone. "How big is his problem?"

"More like everyone else has a problem, because

when Little Pete's drunk, he's mean as hell. He hit a guy in the head with a hand-held radio once because the guy changed the channel on the TV."

"Why is he still working here?"

"That particular time, Lenny made a deal and brought him back. The guy he hit went on permanent disability."

"Why would Lenny bring him back? If he's as truly self-serving as everyone says, I wouldn't expect him to take that kind of a risk."

"I told you about the deals, and Lenny's made a lot of 'em to protect this kid. Every time he gets into trouble, they send him to rehab. He's been twice." Dan was drumming his pencil, eraser end, on the table, making a noise that seemed loud in the quiet lobby. "I can't see Terry jumping anyone," he said, "but I can see it the other way around, with Terry the one who was defending himself."

"I don't suppose there's a chance in hell he'll tell us what happened."

"No. The Dwyers and the McTavishes hate each other. But still, Terry's not going to rat out a union brother and get him fired."

"Would he give up his own job to protect a drunk? Because if I have to get rid of them both to get Little Pete off the ramp, I will."

"With what I've got now, you'd have a hard time busting Little Pete. With no test and no witnesses, I can't prove he was under the influence, and without a statement from Terry, I never will."

"How about this? We keep them both out of service while we conduct our investigation and do some interviews. If we can prove Little Pete was drinking on the job, we get rid of him for good. At a minimum, we can force him back into rehab. In the meantime, maybe Terry reconsiders his story."

"If he doesn't?"

"Then screw him. I don't care about the union and the brotherhood and all that crap. If he's comfortable letting a drunk work next to him on the ramp, he deserves to be gone, too."

"If it comes down to him losing his job, we might see one or two of the decent guys come forward. The McTavishes have a lot of support around here, which we're going to need. I have to tell you, if you terminate Little Pete, you're going to start a war."

"Are you suggesting we leave him out there?"

"I'm just telling you the facts, boss. That's my job."

I sat back in the cushy, crushed velvet love seat and considered my limited options. That seemed to be the drill here—separate the bad options from the worse options and pick one. "Can you handle a backlash on the ramp if we end up terminating?"

"Like I said, the guys like Terry and his brother's got some influence. I think we can ride it out. But it won't be much fun."

"I'll bring Angelo back. That might take some of the pressure off. It'll certainly get Lenny off my back. What do you think?"

"It's about goddamned time. You've been talking about doing it since you got here."

We both turned as we heard the sound of the doors sliding open. The coffee shop was open for business. I reached for the file I'd brought down from my room, stood up, and stretched again. I couldn't seem to get all the kinks out. "Come on," I said. "I'll buy you breakfast. I've got something else I need to talk to you about."

Dan was staring out the window. If it had been summer, he would have been gazing at a lush, terraced courtyard, a carpet of flowering plants, and a swimming pool. But it was darkest January, the floodlights were on, and instead of a shimmering, turquoise blue surface, he was staring at a heavy brown tarp covered with winter's debris. In his hand was the death certificate for Ellen's mother. When he finally spoke, his voice was as blank as his face. "She never said anything about this to me."

"I don't think she told anyone," I said. "Not anyone at work, anyway. You'd have to think if someone knew about it, they would have spoken up. It wasn't in her personnel file." I scanned the obituary again. "Ellen was fourteen when this happened. It had to be painful for her to talk about."

When he didn't respond, I didn't know what else to say, so I drank my orange juice. It was canned, but tart enough to wash away the taste of going to bed too late and getting up too early. The only other patron in the coffee shop, a blonde woman, sharply professional in a sleek suit and sleeker haircut, sat across the floor at a table by herself. We both looked at her when she sneezed.

"Someone knew," he said, turning back to the conversation, his eyes bright with the energy of a new theory.

"Someone knew what?"

"Whoever killed her knew about the mother's suicide. That's why he hung her, to make it look like she killed herself, too. Don't you see that?"

I was about to answer when the waiter arrived. As he served us, I sat back and marveled at Dan. He was either so deep in denial he couldn't see straight, or the most resilient man I'd ever met. Maybe both. The other possibility was that Lenny had been telling the truth, that this unnatural obsession of his was driven by the deepest guilt. "Dan, you have the ability to take any set of facts and form them to support your own theory. Don't you *see* that? I don't understand why you're being so obstinate about this."

"I told you—"

"I know," I said, "she was a good boss and your friend and you're loyal, but this is getting a little absurd. Look at that death certificate and think about what it means."

He picked up his fork and poked at his four runny eggs, a side of pancakes, three strips of soggy bacon, and a stack of toast. The spread looked like something he'd usually enjoy, but not today. He put the fork down. "Okay, what's your theory?"

"Dan, I didn't know Ellen, so all I can do is draw my conclusions from the facts. She came to Boston from staff with a sterling reputation and lots of enthusiasm. She took on a job here for which she wasn't qualified. After thirteen months of trying as hard as she could to turn the station around, she wasn't any further along than the day she arrived. She might have even lost ground. And she was being harassed in the most contemptible way for trying."

He was staring at his eggs.

"It seems to me that something went really wrong for her, Dan. The police have no evidence of murder. Ellen was being treated for chronic depression. She didn't have much in her life besides her job. She was used to being successful, and when it looked as if she might fail in Boston, maybe she felt that her whole life was a failure. It can feel that way sometimes, believe me. And now we find out that her mother killed herself."

I picked at my breakfast, too. The oatmeal with brown sugar had sounded better than it tasted, and I was getting depressed just watching the way Dan was hurting and thinking about Ellen's situation. I abandoned the gummy substance in my bowl and went to the all-liquid breakfast of orange juice and milk. I waited a few uncomfortable moments for a response. When nothing was forthcoming, I went right to the bottom line. "Lenny called me yesterday and asked us to back off this thing, Dan. Maybe it's time."

"Sleazy bastard," he muttered.

"He didn't seem sleazy about it. He seemed to be covering the company's ass and maybe his own. What is it between the two of you?"

"Why? What did he say?"

"He said . . . he said that you were the one who pushed Ellen into taking a hard line with the union and that the reason you're so adamant about how she died was because you feel guilty. You can't accept the fact that she might have killed herself."

Dan's face started to flush. "And you believed him?"

"I don't know what to believe. I know that there's something going on between you and Lenny that you won't talk about. And I feel that there has to be more to your relationship with Ellen that you're not telling me about. Did you two have a thing, because if you did, it doesn't make any difference to me—"

"Don't ever say that, Shanahan. Don't ever say that again. Everything I told you was the truth."

"But are there things you haven't told me?"

We stared at each other, and it became clear that he wasn't going to dignify my question with a response. He countered with his own question. "Did Lenny offer you a promotion if you could make me stop asking questions?"

"What?"

"A promotion. That's what you care about, right? Your career?"

I slipped back in my seat and took a deep breath. I tried to keep in mind that he'd been up all night dealing with recalcitrant employees. But I wasn't one of them. "You're right," I said evenly. "I do care about my career, and I don't want to be made to feel that the things I want are any less important, or in some way less noble, than what you want. I don't believe the issues are that simple."

He sat back, clasped his hands across his stomach, and stared up at the ceiling. His eyes were red and tired, and when he looked back at me, something in them had changed. "I'm sorry," he said quietly. "It's easy for me to say I don't care about my career because I don't have one. And it's been that way for so long, I forget sometimes what it might feel like if I did have something to lose. You're right. This is not your fight."

He had an amazing ability to make me feel validated and guilty at the same time. "This isn't my fight, but I do have a stake in how things turn out. If we can find a way to get rid of the Dwyers, I'd be most pleased. And you do have something to lose—at least Lenny thinks so."

"What else did he say?"

"He said that if I wanted, he'd bust you down to ramp supervisor and move you out of Boston to a station as far away from New Jersey as he can find."

Dan's face turned ashen, then, almost immediately, heart-attack red. "He *said* that?"

"That's exactly what he said."

"Son of a *bitch*." He flung his napkin onto his plate. "Mother*fucker*." When he shot out of his chair, he nearly tipped it backward, bumped the table with his thigh, and rattled all the silverware.

The sleek one glanced up, but only long enough to turn the page of her newspaper.

Dan paced an intense loop around a row of empty tables, came back to ours, then made the loop again. All I could do was hope he stayed in the coffee shop long enough to tell me what I'd said.

"He couldn't even say it to me directly," he mumbled, making another loop. "Yellow ratfuck scumbag."

"Do you want to sit down and tell me what's going on?"

I could see a vein pulsing in the side of his throat as he settled back in and shoved the remains of his breakfast out of the way. "My kid lives in New Jersey. He's threatening to send me away from my kid. That's what's going on."

I wasn't sure I'd heard right. "Did you just say you have a child?"

"She lives with her mother and grandparents down in Newark. I can't fucking believe he would even say that." He banged the table with the heel of his hand and got jelly on his cuff. I gave him my napkin and he wiped it off, carelessly at first, then more deliberately. Even after it was clear the spot wasn't going away, with his mouth set in a grim line and his eyes losing focus, he kept working it.

I reached across the table and took the napkin away. "What's her name?"

"What?"

"Your daughter, what's her name?"

"Michelle. Michelle Marie. She's six."

"She lives in Newark, you said?"

"Belleville. Just outside." He checked his watch.

"What are you thinking?"

"I'm gonna call him. As soon as he drags his ass to work, I'm gonna tell him—"

"I don't think that's a good idea. Tell me what is going on between you."

He sat unusually still, avoiding eye contact. No fingers drumming, no knees bouncing up and down. "I need the key to the house."

"You need to go home and get some sleep."

"Just give me the goddamned key."

This time he got the sleek woman's attention. And the waiter's. And mine. I stared at him, more confused than angry and hoping to chalk the outburst up to too much frustration and too little sleep.

He let out a long, deflating sigh and appeared to regroup. "All I want is to put an end to this. I can't take much more. I'm too tired and I'm afraid of what I'm going to do if Lenny threatens me like that again. If there's a package in that house, I'm going to find it. So can I please have the key?"

The waiter brought the check for me to sign. While Dan waited in the lobby, I went upstairs for the key to Ellen's house. As I watched him walk out the front door with it, I couldn't help but think that he'd never answered my question. Were there things he wasn't telling me?

Chapter Sixteen

Pete Dwyer Sr. was waiting for me that morning, staked out in the reception area with a newspaper, a couple of bear claws from Dunkin' Donuts, and a big cup of coffee. I knew he'd heard me coming down the corridor, but he didn't bother to look up until I spoke.

"Why is it so hot in here?" I asked, sliding out of my coat. It must have been ninety degrees in the office suite. Pete had peeled off most of his outer layers, and still he looked steamy and flushed, maybe because he was sipping hot coffee.

"Damn heating system," he said, almost spitting the words out. "One more thing around here that don't work."

"Are we responsible or is the airport authority?"

"It's the airport. At least once every winter the heating system in the whole building goes wacky. Usually takes them a week to fix it."

"A *week?*" A withering prospect.

He folded his paper, collected his breakfast, and stood right behind me as I unlocked my office door. Once inside, he settled into one of the desk chairs, looking more at home in my office than I did, and watched me with those cool gray eyes, cool despite the ambient temperature and the hot beverage.

"I can't believe you're drinking hot coffee."

"I was outside working all night. It ain't this hot out there."

"Then let's go out there." I didn't wait for an answer, just grabbed my coat and walked out. After a stop for hot tea, we went to the outbound bag room, where it was noisy but forty-five degrees cooler than my office. It was also the heart of the downstairs operation at this time of the morning. Bags and boxes came down in a steady stream from the ticket counter and from skycaps on the curb into the cavernous concrete bag room to be sorted, loaded into carts, and driven to the airplanes—hopefully the right ones.

I leaned in toward Pete and raised my voice to be heard over the grinding of the bag belts and the rumbling of the tugs streaming by with their bag-laden carts. "What can I do for you?"

He stuffed the last of his bear claw into his mouth and licked the sugar off his thumb. "Let's go to the office," he said.

I followed him to the far corner where a couple of flimsy Sheetrock walls with glass windows came together to form an office for the bag room crew chief. He took the desk chair for himself, leaving a rolling secretary's chair with a cracked leather seat and one armrest for me. We could still see the action in the bag room through the windows, but the rumbling of the system was muted, the closed door offering some relief from the constant grinding of the belts. It was quiet enough that I could hear the sound of Big Pete's palms polishing the skin of a grapefruit that had suddenly appeared in his hands. It must have been in the office. He took out a letter opener and began to peel it.

"Is that grapefruit yours?"

"You're holding an innocent man out of service," he announced, completely ignoring my question. "Petey was just an innocent bystander in this thing last night."

"I'm learning that no one is innocent here, and Victor's the union president, so why are you talking to me about this?''

"I don't trust Victor to handle the important stuff"—his eyes cut to my face—"and neither do you."

"Why do you say that?"

"It's true, ain't it?"

It was, of course, and though I didn't want to believe I'd been that transparent, I appreciated the respect he showed by telling me that I had been. It meant I could be equally blunt in return. "If Little Pete was a bystander, why would he have twelve stitches in his head? And I don't think Terry McTavish broke his own hand."

"Man jumps you from behind out of the clear blue and throws you down on the ramp, you're entitled to protect yourself."

"I haven't met Terry, but I'd like to meet the man who could sneak up on your son and throw him to the ground."

He suppressed a smile. "Must have been the element of surprise."

"Must have been. Look, I think I already know what happened last night." He drew back and looked at me all stiff-necked and squinty-eyed. "So instead of you trying to convince me it didn't, just tell me what you want."

He threw part of the peel in the trash, then leaned back and propped his feet up on the desk, his heels resting on the old, stained blotter. "All right. I know you're in a position here. You got appearances to think about, and you got to take some kind of action." As the peel fell away and the fresh citrus smell filled the office, I noticed that he had a hard time stripping the fruit because his fingernails were so short—painfully short—and ragged. They were not much more than nubs, and I knew that he was a nail biter because I had been, too. Big Pete Dwyer struck me as a lot of things, but a nail biter wasn't one. I wondered what it was that made him nervous.

He noticed me staring at his nails and dug his fingers into the fruit, pulling the sections apart. "To my way of thinking," he continued, "Terry threw the first punch. You want to can his ass, we won't fight you. I can guarantee he won't even file a grievance."

"And what happens to Little Pete?"

"He didn't do nothing, so he should come back to work." The grapefruit peel went into the garbage, and a slice of the fruit disappeared into his mouth.

"It's funny how that worked out." I shifted to find a comfortable spot on the cracked leather seat. There wasn't one, so I stood. "You and John McTavish get into a pissing contest the other night. The next thing I know, his brother Terry is in trouble under questionable circumstances. Is Terry aware that his union representative is offering up his job? More to the point, is John?"

"You don't need to worry about what goes on inside the union. You just need to worry about yourself." For a moment he actually made eye contact and held it. "I'm trying to help you out here."

It might have been my imagination, but he seemed oddly sincere even though he was trying hard not to be. There was no question he was trying to help himself and his son, but it was also possible that he truly believed he was helping me, too. "I appreciate the gesture," I said, "but it sounds as if your son is the one who needs help. I understand he has a problem with alcohol."

Pete didn't even stop chewing. "Yeah? Who says so?"

"He's worked under the influence in the past, I think he's doing it now, and I suspect he's the one who instigated the trouble last night, not Terry McTavish."

"My son ain't got no problem like that. If he did, nobody down here would tell you."

His face had betrayed nothing as he sucked another slice into his mouth and spat out a seed, but it wasn't without effort. I heard it in his voice. It was in the measured way he spoke and the precise way he formed his words. The strain was there. It sounded old, scabbed over, and I thought maybe I understood what made him chew his nails. Big Pete was no different than any other father with a screw-up for a son. I almost felt sorry for him.

"How much longer do you think you can cover for him? You can't watch him all the time."

"You don't have no case against my son." He finished off the last wedge and wiped his fingers on a piece of paper from the trash can. "You never will."

"I don't want him working around airplanes," I said.

"If he's working the ramp, he's working around airplanes."

"Then I'm going to have to find a way to make sure he's not working the ramp. What if he causes an accident? Could you live with yourself?"

"You shouldn't even say something like that."

"It scares you, too, doesn't it?"

He stood up slowly, more like uncoiled, and brushed a few wayward flakes of glazed sugar from his uniform shirt. He started toward me and didn't stop until I could smell the grapefruit on his breath. The muscles in my back tensed, and for the first time I felt uncomfortable with him. "My son is my responsibility," he said. "You leave him to me and you won't have no problems. But you push this thing, and you're going to regret the day you ever asked for this job."

I started to breathe a little faster. "Are you threatening me?"

He stepped around me, opened the door, and let the bag room noise come in. Then he leaned down and whispered in my ear. "Think about what happened to the girl who was here before you." I stared straight ahead, fixing my gaze on the letter opener he'd left on top of the desk. "You're all alone out here, just like she was, more alone than you think. I wouldn't want you to get depressed and kill yourself."

I turned to look at his face, but he was already through the door and gone. I would never smell grapefruit again without that awful feeling of my heart dropping into the pit of my stomach.

Molly was at her desk fanning herself and looking as if she might pass out.

"Is someone working on fixing the heat?"

"This happens every year," she said breathlessly.

"So I hear. Why don't you go out and get some fans? Charge it to the company."

"It's the middle of winter in Boston. Where am I going to find fans?"

"How should I know, Molly? *Just do something.*"

I went into my office and slammed the door. I went back to my desk and straight to my briefcase, where I found the fax from Ellen's house, the one asking for a meeting at the same time, same place. I smoothed it flat on the desk and wrote directly on the page, "Saturday, 7:00 PM, Ciao Bella on Newbury Street." It was the only restaurant in town that I knew. I signed my name, went out to the machine, and punched in the number to Sir Speedy in Nahant. My finger froze over the Enter button, giving me one last chance to appreciate what I was doing. I had no idea who had sent this message, and it was just my own instinct saying that it was friend, not foe. But I needed more people on my side, and if this was someone Ellen had trusted, maybe I could trust him or her, too.

I punched the button, the machine whirred to life, and the message was gone.

Chapter Seventeen

Friday afternoon was the worst possible day to cancel a flight. We'd taken two mechanicals back-to-back and cancelled them both. I'd spent the past several hours at the ticket counter helping to rebook a couple hundred inconvenienced passengers. Rebooking is a technical term. It means presenting hostile travelers with a list of terrible alternatives and asking them to choose one. It usually takes a while.

I was almost past Dan's office door before I realized he was in there sitting at his desk, tie loosened and sleeves rolled up. He'd changed his shirt since breakfast yesterday morning, but his eyes were still bleary. He was using one hand to prop up his head and the other to turn the pages of something that had his complete attention.

"If I'd known you were here, I would have invited you up to the ticket counter to take part in our latest disaster."

He responded without looking up. "I just got in. I've been up at Ellen's house all day."

"Which means you've been up for two straight days."

"Here, before I forget . . ." He dug into his pocket and came out with Ellen's house key. "I also went to the post office and got her mail forwarded to the airport."

"Good plan." I sat down and peeled off my shoes.

"Did you find anything? Answering machine tapes, perhaps? Or a fish?"

He gave his head a weary shake. "I've searched every square inch of that place. Whatever she was hiding, I don't think it's in the house, unless it's behind a secret panel or something. With that old place, who knows? But I did find out one thing." He lowered his voice to the point that it was almost just a rumble. "I talked to the old guy, the landlord, and he said the alarm went off again the other night. The police came, but no one was there. You know what that means." He didn't need a response from me. "Someone tried to go in who didn't have the new security code."

"Didn't that make you nervous, being up there by yourself and knowing that?"

He looked at me, and I knew there was no point in pursuing the subject.

The item he'd been studying so intently was a wall calendar. "Are you planning your next vacation?"

"This is Molly's calendar from last year. My buddy over at United got me the list of Ellen's destinations from their frequent flyer desk. Altogether she took fifteen trips, and thirteen of them she could have flown on us. The two we don't fly are to Pittsburgh and Charleston. She got miles for every trip, so you were right. She bought tickets like a real passenger."

I turned the calendar so that I could see the dates. "Did you tell Molly? Because she didn't believe me."

"Yeah. Neither one of us can."

The calendar was from an insurance company, the kind they give out free every year. It had pictures of Massachusetts tourist attractions through the seasons. We were looking at November and Bunker Hill in the snow. Dan had penciled in the three-digit city codes for Ellen's destinations throughout the year. Most corresponded with an ELS, Molly's designation for Ellen, and an explanation of a dentist appointment or an off-site meeting or a personal day off. For some, she must have flown out that night and come back the next morning, because there was nothing on the calendar. No time lost.

"Any pattern or interesting sequence?" I asked.

"Nothing jumps out at me, but I'm working on it. My next step is to call the GMs in those stations."

"If she was sneaking around, flying under cover of another airline, it's not likely she'd check in with colleagues while she was there."

"I know, but I don't know what else to do."

"Is there any connection to the Beechcraft angle?"

"I thought of that," he said. "If there is, I can't figure what it is, other than the fact that we fly them out of here. Big deal."

"You said she had questions about the Beeches. What kind?"

"Like I said, a lot of questions about the cargo compartments, how much weight they can take, position of the fuel tanks, that kind of stuff. That's why I made the connection to drugs."

"But we don't think it was drugs, right? So what was it?"

He shrugged.

"Why don't you try to find another copy of that Nor'easter procedures manual?" I said. "If we looked through it ourselves, maybe we can figure out what she was doing with it."

We stared at each other. We were glum. Stumped and glum. Finally, I reached for the calendar and pulled it into my lap. "When was her first secret trip?"

He checked his list. "A little over a year ago. Not too long after she got here."

I leafed backward through the months, reading the various notations Molly had made and charting the station's recent history in reverse. Besides Ellen's travel days, there were employee birthdays and company anniversaries, retirement luncheons, and the annual Christmas party. September of last year had an entry in red with big arrows pointing to it. It was always an event when Bill Scanlon passed through your station.

"You believe Ellen started her investigation a few weeks ago, right?"

"A little longer, sometime before Christmas."

"If her first trip was over a year ago, then it's hard to relate the travel to the investigation. In fact . . ." I flipped a few pages as the idea settled into my brain. I flipped a few more and I knew I was right. "What these look like to me are secret rendezvous, especially those overnighters."

"What, like she was meeting someone?"

"Someone she didn't want anyone to know she was meeting."

"Why?"

"What do you mean, why? Why does a woman usually have a secret rendezvous?"

"You mean like she was having an affair? No way."

I knew I was right. It felt right, but I had to figure out a way to convince Dan without telling him that my conjecture was based on my own personal experience traveling through the shadow land of whispered conversations, furtive plans, and hidden destinations. "Dan, we've already established this woman's ability to keep secrets. I think it's very possible that she was hooking up with someone in these cities."

His pained expression, lips pursed and eyebrows drawn together, was one I was coming to recognize, because he displayed it every time we found out something about Ellen he didn't know or like. He began to roll down his sleeves and button his cuffs. Something under his desk rattled when he bumped it with his foot. He kicked it impatiently and then again before he looked under the desk.

"Oh, *shit.*" He checked his watch, then reached under and came up with an overnight bag. "I gotta get out of here."

"Where are you going?" As far as I knew, Dan didn't travel anywhere except back and forth to Logan Airport.

"Jersey. I'm going down to see my kid."

"Michelle."

"Yeah, I called her last night and told her I was coming. She'll be waiting for me." As he put on his jacket, he couldn't stop grinning. It was an unabashed, I'm-crazy-about-this-kid-and-don't-care-who-knows-it smile. "She's a pisser. I can't believe some of the stuff she comes up with."

I smiled, too, picturing a miniature female Dan racing around at Mach speeds, spewing invectives. "Does she talk like you?"

It took him a moment to get my drift, but when he did, he was horrified. "No fucking way. I don't swear around my kid." He put his hand over his heart. "On my mother's grave, she has never heard me cuss. Not once. Not my kid."

"If you say so." He unzipped the bag and started loading in files and printouts. I snatched them all back, including the calendar. "I'll take care of this."

"You sure?"

"If you're going to be with your daughter, *be* with her. And by the way, why did I have to hear about her from Lenny?"

"I don't know. It never came up." He closed the bag and looked at me. "You got any?"

"Kids? No."

"Ever been married?"

"No."

"See that? I didn't know that about you. It never came up."

I squeezed back into my shoes and followed him to

the reception area. "Hold on, I'll walk you to your gate." I grabbed my coat and briefcase, closed up my office, and we started walking. It was hard to talk as we pushed through the crowded concourse, so I waited until we'd arrived at his gate. The agents on his flight were boarding stragglers, so I had a chance to tell him about my tête-à-tête with Big Pete. I kept my voice low so no one could eavesdrop.

"Am I doing the right thing not bringing back Little Pete?" I asked.

The bag thudded to the floor as he leaned back against one of the windows. "I think you're doing the right thing—" He caught himself and started again. "I *know* you're doing the right thing. The question is, can we deal with the consequences? And I'm not just talking about here in Boston. Have you talked this over with your boss?"

"Not exactly."

"I'll tell you what's going to happen. Assuming we could even get Terry McTavish to talk and we can nail Little Pete in the first place, Lenny is going to find some way to make a deal with the union and bring him in through the back door. Lenny will be a hero and we'll look like idiots."

"If we can prove that the guy was drunk on the job and physically attacked another employee, I can't see how Lenny could bring him back, if for no other reason than self-preservation. Setting aside all the issues of moral responsibility and self-righteous breast beating, in terms of pure self-interest, knowing what we know—"

"Suspect. What we suspect. Right now we can't prove anything."

"You're right, but if we get to the point where we can prove it, we would have no choice but to pursue his termination. And if Lenny was aware of the same facts, he'd be on the hook, too."

"You're going to threaten him?"

"I'm simply going to make him aware of all the facts. Maybe in writing."

"Sneaky, but be careful. Lenny has no problem looking out for his self-interest. It's your interest I'd be worried about. He'll find a way to get what he wants and blame all the bad stuff on you. He did it to Ellen over and over." He checked the activity at the boarding door. "By the way, is next week soon enough on Angelo? I thought I'd call him when I get in on Monday."

"Monday's fine," I said. "I can't wait to meet the famous Angelo. In my mind, he's almost achieved mythic stature."

"What are you doing this weekend, boss? Looking for apartments?"

"No. And I won't be having as much fun as you will. I'm going to keep an eye on the operation, and if I have time, I might also go back to Marblehead."

"You're going back up?" He hoisted the bag onto his shoulder. "I thought you gave your word to Lenny."

"I only said I wouldn't go into the house. I'm going to check out Ellen's athletic club, talk to her trainer. If I'm reading her invoice correctly, she did a training session a few hours before she died, which seems odd to me. I've also got this mystery woman, Julia Milholland. If she ever calls me back, there might be something to do there."

He was grinning. "I knew you'd come around."

"I haven't come around. I'm simply getting a few questions answered to my own satisfaction."

"Whatever you say." The gate agent motioned to Dan. I walked with him through the boarding lounge.

"One more thing," I said. "Remember I showed you that fax I found on Ellen's machine at her house?

The one setting up a meeting? I faxed it back with a request for a meeting of my own."

"For when?"

"Tomorrow night."

"Shanahan, you sure you want to do that alone? We don't know who this is."

"If it was someone who was working with Ellen, giving her information, he could be helpful."

"What if it's not that person? What if it's the person who swiped the answering machine tapes? Ever think of that?"

Actually, I hadn't. "I set it up at a restaurant, so it'll be crowded, lots of people around. Besides, he probably won't even get the message. I thought it was worth a shot."

"We've got to go, Danny." The gate agent was getting nervous.

Dan went to the podium and jotted a phone number on an empty ticket jacket. "This is where I'll be in Jersey. It's my cousin's place. I'll be back no later than Sunday morning, but you call me if you need me. I'll come back."

"Nothing's going to happen, and I don't want to take you away from your weekend with your daughter."

"Just take it, Shanahan."

I took the envelope. Then I followed him as far as the boarding door and watched him stroll down the jetbridge, chatting with the agent.

"Dan . . ."

He stopped and turned, while the agent kept going. "Yeah, boss?"

"Have a great weekend with Michelle."

He was wearing that high-beam grin again as he turned to board the aircraft. He went off to see his little girl, and I went back to my hotel.

Chapter Eighteen

Marblehead was different in daylight. Twenty miles
north of Boston, it was one of those classic New England seaside communities. It had the dense, layered
feel of a European village with narrow, winding streets
nestled among the hills and tall trees. The houses were
immaculate, three-hundred-year-old clapboard boxes
painted the perfect shade of peach or gray or blue or
yellow with shutters to match, wreaths on the doors,
and brick driveways with flowerpots. All of them.
They looked more like museums than houses, and I
had the impression that the people who occupied them
lived among us but not of us, which, come to think of
it, was not inconsistent with how Ellen had lived.

A brunette, milky-skinned twenty-something named
Heather was behind the counter at the Marblehead
Athletic Club. When she saw me approaching, she laid
two big, fluffy towels on the counter. This must be a
good club. You could always tell by the quality of the
towels. And since they had to be doled out by the
staff and not left lying around for anyone to use, it
must be a very good club.

"What locker can I get for you?"

"I'm here to see Tommy Kerwin. I have an appointment."

"Oh." She whipped those towels back and secured
them in a safe place behind the counter. "I'll page
him for you."

"Thank you."

Ellen's personal trainer was in his twenties, a solid block of muscle in a forest green Marblehead Athletic Club T-shirt and black shorts. His build reminded me of those Rock'em Sock'em Robots, the kind where the head pops up when you hit them just right.

"You have her same job," he said, studying my card.

"I have Ellen's job, yes."

"Do you know why she killed herself?" I was glad to see genuine interest in his eyes and not morbid curiosity.

"We're trying to figure out why. That's why I wanted to talk to you."

"Me?" His eyes widened as he handed the card back.

"I think you may have been one of the last people who saw her that last day."

He shook his head emphatically. "I didn't see her."

The invoice I'd found in Ellen's mail was in my organizer. I pulled it out and pointed to the PT entry. "Doesn't this mean she had a session with you that day? I took it to mean Personal Trainer."

He squinted as he studied the statement. "She was scheduled, but she canceled that afternoon. She just missed the cutoff by like a half hour and I had to charge her. It's club policy. She understood."

"When was her appointment?"

"Regular time, seven o'clock on Monday night."

"And what's the cutoff?"

"You have to cancel at least six hours in advance not to get charged."

Which meant she'd probably called from the airport sometime after one o'clock. "Did she say why she was canceling?"

"No. I asked her if anything was wrong, because

she hardly ever missed, and if she did, she always gave me a reason. Not that I needed one. She was paying me. Anyway, she said something had come up and she didn't want to reschedule, but she'd call me later. That was it."

"How'd she sound?"

"What do you mean?"

"Well, she did what she did only a few hours after you spoke to her. I wondered if she might have sounded depressed or sad or, I don't know, anything out of the ordinary."

His face tightened as he seemed to consider for the first time his place in the sequence of events leading up to Ellen's death.

"She was maybe, I don't know, distracted. It was hard to tell."

A sharp outburst ricocheted out of the racquetball court and bounced around the small lobby where we were seated. Tommy, a man of few words, was staring at me waiting for the next question, and I wished I was better at this sleuthing stuff. I didn't know what to ask, or even what I was looking for. "What kind of a workout did she do?"

"It was a killer," he said, warming quickly to the new subject. "It would all be on her workout card in here."

I followed Tommy into the weight room, where two men and a woman were working through the Nautilus circuit and enduring the loud, pounding disco music that seems to be the required soundtrack at health clubs everywhere. While he searched a two-drawer file cabinet, I stood around feeling overdressed in jeans and a sweater.

"Here it is."

I looked down at the stiff pink card he'd handed me. Tommy was right. Ellen's workout had been a killer, with three reps of squats, leg presses, preacher curls, back extensions, lat raises, and lots more. She even did pull-ups. Twelve of them. On my best day I could maybe do three, and that was only with lots of grunting and cheating. "She worked hard," I said.

"No matter how hard I made it for her, she wanted more. And she did everything I gave her." He pushed the drawer closed and leaned against the cabinet with his arms crossed. "When I read about her in the paper, that's the part I couldn't believe. Why would she work so hard to stay in shape, to stay healthy, then . . . do that?"

I tapped the card with my fingernail. "I don't know," I said. But what I thought was that it was the same compulsion that drove her to work like a dog, to organize and label everything in her life, to try to be perfect in all things. Working out was just another way to try to achieve perfection.

Tommy's name came over the loudspeaker for a call on line one. He looked relieved to have an excuse to end the conversation.

I held up the card. "Can I keep this?"

"I guess. I'd just throw it away."

I thanked him, and while he found a phone, I headed out through the lobby and toward my car.

"Excuse me, miss?" It was Heather calling from behind the front desk, catching me just as I hit the door. "Is someone going to clean out her locker?"

The trainer was trying without luck to remove Ellen's combination lock with a set of jumbo wire cutters. They'd sent a female trainer into the locker room with me, and she was not familiar with the tool. The longer she struggled, the more I wilted in the eucalyptus-scented humidity from the sauna. When the cutters slipped for the third time, I reached up and held the lock steady, albeit with the very tips of my fingers.

Using both hands, she found the right leverage and, with a mighty squeeze, sliced through the thick metal hook. The lock fell away, I opened the door, and we both looked inside.

"I'll see if I can find you some sort of a bag," she said.

I started at the top and worked down. On the top shelf was a tray well stocked with tubes, squeeze bottles, Q-tips, cotton balls, combs. Her brush still had strands of her red hair. Hanging on hooks on the walls were sweat pants, T-shirts, and a couple of baseball caps. An old, faded sweatshirt turned out to be from Wharton, Ellen's business school alma mater. In a strange way, I liked that it felt stiff when I pulled it out, and it smelled of dried sweat. Almost every other aspect of Ellen's life for me was past tense, but the fragrance of running was so familiar that I could imagine the living Ellen in that sweatshirt, just in from a long, exhilarating run through a bright New England winter morning. Or an evening jog along the Esplanade.

At the bottom of the locker was a pile of clean socks, a few running bras, and two pairs of neatly folded tights. When I reached down to pull the clothes out, my fingers scraped something hard, something that was definitely not wearable. I pulled it out. It was a video. A *video?* In her gym locker? And not just any old video. If the cover was any indication, it was pornographic—really pornographic. What in the world was she doing with this? And where was the actual video? When I picked it up, all I had in my hand was an empty box. I hoped to hell we weren't going to find some dark and twisted corner of Ellen's soul because I didn't want to. I had started to like Ellen, at least the parts of her that I could see, and the parts that I could see were helping me understand the parts I couldn't.

Somewhere out of the steam I heard the voice of a

woman, then the response of her little girl. I stuffed the box underneath the stiff sweatshirt and dropped the whole thing in the pile on the floor.

There was more in the bottom of the locker, and as I shoved aside the rest of the socks, I felt a tingle, an all-over buzz because right there in the locker was a binder with the Nor'easter logo. It was Dan's missing procedures manual, and when I saw what was underneath that, the tingle turned electric. Bulging, well used, and fuzzy at the corners, it was Ellen's Majestic/ Nor'easter merger file, the one that had been missing from her desk. I trolled around in the gym clothes, thinking the answering machine tapes might be in there. I was looking inside the socks when the trainer returned.

"This is all I could find," she said, holding open one of two brown paper bags.

"That'll work." I quickly stuffed the clothes and toiletries into the first bag, the files, the video box, and the procedures manual into the second. "Thanks for your help."

A bag under each arm, I backed through the swinging locker room door, walked past Heather at the front desk, and out into the morning air, cool against the eucalyptus dampness on my skin and in my hair. The bag of clothes went into the trunk, the files up front with me.

I didn't even wait to get back to Boston. I pulled into the first coffee shop I could find—they're called crumpet shops in Marblehead—ordered my morning tea, and started with the procedures manual. It was thick and dense and filled with pretty basic stuff, like how to load airplanes. I learned a lot about Nor'easter's ramp procedures, which hadn't been much different from everyone else's, and nothing about why Ellen had found the manual so interesting that she'd taken it with her to the gym. It wasn't exactly a book you'd prop up in front of you on the stair climber. Occasionally, I'd come across notes in the margins, but not in Ellen's handwriting. They always pertained to information on that page, and I assumed they were Dan's. But the first page of the Beechcraft section was marked with a paper clip. So was a diagram of the aircraft, which showed top and side elevations, positions of seats and the cargo compartments, forward and aft. But that was it. There was no indication of why it would be of interest to her.

Almost an hour later, I was drowning in Irish breakfast tea. I'd finally broken down and bought a scone. I don't like scones—to me they taste like warm rocks, sometimes not even warm—but it was all they had. What would have been wrong with serving a bagel or a piece of wheat toast? I was turning pages in the merger file, reading tedious notes, memos, legal documents, and remembering exactly what I had so disliked about my assignment in headquarters. Then I found it. Nestled in among the other papers was a check stub. It was dated April 1995. There was no name, but it was in the nice round amount of ten thousand dollars, and it had been issued by none other than Crescent Security, same as the name on the invoice I'd re-suspended twice. Molly had described Crescent Security as a nickel-and-dime firm that did background checks, which couldn't have been more than a couple of hundred bucks apiece. I tried to remember the amount on the invoice. I didn't think it was more than a few hundred dollars. I knew it wasn't anywhere near ten thousand.

The shop had filled up since I'd been there, and several heads turned my way when my beeper went off. They looked at me as if my cell phone had gone off in church. I checked the display and was surprised not to see the number from Operations. It was a number that was vaguely familiar, but I couldn't place it, so I ignored it. With only a few pages left in the file, I wanted to get to the back. When I got there, I was glad I did.

Stuck in the back of the file as if it didn't belong there was a single sheet of paper folded in half. Handwritten in black ink on the white page was one paragraph.

I think of how my life would be without him, and the thought of letting go scares me to death. I can't think about it directly, so I creep up close to the thought, walk around the feeling, touch it, pull back. When I get too close, I have trouble breathing. My lungs fill up with something cold and heavy, and I feel myself going under. And then I think about my life before him, about the work that filled my days and the ghosts that walked the nights with me, and I feel myself going under again and the only thing that keeps my head above water is the motion of reaching up for him. And I can't let go. Because when I'm with him, I exist. Without him, I'm afraid I'll disappear, disappear to a place where God can't save me and I can't save myself.

The air suddenly felt thicker, harder to breathe. Even if it hadn't been in her handwriting, I would have known that Ellen had written those words. I recognized her voice—the *longing* in her voice. I read it again. Who was she writing about? Had he left her? Is that why she'd 'disappeared'? Because she hadn't known how to save herself? I put the page down, pushed back from the table, and leaned over. I took a few deep breaths, releasing each one in a long exhale. In my mind I saw Ellen writing those words. I saw her reaching out, reaching up for him and trying not to drown. What I couldn't see was his face, the face of the man she was reaching for. And I couldn't see him reaching back for her. She was reaching into emptiness, and I knew what that felt like.

A large woman pushed behind my chair, trying to get by. She brushed against my shoulder, and her touch made me shrink away, pull into myself. It was time to go.

Out in the car, I sat with the door open and the note in my hand, feeling the fresh ocean air on my face and listening to the calls of the seagulls. Up until then Ellen had been elusive to me, hiding amidst the color-coded labels and the calligraphic handwriting and the bare walls of her office. But on this page, in these words, she didn't hide, and it was almost painful to see her so clearly, like looking into the sun after a long walk in the dark. I flipped the page over hoping for a signature or a date, some clue as to who inspired it. Nothing. It could have been written a month ago. It could have been written five years ago. I had a strong feeling based on nothing more than instinct that it was more like last month.

I read it again, this time more slowly. There were no cross-outs, no corrections. The thoughts and words seemed to have flowed out onto the page fully formed, as if she couldn't hold them back. Toward the end the handwriting loosened, almost a tangible representation of the author coming unraveled.

Maybe Ellen had left a suicide note after all.

"Harborside Hyatt, how may I direct your call?"

No wonder the number on the beeper had been familiar. It was my own hotel.

"This is Alex Shanahan. I'm a guest and someone from the hotel beeped me."

"Hold on." I used the Muzak moment as an opportunity to turn up the volume on the cell phone so I could hear over the road noise. Traffic on Route 1A was beginning to build.

"This is the front desk. May I help you?"

I repeated my story to the clerk and waited after he, too, put me on hold.

"Miss Shanahan, this is the concierge." Yet a third hotel employee, this one female, and yet another opportunity to repeat my explanation.

"We received an urgent fax for you this morning," she told me, "with instructions to contact you immediately."

An urgent fax. How dramatic. Probably from Lenny. "Do you have it there?"

"Yes. May I read it to you?"

"Go ahead."

"It says, 'Meet tonight, seven o'clock at Ciao Bella.' "

My scalp began to tingle and my eyeballs went dry. Ciao Bella. The secret code word. "That's it?"

"Yes, it seems to be. There's no signature or cover page."

"Could you look at the time stamp across the top and tell me where it came from?"

"It was sent at nine-forty this morning from Sir Speedy in Nahant."

The meeting was on. "Thank you. Leave it there for me, and I'll pick it up when I get in. Oh . . ."

"Yes?"

"One more thing. Where did you get my beeper number?"

"It was on the fax with the instructions to contact you."

"Okay, thanks again."

The steering wheel had become hard to manage because my hands were sweating so much. I couldn't get the temperature right in the car, and the eucalyptus smell from my hair was too strong in the enclosed space. I should have taken my coat off for the ride back. I had no idea who Mr. Nahant was or even if he was a he, for that matter. Whoever it was, he knew my beeper number, which was a whole lot more than I knew about him.

Chapter Nineteen

The hinges squealed, the door to the restaurant opened, and yet another party arrived at Ciao Bella not to have dinner with me. Fifteen minutes had stretched to thirty, thirty to forty-five. I had eaten too much bread with garlic-infused olive oil and watched a silent hockey game on the set over the bar. Anticipation had given way to frustration, frustration to starvation, and finally to ravioli. Twenty minutes after I'd finished eating, I was still there and still alone. I gave the waitress a big tip for holding her table so long and went out to Newbury Street.

I'd wasted an entire afternoon clenched in nervous anticipation, pacing around my hotel room, speculating as to who the mystery man was and what he could tell me. I'd worked up a good head of anxiety, and now I had no place to put it. The bright New England Saturday had disappeared, turning first to gray, then to a cold, steady rain that had lasted all afternoon. It wasn't exactly ideal weather for strolling, but it had stopped raining, so I decided to anyway.

Most of the shops on Newbury were closed, but their elegant bay windows up and down both sides of the street were dazzling, especially dramatic on a moonless night. Filled with four-button Armani suits, Cole-Haan shoes, and soft leather Coach bags, the bright lights of commerce lit up the red brick sidewalk as the quaint iron street lamps never could.

I lingered at a few of the windows and stopped at one to look at a pair of pleated slacks. I was trying to remember the last time I'd bought something for myself when I saw—felt, really—a quick, cutting movement out of the corner of my eye. The street was alive with foot traffic, but this was too quick for that leisurely pace, and more furtive, like a rat dashing for its hole. I searched the passing faces, but these were no more familiar to me than the ones at the restaurant had been. Too much pasta, maybe. Definitely too much tension.

I forgot about the slacks and kept moving, bundling up against the gusting wind as I crossed Arlington and headed into the Public Garden. I'd been there a couple of times since I'd come to town. On the one occasion that I'd actually kept an appointment to look for an apartment, the realtor had made a point of walking me through twice, and for good reason. It was enchanting in daylight, even in winter. But at night when you're already edgy and sluggish and overstuffed, it's a different story.

Inside the wrought iron fence, sheltered by the old trees, the wind died down and it was much quieter. Quiet enough that I heard the twig snap behind me. Or did I? It was hard to hear anything over the rising tide of panic pounding in my ears. Yes, someone was there, I was sure of it, and if I couldn't hear him or see him, I could feel his presence the way you could feel a shadow moving across the sun.

A tendril of a cold breeze found some exposed skin on the back of my neck and sent a wicked shiver underneath my jacket. He could be anywhere, behind a tree or a statue. The park was closing in on me, and at the same time I felt completely exposed.

I put my head down and walked faster. I was listening and concentrating so hard that I almost rammed headfirst into a couple coming toward me. I had to pull up short and stop abruptly to let them pass. I turned to watch them. They were arm in arm, laughing and pushing close for warmth. Seeing the two of them together made me feel even colder and more alone.

As I turned to go, a voice came out of nowhere: "You picked a bad place to meet," he said—and he was talking to me. For a moment I couldn't move at all. That's the moment I considered running away as fast as I could. I probably should have. Instead, I turned back to find him.

I scanned the area behind me and couldn't see anything. My hands were stuffed into my pockets, and I could feel my shoulders squeezing together, could feel my body almost on its own trying to get narrow so I could hide in plain sight. I tried to swallow, but the cold air had long since stolen the moisture from the back of my throat.

"That restaurant was too crowded."

"Do I know you?"

"I work for you." When he spoke again I spotted him, at least his silhouette, about twenty feet away next to a large tree and well back in the shadows. He was bulky and solid, built like a ramper and dressed in dark clothing. I couldn't see his face, but I knew I'd heard the voice. I just wished I knew if that was good or bad.

He stepped out of the dark. I strained to see as he walked out of the shadows. He came closer and closer, but I still couldn't see. I was reconsidering the running-away alternative when he finally stepped into the light and I could see his face. It was a face I recognized. "John McTavish, right?"

"Yeah. I didn't mean to scare you. I'm sorry."

I started breathing again; then I took off my glove and offered my hand. He quickly averted his eyes, as if this naked appendage, pale and vulnerable in the dim light, was a part of my body he wasn't supposed to see. He made no move to return the gesture, so I stuck my hand back in my pocket.

"How'd you know it was me?" he whispered.

"I didn't know it was you," I said, matching his whisper, "but I know who you are. I would remember anyone who stood up to Big Pete."

He was perfectly still, as I'd seen him in the ready room, the only movement coming from his eyes, quick and alert, locking onto the faces of occasional strangers who happened by, making sure, I presumed, they were strangers. It was disconcerting to see him this nervous.

"Then why'd you send the fax?"

"On a hunch. I found your note to Ellen on the fax machine at her house."

He thought that over. "You took a big chance."

I didn't even want to think about all the chances I'd been taking. "Could we go someplace where it's warm and talk about this? My ears are so cold they're burning. I think that's a bad sign." I took a hopeful step in the direction of Charles Street, but he didn't budge. He didn't even turn in my direction.

"Why'd you want to meet?" he asked.

"I want to know why Ellen Shepard killed herself."

"Is that what you think? That she did that to herself?"

I walked back and stood right in front of him, sniffling. My nose was starting to run from the cold, and I didn't have any tissues. "Do you know otherwise?"

He still wasn't moving, and I knew what he was thinking. If he knew or he didn't, why tell me? I reached back for what I'd been feeling the moment I'd sent that fax. "I'm having a hard time with the union, with Big Pete, and maybe even with my own boss. I'm feeling overmatched and I'm looking for help. That's why I sent it. I need help, and I thought that if you were willing to help Ellen, you might help me, too."

He stood for a moment longer in his zippered jacket, T-shirt, and jeans, an ensemble that struck me as lightweight for the conditions. Then he offered his hand, big and callused, and I grabbed it. He wasn't wearing gloves, but his skin was warm anyway. For the first time he looked me in the eye. "Let's go," he said. "You shouldn't be out here by yourself."

"Too many windows," he explained, referring to Ciao Bella. "We would have been sitting right out on the street in one of the busiest parts of town."

"Would it be that bad to be seen with me?"

"By the wrong people, yeah, it would."

No one was going to see us here. We'd tried two other places before he'd approved of this one, a basement space off Charles Street with exposed brick, a big fireplace, but no windows and only two patrons besides us. I noticed how tiny the coffee mug looked in John's hands. I remembered his quiet confidence as he'd stood in the middle of the ready room and stared down Big Pete. And now he was telling me there was something at the airport that scared *him*. We were sitting in front of the fire, but I couldn't seem to feel its warmth.

"I told you why I sent the message," I said. "Why did you respond?"

He set the mug aside and rested his arms on the table, making a solid piece of furniture feel rickety. "My brother, Terry . . . I heard Big Pete offered him up in a deal for Little Pete."

"He did."

"I also heard you didn't take him up on it, so I figured you would maybe listen to the whole story before you made a decision."

"I'm more than willing to hear your brother's story,

but he's not talking. I'm beginning to wonder if he was even at his own fight."

"He was there, and it's a good thing."

I sat back and studied John's face. It was a big face with a slightly crooked nose, a wide forehead, and a look of disgust that he was trying unsuccessfully to hide. "Little Pete was drunk, wasn't he?"

"They didn't do the test. How'd you know that?" He looked at me hard. "Is someone else talking to you?"

"No. I hear things. And next time, if there is a next time, there will be a test. The supervisor is being disciplined."

"For all the good that will do."

"Tell me what happened. If you want help for your brother, I need to know."

He let loose a long, dispirited sigh, then began, reluctantly, to tell me the story. "Little Pete was tanked up when he got to work that night. He sat in the bag room for a few hours drinking, from what I hear, about a dozen minis straight up. Myers's Rum—dark, that's what he likes. Then he got in a tractor, and while he was driving across the ramp, he fell out."

"He *fell out* of a tractor?"

"That's how he cut his head."

My chest started to tighten as if something were squeezing the breath out of me. Sometimes I threw my anger right out like a fishing net, catching what and whoever happened to be in range. But I couldn't be angry with this man. How could I? This time the anger seemed to settle in my chest and stay there like asthma. "Did Terry tell you this?"

"Yeah. But I also checked with enough guys I know it's true."

"So there were witnesses."

His back stiffened and he stared into his coffee cup.

"I'm not giving any names. I'm only speaking for my brother here."

"I understand."

"So Little Pete's down on the ramp bleeding, but the tractor is still going. It misses the aircraft on Forty by about a foot and rams a bag cart instead. Also runs over a B727 tow bar. Terry sees all this and tells him to get somebody to drive him home. Little Pete says go to hell and starts staggering for the tractor. Terry tries to stop him and that's when Little Pete jumps him. You can check it out. The maintenance log will show a tow bar out of service that night."

I didn't need to check. He was telling the truth.

"And that's not even the worst of it."

"It's not?" I was almost afraid to hear the rest.

"Little Pete was running a crew that night, and one of his guys figured out while they were loading the airplane that he'd reversed the load."

I sat back in my chair. I couldn't even find the words to comment.

"Fortunately," John said, "they caught it before it ever left the gate. His crew sent him inside while they fixed it."

I felt numb just thinking about what could have happened. It's one thing to lose a bag or delay a flight and ruin someone's day. It's quite another to put them on an airplane that won't stay in the air because the load's not properly balanced and the load is not properly balanced because the crew chief was so drunk he couldn't tell the front of the aircraft from the rear. That would be hard to explain.

"Terry has to give a statement, John."

"He's waiting to see what you'll do to him if he won't."

"I'll fire him."

He nodded. "That's what I told him. If he says what happened, will he keep his job?"

"It's the only way he'll keep his job."

"And Little Pete gets canned?"

"If it's the last thing I do."

He angled toward the fireplace, turning his entire upper body, moving the way heavily muscled men have to move. His eyes were fixed on the dying flames, and he looked tired. More than tired, bone-weary. It was the same look I'd seen on Dan a few times. I waited. I knew he'd talk again when he was ready.

"When I first started at the airport," he said, still staring into the fire, "I was working down on the mail dock. My second or third day on the job, the union sent down a steward to tell me to slow down. He told me I was showing everybody up and if I wanted to keep working there, I should ease off. I told him to go pound sand."

"How'd they take it?"

"They gave me one more warning. Then one night in the parking lot, these two guys come up from behind and jump me. The one tried to grab me, I broke his arm. The other one ran away when he heard the bone snap."

The fire popped and I winced. "You broke his arm?"

"He had a baseball bat. They didn't bother me much after that."

I checked out the bulging biceps underneath his T-shirt and wondered what had possessed anyone to come at him in the first place. "Is this job that important to you?"

His chair creaked ominously as he leaned back. "I worked on my pop's fishing boat when I was growing up, me and my brother both. Out in the morning when it was still dark, home after dark. Miserable, cold, and wet, and you worked all day long. Pop didn't pay us much, but he taught us one thing—someone pays you to do a job and you agree to do it, then you do it.

That's it." He turned back to the fire. "We get good money and benefits for throwing bags a few hours a day and sitting around in the ready room watching TV the rest of the shift. On top of that, you and your whole family get to fly around basically for free. It's not like we're skilled labor. This is a good job for someone like me. It's how I'm going to put my kids through college, and nobody's going to run me off."

"You have a family?"

"I got a wife and two kids, three and seven."

"It sounds as if they tried to run you off and failed."

"I can take care of myself. But it's different when it's your family, and I'll tell you something else, Little Pete scares the shit out of me. There's something wrong in the head with that kid. He's okay when he's around Big Pete, but when he's not, it's like he goes crazy or something. And when he's drunk, forget about it. When he's sober you never know what he's going to do, and when he's tight it's getting so it's tough even for his pop to deal with him."

"Do you believe he could kill someone?"

The lines in his forehead deepened. "If Petey'd been one of the guys who jumped me that night in the parking lot, he wouldn't have run off. I can't watch Terry all the time and no offense to you, but I'm sure as hell not going to count on the company to protect him. The company's just as likely to cut a deal and bring Petey back to work."

I wanted to say that that would never happen. I wanted to assure him that once Lenny had all the details, as I had now, there would be no way we'd bring Little Pete back to work and no way Terry would be fired. I couldn't tell him that because I didn't know it. Lenny was still a mystery to me. "Tell your brother to sit tight while I figure out what to do. I'll find a way to work all this out."

"How?"

"I have no idea. And tell him thanks."

"I will."

I sat quietly while he found a poker and tried without success to get the fire going again. When he'd settled back in, I asked him if he wanted more coffee.

"I'm working a shift starts at four in the morning. I gotta get some sleep tonight."

That may have been a clue that he wanted to go home, but I liked sitting with him. In spite of how I felt about everything else, I felt safe with him, and that was something I hadn't felt for a while. "John, you said something outside about Ellen's death not being a suicide. Do you believe she was murdered?"

"I don't know." He said it in a way that made it clear we weren't going to talk about it that night, or maybe ever, and I had to respect that. I tried something easier.

"How did you hook up with Ellen?"

"I was trying to get my brother a job at the airport."

"That doesn't seem so hard."

"The union didn't want another one like me around, so they poisoned him with the supervisors. They said if Terry got hired, they'd slow down the operation, set something on fire. I told her about it, and she interviewed him personally and made them put him on. After that, I told her if she ever needed help to call me."

"And she did."

"Yeah."

"What about?"

He did yet another visual sweep of the restaurant, but no one we knew was there, including our waiter. "There was something she needed . . . this package."

I sat bolt upright, nearly tipping the table into his lap. "What kind of a package?"

"I don't know, about this big"—letter-sized—"a plain brown envelope with tape and dust all over it."

"What was in it?"

"She didn't say I should look in it, and she didn't open it in front of me, so I don't know what it was."

In this one case, I wished he'd been a tad less principled. I couldn't ask the questions fast enough. "Why did she need you to get it?"

"It was in the ceiling tiles in the men's locker room. Dickie must have tossed it up there sometime when he was working here."

"Dickie Flynn?"

"He's the one told her where it was."

"Why was it in the ceiling?"

"Guys use the ceiling for a hiding spot when they're in a hurry."

"Doesn't seem all that convenient."

"Say they're helping themselves to the catering cart, stealing minis. After cocktails, they don't want to walk around with empty bottles knocking around in their pockets, and they don't want to leave 'em lying around in trash cans, so they toss them up there. The ceiling has rattled around here for years, decades even."

"But no one ever came upon this package?"

"It was way off in the corner. You wouldn't find it unless you knew what you were looking for."

"That means it could have been up there for a while. And you can't even hazard a guess as to what this was about? She never said?"

"No, I don't know. But I think Angie might."

"Angie as in 'Angelo'?"

"Yeah. He had something she needed, and she wanted to put the squeeze on him."

"DiBiasi?" I had to pause for a moment and regroup. I had clearly hit the mother lode, and I was having a hard time assimilating all the new data. "I thought Angelo was small-time. An afterthought. Wrong place, wrong time, that whole story."

John shook his head. "Angelo was the target all

along. That whole stakeout thing was just to make it look like they grabbed him up by accident. I gave her some help on the thing."

"Ellen set him up?"

"As far as I know, the whole thing was her idea."

"I'll be damned." I sat back and let this new information settle over everything else that we knew. It added whole dimensions to what I knew about Ellen. And it forced a new appreciation for how deep the swamp was getting. Packages, setups, stakeouts. Missing files, missing tapes, missing videos. Maybe a mystery lover. I didn't know if we'd ever find the bottom or what we'd find if we got there. What I did know was that I was following Ellen's tracks right into the depths.

"This Angelo thing," I asked, "was it before or after the package?"

"After."

"So he might be connected somehow to that envelope. Maybe that's why the union's pushing so hard to get him back," I said. "And Lenny, too, I suppose. They're trying to take away my leverage. I didn't even know I had leverage. John, I know you don't know what was in the package, but did Ellen ever say anything about the Beechcraft?"

He looked puzzled. "No. Not to me."

"How about fish?"

"Fish?" More puzzled still. "Like scrod?"

"I don't think so, but I don't know. Crescent Security?"

He shook his head.

"Ellen seemed to be working on something, collecting information. It may have something to do with the Majestic-Nor'easter merger or the Beechcraft. We were even thinking Little Pete might have been involved in drug running."

"No. That I would have heard about. Besides, Big

Pete would kill Petey with his bare hands if he found out he was into drugs. He's already close to killing him over the booze."

"Does he really care about him as much as it seems?"

"Yeah, he cares about him, but part of it is he feels guilty, too, like he passed on the disease. Big Pete was a boozer himself until just a few years ago—the whole time Petey was growing up, anyway. He's always trying to get him to go to A.A. meetings with him. The kid won't go."

Big Pete's chewed-up fingernails started to make some sense. We sat for another few minutes in silence before he started fidgeting, making it clear he wanted to leave.

"John, would it be all right if I contacted you again?"

"Do you have something to write with?"

I found a stubby pencil in my jacket, down with the pocket lint and old movie ticket stubs.

"You can leave a message at this number," he said, writing on a cocktail napkin, "and I'll get in touch with you."

The number was familiar. "Where is this?"

"Sir Speedy up in Nahant. My sister works there."

One mystery solved.

Charles Street, still damp from the rain, was threatening to freeze over, and the brick sidewalk was slick and precarious. John offered to drive me back to the hotel, but I knew he didn't want to be seen with me and I wasn't keen on lying in the backseat under a blanket.

"John, did anyone know you were talking to Ellen?"

"Not even my brother. And you can't tell anyone. Even Fallacaro."

"You don't trust Dan?"

He didn't answer, so I put my hand on his arm and made him stop walking. "Are you saying you don't trust Dan?"

He looked away for a long time as if trying to find the words. "Here's the way I see it," he said. "If she had trusted him, she would have had him get her the package, right?"

He didn't wait for an answer, which was good because I didn't have one. I watched him disappear down a side street and into the shadows; then I turned and started for a cab stand. I was still trying to digest that last thought when it occurred to me that the address on Julia Milholland's postcard was somewhere on Charles. One-forty-two . . . 146, maybe. I went from door to door reading labels on buzzers and peering through plate-glass windows into dry cleaners, drugstores, and gift shops. I came to 152 Charles Street and found it occupied by something called Boston-in-Common. An article written by Ms. Milholland herself was posted right in the window. It was advice on how to find your perfect mate. Boston-in-Common was a dating service.

The cab dropped me off in front of my hotel. I reached through the window to pay, and when I turned around, I felt him out there, felt him before I saw him standing off to the side in a leather jacket with the collar turned up in front of his face. I didn't need to see his face to recognize Little Pete.

"What are you doing here?" I asked, trying not to show surprise. Or anything else.

"I came to see you."

It had stopped raining, but it hadn't stopped being cold, so the perspiration dripping down his face was disturbingly out of place. Rivulets tracked around the ugly, swollen row of stitches that snaked through his right eyebrow. The thought of how he had gotten them made me even more nervous, and I wondered if he was drunk again.

"If you want to talk to me, do it at work." I hoped I was sounding annoyed and in command.

His fist shot into the air. I flinched and stepped back, almost stumbled backward, certain that his arm, like a tree limb, was about to crash down on my head.

"I can't come to work," he whined.

The blow never came; it was only a gesture of his frustration. No matter. My pulse was racing. I wasn't nervous, I was scared. He wasn't staggering and I didn't notice any slurring, but he was wasted. I could see it now that I could see his eyes.

"That's what union reps are for," I said, inching backward and plotting my path to the front door of the hotel.

"I don't *need* my *fucking pisshead union rep mouthpiece* talking for me." A man coming out through the door of the hotel reacted to Little Pete's harsh tone—or maybe the harsh language—with a grim scowl. I reacted by moving closer to the door.

"What happened," he said, his voice elevating with each of my steps back, "wasn't my fault. It's that fucking McTavish."

It was there, that flash of rage, the one I'd seen in his eyes when he'd looked at me during his hearing. I still had no idea where it came from or why it had anything to do with me. All I knew was that seeing it in those dull, drunken eyes sent a cold shiver right through my soul.

"Don't ever approach me like this again."

I turned and headed for the door. Thankfully, he didn't follow, just yelled after me. "I'm not losin' my fucking job over this. *You're not takin' my fucking job.*"

Inside the elevator I reached out and pushed the Door Close button. When it didn't close fast enough,

I pressed again and again and again. I don't think I took a breath until I got into my room and locked the door. I know that my heart rate didn't come down until hours later when I finally fell asleep.

Chapter Twenty

Dan's sneakers squealed on the varnished floor as he looped under the basket and in one fluid motion rolled in a left-hand runner.

"High school ball?" I asked.

"Yeah, but that's not where I really learned to play." His perimeter shot was equally good. He knocked it down, grabbed the ball, and stood in front of me, sweating in an old hooded sweatshirt and what appeared to have been sweat pants at one time. They were cut off at the knees. "Playgrounds in Newark. Me and my cousins played for money."

"Hustler, huh? In Newark, no less. You're probably lucky to be alive."

When I dropped my backpack and pushed up the sleeves of my sweater, he handed me the ball and cut to the basket. I passed it back and he sank a twelve-footer.

"How was your trip?"

"Good."

"Why did you come back last night?"

"I thought the weather might get bad here. Besides, Sunday is family day down there. They all go to Mass and come home and put on a big spread, and everybody wants the kid around for that." He shrugged. "I'm not part of the family anymore." He bounced the ball to me. "You didn't have to come over here," he said. "I would have met you somewhere."

I dribbled a few times and hoisted a shot that banged off the rim. I used to do it better in seventh grade, but at least I didn't heave it underhanded. "My hotel room was closing in on me. I'm just glad you take your beeper to the gym. Or whatever this is."

"This is my neighborhood rec center."

"How come there aren't more people recreating?"

"This place will be jammed this afternoon with a thousand screaming kids, which is why I come in the morning. But when I get more time, I'm going to coach a kid's basketball team."

"Teach them how to hustle?"

"Sure," he grinned, "why not?" He looped up one last shot from under the basket, missed, and followed the ball as it bounced over to a row of wooden bleachers. I followed him, and we sat on the bleachers in a wedge of sunlight that came through a row of high windows. With the mint green cinder-block walls, the heavy double doors, and light mildew odor, I could have been back in gym class.

"I've got to ask you something before I forget," I said. "You haven't talked to Angelo yet, have you?"

"I was going to call him tonight, tell him to get ready to get his ass back to work. He's got Sunday-Monday off, so he wouldn't be in until Tuesday. That's what you wanted, right?"

"I changed my mind. I don't want to bring him back yet."

"Why not?"

I really wanted to tell him the whole story about how Ellen set up Angelo. I wanted to tell him about the package and ask him what he thought Angelo might know. But I couldn't. "I want to wait another day or two and see what happens." I watched for a reaction, wondering if that reply sounded as tepid as it felt. But if he was any more curious than that, he didn't say.

"We've got no problem with Angie because he's already terminated, but we have to do something about Little Pete and Terry McTavish. Wednesday night will be a week, so I have to either start termination proceedings or bring them back."

"I don't suppose Vic might agree to an extension."

"I can talk to him, but if I do they're going to be pissed. They know that Terry hasn't said a word. They know we haven't got jackshit and they're going to want him back. Not Terry, but Little Pete."

"Ask him anyway."

"All right."

"He came to see me last night."

"Victor?"

"Little Pete. He was waiting at my hotel when I got back from dinner."

"I'm going to kill him," he fumed, squeezing the ball until I thought it would burst. "I'm going to go over to his fucking house—"

"Good, Dan, that's all I need, to be working on this by myself." I unbuckled the pack and started unpacking. "At least wait until you see what I found yesterday in Marblehead. I was very busy up there yesterday." Exhibit one was his Nor'easter procedures manual, and exhibit two was the merger file. "These were in Ellen's locker at the health club."

"No shit." He threw the towel around his neck and grabbed the manual. "You're pretty good at this, Shanahan."

It was nothing but a throwaway comment, but it still gave me a lift, the kind I seemed to get from any pat on the head for any reason. "Guess what else was in there?"

I whipped out the porno video box and he grabbed it, eyes wide. "Jesus Christ, Shanahan. What are you doing with this?"

"It was in Ellen's locker with all this other stuff."

"She had this? No way. Ellen was a Catholic, and a good one, too. Not like me. I never even heard her swear." He popped it open. "Where's the tape?"

"I found it that way."

He turned the box over a few more times, reading everything that was written on it, which wasn't much, then set it aside with a look of complete bewilderment. Still shaking his head, he reached for the merger file. "Anything in here?" The check stub from Crescent was right on top. He glanced at it and went on. "Anything in this file about fish?"

"No fish. And no answering machine tapes, either." I reached across, pulled out the stub, and showed it to him. "Have you ever heard of this company?"

"Means nothing to me."

"When did you say you came to Boston?"

"May 23, 1995."

"Just a month after this check was issued. But it doesn't ring any bells?"

"Nope. Why?"

"Ellen had a copy of an invoice from Crescent Security in her follow-up file. Here it is again popping up in the merger file. A couple of things are starting to feel significant to me, even if it's just because they keep coming up, and the Majestic-Nor'easter merger is one of them." I slowed down and reminded myself not to reveal things I'd learned from John, things I wasn't supposed to know. "First, Ellen came to work in Boston fresh off her assignment on the Nor'easter acquisition task force, which might not mean anything except that a few weeks ago she pulled this file," I tapped the manila folder on his knee, "and ended up hiding it under her gym socks. At the same time she developed a keen interest in your Nor'easter procedures manual—specifically the Beechcraft—and also stashed it away with the socks. She contacted a colleague from the merger project and asked him where to find documents that had to do with the deal."

"What kind of documents?"

I explained what I had learned from Matt. "She was explicit about what she wanted. These were schedules having to do with a certain kind of pre-merger expense, something called purchase price adjustments, which is a fancy way to describe a list of vendors and how much we paid them for services related to the deal."

"What would the merger have to do with Little Pete?"

"I have no idea."

The last thing I pulled out was the handwritten paragraph. After he took it from me, he read it so fast you would have thought it made his eyes burn. Then he flipped it over to check the back. Finding nothing more than I had, he folded it up and thrust it back without a word.

I took it back and unfolded it. "That's Ellen's handwriting, isn't it?"

"So? You don't know how old it is. It could be ten years old."

"Why so defensive?"

"I told you she wasn't seeing anyone."

"Let's just postulate that it's current, shall we? I think Ellen was seeing someone in secret, Dan. I believe that's what the travel on United was all about. She could have been flying around to meet him and didn't want everyone to know." The postcard from Boston-in-Common was in one of the side pockets from my backpack. I pulled it out and handed it to him. Thank goodness I'd brought visual aids, because he was turning into a tough audience. "Ellen belonged to a dating service."

"C'mon, Shanahan," he said, stuffing the card back

into my pack. "That's not what that card says. It doesn't say anything."

"The address from that card matches the address of a place called Boston-in-Common on Charles Street. I saw it, and it's a dating service. Maybe she met someone there. Maybe she fell in love. Is that so hard for you to believe? It's possible she got dumped and having cared so deeply for this person—"

"Are you saying she killed herself over some guy?"

"Listen to what she wrote, Dan." I read him the last line. " *'Without him I'm afraid I'll disappear, disappear to a place where God can't save me and I can't save myself.'* She sounds as if she's afraid to live without him."

"Why would she keep it a secret?"

"I don't know, Dan. Ellen had lots of secrets. I'm going to Boston-in-Common tomorrow when they're open to see if they'll give me any information, although I doubt that they will. They strike me as discreet beyond belief, these people."

Dan jumped down to the floor and began pacing back and forth along the front of the bleachers, dribbling the ball as he went. "She didn't kill herself over some guy." He punctuated the thought with one hard bounce of the ball.

"You already said that."

"But you don't agree."

"I don't think we need to agree on that point. I'm curious enough to keep digging, no matter how she died, and I'll share everything I find with you, just as I have so far."

"But you do think that, don't you? That she climbed up on that locker and put a rope around her neck and jumped off."

I finished buckling the backpack, set it aside, and tried to figure out exactly what I did think about this woman.

"I believe there were two Ellens, Dan—the one she showed to the world, and the one she kept to herself. That's why we continue to find things that surprise you. Since I didn't know her at all, it's possible I can see things you can't, or at least see them differently. That paragraph she wrote, it's the truest, most authentic thing I've found so far about her. The dating service, her mother's suicide, these feel like the real Ellen to me, and the real Ellen feels very sad. And I don't know why she kept that from you."

The bleachers rattled as he climbed back up, dropped down to the bench beside me, and wedged the ball between his old-fashioned high-tops. "Do you know when she joined this dating service?" He spat out the word "dating" as if it were an anchovy.

"Hopefully I can find out tomorrow."

He leaned back on his elbows and squinted up into the windows. "The reason I can't believe she had any kind of relationship going on was because of something she said to me once. She was always talking about how great it was that I had a kid and how I should never take it for granted. So one day I said something stupid like, 'It's not rocket science. You can do it, too.' She said it was too late. Here she is thirty-five years old and she's talking like she's eighty-five. She just laughed and said, 'What am I going to do? Quit my job, get married, and raise a family with someone I haven't even met?' I said, 'Why not? People do it all the time.' She said she'd made her choice a long time ago without even knowing it. And she said I wouldn't understand because I'm a guy."

"Did you understand?"

"No."

"She was saying she chose work."

"But that's not a choice she made without knowing it."

"I would say it differently. To me, it's not the choice

that's unknown, it's the consequences. Like choosing a path you think is going to . . . I don't know, Paris. But you end up in Tulsa, Oklahoma, and you can't figure out where you made the wrong turn. The truth is, you've been on the road to Tulsa all along, and the day you wake up and figure it out is probably a day too late."

"It's never too late for anything."

"You begin to feel that it is, and that's all that matters. It becomes a self-fulfilling prophecy."

"She could have quit her job."

"That's easy to say, but I love what I do, and I believe Ellen did, too. When I dispatch an airplane every night that's going to be in London the next morning, or reach up and put my hand on the side of an aircraft engine, I still get the same charge I got the first time I ever did it. I love this business. I love the moving parts and every different way things can get screwed up. I love how hard it is to put it all back together, or to just keep it together on any given day. I love Majestic Airlines, and being part of a great company, even with all the demands that come with it. It's my home. It's more of a home than I ever had. I don't know who I'd be if I wasn't the person who did this job."

I took the ball from between his feet, stood up, tried another shot, and missed again. "Maybe that's why Ellen joined the dating service."

"Why?"

"To find out who she was outside of this job. Could be you talked her into believing it wasn't too late."

I walked across the court to retrieve the ball. My arms felt heavy as I leaned down to pick it up. It was the same heaviness I always felt when I allowed myself to think about my life, my choices, and the things I wished I'd done differently.

"You gonna tell me you feel that way, too?"

"I'll be thirty-two in a few months. I have no husband, no kids, and no prospects. I don't even have a dog. My apartment in Denver is filled with boxes I never unpack. Boston is supposed to be my new home, but I've been here two weeks and I've spent about five minutes thinking of finding a place to live. If it were up to me, I'd probably stay in temporary housing until it's time to move again. It makes it easier to leave that way."

I squared to the basket, dribbled twice, and really focused. If Ellen had believed that it wasn't too late, I envied her. When I let the shot go, it arced perfectly, angled off the glass, and swished through the net. The bank was open, as my dad always used to say. I looked over at Dan. He was watching me with his chin in his hands, elbows on his knees.

"No," I said, turning back to face the basket, "I don't think I'll be seeing Paris. But maybe Tulsa's not such a bad place. At least that's what I tell myself."

The ball rolled into a corner and died.

Chapter Twenty-one

Boston-in-Common looked more like an art gallery than a dating service. It had polished hardwood floors, subtle indirect lighting, and small photographs with large mats punctuating smooth bare walls. It felt expensive and minimalist, and I felt out of place. I'd never been near a dating service before, and as far as I was concerned I could have gone my entire life without visiting one. Not that I'd ever had much luck on my own, but there was something about the *arranged* aspect of the whole affair, the forced conviviality that seemed so artificial. The very idea gave me the willies.

"Welcome to Boston-in-Common. May I take your coat?"

A young Asian woman with perfect, pale skin, red lipstick, and a helmet of precisely trimmed, gleaming black hair came out from behind her chrome desk and waited for me to slough off my coat.

"Sure, but it's pretty wet." I pushed a clump of matted hair out of my face. My newspaper-umbrella hadn't provided much cover, and it was not a good day for suede pumps, Scotchguarded though they might be. I felt as if I was standing on two wet sponges. "I have an appointment with Julia Milholland."

"Yes, we've been expecting you, Ms. Shanahan. Would you like to freshen up?" I took that to mean, "You look like hell and you ought to at least comb your hair," but I smiled and she pointed the way to the ladies' room.

When I looked in the mirror, I had to admit she was right. I hadn't been sleeping well, my running schedule was screwed up, and I wasn't eating right, all of which made me grumpy. I was spending my time either at the airport or digging around in Ellen's life, and my complexion was beginning to take on that Dan Fallacaro pallor. I felt even more disheveled thinking about what kind of place this was and why people came here. There wasn't much I could do except pass a comb through my damp hair and pretend I was supposed to look this way. I'd never been much good at primping.

The sound of heels on hardwood preceded the arrival of Julia Milholland. She was what people called a handsome woman, impeccably dressed with unusually good posture. Though she was probably closer to sixty, she looked fifty, and when she introduced herself she asked me to call her Julia. How convivial of her. Perhaps it was my own state of mind, but as I followed her back to her office, she appeared exceedingly well rested to me.

After she settled in behind her desk, she clasped her hands together and smiled at me across her desk as a pediatrician would smile at her patient. "Now then, Alex, let's get you started."

"I apologize if I misled you, Ms. Mil—Julia, but I'm not here to sign up for the service. I'm here to ask you about one of your members." I handed her my business card. "Ellen Shepard."

She didn't even glance at the card, much less take it. I laid it on the desk.

"I'm sorry," she said stiffly. "If I had known, I would have told you over the phone and saved you the trip. We are very protective of our clients' privacy, and I can't tell you anything unless you have Ellen's permission."

My shoulders sagged. I'd assumed she knew about Ellen. I don't know why. It's not as if someone had sent out announcements. Now I was going to have to tell her. I sat up straight in my chair and pushed that stubborn hair out of my eyes. "I have some bad news, Julia. About Ellen."

She turned her head slightly. "Oh?"

"She died. Two weeks ago."

An elegant gasp escaped from her lips as she touched her chin lightly with her fingertips. "Oh, my. I just talked to her last . . . oh, dear. What happened?"

"It appears that she took her own life."

Her hand moved to her throat, her fingers searching for an amulet hanging from a gold chain around her neck, some kind of a Chinese character. She found it and held on tight. "That poor, poor woman."

"Did you say you just spoke to her? Because I saw in her mail that you were trying to contact her. I had the impression you were having a hard time."

Julia, still holding the amulet, was considering my business card again and not listening. At least she wasn't answering.

"Ellen didn't leave a note," I said, "and when I found your name in her mail, I thought you might be able to help. I assumed that she was a client."

"Yes and no."

"I beg your pardon?"

"Let me tell you how our process works, and I think you'll understand." She let go of the necklace long enough to peel a form off a stack at her elbow and pass it across the desk. "When a client signs up at Boston-in-Common, we ask them to fill out this questionnaire, and then sit for a seven- to ten-minute video."

I looked at the form. A background check for a

cabinet post couldn't have been more thorough. The questions were what I considered to be personal, some deeply, and I felt exposed just reading it.

"Information from the questionnaire goes into our database. We run comparisons until we find a match. The two clients, the matches, read each other's questionnaires and view each other's videos. If they both like what they see, we get them together."

"Did Ellen do the questionnaire and the video?"

"She sat for the video over a month ago, I think." Julia paged back in her desk calendar. "Yes, it was Tuesday, December 2. She brought her questionnaire with her when she came in. I made a match for her almost immediately. It wasn't hard. She was shy, but I found her to be very attractive and quite charming with a wonderful sense of humor."

"Would you be willing to give me the match's name?"

"Of course not. It wouldn't help you anyway because she never met him. I couldn't reach her to give her his contact information, which is why I sent the card. When she finally did call back, it was to cancel the service."

"Cancel the service?"

"Yes. She said something had come up. She didn't want her money back, but she knew it was not going to work out for her. She resigned her membership before she ever met one man. I was astounded because she had been so . . . so . . ." I waited, but she became transfixed by a spot on the desk, and it seemed as if her batteries had just run down.

"Excited?"

"No. I think determined is possibly more accurate."

"How much money did she forfeit?"

"Eighteen hundred dollars."

"Eighteen *hundred?* What do you get for *that?*"
Julia lifted her chin just enough so that she could

look down her nose at me. "We are a very exclusive service, Ms. Shanahan. The fee is for an annual membership, and it includes one match each month."

I wanted to ask about guarantees and warranties and liquidated damages, but that would have been pushing it, especially since I wasn't here to plop down eighteen hundred clams. "Okay. So if you sign up and pay the fee, you're probably serious about meeting someone."

"We only accept candidates who are serious and"—she fixed me with a meaningful, clear-eyed, all-seeing look—"emotionally available."

I felt exposed again. Worse than exposed. X-rayed. The radiator in the corner, painted off white to match the walls, had kicked in and the office was filling with that dry radiator heat that I always found so uncomfortable. Finally she continued.

"I told Ellen I would keep her account active for a few months in case she changed her mind. She thanked me and told me to close the account."

"She was that sure?"

"Yes. She said she knew she would never be back . . ."

Her voice died and I watched Julia's face transform as Ellen's statement came back to her with new meaning. The lines grew deeper and she was now looking all of her sixty years.

"If you're agreeable, Julia, it would help me to get copies of Ellen's materials." I pulled out Aunt Jo's power of attorney and handed it to her. "As I said, I have authorization from the family."

She put on a pair of glasses, perused the document, and then looked at me over the tops of the lenses. "May I make a copy of this? I'd like to check with my attorney before I release anything, if that's all right." Julia was not a spur-of-the-moment kind of person.

"Would it be possible for me to wait while you did that? Maybe I could use the time to watch Ellen's video."

She took off her glasses, turned and watched the steady rain outside, and I thought she was considering my request. "You meet all kinds of people doing this work," she said, still staring, "and they all come in saying they're ready to change their lives. But it takes courage and so many of them don't have it. I thought Ellen did, which is why I was so surprised when she quit. I thought it had been a long, hard struggle for her, but that she was ready, and though I didn't know her well, I believed that good things were about to happen for her." She set her glasses softly on the desk and looked at me, her face still strong, but her eyes glistening like the wet windowpane. "I find this all very sad, Miss Shanahan, very sad, indeed."

I didn't know what to say and my voice was stuck in my throat anyway, so I just nodded.

A still photograph is perfectly suited to the memory of the dead. An image frozen forever, it captures the very essence of death to the living, the infinite stillness, the end of aging. I'd seen the pictures of Ellen, but when her video image came up on the bright blue screen and when I heard her voice for the first time, she came alive, alive in a way that made me feel the void where she used to be.

The first thing I noticed was her hair. I'd known it had been red, but the color was richer and deeper than I'd imagined, and under the lights it shone like polished mahogany. She wore it in a chin-length blunt cut that softened her square jaw. Her hazel eyes were riveted to a point just off camera, and she wore the same expression that we all do when we're at the wrong end of a camera lens—horrified. But even as uncomfortable as she appeared, I felt her presence. It was strength or determination or perhaps the sheer force of will it took for her to sit there and subject herself to something I knew I couldn't do. I was impressed.

"We'll start with an easy one, Ellen." It was Julia from off-camera, her blue-blooded Beacon Hill voice easily recognizable. "Why don't you tell us about yourself?"

"I'm originally from Fort Lauderdale. I went to college at the University of Florida, then graduate school at Wharton in Pennsylvania." I was surprised at Ellen's voice. It was almost husky with a tinge of a Southern accent.

"What did you study?"

"Finance."

"Your graduate degree is an MBA?"

"Yes."

The pause was long enough to be awkward, and I imagined Julia hadn't expected such spare, to-the-point answers. But she was a pro and she recovered. "I must say, I'm not very good with numbers, and I always admire people who are. I think you have such an interesting job, Ellen. Will you tell us about it?"

"I work at the airport. I'm the general manager for Majestic Airlines here in Boston."

"That sounds like a big job, and a tough one, especially for a woman." Julia was definitely not of our generation. "What exactly does a general manager do?"

"That's the first thing I had to learn when I arrived. I came to the field straight from a staff job, which means I didn't have the experience to do this work, and it's been challenging."

She gave an articulate, detailed description of her job—our job. As she talked about her work, her face relaxed and grew more animated. Her voice grew stronger, and she spoke with such pride about her position, I felt bad for ever having questioned her right to be in it.

"I have the ultimate responsibility for getting our passengers where they want to go on time with all their belongings. But it's my employees who determine how well we do that. My most important job is giving them a reason to want to make it work."

I couldn't have said it better myself.

"Do you get to fly for free?" Julia asked the question with the sense of awe and wonder that always made me smile. For people not in the business, flight benefits are absolutely irresistible.

"Yes," Ellen said, smiling as well, "that's a great benefit. I don't travel as much as I'd like, but I'm hoping for some changes."

Julia jumped on the opening. "Can you elaborate on that? It sounds as if you're making lots of changes in your life."

The quick shift seemed to catch Ellen off guard. She tried another smile, but it was tight and tentative, and it came out more like a grimace. We weren't talking about work anymore.

She began slowly, reaching for every word. "I started working when I was in high school. I worked through college, worked through business school, and started my job with Majestic two weeks after I graduated. I would have started sooner, but I needed two weeks to move. I've been working ever since."

I sat in my curtained cubbyhole at Boston-in-Common with my earphones listening to Ellen talk and nodding my head. Except for the fact that I went to graduate school at night after I'd started working, she could have been describing my life.

"I love my work," she added hastily, "and I have no regrets. I love the airline. But there are long hours and you move every couple of years. It's hard to . . . there are sacrifices . . . you can get fooled into thinking that you're happy and sometimes you make choices that aren't right for you."

She seemed torn between wanting to sell herself and needing to unburden herself. For someone with no regrets, she looked very sad as she stared down into her lap.

"I've always picked people, situations that were never going to work out. I'm here because I want to stop doing that." She reached up with a manicured finger and gently brushed away a strand of hair that had fallen into her eyes. She wasn't even trying to smile anymore. "I hope it's not too late."

"It's never too late, Ellen." Julia's response was automatic, but then there was a pause and I imagined that she was a little stunned by Ellen's frankness. Some of the perkiness had gone out of her voice. "One final question, dear. Describe for me a picture of your life if all your dreams came true."

Ellen turned slightly and for the first time gazed completely off-camera, the way she might if she was looking for her response through a window. But I knew she wasn't. I knew she was looking inside and she was struggling, trying to hold off her natural inclination to close herself off, to deny herself even the simple pleasure of saying her dream out loud. Because if you never say it out loud, you can still pretend the reason you don't have it is because you never wanted it to begin with. Anything else hurts too much.

"I believe it's a gift to know your dreams." Ellen had gathered herself and leveled her gaze directly at me—at the camera. "If I'd known before what my dreams were going to turn out to be, I'd have made different choices. That's not to say that I wouldn't have worked, but my priorities would have been different. I want . . ." She paused, started to speak, stopped, and tried again. "I want to learn to let people know me. I want to meet a man who wants to know me better than anyone else does. I want to be a mother so that I can leave something behind. If there's a place for me in this world, I want to find it. That's my dream."

She smiled into the camera, a radiant, hopeful, almost triumphant smile. That was the last image of her as the tape ran out and the screen went blank.

I stood in Boston-in-Common's sheltered entryway and stared out at the cold rain. It was one of those gloomy days where indoors you have to keep the lights on and outside there's no way to stay dry because of the wind. It was the kind of winter day that seeps through to your bone marrow and makes you feel that you're never going to get warm again.

Ellen's video was under my coat where I could protect it. I'd watched it twice waiting for Julia, thinking both times that she'd been wrong; it can be too late. It had been too late for Ellen, and I had the feeling that when she sat for that video, Ellen had somehow known that.

I turned on my cell phone and dialed the airport.

"Molly?" The rain started to pound the bricks harder, and I had to step back not to get splashed.

"I've been calling you for an hour," she said. "Where have you been?"

"I had to run an errand. I told you I was going out."

"You didn't say you'd be unreachable."

"Can't I have an hour to myself?"

"No skin off my nose." I heard her taking a drag on her cigarette. "I just thought you'd like to know that your bag room blew up."

Chapter Twenty-two

When I saw the news trucks parked in front of the terminal, I knew it was going to be one of the days where I wished somebody—anybody—had my job instead of me. Bombs at the airport always made for good press, but reporters scared me almost as much as anything that could happen in the operation, including bombs.

I went the back way, where I could enter from the ramp. I followed the flashing lights, the official uniformed personnel, and the acrid, sinus-searing odor. I pushed my way through the crowd of employees at the door, wondered vaguely who was working the trips, and flashed my ID at the trooper standing guard. He lifted the yellow tape and let me in, where I joined what must have been twenty-five firemen, state troopers, inspectors, Port Authority employees, mechanics, and various others crowded into the concrete, bunkerlike space. The way they were milling and talking, it almost looked like some absurd cocktail party, except that one wall and part of the ceiling was totally black, fire hoses were lined up on the wet cement, and right in the middle of everything was a blackened bag cart, misshapen and still smoldering, its singed contents splayed around the floor. There were lots of skis—actually, pieces of skis.

I felt the same way I do at cocktail parties, as if the action swirling around me had nothing to do with me, but not for the same reason. I looked around at the destruction, and I knew that of all the people in this room, I was the one, the only one, responsible for what had happened here.

I spotted my rotund supervisor talking to someone who looked important. Norm introduced me to George Carver, the fire chief. The chief was a large man, late fifties, with stern hazel eyes.

"It could have been a lot worse, Miss Shanahan," he said.

"Was anyone hurt?"

"No. As luck would have it, there was no one at all in the bag room when the device went off."

I wasn't feeling that lucky. "Can you tell me what happened? I was off-site and just got back to the field."

We stepped over a fire hose as he led me over to the bag cart, basically a metal box on wheels with two open sides covered by plastic curtains and a bisecting shelf. This one was slightly cockeyed, and the curtains were shredded and melted. I could smell the burned plastic.

"You had some kind of a small homemade explosive device that was probably about here." He pointed with his pen to a spot on the floor of the cart. "You see how this is bowed up?" He was referring to the shelf, which now looked like one of the golden arches. "And it was on this side. You see how the blast went out this way?" The concrete wall on the ramp side was covered in black soot. A computer that had been sitting on a rickety table lay shattered on the ground. He took me around to the other side. "Virtually no damage over here to your bag belt. This side of the cart was packed to absorb the shock and force the damage the other way."

Damned considerate. "You said there was no one in here at the time?"

"Right."

"And it was a single bag cart in the middle of the floor? Not a train?"

He nodded. "You people will have to do your own investigation to rule out whether or not the thing came in on an aircraft. I don't think it came in in a checked bag. My eyeball opinion is that someone rolled this cart in here, packed it, stuck in a device, and ran like hell."

"Jesus." I stared at a B727 parked on the gate less than two hundred yards away. Through the porthole windows I could see passengers moving down the aisle to their seats. My knees felt weak as I began to absorb the enormity of what could have happened.

Chief Carver followed my gaze. "Like I said, it could have been worse. We'll be conducting our own investigation and giving you a complete report. I should be able to tell you what kind of a device it was. We'll put it with all the rest of our reports on Majestic Airlines incidents at Logan."

"You've seen this before?"

"Bombs, bomb threats, fires. You name it. Your guys are real flamethrowers. I keep warning you people that someone's going to get hurt."

"Have you ever identified any of these flame-throwers?"

"No, and unless someone who saw something or heard something steps up, we won't catch this guy, either."

"If anyone knows about this, we'll find them." I tried to look and sound confident, but I knew full well how the union closed ranks. So did he. He responded with a look that was the equivalent of a pat on the head.

We had to step out of the line of sight of a trooper taking photographs. Someone from the Port was motioning to me. "Chief Carver, I'm glad to have met you, although I'm sorry about the circumstances. I'd like to come over and talk about some preventive measures we could take to avoid this sort of thing in the future."

"That would be refreshing. You know where to find me."

I grabbed Norm, who seemed to be standing around observing. "Where's Dan?"

"He heard you were on your way, so he decided someone had to keep the operation going."

"Good." I turned him toward the faces peering in at us through one of the open garage doors. "You see all those people? Get the ones in Majestic uniforms to work and tell the rest of them to go back to their own operations." I pointed out a train of carts on the ramp filled with inbound bags. "Then figure out how we're going to get all those bags back to the pissed-off people on the other side of that door. See if we can use USAir's claim area for the evening."

"They're going to want to get paid."

"We'll pay them. Let me know what you find out. And get as many agents as can be spared down to baggage claim. It's going to be a nightmare out there."

I took one quick look to see if Big Pete was among the gawkers, but I didn't see him. It wasn't his shift, and that wouldn't have been his style anyway. But I felt his presence. He might as well have written his initials in the black soot on the wall.

I stood in front of the damaged cart with my hands in my pockets so that no one could see how they were trembling. Things were getting out of hand, and I had to start asking just how far they would go. Norm was herding people back to work, but some remained in the doorways staring at me. I was in charge. I was supposed to know what to do, but nothing in my experience had prepared me for anything like this.

I kicked at the remains of a suitcase at my feet. The Samsonite logo was still intact, and the handle had a tag with a business card inside. I did the only thing I was sure I could do. I picked it up, walked through the door to the passenger side, and started looking for its owner.

Chapter Twenty-three

I was hoping my phone would stop ringing by the time I'd found my key and opened the door to my hotel room. No such luck.

"Hello?"

"God, what's the matter with you? You sound like you're on your last legs."

It was Matt. I dropped down on the bed and just kept going until I was horizontal. My left hamstring—a constant reminder of an old running injury—was throbbing, my neck was stiff, and the rest of my muscles were tightening so rapidly I'd be lucky if I didn't fossilize right there, staring up at the spackled ceiling. "My bag room blew up today. The union planted a bomb to send me a message."

"Back here we use e-mail for that."

Usually Matt could make me laugh, but not tonight. There wasn't much that could make me happy tonight. I found the remote and turned on the TV, leaving the sound off, so I could see if I'd made the late news. Then I dropped my shoes on the floor and shimmied on my back closer to the middle of the bed so I could elevate my feet. "Obviously, you've already heard."

"It would be hard not to. That's all anyone's been talking about around here. Your name is on everyone's lips."

I knew Matt was right, and that was not a good thing. You never wanted to be a topic of conversation around headquarters, especially after the story had time to marinate into a juicy rumor. For the first time since I'd been in Boston, I wondered what Bill thought about my situation. I worried about what he was being told, and I really, really wanted his advice. Or maybe I just wanted someone to talk to, someone to be there for me the way he used to. That was one of the things I missed most of all.

"Tell me you're calling because you have my files, Matt."

"The archivist can't find them. He's still looking."

"That seems odd."

"You wouldn't say that if you'd seen the archives. It's a big warehouse filled with thousands of boxes and one poor guy who's supposed to keep track of everything. I'm surprised he ever finds anything. Which brings me to my next question. Do you want the other thing she asked for, the invoices? Because if you do, I have to go to a separate—"

"Ellen asked for invoices?"

"She wanted copies of the actual invoices to go along with the purchase price adjustment schedule. I suppose you want hard copies, too."

"As opposed to what?"

"Fish."

I sat up so abruptly I had to wait for the blood to rush back into my head. "Did you say fish?"

"Fish, feesh—whatever you want to call it—the microfiche is here in the building."

Microfiche? How was I supposed to have figured that one out?

"But she didn't want the fish. She said she needed the hard copies, which are over in Accounting. If you want those, too, I have to put in a separate request."

"Hang on, Matt."

Ellen's stuff was starting to get mixed up with my own. I stood in the middle of the room in my stocking feet and tried to divine the location of that page from her calendar, the one Dan had given me at the house for safekeeping. Where exactly had I put it to keep it safe? Briefcase? No. Table stacked high with things I didn't know where else to put? No. The box on the floor . . .? *Yes.*

The page with the fish reference was mixed in with the mail. "1016.96A. Is that the reference on the microfiche?"

"I don't know. I told her to call Accounting, but that doesn't sound like their filing system. Usually they have a date embedded in there somewhere, and besides, I just told you she wanted hard copies, not fiche."

"Oh, yeah. You did say that."

"Thank you."

The moment of enthusiasm passed. I sank back down on the bed and took off my pantyhose, which wasn't easy with one hand holding the phone. "What would hard copies have that microfiche wouldn't?"

"Signatures. I assumed she wanted to see who approved payment of the invoices. That's all that prepurchase schedule is—a list of invoices."

"Invoices." I said it almost to myself. "Like Crescent Security."

"What is that?"

"A local vendor. It keeps turning up in Ellen's things. I found a copy of an old invoice, and she had a check stub from Crescent stuck in her merger file. What would a local vendor in Boston have to do with the merger?"

"If it was a Nor'easter vendor, nothing. Majestic and Nor'easter were two separate entities before the merger. Separate management, separate accounting, separate operations."

Without my pantyhose on, I could think better and I remembered the conversation with Kevin. "But there is something that linked Boston to the merger. It's the IBG contract, the last one before the deal. From what I understand, the failure of that contract triggered the sale of Nor'easter.''

"That wasn't just Boston. That was a company-wide IBG vote, and I'm going to have to go soon or I'm going to be late for my condo association meeting.''

"But it's true, isn't it? If the contract had passed, there wouldn't have been a deal.''

"Very true. In essence, the Nor'easter board rolled the dice and put the future of the company into the hands of the IBG.''

"And they lost.''

"No, they won. At the time Nor'easter's largest shareholder was a group of venture capitalists. They'd already sucked all the cash out of the business and were looking to bail out. They figured the union would vote down the contract proposal, which meant the VC's could cash out and blame it on them. Of course it was good for us, too. The night we found out it was dead, the entire task force went out to a bar and celebrated. Even Scanlon came.'' He was talking faster and I knew he wanted to hang up.

"So the venture capitalists would have had incentive to make sure the contract failed. But wouldn't that have lowered the value of their investment?''

"Nor'easter would have been worth more with a signed agreement with their largest union, but these guys bought into the company originally on the cheap, so even at a reduced price they all made out. I really do have to go, but if I find this stuff for you, you're not going to ask for anything else, are you?''

"I don't know.'' Matt was shifting into serious self-protection mode, and his tone had taken on an everyman-for-himself quality. I reached for the remote control and started surfing the dial. "Is someone giving you a problem?''

"I don't want to get on Lenny's shit list. You've heard what he's been saying about you, right?"

My finger froze mid-surf, and my hamstring started throbbing again. "What has he been saying?"

"That you can't handle the union and he's probably going to have to come up there himself. And if he does that, then he's going to have to bring someone else in, and he's all concerned about the management turnover in the station and what it's doing to 'those poor employees because they've been through so much already.' You see why I don't want him mad at me?"

"He said he's going to replace me?" I dropped the remote behind me. It fell off the edge of the bed and clattered to the floor. "Who's he been talking to?"

"The only guy who counts."

"He said that to Bill Scanlon?" That was one question answered. I now knew what Bill was being told. What I didn't know was what he believed. "How do you know?"

"He told Scanlon's entire staff. He brought it up at the monthly planning session. If you ask me, he's covering his ass in advance in case anything else goes wrong."

"Goddamn him. He is such a liar. I just got off the phone with him at the airport. He was unbelievably supportive. 'These things happen,' he said, 'don't worry about it, it's not a reflection on you.' He's flying up here tomorrow."

"We don't call him the Big Sleazy for nothing."

"The what?"

"He's from New Orleans. That's what we call him."

In spite of everything, I had to smile. The Big Sleazy. I'd never heard that one before.

"You still want all this stuff," he asked, "if I can find it, right?"

"Yes, and call me when you have something."

He hung up and so did I. My channel surfing had stopped on the Animal Planet station. The mute was still on. In the silence I watched a baby turtle on his back in the sand on a beach. He was fighting to roll over, to right himself so that his shell was on top. His tiny turtle flippers flapped desperately as he rolled from side to side. I knew how he felt. I was starting to understand how Ellen must have felt. Lenny was my boss. He was supposed to be on my side, to provide cover while I was fighting it out on the front lines. Everything I found out about Lenny made him more contemptible to me. But in the end, I knew I could deal with Lenny. What I couldn't deal with was the thought that Bill Scanlon might start to question my abilities, to believe that I was failing out here. I went to my briefcase and found my address book. The phone number was right where I'd put it, unlabeled and written lightly in pencil inside the back cover. I hadn't used it in over a year, had even made myself forget the number that I had known by heart. But I'd never erased it and I never forgot it was there.

I sat on the bed staring at the phone until I could make myself pick up the receiver. Even after I'd dialed, the pattern on the keypad so familiar, it was an effort not to hang up. The call rolled to voice mail and I thought I was saved, but then I heard his voice. It was a recorded message, but it was *his* voice and my entire being responded as it always had to the timbre, the cadence, the rhythm of his voice. It was the perfect pitch to reach something inside of me, and the sound of him reminded me of the feel of him, the taste of him. All I had to do was speak, to leave a simple message, to say what I needed, but all I could do was sit on the edge of the bed, the room blurring around me, listening as the electronic operator demanded that I put up or hang up.

I hung up.

The baby turtle was gone when I checked the screen. I found the remote under the bed and waited a few seconds before turning off the TV, but he was nowhere in sight. I would never know if he had walked away or been carried away.

Chapter Twenty-four

Dan turned from the window and paced the length of my office. He'd rearranged the chairs to give himself a lane in front of my desk. As he paced, he continued his report, ticking off the points one by one. "We're using USAir's inbound claim until we can get ours up and running again, which might take up to two weeks. They're charging us an arm and a leg for it, but we don't have a choice. We're closing off all access to ours while we put it back together. No damage to any of the aircraft, but Maintenance had to check out everything that had been parked at that end of the building when the thing went off. We delayed three flights, canceled the last, and rebooked everyone on United and American."

"We lost the revenue?"

"We didn't have any choice, boss. Nothing of ours was going that way that would have gotten them to Denver last night. A few people were so spooked they didn't go at all."

"I guess we ruined a few vacations. How many bags were lost?"

"Thirty-seven items for twenty-two passengers. Everything in the cart was blown up or burned beyond recognition, mostly skis."

"I know about the skis. I spent several hours in baggage service last night letting people scream at me. It's amazing how attached people can get to their skis.

A couple of guys even wanted the pieces back. It was painful."

"We've got inspectors all over the place," he said, "Port Authority security, investigators, state troopers. I'm dodging the media and trying not to trip all over the headquarters people who've come out to 'help' us."

"As far as the media," I said, "I called Public Relations again this morning. Refer all inquiries to them." I stood up and leaned back against my credenza, resting my hips against the edge of the work surface. Somehow, it didn't feel right to be sitting down through all of this. "This is because of Little Pete, isn't it? About not bringing him back to work?"

"If it's not, it's an incredible fucking coincidence. I talked to Vic yesterday morning about delaying the decision, yesterday afternoon the bag room blows up. I'd say the two could be related."

I didn't know whether to be nervous or angry. I settled for being generally uncomfortable and continuously on edge. "What do you think we ought to do, Dan?"

"We've got the employee meetings set up. You had your say with the Business Council last night."

"Sure, that was effective. 'We'll do everything we can to help you through this,'" I said, mimicking Victor's insipid tone, "'but we need to know exactly how you're gong to protect our men.'"

Dan stopped pacing. The second he slipped down into one of my side chairs, I took his place. The distance from wall to window was exactly seven paces. On one of my laps, I closed the door. "There has to be something we can do that will get their attention."

"I think you've already gotten their attention, boss. As far as doing something about it, here's what's going to happen. We'll do our investigation, the fire department will do theirs. No one will talk, which means nothing concrete will come out of it, which means you can't blame the union because you can't prove they did it, which means you can't take formal measures against them."

"I don't want to back down on this, Dan."

"You might not have much choice. If Terry McTavish was not talking before, he sure as hell is not going to be talking now. Besides . . ." He gazed out the window at an empty expanse where an aircraft should have been. The gate closest to my window was out of service while the jetbridge was being repaired. "I'm not sure it's the best thing for you to hold out against Big Pete."

I turned and stared at him. "How can you say that? Should we give them what they want because they blew something up? Or set something on fire? Or slowed down the operation? That's why we're in this spot to begin with."

"No, it's not. It's not because of something you did, or I did, or Ellen did. It's Lenny. This station went to hell while he ran it, it got nothing but worse when Dickie was in charge, and as long as Lenny's your boss, nothing is going to change. You can't take on this union without the company's support, and as far as it goes out here, Lenny is the company. Makes no difference to me. I'm not going anywhere. But you were right the other day. You've got something to lose."

The mention of Lenny reminded me of the upended turtle. I'd been so tired after yesterday, but after what Matt had told me about how my own boss had been trashing me behind my back, I'd spent most of the night stewing instead of sleeping. I'd gotten out of bed this morning exhausted, but clear on one point—if I was going, I wasn't going out on my back. I stood in the window and stared down at the empty ramp. "Do you think Scanlon knew what was going on in Boston while Ellen was here?"

"No."

"Do you know that for sure?"

"Think about it. You know Lenny's not going to let on to his boss, and I know Ellen wouldn't have filled him in."

"No?"

"She always thought that she could handle Lenny, that he would help her if he understood what was really going on, and if she couldn't make him understand, then it was her fault. She felt like she owed him for giving her the job. She said he was the only guy in the field operation who would have taken a chance on her."

I turned back to the window, thinking that Ellen was the one who had taken the chance, not Lenny. Taken a chance and lost.

Dan came and stood next to me. "Speaking of the asshole, when's Lenny due in?"

"Not until two o'clock. Why? Do you want to meet his flight?"

"After what he said about my kid, I might kill him if I see him. Besides, that's your job. That's why GMs get the big bucks. Do you need anything else before he shows up?"

"Maybe some oxygen. Do we have extra coverage while he's here?"

"I called in a couple of supervisors from their day off, and I had a talk with some of the better crew chiefs. As soon as I can find him, I'm going to have another long chat with Victor just to let him know that I'm watching. Things are going to smooth out if I have to break balls personally."

"Listen"—I turned to check the door, forgetting that I had already closed it—"I talked to my Finance guy again last night, and I found out what fish means. It's microfiche."

"No shit?"

"He also told me that Ellen asked for invoices related to those pre-purchase adjustments, but she asked specifically for hard copies because she wanted to see the signatures. We're thinking she wanted to see who had approved payment of those invoices."

"Do you think those invoices are somehow related to the one you found from . . . what was it called?"

"Crescent Security. I think there's a link between the deal and the Nor'easter operation in Boston, I think it has something to do with the IBG contract that failed, and I think Crescent Security is part of it. Molly's going to pull all the information she can find on them in the local files. If Matt ever sends me the documents, we might find the connection."

As we watched, a driver pulling a train of three carts came out of the outbound bag room too fast, made a sharp turn, and sent two boxes and a suit bag flying across the ramp. He never looked back.

"Fucking moron." Dan moved toward the door. "Tell Finance Guy to hurry up. If Lenny's coming up here, we may be running out of time. By the way," he said, pausing in the open doorway, "you looked good on TV last night, really in control. Even I was reassured."

He dashed out laughing at my expense as Molly strolled in with the morning mail. "You should have worn some lipstick if you were going to be on TV."

"Believe it or not, I didn't get dressed yesterday morning with the idea that I would end the day on WBZ."

"You should never leave the house without a tube of lipstick."

"Thank you, Miss Manners."

I took the pile of mail and went back to my desk.

Molly was in no hurry to get to work. She stood in front of my desk, perusing the office like an interior decorator. "When are you going to hang something on these walls?"

"I don't know. I think all that stuff is in storage right now."

I sifted through the mail quickly, threw half of it away, and tossed the rest into my in-box. Molly hadn't budged.

"Danny showed me Ellen's frequent flier card," she said, "and that list of trips she took."

"Are you convinced now?"

"I have a theory," she said, sounding more provocative than usual. "I think she was having an affair, a secret affair."

I leaned back in my chair. "Why do you think that?"

That's all she'd been waiting for. She closed the door and dragged one of the chairs in front of the desk and settled in. "I'll grant you, I didn't know anything about this travel business, but I thought something had been going on even before that. She used to get these phone calls. Usually she'd close the door, but sometimes I overheard and whoever she was talking to"—she raised her eyebrows—"she had the tone. You know the one I mean?"

I thought about Ellen's note, I thought about the voice I'd heard on the phone last night, and I knew exactly what she was talking about. "It's the way you talk to someone you love."

"Exactly. It's the tone. Kind of low and sexy and quiet. After one of those calls her whole mood would change. She'd be happy for the rest of the day. And sometimes she'd come in all dressed up for nothing in particular. If you ask me, those were the days she was going to meet him and wanted to look her best. That's what the travel was all about. She didn't want anyone to know."

"Did she ever talk to you about it?"

She dismissed the idea with a quick shake of her head. "Ellen was way too private for that. But sometimes a girl just knows, and I knew something was going on."

"Did you know about the dating service?"

"Dating service? When was this?"

"Recently. She joined and quit all within the past two months."

Again with the abrupt head shake. "Whatever was going on with her started right after she got here and went right up until the end. In fact, remember I told you about that last day, when she came out of her office crying? Maybe she got dumped. Women have killed themselves for less."

Even with all the intrigue and threats, the questions, the mystery package, it was still hard to argue with depression, alcoholism, Detective Pohan, and genetics. Ellen's mother had killed herself. And when you added a possible broken heart . . . Molly and I were definitely on the same track, but did that make it so?

"Dan doesn't believe she was having an affair," I said. "In fact, he emphatically disagrees."

She ran one of her perfectly lacquered nails along the edge of her gold bracelet. "Danny doesn't want to believe anything bad about Ellen."

"If having a boyfriend makes you bad, we'd all be in trouble."

"Oh, it's not the *what* that bothers him, it's the *who*." She raised her dark eyes, and I realized this was the point she'd been building to all along.

"Do you know who it is?"

"It was Lenny."

I think my jaw might have actually dropped. I

leaned forward until my chin was almost on the desk. *"Lenny?"*

"I think she always had a little thing for him ever since he gave her this job, and he's not hard to persuade in that area. I've lost track of his extracurricular activities since he left the station, but more than a few of the girls around here got to know Lenny when he was the boss, if you get my drift."

"Lenny *Caseaux?*"

"Sure. He's a good-looking guy, and that Southern accent of his can be charming in a deep-fried sort of way. Besides, he's the boss. Power is always sexy."

"I guess so. I just never thought of him as anything *but* my boss. Isn't he married?"

"Why do you think they kept it a secret?"

I could see why Dan would be upset by the idea. "Do you really believe she would have killed herself over Lenny?"

"Here's what I think. Ellen worked too hard, she had no life, and she felt like she was getting old. If he showed the slightest interest in her, she might have decided that it was better than being alone."

I thought about Ellen's dating video. By her own admission, she'd picked situations that were never going to work out. This one certainly would have qualified. I reached up to rub my eyes and it felt good until I remembered, too late, that I was wearing mascara.

Molly just shook her head. "I can find out for sure," she said as she handed me a tissue from her skirt pocket. "I can check the list of her destinations against his travel schedule. The executive secretaries post the officers' travel calendars in the computer. We can see if they were together in the same cities."

"You need a password to get into the site."

Her full red lips curved into a feline smile. "Give me a few days."

The phone rang and she answered it in my office as

I used a small mirror from my desk—Ellen's mirror—and tried to repair my raccoon eyes.

"Speak of the devil," she said, hanging up.

"Make my day and tell me Lenny's not coming."

"He's not coming." She walked around to the front of the desk. "He's here."

"He's here. *Now?*" I bolted from the chair and threw on my suit jacket. "He's not supposed to be in for three hours." I opened the door and ran out, trying to smooth my collar on the way. I was halfway out to the concourse when I had to double back.

"Where is he, anyway?"

Chapter Twenty-five

Lenny was on the phone when I arrived at the USAir terminal, which was good because I needed time to catch my breath. He was talking on the last in a long bank of pay phones, the only voice in an otherwise deserted departure lounge. When I moved into his line of sight, he turned away and I was left staring at his back. Hard to give that a positive interpretation, but then I wasn't too pleased with him, either.

Few people were in evidence this early afternoon, mostly stragglers moving on sore feet toward baggage claim.

I felt him approaching behind me before I heard him. I turned and looked, and for a fraction of a second he was just staring down at me. Then a broad smile spread across his face and his eyes crinkled at the corners. "I apologize for being early," he said, sounding like a colonel from the Confederate army. "I hope I have not disrupted things too much for you."

Molly was right. He could be charming when he wanted to. "I'm happy to accommodate your schedule," I said, trying not to sound like a Southern belle.

"It's understandable you weren't here to meet my trip. I should have called you. Just remember when the chairman comes through your city, you have to keep better track because he is always on time, no matter when he arrives." He gave me that smile again, only this time it was less charming than condescending. "I make it a point never to let him wander around one of my stations without me. You never know what he might turn up."

He started walking, and I had to move briskly to keep up with his long-legged stride. My two-inch heels made me five foot ten, and I still only came up to Lenny's chin. He was tall and quite narrow and wore only custom-tailored European suits. There was a story floating around about how he used to expedite his shirts to Paris on one of our overnight flights to have them dry-cleaned there. I didn't know if it was true, but judging by the way he wore his clothes, the way he carried himself, and especially the way he lightly touched his collar when he smiled, I could believe it.

"Anything blow up today?"

"Nothing today," I said, ignoring the sarcastic tone. I was determined not to let him get to me.

"Well, that *is* a positive sign. I'd like you to fill me in on the situation with Petey Dwyer. How is it he was attacked by another employee and you're holding him out of service?"

"That's not what happened." And since when did Little Pete become Petey to Lenny?

"It is what happened according to the statements of the two people involved." He looked across his shoulder and down at me. "I wish I had heard that from you."

"I'm sorry I didn't brief you. I should have." I really should have. That was a tactical error that gave him an excuse to be self-righteous. "No one has the full story yet on what happened that night, but the situation is more serious than it might look on the surface. Little Pete caused the fight, he was drunk when it happened, and he consistently works his shift under the influence. We're trying to find—"

"Do you have any proof of what you're saying?"

"Not yet, but we're working on building a case."

"But you're not going to be able to do it, are you? You and I both know that. Therefore, I find it puzzling that we are going through all this upset. Can you enlighten me?"

More passengers were beginning to fill the concourse as we walked. A woman dragging a rolling bag was coming straight at me, reading her ticket and not paying attention. I had to step around her to avoid a head-on collision. Lenny kept going.

I was prepared to enlighten him, to try anyway, but when I caught up he was still talking. "You were supposed to come up here and calm things down," he was saying. "So far the operation has deteriorated, you've completely alienated the union over some meaningless shoving incident, and now you've reneged on your deal with Vic to bring back Angelo. Oh, and the bag room blew up. Is it any wonder the place is in an uproar? I thought you could handle this operation, Alex, but I'm losing my confidence in you. Your performance has been staggeringly disappointing."

I was losing patience, in no small part because I couldn't even keep up to talk to him.

"With all due respect, Lenny, even if all of that were true, I can't see how it justifies setting off a bomb in the bag room. I think we have to deal with that situation separately. If you want, I can address your other concerns individually."

Now he was getting frustrated, and it gave me a warm glow inside. He glanced at me and I smiled sweetly.

"What's going on with Angelo?" he asked.

"In light of recent events, I've decided to freeze all negotiations with the union. Angelo's status is on hold."

"I see. Well, I'm here to help you get it off hold, and here's how we're going to do that. We're meeting with the union, you and I, and we're going to find a way to work things out. What I mean by that is at the end of the meeting, we will have a plan for returning Angie to service and for Petey coming back to work. I'm afraid we'll have to fire the McTavish kid since he instigated the fight. He will surely grieve the action, and when he does I'll be happy to hear his grievance. That should help you remain focused on what it is you have to do here."

"I am focused, Lenny. I'm focused like a laser beam on the problem we have with Pete Dwyer Jr."

"What problem?"

"Little Pete is drinking on shift. He's a danger to himself, his fellow employees, and the operation. The other night before the fight, he was so drunk he reversed the load on one of his trips. We're very fortunate his crew caught it before it left the gate. If I can prove what he's doing, I won't bring him back to work under any circumstances." I didn't look at Lenny, but his pace slowed and I could feel him tensing. He seemed to be growing taller. I wet my dry lips and went on, trying to stay calm but getting more and more wound up. "If you force me to bring him back or make that decision yourself, it's going to be on you because I'm going to go on record and document my concerns in writing."

He stopped so abruptly that I shot ahead and had to backtrack.

"I understand your concerns, I do," he said. "And I wouldn't want you to do anything that makes you uncomfortable, so I'm going to find a way to allay those concerns. But let me give you a word of advice." He was smiling, his tone was sickly sweet, and I was concentrating on breathing, having lost the natural rhythm of respiration. "Unless and until you can prove any of what you're saying, it would be unwise to generate even one word of documentation. Because if you did, I would have to consider you to be reckless, unnecessarily hostile to the union, and lacking in the judgment it takes to run this station, in which case I would be forced to terminate your employment with this company. Understood?" He turned to go, then stopped again. "And that's not even taking into account the insubordinate and deceitful manner in which you've engaged yourself in the matter of Ellen Shepard's death. Shall we discuss how you came into possession of that power of attorney and what you've been doing with it?"

We were standing in the middle of the vast ticketing lobby, where we were surrounded by a swirl of people and bags and skycaps and carts and animal carriers. But all I could hear was the edge under the drawl, and it was sharp enough to cut diamonds. I knew I'd crossed the line, and I knew I had been stupid to threaten him. I could have anticipated the consequences. But having him articulate them with such cool confidence made my knees weak.

When it came down to it, I figured Bill would intervene if Lenny tried to fire me. But I didn't want to put him in that position, and besides, it would be tricky with Lenny involved. Lenny wasn't stupid. No matter what happened, my career at Majestic would be forever compromised. I felt my self-confidence crumple. I felt my anger deflate. "I understand."

He moved in close enough that I could smell his tangy aftershave. Then he actually put his hand on my shoulder. It felt like a rat had perched on my suit jacket, and it was all I could do not to smack it off. "Let me give you some advice," he whispered. "Don't ever threaten me again. If you do, you'd better have what it takes to follow through, or it will be the last thing you do in this company. Now," he said with a jaunty smile, "let's go see your operation."

Chapter Twenty-six

I'd spent the entire excruciating day with Lenny crawling through every inch of the operation, including the bomb damage. It had taken a monumental effort just to be civil around him, partly because I couldn't stand him, mostly because I couldn't stand myself with him. The last thing I wanted to do when I got back to my hotel was go out again. I'd collapsed facedown across the bed, fully clothed. If the carpet had been on fire, I'm not sure I could have roused myself to run for safety. But the phone rang and it turned out to be the one guy who could change my plans.

"I been trying to reach you most of the day."

John didn't say hello, but I recognized his voice. Boarding announcements blared in the background over the constant hum of milling crowds, so I knew he was at the airport, probably at a pay phone upstairs. I always pictured him on a pay phone when he called, huddled over with one hand cupped around the receiver and the other hiding his face.

"Are you on break?"

"Yeah, but I'm off in an hour. I got your message. What's up?"

If I had told him over the phone that his brother was about to be fired, I could have saved the trip. I could have stayed on the bed, ordered room service, and spent the evening feeling sorry for myself. But I was talking to a man who had gone out on one long limb for me. I changed my clothes and dragged myself out to meet him.

He came around the bend at Tremont, and I immediately picked him out of the crowd by his stevedore's build and his lightweight dress. What was it with this guy? Everyone on the street, including me, had every inch of flesh covered, and he looked as if he was going to a sailing regatta. Topsiders, jeans, a sweater, and a windbreaker. His one concession to the cold was a knit cap pulled down over his ears.

"Don't you ever get sick dressing like that?"

"Never. I love this weather. Great for working. What I can't stand is the heat in the summer. It makes you slow."

He took a deep, sustained breath and indeed seemed to draw energy from the cold. Just watching him made my lungs frost. "Can we at least get out of the wind?"

"Sure."

We weren't far from the Park Street T stop, so I suggested we get on a subway to nowhere.

"There's lots of guys on the ramp take the T to work," he said, shaking his head. "But that gives me another idea."

I followed him past a knot of sidewalk vendors clustered around steaming carts filled with roasted chestnuts and hot pretzels. We went through the swinging doors, down the wide concrete stairs to the underground station, and for the cost of two eighty-five-cent tokens, into the bowels of Boston mass transit. As we moved down the crowded platform, I noticed that most of the rush-hour commuters were dressed too warmly for the underground air, but seemed too tired to do anything but sweat. I could feel their collective exhaustion. It felt like my own.

John disappeared down another set of concrete

stairs, into a narrow subtunnel. When I caught up, he was leaning against one of the tiled tunnel walls.

"Here?"

"You said you wanted to get out of the wind."

The sound of the trains grinding and creaking above rolled down into the tunnel, but didn't seem to disturb the man curled into a drunken fetal stupor to my right. He was breathing—I checked—and by the smell of him, other bodily functions were also in good working order. I wrinkled my nose and tried to shut out the fetid air. "You're comfortable down here?"

He laughed. "I told you I used to work on a fishing boat. What's the news on Terry?" he asked as I peeled off my hat, gloves, and scarf.

"Lenny Caseaux's in town."

"We heard."

Of course they had. "He's not enthusiastic about the way I've been handling things. He's going to bring Little Pete and Angelo back to work, and he's going to hear Terry's grievance himself."

"That's it then for Terry."

It would have been easier if I had seen some anger in him, or even cynicism. But there was nothing like that, just the hopelessness, and the bleak acceptance that showed on his face and made me ashamed to be in the same chain of command with Lenny. John deserved better. So did his brother. So did I, for that matter, and I was feeling like a total loser for not standing up to Lenny on behalf of all of us. "I can keep pushing him," I said, "but he's already trying to take me out of my job."

"He said that?"

"Pretty much."

"I know you did what you could," he said, showing at least as much concern for me as for his brother, "and it's not worth giving up your job. Besides, I'd rather have you as GM than some of the others he could bring in."

We were quiet, both staring at the floor. The ground was covered with discarded handbills, some wet and soaked through, promising all manner of lewd exhibition at a gentlemen's club down the street. I pushed a few of them around with the toe of my boot, trying to find a way to ask what I wanted to know. I decided on the direct approach. "John, do you know who planted the bomb?"

He shook his head. "No."

"Would you tell me if you did?"

He pushed his knit cap higher, then whipped it off altogether and wiped the sweat off his forehead with the back of his sleeve. "I wouldn't tell you everything that goes on down there, but I would tell you that. Settin' off a bomb on the ramp so close to the fuel tanks, an aircraft sittin' right there on the gate—that's just stupid. People coulda been killed."

"I'm thinking it was Big Pete's idea."

"Nothing that big would happen without Big Pete knowing about it. But he didn't plant the thing, and you'd never find a way to prove it was him told someone to do it."

"What's the message?"

"They're trying to scare you, to let you know you're not in charge. You pissed 'em off when you took out Little Pete. They're not used to being challenged like that. The only other one ever did it was Ellen."

"And look what happened to her."

"What? I didn't hear you."

"Nothing." I hadn't even been aware that I'd said it out loud. "John, tell me what you know about the IBG contract vote, the one that triggered the merger."

"Why? You think it has something to do with all this?"

"Maybe. I keep running into references to the

Majestic-Nor'easter deal, and the only link I can find to Boston is that IBG contract."

"Maybe it has to do with Big Pete tanking that contract."

I stared at John and not because I didn't believe him, because I did. It was just so amazing what came out of his mouth when I figured out the right questions to ask. And it all seemed to be common knowledge floating around downstairs that never made it upstairs. "How did he do that? I thought it was a company-wide vote. Would he have had that much influence?"

"He had as much as he needed. Back then at Nor'easter, Boston was the biggest local of the IBG by far. However the vote went here, that was how the vote was going to go for the company, and Big Pete wanted it killed."

"You wanted the proposal to pass?"

"The way I saw it, the union shouldna had to give nothing back, but I knew if we merged we'd lose jobs. It happens every time. A lot of guys agreed with me till their tires started getting slashed, or their windows got broken, or they got acid poured on their car. One guy's Rottweiler turned up dead. Broken back."

"Someone broke a Rottweiler's back?" My own vertebrae stiffened at the thought.

"I told you about Little Pete, how he acts when he gets drunk."

"It was him?"

"He couldn't keep his mouth shut about it. Wanted everyone to know how he used a baseball bat. The way I look at it, it was a lucky thing it was just the dog."

"Jesus Christ. What would be in it for Big Pete to kill the contract? What would he care? He was senior enough not to lose his job. So was the kid, right?"

"He was paid off, pure and simple. He tried to make it look like he was taking a hard line for labor, but that guy doesn't believe in anything, doesn't stand for anything."

"Who paid him?"

"I don't know. There were so many deals and pay-offs back then, it was hard to keep them all straight."

I began sorting through the list of loose ends, hoping to find one that he could shed light on in his matter-of-fact way. I'd already asked him about the Beechcraft. I'd found out what "fish" meant. Still unexplained was the porno video and Ellen's secret liaisons.

"John, this is awkward . . . I'm not sure how well you knew Ellen, but I've found a couple of things I'm wondering about. We—I think that Ellen may have been seeing someone, taking secret trips to meet him. Given the amount of scrutiny she received, I was wondering if anyone downstairs—"

"You think she was going with someone on the ramp?"

He began shifting his considerable weight from side to side, foot to foot, and I had the momentary thought that it might have been him. Nah. "I was actually thinking that someone from the ramp might have seen or heard something. It seems like a subject that would draw interest among your colleagues." He was shifting faster and faster, and I knew I was on to something. "Is it true, John? Has someone said something to you?"

He turned and leaned one shoulder against the wall and looked straight down so I couldn't see his face. "I don't think I should talk about this. What good would it do now?"

A surge of excitement pushed through my tired muscles and exhausted brain. He *knew*. "It might help us figure out what happened to her."

He considered that for a moment as he let out a long sigh. "One of my guys was in Miami last year for a wedding. He had to fly back on United on an overnight to get back for his shift, and he saw the two of them at the airport that night. He was on Majestic and she was on my guy's flight on United. When she saw my guy, she started acting really antsy, trying to hide.''

"Who, John? Who was the man on Majestic?"

"Lenny Caseaux."

I leaned against the wall next to him. "Your guy saw Ellen and Lenny together in Miami?"

"Yeah, but they were acting funny, like ignoring each other."

"Like two people act," I said, "when they don't want to be seen together." What a dispiriting thought. "So it's true after all."

"I made my guy promise not to tell anyone, and I don't think he ever did. I never heard anyone else talking about this."

"Ellen was good at keeping secrets"—I looked at him—"and you were a good friend to her." My second wind had blown out, and I was ready to go. "I think I'm going to get on one of those trains and head back to the airport. I'm out of gas."

"Before you do, there's something else I gotta tell that I wish I didn't have to."

I could tell by the catch in his voice that it was something I wasn't going to like. In fact, he was so uncomfortable that he couldn't even look at me. It was alarming. "What? What is it?"

"There's been some talk downstairs . . ."

"About what?"

"About you. About Little Pete. He's got nothing better to do these days but sit around and get plastered, and he's worked up a pretty good hard-on about you—" He caught himself and blushed. "I'm sorry, I—"

"Go on, what is he saying?"

"The word is that he's talking about how something could happen to you like it did the last one, to Ellen."

He was staring straight down, talking slower and slower with every new revelation. I wanted to grab him by those broad shoulders and shake him. "What *else*?"

"He's saying that suicide's no good. Who would believe two in a row, right? But an accident, maybe . . ." He didn't have to finish. He had finally made eye contact and was looking at me as if I was in real trouble.

"Oh, my God." I started pacing the narrow tunnel, back and forth, the soles of my boots slick on the damp floor. "This is . . . how can he . . . *what kind of a place is this?*"

"I know," was all he could come up with.

We stared at each other for a moment, the dank air pressing in, feeling like more of a presence in the tunnel than the live human being curled up on the ground.

"Does he mean it? Should I be worried, or is it just talk?"

Before he could respond, a train rumbled overhead. He waited for the train to pass before answering. But I saw the answer in his eyes, and even standing in that stuffy passageway wearing too many clothes, I felt a chill, one that came from someplace deep and refused to pass. When it was quiet again, I asked him, "John, do you believe that Ellen was murdered?"

He checked the tunnel both ways and moved closer. "When you're downstairs, you worry most when it's quiet. A thing happens, something's going on, you can't go nowhere without you hear all about it, the stuff that's true and especially the stuff that isn't. GM dies. Kills herself. You'd expect nothing but talk about it, all day, every day."

"Nobody's talking?"

"Everybody's looking over their shoulder, but no one's talking."

"But you haven't heard anything definitive, right? You don't know anything for sure."

"That's the thing I'm saying. Nobody ever says it for sure, but that don't mean they don't know."

I started piling the rest of my layers back on—coat, hat, scarf. I felt claustrophobic in the tunnel. I wanted to be out in the open, around people. "I don't want to do this alone, John. I can't."

"I'll help you best I can."

"I know you will, but I'm talking about Dan. I want to tell him all this stuff."

He sucked in his upper lip and raised his eyes to the ceiling, and I knew I'd put him on the spot. Frankly, I didn't care. "I have to tell him I have a source, John. I won't tell him it's you, but I need his help, and if I don't tell him I'll never be able to explain where all this information is coming from. And I want to tell him about these threats. Please, John."

He switched to staring at the knit cap, which he was working with both hands. "You trust him?"

"I do trust him, and if you don't, I wish you'd tell me why."

His answer was a shrug. "All right. If you think you have to. But it's under the condition that you never use my name."

"Thank you. I've leaving and I know you don't want to walk with me, but will you keep an eye on me from a distance until I get onto the train? Better yet, I think I'll take a cab."

"Sure, and I'll tell Terry what you tried to do for him."

I started to walk, then remembered something else I'd meant to ask before I'd become terrorized. "Was Angelo involved in this vote fixing? Is that why Ellen would have wanted to talk to him?"

"Whatever Big Pete's into, Angelo knows about it."

"They're friends?"

"For years."

"Do you have any influence with Angelo?"

"Nobody influences him except his wife, Theresa."

"Okay." I wasn't sure how that helped me. "Thanks."

I turned one way in the tunnel, and he went the other over to the inbound platform. As I reached the top of the stairs, I turned and looked for him. He'd been watching me from behind a post, and as I headed out of the station and to the street, he stepped onto a train and didn't look back.

I had once felt safe with John. Now I didn't feel safe with anyone.

By the time I slid the plastic card key into the slit in my hotel room door, it was almost ten o'clock. My clothes felt damp and heavy, and I couldn't wait to peel them off.

The orange message light on my phone was on, its reflection blinking in the dark room like some kind of a coastal beacon signaling a warning in the night.

I flicked on the light, took one step in, stopped short. I took another halting half step and my mind went blank, short-circuited by the scene right in front of me. All the dresser drawers were open. My clothes were on the floor. My briefcase was on its side, its guts spilled out on the table. I stood in the silent room with both hands pressed against my heart, trying not to panic. Only, it wasn't silent. A noise—a sweeping sound, back and forth. It was . . . Jesus, it was coming from behind me and it sounded like . . . I made myself turn around, and when I saw it, my heart turned to ice and all the blood pumping through it turned cold.

It was a *noose,* a big, stiff noose with a big knot, and someone had looped it over the thing—that metal door thing, the pneumatic arm. I'd set it in motion when I'd walked in, and it was still swinging like a pendulum, scratching lightly against the paint. I tried to make my brain work, but it wouldn't. I tried to make my body respond, but it wouldn't. I couldn't take my eyes from the noose. It felt like a living thing, like a bird that could fly off the hook where it was perched and ensnare me, wrap itself around my neck, and squeeze the eyeballs out of my head. The sick drawing of Ellen emerged from some feverish corner of my memory. I stumbled back, then a thought, a horrible thought as my gaze flew around the room— he could still be *in* here. I blew straight out the door and down to the lobby, where I had the front desk call security.

An hour later, I was checked into the Airport Ramada, the seedier of the two airport hotels. I walked into my new room, went straight to the phone, and dialed the number from my address book, the one I had never really forgotten no matter how hard I'd tried. This time when his voice came on I closed my eyes and counted to myself and after the beep I left my number and my message, "I need to talk to you. Please call."

Chapter Twenty-seven

"So the only thing missing was this tape?" Dan was trying to be somber and concerned as we stood in the window at Gate Forty-two, but he couldn't completely hide his excitement. A hotel room invasion was exactly the kind of thing that got his blood flowing. Too bad it had happened to me and not him.

"A tape is missing, but it's definitely not the one he was looking for. The East Boston Video Vault is not going to be pleased with me. It was their only copy of *The Wild Bunch*, the anniversary edition."

"What's that?"

"It's an old western. A classic."

He stared.

"Sam Peckinpah? William Holden? Ernest Borgnine?"

"I never would have pegged you for westerns, Shanahan."

"I love westerns, but this is not just a western. It's a—"

A crashing noise rattled through the silent concourse. I flinched, then realized it was the wire-mesh gate at the throat of the concourse. Someone at the security checkpoint had rolled it up into its nest in the ceiling, probably Facilities Maintenance doing their daily calibration of the metal detectors. It was four-thirty in the morning, and the Logan operation of Majestic Airlines was open for business.

"Take it easy, boss."

"I'm edgy."

"Do you think it was Little Pete who was in your room?"

"Yes, I do. He touched all my things. My clothes were all out of the drawers. In the bathroom my toothbrush and my razor, all my makeup, it was all there but moved, everything moved so that I would know that it had been touched. It felt personal. I felt him there. It made my skin crawl."

Dan leaned back against the window, hands in his pockets, and crossed one foot over the other at the ankle. He looked as if he'd gotten dressed in the dark this morning. His shirttail was out, his tie was draped around his neck, and one button was missing from his shirt. I probably didn't look much better, although I had fewer parts to deal with. I had on a simple dark brown and slate blue turtleneck sweater, a long, heavy one that came down almost to my thighs. I wore it over a brown suede, shin-length skirt and leather boots, and is it any wonder I had every inch of my body covered up this morning? Our coats were in a pile on one of the chairs in the row behind us.

"We know he knows where you were staying," Dan said. "He's got plenty of free time on his hands since he's not working, and he hates your guts." He threw me a sideways glance and grinned.

"This is not funny to me."

"I'm sorry, boss. I'm teasing you. I'm getting you back for not telling me that you found Ellen's snitch."

"I did what I thought was right. He's paranoid about someone finding out what he's doing, and I can't blame him. Everyone knows everything that goes on in this place."

He tapped his knuckles and then his St. Christopher's ring on the vertical metal strut that separated the large windowpanes. It was the only noise in a quiet concourse that felt cavernous at that time of the morning. "Well, fuck him," he said finally, almost to himself.

"Excuse me?"

"Fuck him if he doesn't trust me."

"It's good that you're not taking this personally. Let's focus on his information and not him."

"Okay. Why would Little Pete take your copy of— what the hell is it? *The Wild Bunch?*"

"Obviously, he thought it might be something else. Now I have a box with no video. Sound familiar?"

"The porno box in Ellen's gym locker."

"Exactly. I had plenty of time to think about this when I was lying awake all last night staring at the ceiling. I think that Dickie Flynn sent Ellen a videocassette. That's what was in the mystery package."

"Why would they think you have it, especially when you don't?"

"All I can figure is that someone found out I rented a VCR, jumped to the conclusion that I had found the tape, and came looking. But *only* for the tape. All the stuff from Ellen's box, her files and mail, it was dumped on the floor but it was all still there."

"What does the snitch say?"

"I haven't had a chance to ask him, but the package he described would have been about the right size. It could have been a videocassette, but he never looked inside the envelope, so he wouldn't know for sure." When I leaned against the window next to Dan, the glass felt cold on my arm all the way through my thick sweater. "I think we're looking for Dickie Flynn's videocassette, I think it's the key to whatever happened to Ellen, and the Dwyers think we already have it."

Dan tilted his head from side to side, trying out the idea. "What's on the tape?"

"I don't know. Let's start with why Dickie Flynn

would send his package to Ellen in the first place. Did he even know her?"

"He knew her. She went to visit him when she heard he was sick. Between Nor'easter and Majestic the guy had given thirty-five years to the company, and she figured someone should pay their respects. Lenny couldn't be bothered."

"Did you go?"

"No. Dickie was an asshole. Just because he was dying didn't make him any less of an asshole. Don't get me wrong. I didn't wish stomach cancer on the guy. God forbid anyone should have to go that way, but he always treated me like dirt, and I didn't want to be a hypocrite."

Out of the corner of my eye, I caught sight of an agent hurrying through the concourse on her way to start an early shift. She waved as she went by, and we waved back. If she was surprised to see us there at that hour she didn't show it.

"When did Ellen make this visit?"

"When we first heard he was dying, maybe six months ago. Sometime late last summer." He laughed. "Ellen came back and she said he was an asshole, too."

"Last summer's too early. When did he die?"

"Around the holidays. Thanksgiving, I think. Molly went to the funeral. She'd know."

That timing worked better. I took a few steps toward the podium at the gate, unmanned and locked up at this hour. When I had it straight in my mind, I came back. "Right before he died, sometime around Thanksgiving, Dickie Flynn sent Ellen a secret tape, something he'd hidden away years before when he still worked here. She watched it and whatever she saw caused her to start an investigation. We don't know what it was about, but the next thing she did was call Matt Levesque wanting to know where she could find her old merger files. We found her own personal merger folder hidden in her gym locker. She was on the task force and knowledgeable on details of the transaction."

"So she found out something hinky about the merger."

"I think so, and it has to be the IBG contract, the one that was voted down because that happened right here in Boston. And it was significant. That contract failing as much as guaranteed that the deal would go forward. My source tells me that Big Pete was paid to tank it."

"That's a rumor. It's always been the rumor, but no one knows for sure."

"I'll bet Dickie Flynn knew for sure. Maybe he sent Ellen some kind of proof of the contract fraud or tampering or whatever you'd call it, and she was trying to put together a case. The package is evidence, and that's why Big Pete wants it."

"You think this proof is on a tape?"

"That's part of what we don't know. I also don't understand why Ellen wanted your Nor'easter procedures manual. What the heck was her interest in the Beechcraft, anyway? And Crescent Security. We don't know the significance of that."

I felt my shoulders sag with the weight of all we didn't know, but Dan was looking at things from a different angle. "We know a lot more than we did this time last week," he said brightly.

A passenger settled in not far from us, a businessman with two newspapers and a cup of coffee. We moved a couple of windows farther down the concourse.

"We know something else, too, Dan. Ellen was spending time with Lenny. They were seen together in the same airport ignoring each other. Molly's going to check Lenny's travel schedule against Ellen's list of destinations. That will tell us for sure."

He had turned toward the window and was looking down on the ramp, where a three-inch blanket of snow had fallen during the night. He was either wearing down or he'd decided to stop wasting his breath, because even though he was shaking his head, he didn't argue. All he said was, "What next?"

"Angelo."

"What about him?"

"That stakeout Ellen sent you on, the target all along was Angelo, not Little Pete. Ellen set him up. It sounds as if she wanted to fire him and trade his job back for information."

"I guess there's a good reason Ellen didn't tell me anything about what she was doing."

"I don't know, Dan."

He rubbed the side of his face with the palm of his hand. "So Angie knows something, which is why you didn't want me to bring him back."

"I'm sorry I couldn't explain that, but now we have to figure out how to get him to talk and we have to hurry. Lenny's trying to get his arbitration hearing scheduled within the next couple of weeks."

"If he does, we're screwed. The arbitrators will probably bring him back, and even if they don't, after arbitration Lenny can do whatever he wants."

"Yes, but until then it's still my call. This is the station where he was fired, and I'm now the chief operating officer here. Lenny can't do anything, not formally anyway, without an exception from the international, and he needs Scanlon's permission to do that."

Things were beginning to move outside. The pristine white expanses between the gates were beginning to look like abstract paintings, clean canvases brushed with black tire tracks in wide arcs and tight loops.

"I'm going down to check on the deicing operation," he said. "I'll let you know when I get in touch
with Angie."

"Good. Thanks for coming in so early. Hey . . ." I
had to call after him because he'd shifted into airport
speed and was almost to the stairwell. "You left
your coat."

After he was gone, it was just the passenger and
me. I turned to the window for one last look at the
peaceful scene before it was completely obliterated.
There was an aircraft on every gate, and the snow on
their long, smooth spines and broad, flat wings looked
like soft down comforters. Later, when the sky was
brighter and the aircraft were preparing for departure,
all trace of it would have to be cleared off under the
high-pressure blast of the deicing hose. But for now
the dry white crystals softened the rough edges and
brought grace and gentleness to a hard place. If I
stared long enough, I could almost believe the illusion.
Maybe that was Dan's problem with Ellen. He was
having a hard time letting go of the illusion.

I stayed out in the concourse until the first depar-
tures had gone, greeting passengers, lifting tickets, and
assisting the agents. By the time I made it to my office,
Molly was in.

"What are you doing here?" she asked, eyes wide.

"I work here."

"Did you forget about your meeting?"

Chapter Twenty-eight

They were staring at me. People gaping from the window of a passing city bus couldn't have looked more vacant. Except for feet shuffling and throat clearing, a random cough here and there, I could get no reaction out of the twenty-five or thirty rampers gathered in front of me. They were slumped on benches and in chairs, clustered in the doorways, and arrayed around the walls of the ready room among raincoats hung from hooks. The rain gear showed more animation.

I'd already done my short presentation, giving them the facts on the bag room bombing, passing around pictures of the twisted cart and ruptured skis. We—rather, I had already discussed the costs of reconstruction, interim use of USAir's bag claim, and passengers' belongings blown to smithereens.

"Does anyone have any questions?"

Silence.

The apathy was so impenetrable, it felt like an act of aggression, and one that had been coordinated in advance. I didn't need to be liked by these people, but I could not walk out of there without some acknowledgment, no matter how tiny, that bombing the bag room—or anything else—was not okay.

Big Pete, coming off the end of his shift, was leaning against a wall in the opposite corner. Still in uniform, he was, as always, outwardly nondescript with several layers of shirttails out and uncombed hair.

"Pete, as the union representative, do you have anything to say?"

For the longest time he didn't move or respond. Finally, he shifted slightly so that he was more angled toward the room, gave me one of those languid, crocodile-in-the-sun blinks, and began to hold forth. "First off, I want to say that the union don't condone this sort of activity."

At the sound of his raspy voice, some of the congregation turned their eyes in his direction. The ones that didn't looked out the window.

"Second, I want you to know I don't think none of you was any part of this. To me, it was someone from off the field who breached security, come onto our ramp, and did this thing. Maybe some kind of a terrorist like we're always hearing about."

Even some of the rampers were having a hard time keeping straight faces.

"I want everyone to be alert. The fact is, we ain't as safe here as we'd like to think. Anyone not wearing his badge, don't be afraid to challenge him. And if you got something on who might have done this thing, the union wants you to come forward and give it to management." He nodded graciously, and when he turned the floor back over to me, it was with a smug expression that seemed to ask, "Great performance, eh?"

I went back to my flip chart and found a great big red marker, the perfect symbol for how I was feeling. "I want to say one more thing just to add to Pete's point. No matter who perpetrated this act, this number"—I underlined the total cost of the bombing, twice—"translates into seven or eight full-time *union* jobs a year that could go away because someone was trying to send a message"—I looked at Pete—"no matter who that was." I capped the felt-tipped pen and checked my hands for leaking ink. "We can't even calculate the revenue we'll lose because passengers generally try to avoid airlines that have been bombed. You junior employees should pay particular attention. You're at the bottom of the seniority list, and you're the ones who will be out on the street. Given the sliding salary scale, it's going to take about ten to twelve of you to get to this number. Pete's right. It's in all of our best interests to make sure this never happens again."

I was encouraged by a stirring in the hallway, a murmuring that seemed to move into the room and run through the group like a lit fuse. I was getting through to them.

"That may be," Pete said with a polite sneer, "but we're all in the same union, and it ain't gonna work to try and set us against each other. Besides, management is responsible for the security of the operation. If you can't keep the ramp safe for us to work, you might want to start worrying about your own job."

The room fell quiet. Blood rushed to my head. I could feel my face heating up. An appropriately clever response would deflect attention from me and put him in his place, but with thirty pairs of eyes trained on me, I couldn't quite grasp it.

"Friend"—the voice exploded through the doorway and into the room—"her job is none of your concern."

My head snapped around so I could see if my ears were deceiving me. The crowd at the door parted as if they were being unzipped, and in walked Bill Scanlon—chairman, CEO, airline legend.

I was stunned—suddenly and completely struck dumb in front of a room full of my employees. I should have stepped forward, extended my hand in the usual professional greeting, and welcomed him into the room. Not that he ever needed any welcome, but it would have given me something to do besides stand rooted to the painted cement floor. But I couldn't. I couldn't even summon the will to take my eyes off him.

The dull murmur grew to an excited buzz as he strode on long legs into the center of the room, right where he was most comfortable.

"Sorry to drop in on you like this." His smile was crisp and, I felt, coldly impersonal.

I was swamped by a flood of emotions, none of which I could show, and for what seemed like the longest time, my mouth was open but I was afraid to speak, afraid of what might come out and when something finally did—'That's all right' is what I think I said—it sounded once removed, as if I were speaking in the voice of a passing stranger who had found my empty vessel of a body and moved in. But I knew it wasn't a stranger in there because the one emotion that kept crashing forward like the biggest wave in a pounding storm was fear. I was afraid that he was angry, that he had come all the way to Boston to fix what I couldn't fix. I was profoundly worried that I had let him down and that he was here to tell me.

But when he turned to slip out of his long cashmere coat—midnight blue—his eyes locked on mine for just a second longer than necessary, and for that one second it was as if he'd taken all the excitement he'd brought into the room, pulled it into a bouquet, and offered it to me as a secret gift. His eyes said what he couldn't say out loud: I am so excited to see you.

While he handed his coat and then his suit jacket to Norm, who had sprung from his seat to take them, the storm inside me ceased, the churning stopped, and the sun came out.

Bill smiled graciously at Norm, thanked him without the slightest trace of condescension, and turned to me. He was ready to go to work. "With your permission—"

"The floor is yours."

"You might want to get someone to take notes."

"Of course." As if I wouldn't remember every word that was about to be spoken. I was noticing how warm it was in the room, at least ten degrees hotter since he'd walked in. But maybe that was just me.

The group did not accommodate me as it had the chairman, and I had to elbow my way to a spot near the door where I could be available yet unobtrusive. The room was getting more crowded as ticket agents filtered down from upstairs. Majestic employees never missed a chance to see up close "the man who'd saved the airline," and to see him in a surprise visit was a double bonus.

I asked one of the agents to call Molly and have her track down Lenny, and then settled in to watch the show.

He stood in the center of the room in his pressed cotton shirt, exquisite but understated tie, and suit pants that were perfectly tailored to his lanky build. Some men might have felt out of place in that dingy room, just as I almost always did. But he was a man with the unwavering conviction that where he was was where he belonged and that the surroundings— whether it was a maintenance hangar or a Senate chamber—would conform to him.

"Ladies and gentlemen," he said quietly, letting his voice draw them in, "we have picked a tough business in which to make our livings, you and I. Don't you agree?"

No one moved. Everyone agreed.

"I look at some of these other hotshots who run businesses, and I think to myself every day, they've got it made compared to us. Think about the software business. Those guys in Silicon Valley, they've got a high-margin business, markets that are growing exponentially, new markets opening up every day, and they get to come to work in shorts and sandals." His smile let us all in on the gentle teasing. "Who couldn't make money doing that? Or take the money guys on Wall Street, investment bankers and fund managers. In a market as robust as the one we have today, they don't even have to come to work to turn a profit." He was gliding around the small space, making it look bigger than it was, stopping now and then to pick someone out of the crowd and focus his entire being on them. "But you and me, we don't have it that easy. We have this massive, complicated machine"—he opened his arms wide, as if holding the entire contraption in his own two hands—"with more moving parts than any human and most computers can comprehend. We've got weather issues, we've got scheduling issues—airplanes, pilots, and flight attendants who all have to be scheduled according to their specific labor contracts. We've got regulatory requirements, environmental requirements, and constraints of air-traffic control. And we deal with machines, so we have the ever unpredictable maintenance variable."

Heads around the room bobbed in solemn agreement.

"You're on the front lines here," he said. "You know better than anyone how every day we have to mesh it all together in a way that works best for the customers, the employees, and the shareholders. We go home every night, and every morning we have to get up and do it all over again from scratch, because we have no inventory. Am I right?"

Of course he was right. He was tapping into the mother lode of truth for these people—for any people—telling them how difficult their jobs were, how hard they worked, and how no one understood them better than he did. He could communicate with anyone on any level about anything. And he could make you agree with him. He could make you want to agree with him. That was his gift. He had the ability to find a way to lead you wherever he wanted you to go. I tried to remember that there were good reasons why we weren't together anymore. Watching him work, it was hard to think of exactly what they were.

"We don't make money in this business unless we grind it out every day, seven days a week, twenty-four hours a day. We do this at Majestic with more success than our competitors. How is that?"

"We're better than they are," someone yelled from the back, one of the rampers who had been unconscious for my segment.

"Are we?" Bill picked him out with his eyes and challenged him for giving the easy answer, but obviously the one he had expected. "Our planes look just like their planes, our cabins are just as crowded, and our leg room equally deficient. We don't fly any faster than they do. Why are we better?"

No one dared risk another response that didn't work. A brief pause stretched to a long one, and still no one spoke up, and still he didn't say anything. He waited until the moment when the silence was unbearable, then answered his own question.

"The way we make money, the only way anyone makes money running an airline, is by running it better," he waited a beat, ". . . and faster," another beat, ". . . and cheaper than the next guy, by demonstrating a deeper commitment to our customers, and by being nothing less than relentless when it comes to keeping our costs down. *Relent*less, ladies and gentlemen."

He had ended up next to the flip chart and stood there now, scanning the audience, seeing everyone and everything, letting no one off the hook. When he stopped, he was staring at me. "I'm not going to speculate on the identity of the person or persons who set off a bomb in my operation the other night," he said. "That would be a waste of time—yours and mine."

It was as if he had set off his own bomb in the

crowded room. No one was moving; they might have all stopped breathing. He swept the room again with eyes that seemed darker. "And I would never accuse anyone of doing something like that deliberately. You have a fine management staff here in Boston and capable union representation, and I'm confident they will work this situation out. When I came in, your manager was talking to you about how incidents like this can affect people's jobs, people who had nothing to do with what happened. That doesn't seem right, does it?"

Every muscle in my body stiffened, down to the arches in my feet. I'd seen him too many times not to know that something was coming. I watched him walk the perimeter of his stage, moving slowly enough that everyone could see him as he passed. "I'm going to go one better." When he stopped, he was staring at Big Pete, holding eye contact as if he had his hand on the back of his scruffy neck. "If I ever find out that someone who works for me planted that bomb, that they put themselves, their fellow employees, our passengers, and our equipment at risk, I'll shut this operation down."

People turned to look at each other, to see if they'd heard what they thought they'd heard. As they began to absorb what he was saying, Bill waited, milking the moment for every bit of drama. "I'll take every last job out of this city and move them to Philadelphia or Providence or Wilmington, Delaware. I don't care."

He spotted the spring water dispenser, and we all watched as he went over, plucked off a paper cup, and filled it. "And if you don't think I'll do it, my friends, try it again." He knocked back the water, turned, and searched the crowd.

"Any questions?"

"Nice of you to show up for work, Leonard." Bill eyed Lenny as the three of us stood around the table in a small conference room in the Peak Club, our haven for first-class passengers and very frequent fliers. Lenny looked as if he'd been dragged out of bed early, which is apparently what had happened.

"Bill, we had no idea you were coming"—he shot me a suspicious look—"did we?"

"No one knew," Bill snapped, "which is exactly what I wanted. My meeting in New York canceled this morning, so I decided to come up here and shake these people up. How was that?" he asked me. "Will that help you out?"

"Tremendously," I said evenly, playing my role in the charade. "Thank you. Do you want to meet with anyone else, maybe the next—"

"You won't need any more meetings. The message has been delivered."

I nodded. Here was a man keenly aware of his own impact.

He reached into his briefcase for a single, wrinkled piece of paper and put it on the table in front of us. It was a copy of the awful drawing that had been delivered to me on my first evening in the station, the one of the hangman's noose with Ellen at the end of it. "I want to know about this."

"Bill, you know what that is. It's just the guys downstairs blowing off steam—"

"No, it's not, Lenny. What this is, Lenny, is bad for business. People who have time to draw pictures and send them to me have too much time on their hands. People who are spreading rumors are not working."

Lenny stuck his hands in his pockets and decided not to pursue the point.

Bill turned back to me. "Now, what about this bomb? What have you learned?"

"The fire department is investigating," I said, feeling more confident. This was a subject I knew something about. "They don't expect to find anything. We have Corporate Security and Aircraft Safety on site. We're almost certain a ramper planted the bomb—"

"There's no evidence of that, Bill. We have to be careful about making accusations."

Bill glared at him. I expected burn marks to appear on Lenny's ecru cotton shirt. "What we have to be careful about is that the thieves, thugs, and criminals that you hired in your day do not get it into their heads that they can threaten or intimidate any member of my management staff and get away with it. You just lost one general manager in a most unpleasant manner." He held up the page again. "Do you really think it's a good idea to have this stuff floating around?"

I didn't look at Lenny because if I had, I surely would not have been able to hide the warm satisfaction that was welling up inside me.

"I just want to know one thing from you." Bill had turned to me. "Do you feel safe?"

Lenny looked at me. I looked at Bill. "Excuse me?"

"You're the one who has to live and work here every day. I want to know if you feel comfortable in this station, and I want you to tell me if you don't."

Well now, here was a loaded question if there ever was one. Lenny was still watching me closely. If I admitted I was sometimes afraid, would I be taken out of the job? And never offered another good one again? If I didn't, was I giving up all future rights to being scared? For the first time I noticed the music that was being piped into the room through an undersized overhead speaker—a tin can version of *I Honestly Love You*. It seemed as if the entire song had played through twice before I came up with my answer. "I'm fine here."

Bill's eyes narrowed slightly, and I had the feeling he was trying to decide if that was my real answer or my for-show answer. The real answer was that I wasn't always comfortable there, and I didn't want to leave Boston. Lenny had no reaction.

"Okay," Bill said, plowing on to the next subject, "here's what you do. You get that bonehead in here who runs the local. What's his name?"

"Victor Venora."

"Get him in your office and tell him exactly what I just said in the meeting. One more incident that even looks suspicious, and I will shut this operation down so fast, it will make his empty head spin."

"Would you really do it?" I asked.

The expression on his face left me feeling stupid for asking.

"You run this station, Alex, not the union. Don't let them push you around, and don't be afraid to be an asshole." Simultaneously, I was nodding, looking serious, and berating myself for being so thrilled at the sound of him saying my name again. "And you, Leonard, I expect you to give her whatever support she needs to get that done."

As he closed his briefcase, he addressed us both. "I want to see this place turn around, and fast. If it doesn't, I will hold both of you responsible. Do you understand?" He waited until we acknowledged what he had said. "Good. I'm going downtown to meet with some portfolio analysts. Lenny, you come with me and let her do her job."

He blew out the door with Lenny in tow and left me standing there. When I checked my watch, I realized how completely disoriented and out of sync I was. The whole encounter had taken a little over an hour. It wasn't even ten o'clock in the morning.

Chapter Twenty-nine

It was one of those yawns that brought tears to my eyes, the kind so wide and deep, it threatens to turn your face inside out. The black-and-white pictures on the closed-circuit TV monitors blended into one big, blurry gray image. Sort of how my day had gone.

"I hear I missed all the excitement this morning," said Kevin, coming through the door and sounding uncommonly bright. Either that or I was uncommonly dull.

It was the beginning of his day while mine was thankfully coming to an end. "That's what you get for bidding nights."

"Indeed, but had I known, seeing Himself in person would have been worth bounding out of bed early."

"No one knew. He just materialized in the ready room like a bolt of lightning. It was vintage Scanlon."

"So I heard. The whole place is a-twitter." He chuckled as he hung up his coat, walked over, and stood next to me. "Did he really say he was going to shut us down?"

"Unequivocally."

"I hope the message got through. I don't want to be unemployed." He surveyed the wall of electronic windows to the ramp, then reached up and wiped a smudge off one of the screens. "What are we looking at here?"

"Are these cameras set up to record?"

"No."

"Were they ever?"

"They were never intended for that." His rolling chair squealed as he settled in and immediately started cracking his knuckles, one by one. "You're not thinking of surveilling the ramp, are you?"

"No, but why not? Other stations do it."

"Obviously, you haven't heard about Dickie Flynn's fiasco."

I walked over and leaned against his work counter as he began his ritual, the kind we all go through to get ourselves prepared for another day of work. "Dickie Flynn surveilled the ramp?"

Kevin's motions were efficient and practiced, and he talked to me without once ever interrupting his flow. "Dickie used to go through his phases, his different kind of management phases. He tried management by intimidation, but no one was ever scared of him. He tried management by consensus, but no one ever agreed with him, much less each other. At one time he got frustrated and tried management by spying."

"Spying?" I tried to sound only casually interested. "With video cameras?" It wasn't easy.

"Cameras everywhere. The bag room, the ready room, the lunchroom. What he never quite accepted was the fact that you can't have secret surveillance in a twenty-four-hour-a-day operation, which was the fatal flaw in his scheme."

"People knew about the cameras."

"Of course they did. He even tried moving them every few days, but within hours the union would have the locations posted on bulletin boards all over the field. He finally gave up the ghost after one night when someone swapped all of the tapes with several—how shall I put this delicately—adult entertainment features."

"Porno tapes?" I straightened up so abruptly, I drew a quizzical look from him.

"From what I understand, the full range. Something for everyone—heterosexual, homosexual, bestiality . . ."

As he talked, I stared down at the toes of my boots, glassy-eyed, and let the outside world drift away as the pieces began to coalesce in my head. The monitors drew me back, and I studied each one closely as figures moved across the black-and-white screens setting up gates and working the flights. The pictures were clear and the cameras high-quality, but far enough away that I couldn't distinguish faces.

". . . yes, indeed, shocking stuff," he was saying, "but not so shocking they didn't all gather in the ready room for a matinee, mind you—"

"Kevin, are you saying someone brought a bunch of porno videos to the airport one night and swapped them out for surveillance videos?"

"It would appear so."

"Which means it's likely that Dickie's surveillance videos came right out of the machines . . . and straight into the porno boxes." I was talking more for my own benefit now and feeling less and less fatigued.

"I can't say, but I would imagine so."

The sound of my beeper was usually an intrusion, but particularly so when it erupted at that moment. I didn't recognize the number.

"Kevin, did they ever find out who stole the tapes?"

"Surely you jest?"

"Were these good-quality cameras he used? Like these?"

"Dickie never spared any expense when it came to spending the company's money."

I checked my watch. Four o'clock. "Can I borrow your ramp coat?"

"I would be honored."

"Thanks." The phone rang, and when he picked up I grabbed the coat and a set of truck keys from a hook on the wall and made for the door. Dickie Flynn had sent Ellen a surveillance video. A *surveillance* video. I couldn't wait to tell Dan. If I was lucky, I could still catch him at his meeting across the ramp at the post office. As I rushed down the corridor, my beeper went off again.

Whoever it was didn't want to wait.

Chapter Thirty

The maître d' at Locke-Ober was a small-boned man with a black suit and a face as stiff as his starched white cuffs. The gold name tag on his jacket read Philip.

"Good evening," I said.

He glanced past me into the empty foyer. Locke-Ober had not even admitted women until 1970, so he was no doubt searching for my husband. Finding no escort, he defaulted to me. "May I help you?"

"Yes, thank you. I'm meeting someone for dinner." Although the way my stomach was flipping around, it was going to be hard to eat.

He hovered over his reservation book. "What is the gentleman's name, please?"

"The *party's* name is William Scanlon." Jeez.

Philip's demeanor transformed instantly as I grew in social stature right before his very eyes. Twit.

"Indeed, Mr. Scanlon is here. He's in the bar. I'll let him know his guest has arrived."

"I'll find him, if you'll point me in the right direction."

"Certainly. The bar is right this way." He tugged on one cuff and motioned toward the bar. "Tell Mr. Scanlon we'll hold his table as long as he'd like."

That's what I'm here for, Philip, to deliver messages for you.

The prevailing theme in the bar was dark, dense,

and heavy. Polished paneling covered the walls, thick and ponderous furniture filled the floor space, and reams of suffocating fabric absorbed all light from the windows. The air was filled with the blended odor of a dozen different cigars.

I peered through the mahogany haze and found him at the bar, holding court. He was wearing the same gray suit from this morning with a different but equally spiffy silk tie and that electric air of self-confidence the rest of us mere mortals found so mesmerizing. Take the people in this bar. Nobody here worked for him; I doubt anyone even knew him. Yet when he laughed, they smiled. When he spoke, they leaned in to hear what he had to say. He effortlessly commanded all the attention in the room through the sheer force of his personality.

"Alex Shanahan." His voice cut through the dampened acoustics, calling everyone's attention to—me. The stares were discreet, but intense enough to raise the humidity level inside my suit a few damp degrees, and he knew it. He smiled serenely as he reached for his wallet and turned toward the bar.

Rather than stand in the doorway on display, I worked my way through the room and ended up standing right behind him. Too close, it turned out, because when he turned to leave, he almost knocked me flat.

"Ah," he said, reaching out to steady me, "and here you are."

I thought he let his hands linger. I thought he did, but couldn't be sure. What I was sure of was the jolt that moved from his hands through my arms and all the way down my spine, almost lifting me off the floor, the stunning reminder of the powerful physical connection that had always been between us—and how little it would take to reignite the flame. He felt it, too. I saw it on his face. I saw it in his eyes, and I knew that if I'd had any true desire to keep my distance from him, I wouldn't have come here tonight.

"Thank you for coming," he said, adjusting his volume down for just the two of us. "Hungry?"

"Yes." Not really. "They're holding your table."

"Then let us go and claim it." He gave my arm one last squeeze.

Philip, with his maître d' sixth sense, was waiting for us with two menus. He personally escorted us upstairs to our table, draped a napkin across my lap, and addressed himself to Bill. "Sir, it's nice to have you back with us."

"It's always nice to be back. Ask Henry if he has any more of that cabernet I had last time. That was quite nice." He looked at me. "And a white burgundy, also. Tell him to bring the best that he's got."

"Yes sir, I'll send him right over. Enjoy your dinner."

Philip melted back into the dining room while Bill leaned back, stretching his long legs out and making the table seem even smaller and more intimate. I kept my hands buried in my lap, my feet tucked under my chair.

He touched the silver on each side of his plate, tracing the thick base of his knife and the flat end of his spoon. "It is white burgundy, isn't it?"

He looked at me in the dim glow of the table candle flickering between us, and a slow smile started—an open, ingenuous smile that was not for the entertainment of the masses but just for me. When he smiled that way, it changed him. When he smiled that way, it changed me.

"You know I like burgundy," I said. "You never forget anything."

He pushed his plate forward and leaned on his elbows as far toward me as the table would allow. "I haven't forgotten anything about you. Until I picked up your message, I thought you'd forgotten about me."

I studied his face: the long plane of his cheeks, the curve of his forehead, the shape of his eyes, the way they sloped down slightly on the sides in a way that kept him looking almost boyish. No, I hadn't forgotten anything. That was the problem. No matter how hard I tried and no matter how much distance I put between us, I couldn't forget him.

"That was quite an entrance you made this morning."

"Dramatic, wasn't it?" He brightened at the memory, like a little kid on Christmas day. He did love being Bill Scanlon. We both leaned back, making way for the wine steward, who had arrived with a silver ice bucket, two bottles, and other assorted sommelier paraphernalia.

"You surprised me," I said.

He shook his head and grinned. "I don't think so. If you hadn't wanted to see me, you never would have called. You opened the door. All I did was walk through it."

"More like blew it up."

He laughed and so did I. It felt good to laugh with him again.

Henry poured our wine and, after more gratuitous bowing and scraping, receded into the background.

Bill offered a toast. "Here's to blowing up the door . . . and any other barriers left between us."

We touched glasses. This morning when he had stared down Big Pete, his eyes had seemed almost black. But in this light they were clear amber, almost sparkling. It was like looking into a flowing stream and seeing the sun reflected off the sandy bottom. I had missed seeing myself reflected there.

I put my glass down, searching for and finding the

precise depression in the tablecloth where it had been.
"Where did you get that hangman's drawing?"

"Someone sent it anonymously. I usually throw
things like that away, but since it was your station—"

"I know, and I'm sorry about that. I can explain—"

"Are you seeing anyone?"

I blinked at him. He waited, eyebrows raised. I took
another drink of the chilled wine, letting it roll over
my tongue. "No."

"Why not?"

Because I haven't gotten over you. "Do you know
what that drawing means? Has Lenny told you—has
anyone told you what's been going on around here?"

"Lenny makes a point of not telling me anything,
which is one of the reasons why I'm here."

"Are you saying you don't know anything about the
rumors and why they set that bomb off?"

"I didn't say that. I said that Lenny didn't tell me.
And I don't want to talk about him. Were you seeing
anyone in Denver?"

I inched back. He didn't move, and yet he felt so
much closer. In our good times I'd always felt better
with him—safer, surer of my footing. He had confidence to burn, and sometimes when I'd touched him,
I'd known what that felt like, not to be afraid of
anything.

"Why do you want to know if I was seeing
someone?"

"Because I heard that you were."

"And why would that matter to you?"

I didn't feel the pointed end of that question until
he straightened up as if he'd been poked in the stomach. He reached for the bottle of red and poured another glass. When he drank the wine, I could almost
track its warming flow through his system, and it
seemed to me that he was trying to relax, trying to
get the words just right. That he didn't have the right

words and exactly the right way to say them was disarming.

"I used to see you around headquarters," he said, "across the cafeteria, turning a corner at the end of a corridor. Or sometimes I'd be sitting in a meeting and I'd see you walk past the open door." He shook his head and smiled, as if the memory gave him pleasure. "You know how my office looks out over the parking lot? I'd watch for you in the evenings going out to your car. I'd stay at my desk waiting, finding something to do. I never wanted to go home until I saw you."

I stared down at my hands in my lap and remembered all of the times I'd stood at my car and glanced up for him—quickly and furtively so that no one, especially Bill, would catch me—just to know that he was there. And I remembered the emptiness I'd felt when the light was off and he was gone. I'd never seen him looking back. But then, that had been the story all along. I'd always reached for him and never felt him reaching back.

"Alex, I couldn't stand the thought that you were with someone else. It made me crazy. A hundred times over the past year, I almost called you."

"Why? To find out if I was seeing anyone else? Because in the end, Bill, when I wanted you to call me, when I needed to hear from you, you weren't there."

"As I recall, you dumped me." He said it with a little smile, trying but not succeeding to sound light. "You didn't want to see me anymore."

I caved back into my chair, instantly weary from the notion that as hard as I'd tried to help him understand, he hadn't gotten it then, and he still didn't get it. "It was not you, Bill. It was never you. It was the circumstances. For me, they began to overwhelm everything, and you wouldn't change them."

"Alex, I couldn't go public about us."

"I wasn't asking you to call a press conference. All I wanted was to stop sneaking around like a couple of fugitives. I wanted to be able to go out to dinner without worrying that someone might see us together. I wanted to stop feeling as if I wasn't worthy of being with you. The longer that went on, the more I started to feel that you . . . you were ashamed of me."

"You know that wasn't it. I was about to be named chairman, and I could not be involved with a woman who worked for me. The company has rules about that. And it wouldn't have been good for you, either."

I resisted snapping back. I had always hated it when he'd made a decision that clearly benefited him, then turned it around to make it sound as if he were really doing it for me.

He reached for the bread, which I hadn't even noticed had arrived, and tore off a piece that was dark and dense. "All I'm saying is you could have given it a little more time. You could have waited."

"The minute I raised the issue, Bill, the very second I spoke up and finally asked for what I wanted, you backed off. You were suddenly unavailable. You were in meetings. You were traveling. You stopped calling." I took a breath and tried to steady my voice, which was starting to inch up the decibel scale. I wanted to tell him how deeply painful that had been, how thoroughly destabilizing, how it had removed from me any sense of security and self-confidence I'd managed to nurture in the shelter of our relationship. But I thought if I did, I would start crying. "It wasn't about timing, Bill. It was you not wanting to be with me as much as I wanted to be with you."

There. I'd said it. I'd ripped off the scab, and it hurt as much now as it had then. Maybe more.

"And the worst part, the worst thing you ever did

to me, was to not tell me. You disappeared. First, you didn't want to be seen with me—"

"That is not true, and you know it."

"—then you vanished from my life. And I had to keep going to meetings with you and sit across the table from you and watch you give presentations. And you, all the while ignoring me, or pretending I wasn't there. I couldn't stand it anymore. That's why I left." I reached out and touched the base of my wineglass. "At least I told you I was leaving. You were gone long before we ever said good-bye."

The words were old, the feelings familiar, the hurt still there. This was well-trod territory for us, and I was disappointed to realize that there was nothing new here.

Henry reappeared to top off our glasses. As he served, I looked out at the other tables, because I couldn't look at Bill. What do you know? We weren't the only two people in the world tonight. A sprinkling of women dotted the dining room, but I could hear only men's voices. It was as if the years of exclusivity in this place had filtered out the sound of a female voice. I tried to tell from their faces what they were saying. Were they happy? Sad? Hurt?

The cubes rattled as Henry slipped the bottle of burgundy back into the ice bucket. I looked at Bill. "Why would you come here like this? Why would you want to dredge all this up again?"

"You called me."

"I called for professional support."

His gentle smile acknowledged my stubborn self-deceit and, at the same time, let me get away with it. "You're so smart about these things, Alex—smarter than I am. I thought you would have figured it out by now."

"I haven't figured anything out, Bill."

It was his turn to look around the room and gather his thoughts. "You scared me."

"I what?"

He leaned forward and lowered his voice. He was speaking quietly, but with so much urgency, I couldn't look away. "You're right. I did back off. At the time I thought . . . I don't know what I thought, that it was best for you, that with two careers, both of us in the same company, it was never going to work out. But the truth was, I was thinking about you all the time. When I was with you, when I wasn't with you. I couldn't get you out of my head."

"That's how people feel when they're in love. It's how I felt about you."

"I never felt that way about my ex-wife—or anyone else, for that matter. I thought that because I couldn't control this thing, it was a weakness, some kind of a failure of will. I've never lost control like that. I thought the best thing was to take a break, to let things cool off a little."

"If you had just told me that's what you were doing—"

"I wasn't thinking about what that might do to you. It was a mistake and I came here to apologize to you. I'm sorry, Alex. I'm sorry."

I sat back in my chair and felt the resentment I'd been carrying around, the intractable knot of bitterness, begin to melt like the butter softening on the plate in front of me. I looked at his face. He'd shaved since this morning, shaved for me. I remembered how it felt to touch his hair. It was thick and dark and rich, the kind of hair Italian and Greek men take to their graves.

"All I can tell you is that I miss you. I miss talking to you and holding you and laughing with you. There's no one else in my life that I feel that way about. And I miss being with you, making love to you. When I got your message, I can't tell you how that made me feel after so long. And when I saw you today in that meeting, being that close without being able to touch you, I thought I was going to grab you right there in front of all those people. I took it out on poor old what's his name with the funny hair."

"Big Pete."

"Even now . . . just seeing you again . . ."

I could feel his eyes on me, on my hair, on my eyes, my lips, my throat, and I began to feel a flush rising under that big sweater.

"I need you," he said. It was a statement so elegant in its simplicity and so powerful, I felt the distance he had come to say it to me, and not geographical distance.

His hand, when he offered it to me, palm up, looked like a cradle. The candle in the center of the table threw an odd light on it, making it seem to glow in the dim corner where we sat.

Leaving him had been painful beyond belief, like cutting off one of my arms at the shoulder with a dull knife. The wound still throbbed, especially at night. Or early in the morning before dawn when my room was silent and my bed was empty and I was thinking about starting another day alone. I always told myself that it had been the best thing for me, that there had been good reasons. But time and distance had made it harder to remember what they were. And even if I could, this close to him, it wouldn't have mattered. It might not have mattered even if he hadn't said he was sorry. What mattered at that moment was his hand reaching out to me. What mattered were the things my body still remembered when I closed my eyes. I felt him in my skin, my muscles, my bones—every part of me, the deepest part of me remembered how I'd felt with him and wanted to feel again.

*　　*　　*

I woke up in the dark and he was breathing next to me, the long, measured breathing of deep sleep. When my eyes adjusted, I could see his face, half buried in the pillow, lips parted like a boy's. His hair had fallen down over his eyes, and I resisted the urge to push it away, to put my lips softly on his. I didn't want to wake him.

As I turned to the other side, he put one arm around me and pulled me close until my skin was next to his. I put my arm over his and it felt exactly right, as if we were two pieces of broken ceramic fit back together, fit together so tightly that the wound disappears.

I went to sleep thinking I could feel his heartbeat, thinking that I never wanted to wake up alone again.

Chapter Thirty-one

The air felt steamy when I opened my eyes, and warm, like a tropical rain forest. I expected Bill to appear from the bathroom, an apparition in the moist vapor, but his voice came from across the room. He was at the desk talking on the phone. I smiled at the sight. He was obviously discussing weighty issues because he had his professional voice on. But he was sitting, legs crossed, wearing nothing but a thick white towel across his lap. He caught me watching and signaled that he'd be off soon. I stretched lavishly in the big Four Seasons bed—I couldn't reach the bottom with my toes or the sides with my fingertips—then curled up into a twist of cool, extremely high-thread-count hotel sheets.

"Call me back when you figure it out." His tone suggested it should have already been figured out. "I've got a conference call in an hour. Don't make me late."

He hung up and sat at the desk, staring at me, forehead wrinkled, looking concerned.

"Who . . ." I cleared the sleep out of my voice. "Who was that?"

"Tony Swerdlow."

"In Denver?" I checked the bedside clock-radio.

"I'm about to negotiate one of the biggest aircraft deals in the company's history, and this guy's home in bed sleeping."

"Bill, that's what people do at three-thirty in the morning."

"Not if they haven't done their work. He's a week late with my performance data, I'm talking to Aerospatiale in an hour, and I can't wait any longer."

"No one sleeps until the Big Cheese is satisfied."

The teasing brought a smile. He wrapped himself in the towel and came over to the bed, leaned down and kissed me. "Especially you."

The feel of his smooth chest against the palm of my hand, the smell of him, the taste of him—after going without him for so long, one night was not enough. "Come back to bed."

"I have to shave."

"For a conference call?"

"I don't want to be late. They're already going to be ticked off."

"Why?"

"Because I'm supposed to be there in person." He smiled, waiting for me to catch on.

"And instead you're here with me."

I had to let that sink in. In all our time together, I'd been the one to arrange my life around him. I couldn't remember a single time when he'd done it for me. The fact that he had this time was surprising. More than surprising. It was shocking—and really sexy.

He straightened to go, but I reached out and barely caught the corner of his towel. It came off easily with a quick flick of the wrist. When he tried to grab it, I drew it under the covers with me.

He stood for a moment looking at the clock, but I pulled back the sheets to invite him in, and he slipped into my arms and stretched out beside me.

"You make me stupid," he murmured softly in my ear.

His skin was warm, his hair still damp from the

shower. Last night in the dark, I had rediscovered his body—the way his back curved under my hand, the feel of the rough scar on his knee when it brushed against my leg, the way his long eyelashes felt soft on my face when he closed his eyes.

I found the line of his backbone and traced it up and down, going a little farther each time until I heard the catch in his breath and felt his hands on my back.

"How am I ever going to work around you? I can't keep my hands off you." And he couldn't. "You made me crazy yesterday in that meeting. I was imagining you under that sweater, thinking about what it would be like to take it off you."

"Show me."

I felt his hand on my hip. "This is where it started, right? About here?"

"More like here." I pushed his hand down until I felt it on my thigh.

"Mmmm, I think you're right." Then slowly, very slowly, he pushed the imaginary sweater up—a millimeter at a time, his fingertips like feathers tracing the shape of my hipbone, the curve of my waist, stopping to linger on all those good places he still remembered.

"Don't stop doing that," I whispered.

He lifted my hands over my head and ran a fingertip up the underside of each arm. I closed my eyes and as he moved over me, I wrapped myself around him and felt the letting go. Boston, the ramp, Lenny and the Petes, Ellen Shepard and Dan Fallacaro—none of it was important. Nothing mattered except the feel of him inside me and this moment.

"I have to get dressed." He was lying on his back with his eyes closed. Untangling his legs from mine, he rolled off the bed and found his towel, which had somehow ended up on the floor. Before he went into the bathroom, he pulled the sheet and then the blan-

ket all the way up and tucked them under my chin.
"Don't distract me anymore."

By the time he came back out, I had gathered in
all the pillows on the bed and propped myself up so
that I could watch him. I'd always loved watching
him dress.

"I need to ask you something," I said.

"What?"

"Why do you have Lenny working for you?"

"Because he's got valuable contacts in Washington,
which has proved very helpful on some of these big
route-authority cases. He's not my best operating guy,
he's definitely high-maintenance, but I can get what I
need from him." He chose two ties and held them
against his suit for me to see.

"I like the darker print," I said, "and Lenny doesn't
get the job done. He hires fools like me or like Ellen
who will go to any lengths not to fail, which means
he won't fail."

"Which means I won't fail. What's wrong with
that?"

"Don't you care about his methods?"

He put the rejected tie back, then sat on the edge
of the bed with his back to me, pulling on his socks.
"Is that why you called? Because you're having problems with Lenny?"

"Do you think I would call you to intervene in a
dispute with my boss?" When he didn't answer, I
poked him through the covers with my big toe. "Do
you?"

"No. So what is going on? And tell me fast because
I've only got twenty minutes." He went into the bathroom, then came out searching. "Have you seen my
watch?"

"It's right here." I plucked it off the nightstand and
tossed it to him. "I get twenty minutes?"

"We would have had more time if we hadn't—"

"All right, I'll give you the Cliff Notes version." I adjusted the pillows so that I could sit up straight. "I'm not sure that Ellen Shepard killed herself."

He paused while buckling the watch and looked up. "That's a provocative statement."

"It's possible someone killed her and made it look like a suicide."

"I had a feeling that's what this was all about."

"Why?"

"Because it's a perfect setup for you. It appeals to all of your instincts as defender of the weak, pursuer of justice, she who rights all past wrongs—"

"I take it you don't believe the rumors about Ellen's death."

"All this talk, those dreadful drawings, that's the kind of mean-spirited gossip traded in by people with small minds who live in small worlds and have nothing better to do but chatter on about this sad woman. It's a tragic, tragic situation, and no one should be using it for their entertainment."

"I don't have a small mind, I don't find this entertaining, and this is *my* twenty minutes."

"It makes me angry."

"So you said. You also said you'd listen to me."

"I'm sorry. Go ahead."

"Ellen got involved in something right before she died. It had to do with Big Pete Dwyer and his son and some guy who works on the ramp named Angelo who might be the key to everything. I think what it all may have to do with is someone paying off Big Pete Dwyer to tank the IBG contract vote that made the merger happen. I suspect Lenny's involved, too, but I don't know how yet."

"First of all, Lenny didn't make the merger happen and neither did this Big Pete asshole. I made that deal happen. Second"—he was making one last check in

the mirror, straightening his tie, smoothing his hair—
"I hate to tell you this, but none of this is news."

"It's not?"

"That business about the contract has been rumored for years. And I can tell you exactly how Lenny would have been involved."

"You can?"

"He's the one who was supposed to have made the payoffs, and the reason is, when Nor'easter sold, he cashed in all his stock options. Don't ask me how he got them, but he had a pile of them with really low strike prices."

"He did?"

"The guy made a fortune."

"So Lenny is part of this after all."

"I didn't say that. I said it's been rumored. No one has ever proved anything."

"The proof is in the package," I said, connecting the dots.

"What package?"

"Do you know who Dickie Flynn was?"

"The drunk who used to run your station."

"He died last year, but before he did, he sent Ellen a packet of material that he'd hidden in the ceiling of the men's locker room at the airport. I think it was a surveillance tape from the ramp, but whatever it was, I'm beginning to think she was killed for it."

"Why didn't the police find any of this?"

"No one in this Boston operation ever has or ever will talk to the police. But I've got a source, a guy I've been talking to down on the ramp."

"How do you know he's not twisting you around for fun?"

"He's not. I know he's not. He's the one who went and got the package for Ellen."

"Does he have it?"

"Nobody has it. We think Ellen may have stashed it—"

"Who's 'we'?"

"Dan and I, Dan Fallacaro. We haven't been able to find it yet. One thing I know is, we're not the only ones looking. Someone ransacked my hotel room, and it's pretty clear they were looking for Dickie's package."

"What?"

"That was the night I called and left you the message. I think it was Little Pete."

"You're just telling me about this? Did you tell Corporate Security? I can call Ted Gutekunst right now—"

"I told them, I told the police, I changed hotels, and I've calmed down a lot."

He walked over to the bed, hands in his pockets, looking as if he was ready to handle the situation right then and there. "I'm not sure you should be calm about this."

"I think I can find the package," I said, "this surveillance video. It would help you get rid of Lenny, wouldn't it?"

"Maybe, but—"

"Even if Lenny had nothing to do with any of this, he was guilty of not backing Ellen up. This is a hard job, and when she needed help he wasn't there. I suspect he may have even been working against her, which I can't understand because they were sleeping together. Maybe they had some kind of a falling-out."

"How did you know they were sleeping together?"

I looked at him. "How did *you*?"

"I asked Lenny."

"And he confirmed it?"

"He denied it, which is all I needed to hear. He has a reputation for that sort of thing."

"Then I'll ask you again, why is he still here?"

"Look," he said, "I'm beginning to think we put Ellen in a job she couldn't handle to begin with, and that Lenny put too much pressure on her and made a tough situation worse by getting personally involved with her. He created an environment where she couldn't succeed. He's going to answer for it, don't worry. But in the end when she couldn't handle it, she made the final choice, not Lenny. And if she was involved with him, she made that choice, too. If I tried to police all the affairs in this company, illicit and otherwise, I'd never get anything else done."

"That's a cop-out, Bill."

"Did you know Ellen Shepard?"

"No, but—"

"I did. She was on my merger task force, and I can tell you this—she was more fragile than people think. And high-strung."

"That doesn't mean—"

"I *knew* her, Alex. And I know you. You can't save Ellen Shepard. It's too late. Don't let this thing be more about you than it is about her. You do that sometimes and you know it. I have whole squads of people who are trained for work like this. There's no reason for you to be involved. I don't want you to be. It's not good for you and it worries me." His attention wandered to the clock on the nightstand. "Alex, I have to get ready for this call. I'm sorry. We can talk more later. We should talk more about this." He disappeared into the next room.

I found one of the hotel's thick white robes hanging on the back of the bathroom door. It wrapped around me one and a half times, but it did what I needed. He was out in the sitting area sorting through his briefcase.

"I need just a couple more minutes," I pleaded. "I promise."

He checked his watch again. "Well, they won't start without me, that's for sure. It might even be a good negotiating strategy to be a little late. Go ahead."

"I need your help on one thing, Bill." I told him the tale of Little Pete and Terry McTavish.

"You say you have a source?" he asked.

"It's the same one I told you about before. He's a ramper and he's as close to Terry as you can get. He's not intimidated by the powers that be in the union. He's a good man. I trust him."

"What about this Little Pete person? What are we doing about him?"

"I heard on my way out tonight that Lenny's already brought him back to work."

He didn't say it, but Lenny was in for a bad day. "Can you nail him again?"

"We plan to make it a priority. Guys like him always give you another chance."

"So you want this McTavish kid to have his job back?"

"He doesn't deserve to be fired."

"Done."

"Thank you," I said, "and I'm not finished talking to you about Ellen."

"You can talk all you want," he said, picking up the phone. "Just don't do anything that might get you hurt. Please."

After a night at the Four Seasons, my own hotel seemed alarmingly inadequate when I went back to change. As I passed the front desk, I picked up my messages. The first one said, "Where are you?" Dan had wanted to know at eight-thirty and again at nine-fifteen last night. But the message from Molly was the one that made me sorry to be running so late. "Re: Crescent Security," it said, "You're not going to believe this."

Chapter Thirty-two

Dan savored the last of his fried potato skins. Stuffed to overflowing with sour cream and bacon, the skins made up one-third of the deceptively named Fisherman's Platter. The other two-thirds were fried onions and nachos. The cholesterol extravaganza was his typical order at The Lobster Pot, a cheesy, overpriced airport restaurant and our usual luncheon venue at the Majestic terminal.

He noticed me staring. "What?"

"Does the word angioplasty mean anything to you?"

"Don't start with me, Shanahan." He licked the sour cream off his finger. "This is one of the few pleasures I have left in my life."

The waitress slapped the check on our table while she was yelling something to the bartender. They knew us at The Lobster Pot, knew they didn't have to waste any service on a captive audience.

"What did you want to talk about, boss?"

I looked again around the restaurant, checking the bar and all the corners. "You haven't seen Lenny, have you?"

"Lenny wouldn't be caught dead in a place like this. Besides, I think Scanlon has him running around on something. He hasn't been here much."

I gave silent thanks to Bill. I hadn't even thought to ask him for a Lenny distraction. I scooted my chair around until I was right next to Dan. "Crescent Security," I said, "I know what it is."

"And you waited all the way through lunch to tell me?"

"I waited until Victor and his cronies left. They were sitting two tables over."

He checked the tables across the room, now empty. "What did you find out?"

I pulled the computer printout off the chair next to me, cleared a space on the table, and set it in front of him. He began thumbing through it. "What is this?"

"Molly researched the station files for anything on Crescent Security. She looked as far back as the local files go, which is like—"

"Seven years."

"Right. She found nothing. So she called HDQ and had them run a summary of all payments to Crescent Security by either Boston Nor'easter or Boston Majestic. This is what she got."

He turned the pages, running his index finger down the dollar column. "It looks like . . . what, fifty, sixty thousand a year?"

"It averages out to forty grand a year for five years," I said. "Over two hundred thousand bucks in total."

"What's it for?"

"No one knows."

"What do you mean by that?"

"Molly has no recollection of processing a single payment to this company, there are no local records, and yet Crescent received a couple of hundred thousand dollars in payments which were approved out of this station."

"What about Molly's ledger books? Have you ever seen those goddamned things? Even if the files were lost, she would have had it all in there, chapter and verse. That's why she does it that way, so nothing gets paid that's not supposed to."

"I'm telling you, there are no local records. But Accounts Payable in Denver had copies of the invoices." I showed him the faxes Molly had given me, slick paper faxes that wouldn't stay flat. We had to be the last office operation in the world without a plain paper fax machine. "Check these out."

He pinned the pages to the table and searched them one at a time. "Looks like they're coded right. These are the accounts Nor'easter used for security background checks, I think. They should have written that in the comments box. Signed by Lenny, but he would have signed if he was general manager. If Molly didn't code them, who did?"

"Lenny."

He let go of the faxes and they immediately curled. "Give me a break. Lenny would rather break his own arm than code an invoice. I don't think he's ever once cracked a chart of accounts since I've known him."

"Molly recognized his handwriting in the coding box."

Dan unfurled one page and looked again, concentrating on the handwritten account codes. He got the connection; I could see it on his face when he looked up at me. "The sevens."

"Exactly. She says Lenny crossed his sevens like that, European style."

"She's right. Fuckin' Lenny. Wants the world to think, he was born in France. In the meantime, he's from some backwater hick town down in Louisiana."

"He's from New Orleans."

"That's what I said. What did Crescent do for us? Forty grand is a lot of background checks."

"I don't think they did anything. Here's what I think. Lenny had Crescent send these invoices to him directly. He'd code them, sign them, and forward them to Accounts Payable. Molly never saw them, and he kept no copies around for her to stumble over. Accounts Payable would cut the check and send it directly to Crescent."

"But Crescent never did anything for the money and Lenny knew it."

"Right."

"Jesus Christ, you're saying he was stealing?"

"Embezzling."

He sat back and shook his head. "That makes no sense, Shanahan. Two hundred grand is tip money to Lenny. The guy is loaded."

"From the deal."

"Right. He hit the jackpot."

"Why didn't anyone bother to tell me this?"

"I figured you knew."

"I didn't. And besides, this scam was going on before the deal."

"True." He leaned over his plate and rummaged for an onion ring. "You don't know who these Crescent people are?"

"The address on the payments was Elizabeth, New Jersey."

"I know Elizabeth. That's not too far from where I grew up."

"Wherever they were, they're gone now, but I figured out something else, too. Do you know what they call New Orleans?"

"You mean like the French Quarter and Mardi Gras?"

"When you fly into New Orleans at night from the south, you come in over the Gulf of Mexico and you can see the lights of the city. It's beautiful, and it's shaped like the moon—a crescent moon."

He stared at me, onion ring poised over the cocktail sauce.

"New Orleans is known as the Crescent City, Dan. Crescent Security was Lenny. It had to be."

He dropped the onion ring, took the napkin from his lap, and slowly wiped the grease from his fingers. "I'll be damned."

"Lenny was stealing from Nor'easter to pay himself. And I think he was using the money to make payoffs. That's what the stub was doing in Ellen's merger file. Remember the stub for ten thousand dollars?"

"Yeah."

"I'll bet it was a payoff and Crescent was some kind of a clearinghouse for him—a way to make his illegal payoffs look legitimate."

Dan sat staring at the printout. His face was blank. I'd expected more of a reaction than that. Molly had given me the Crescent payments, but the rest I'd figured out, and it all fell into place. I loved when that happened, but he was unmoved. "What's the matter?"

"Do you think this had anything to do with Ellen?"

"Yeah, I do. The way we knew about Crescent was because of the reference in her files. My first thought was that this was the money used to buy the IBG contract. She found out about it, and that's what got her into trouble. That might be the connection."

"But now you don't think so?"

"I'm not sure. The payments started a long time before there was ever any thought of selling Nor'easter. And look at the last page of that printout."

He flipped to the back and almost knocked over the lighthouse peppermill in the process. He was oblivious, but I caught it in time. I pointed at the last entry. "See how the payments stopped in August 1994. Molly told me that the contract vote wasn't until November. She said it screwed up everyone's Thanksgiving, so the timing doesn't work, but even if it did, there's less than thirty grand here for 1994. At first I thought it didn't seem like enough to buy a contract. But then I thought, How would I know? I heard about a guy on the news once who paid a professional hit man five thousand dollars to have his wife murdered. That seemed low to me, too."

Dan was rubbing his forehead, looking worried.

"What's the matter with you?"

"Nothing. It's just . . . the thing is . . . I don't think that's what this money was for. I think that money had to come from somewhere else."

"That's what I'm saying, too, that this was the everyday fraud fund. There was a bigger one somewhere else for special occasions."

"So, Ellen knew about this?"

"She must have."

"What else did you find out?"

"That's it. I've got Molly doing more research. She's into it now. She's taking it personally that Lenny corrupted her system."

"Yeah, she would."

I paid the check. Lunch was on me to celebrate finding the dirt on Lenny. Dan still wasn't excited enough for me, and he was actually walking slower than I was as we headed down the concourse to the office. "Are you all right?"

"What? No, I'm fine. But I got a call this morning from my ex. Michelle's got the flu. I thought I might fly down and surprise her this afternoon. Take her a milkshake or something. Is it all right with you? You can beep me if you need me."

"Don't be silly. Take as much time as you need. In fact, why don't you stay down there for the weekend? The only thing I have on the schedule is this meeting with the third shift tonight about the bomb."

"Are you going to be okay for that?"

"Sure." He stood there, hands in his pockets, shifting from one foot to the other. He was obviously anxious to take off. "Give me a call and let me know how she's doing."

"I will," he said, pulling away at Mach speed. "Thanks."

Chapter Thirty-three

It was a few minutes before one in the morning when I left Operations and headed to the ready room. My version of the bag room bomb speech was going to be a pale imitation of the chairman's, but I still owed the midnight shift a face-to-face meeting. I touched the face of my watch. Bill had left on the last flight to Denver. He should be getting in about now. It had taken months for me to stop thinking about him this way, wondering in any random moment where he was and what he was doing. It was funny—maybe scary—how quickly and how vividly it had all come back. It was almost as if he had never gone from my life.

Thinking of him made me feel good, good enough to bypass my usual moment of insecurity and push through the ready room door without hesitation. I was thinking that I was where I belonged. Too bad all that self-confidence was wasted.

The spicy aroma of a microwaved burrito lingered in the air. The door behind me squealed as it swung back and forth on squeaky hinges, and the room where I was supposed to be holding a meeting was completely empty. And in case that message was too subtle, the one written on my flip chart with a thick black marker was more direct. It said, "Fuck you, Shanahan." Anonymous, of course. I could almost feel my skin thickening as I stood there. This kind of stuff was losing impact with me. I was more upset about having stayed up this late for nothing.

I went through the swinging door and straight back to Operations.

"Pete Dwyer, midnight crew chief, Pete Dwyer, please respond with your location. Over." I released the button on the radio and waited. Kevin had gone home and the Ops office was quiet. I called again, and waited again. The third time, I called for anyone knowing the location of Pete Dwyer. Lo and behold, someone responded. Whoever it was suggested the bag room.

"Outbound or inbound?"

No response.

I'd check the outbound first, but the inbound bag room was still under construction and off limits to employees, reason enough to believe that that's exactly where Pete would be.

Kevin's Majestic ramp coat was hanging where he always kept it, on a hook by the door. It was about a foot shorter than my shin-length skirt and bulky as a fireman's gear, but it kept me warm on the long, gusty walk across the open ramp.

As I suspected, the door to the inbound bag room was open, pinned against the wall by a heavy brick. From outside the doorway, I could hear the quiet shuffling of what I knew were heavy construction tarpaulins hanging from the ceiling inside, but the lights were off and I couldn't see a thing. It was unsettling and I probably should have turned around right then, but more unsettling was the fact that the light switch was not in the obvious place by the door and dammit, I had no clue to where it was. I hated being in a new job.

I called into the bag room for Pete. The only answer was the swishing of the tarps as a rogue gust of wind kicked up, scattering old bag tags and finding all the

parts of me that weren't covered by Kevin's coat. He
still wasn't responding on the radio, and the longer I
stood out in the mostly deserted operation calling
Pete's name, the more duped and idiotic I felt. Best
to go back to my hotel and deal with Big Pete Dwyer
and his recalcitrant shift mates in the light of a new
day. Or evening.

When I turned to go, my heel stubbed against something hard, and I tripped into something—no, some-
one who was standing behind me. Jesus, *right* behind
me. I bounced off, stumbled back, and almost bolted.

"I hear you been lookin' for me." His face was
hidden under the hood of a cotton sweatshirt that
came up from under his coat and engulfed his entire
head. But the raspy voice was unmistakable.

"God*dammi*t, Pete, what the hell are you doing?"
I was tingling from a delayed surge of adrenaline, and
my stomach felt as if he'd stomped on it with that
heavy boot I'd tripped over.

"Lookin' for you."

"Why didn't you answer my radio call?"

"I was answering nature's call."

"You didn't have your radio with you?"

"I said, I was taking a leak. I had my hands full.
Besides, I'm here now, ain't I?"

"And as respectful as ever."

It was eerie the way his voice floated out of the
black hole where his face was supposed to be. He was
like a sweatsuit version of the grim reaper. It bothered
me, bothered me a lot, that he'd sneaked up on me
and I'd been oblivious enough to let him.

"Let's go to Operations," I said, "I want to talk."

"We can talk in here."

He was past me, through the door, and behind the
tarp before I had a chance to react. I heard a heavy
snap and the lights came on. Pete knew where the
light switch was located. When he emerged, his hood

was down, revealing a face that was unshaven and a head full of thinning gray hair that stood up in uneven tufts. Hood hair. Looking at his face, I couldn't understand why he covered it at all. His leathery, lined skin struck me as adequate winter protection.

"This is a hard-hat area, Pete."

"I won't tell if you don't."

The ramp behind me was empty, and I could feel the isolation. We were in a godforsaken spot in the middle of a cold night, and no one knew I was out here. I hesitated.

"I ain't gonna bite you," he said, recognizing his advantage. "I just want you to see something, that's all."

He stood waiting with the tarp pulled to one side. Eventually, my curiosity trumped my cautiousness, and besides, Big Pete wasn't going to bite me. From what I'd heard, he might tell someone else to bite me, but he would never do it himself.

"After you," I said, stepping through the plastic portal, "and show me where the light switch is, if you don't mind."

"Sure." He led me to an open fuse box in the corner. "The switch on the wall ain't been fixed yet, so you got to use these." One breaker was thrown. He flipped another as we stood there. Nothing happened.

"What was that for?"

"You'll see."

We continued through the maze of hanging blue walls, moving circuitously toward the north bag belt. The inbound bag room was smaller than the outbound and served a much simpler purpose. Two oval carousels—racetracks we called them—wrapped around the wall that separated the concrete from the carpet. The moving belts carried bags from the rampers in the bag room to the passengers in claim. The belts were controlled by a panel of buttons on the wall, which is where I found Pete when I caught up with him.

"Ready?" he asked.

"For what?"

He pushed a button. Three warning blasts sounded, the gears began to grind, and the ancient conveyor mechanism sputtered to life, complaining against the cold. This would explain the second circuit breaker he'd thrown.

"Watch the security door." He pointed with one of his stubby fingers to the opening in the wall where the bags fed through to the passenger side. The heavy security door had lifted automatically when the belt had started to move, leaving nothing but a curtain of rubber strips that swayed with the motion of the belt.

"Are you watching?"

"I'm watching."

He hit the emergency shutdown switch. The alarm blasted again, the belt lurched to a halt, and the security door dropped in a free fall from its housing, crashing onto the belt with a force, both thunderous and abrupt, that made me jump about a foot off the ground. "Jesus *Christ*."

"It's defective."

"I hope so."

He was right next to me, once again standing too close for my comfort. I took a step away as he propped his foot up on the belt and took out a pack of Camels—unfiltered. The belt was off, the bag room was quiet, and the sound of his lighter snapping shut was loud in the strange stillness that followed the resounding crash.

"One of my guys got his foot almost took off by that thing about six months back. He was trying to kick a jammed bag through when some idiot over there hit the emergency stop." He nodded toward the wall, indicating that "the idiot" had been a passenger in the claim area.

"Is he all right?"

"He's on long-term disability and his foot don't look much like a foot no more. But thank God he didn't lose it."

I stood, hands down in the gritty pockets of Kevin's coat, shifting from foot to foot, trying to keep feeling in my toes. The cold from the concrete was seeping up through the thin leather soles of my pumps and I shivered, but not from the cold. I was imagining what a bone-crushing force like that could do to a man's foot. It was exactly the reaction he was hoping for and we both knew it.

He was leaning forward on his knee and looking at me pleasantly, as if we'd met in a bar to talk over old times.

"Why are you showing me this?"

He stared at the burning end of his cigarette. "I hear the McTavish kid is coming back."

"So what?" Not a snappy comeback, to be sure, but no one had told me, officially anyway, that Terry was coming back and it ticked me off that Big Pete was continually better informed than I was. "Besides, Little Pete's coming back, and the only thing Terry did was save him from an even bigger screw-up than the one he actually caused."

"I don't know what screw-up you'd be referring to."

"The one where he reversed the load on one of his trips because he was drunk."

The fact that I knew one of his secrets didn't seem to bother him. He offered a nod in my direction that was almost deferential. "That was a ballsy move, going around Lenny the way you did. I gotta give you credit for that. Lenny's a piece of shit, but he ain't easy to push around, neither." He took another deep drag, his cheeks hollowing out as he inhaled, then exhaled slowly, directing the stream up toward the ceiling.

"I also gotta ask myself, how is it you seem to know so much about what's going on down here with us."

"I'm well connected."

"Either that or you got a snitch . . ."

Something in the back of my neck began to tighten.

". . . Which means we got a rat."

The smoke from his cigarette drifted up toward the ceiling, a ceiling still black with soot from the bombing this man had most certainly engineered. I was starting to get the idea. That tightening in my neck twisted a little more. "Say what you mean to say."

"All right. I know about Johnny McTavish. I know he's been feeding you information. I know that's part of why his kid brother got his job back."

I held perfectly still, which was just as well since all sensation had long since abandoned my feet.

"Is that what this demonstration is all about? Is this a threat to make me stop looking for whatever it is you and I aren't looking for?"

"This ain't nothing more than a friendly reminder that the ramp is a dangerous place. Accidents happen all the time, and even though you ain't out here that much, other people are." He looked at me with those chameleon eyes. "We don't like rats down here. That guy who got his foot flattened, he was a rat, and he was lucky it wasn't his head got caught in that bag door. Johnny Mac's a pretty tough guy, but his bones break just like everybody else's. Just like yours." He stepped a little closer. "Just like hers."

My heart thumped against my rib cage. "What are you talking about?"

"I hear that's how she died—broken neck." He snapped his fingers. "Just like that. That's how quick it can happen." He pressed his lips into a thin smile that to me was the equivalent of fingernails on a black-board. "Can you imagine that?"

"You sick, sleazy bastard."

"What happened to that woman should never have happened," he said, "but it did. It's done and nothing you can do will change that. Nothing. This ain't your fight, and what you're looking for, nobody wants you to find it. Nobody."

For the first time I felt real panic, as if I was in over my head, as if something I'd started was about to spin dangerously out of my control. I wanted to run to a phone to call John, to call Dan, to call everyone I knew and make sure they were safe tonight. And I wanted to get out of there. "I'm leaving."

He dropped the cigarette on the cement floor and crushed it out under his boot. Then he stood in front of me, this time at a polite distance, with his hands in the pockets of his coat. "Listen to me. There's nothing happening around here that ain't been happening for a long time, and by the time you figure that out, that it ain't worth it, it's going to be too late. I hate to be the one to tell you, but you got no friends here, including that asshole Fallacaro."

The numb feeling in my toes began to creep ever so slowly into my calves, my knees . . . "What about him?"

"He's been lying to you right from the beginning."

. . . my thighs, my hips, and my stomach . . .

"Who do you think told me about Johnny Mac being a rat?"

"What you're saying about John McTavish is not true. But even if it was . . ." My words couldn't keep up with my brain. "What would be in it for Dan to tell you something like that?"

"He didn't tell me. He told your boss."

"Why would he tell Lenny something . . ." The cold, dry air was sticking in my throat, and it was getting painful to breathe, almost impossible to talk, and now I was completely numb. I didn't feel cold. I didn't feel anything. "Dan hates Lenny. He wasn't even in Boston most of the time that Lenny was here."

"You know about Crescent Security, I know you do. But do you know where it was located?"

I opened my mouth to answer and closed it.

Pete was watching me closely, nodding. "Crescent Security was run by Lenny's brother-in-law in Elizabeth, New Jersey, which is just down the road from Newark. He used it for payoffs. He needed to pay someone off, he made them a Crescent contractor. He needed to collect, he'd send a bill from Crescent. But sometimes he needed to move large amounts of cash in secret, and that's where your buddy came in. It was the Danny Fallacaro delivery service—Jersey to Boston, hand-delivered. Better than FedEx. That's how he got into management. He was just another bag slinger before that . . . one of us."

I tried to find some equilibrium, because the concrete floor was falling out from under me. I wanted to say I didn't believe him, but I couldn't find my voice.

"If you don't believe me, ask him." Pete lifted his hood over his head, and when he turned to go, I could no longer see his face, could only hear his voice. "Ask him about locker thirty-nine. He'll know."

Chapter Thirty-four

The track at the East Boston Memorial Stadium is right in Logan's front yard, encircled by a noisy four-lane road that loops into and out of the terminals. But as I came down the back stretch, the only sounds I heard were my feet pounding the track and my own labored breathing as I sprinted the last quarter mile at a pace I could barely sustain, pushing toward the finish, arms pumping, chest heaving, tapping into my last reserves of energy. When I was finished running this morning, I didn't want to have anything left.

Coming out of the last curve, a sharp, familiar pain flashed like a hot poker from behind my left knee straight up the back of my thigh, and I knew I'd pushed too hard. Again. My hamstring had been aggravated for two years, but I'd never stopped running long enough to let it completely heal. I shifted down to a trot and then a walk, hands on my hips and favoring the left side.

"Shanahan . . ."

I shielded my eyes so I could peer down the track, but I didn't need to see. The tenor and cadence of Dan's voice had become as familiar to me as my own. He was standing in the middle of my lane, completely out of place in his gray worsted suit, pant legs flapping around his Florsheim shoes. He had his hands stuck down in the pockets of his camel-hair coat, which was about an inch too long for his frame. Behind him, the traffic flowed over the access road nonstop, moving like sludge out of the airport. The sky over his head was bright and clean and blue.

"You pick the strangest places to have meetings, boss."

The jaunty tone was jarring. I'd been in a black pit in the hours since I'd talked to Big Pete, unable to sleep, too upset to eat. I was doing the only thing I knew would make me feel better. But there are only so many miles you can run before your body breaks down and you have to face the hard things in life, and there wasn't much that was harder than what I was about to face with Dan.

"How was the meeting last night?" he asked when I was closer.

"The meeting didn't happen," I said, wiping the sweat out of my eyes, "but I had a long talk with Big Pete."

My bag was over on the bleachers. The pain in my leg was getting worse. It felt sharp, serious, as if something important had ripped. Every step hurt worse than the last as I limped across the track and toward the bag. Dan was close on my heels. "What'd that piece of shit have to say?"

The last few words were drowned in the roar of an aircraft leaving the runway on the other side of the terminal. I glanced up, then he did, and we both stood and watched it climb out. The sun glinted off the clean lines and graceful curves of a B767, one of my favorite fleet types. As it banked over the harbor, the royal purple tail with the mountain-peak logo made it easily identifiable as one of ours. I watched until I couldn't see it anymore, then pulled a thin hotel towel from my bag and started wiping down, first my face, then my neck. I was breathing normally again, but the ache in my leg had migrated to my heart, which felt as if it was throbbing, not beating.

"Doesn't look much like there's a blizzard coming, does it? But that's what they're saying." He was still staring at the sky, but toward the west. "Tomorrow night at the latest."

The words came up and caught in my throat, but I finally spat them out. "What's locker thirty-nine, Dan?"

At first he didn't move, just kept staring at the sky, looking for that storm coming. Then he slowly rolled his head back and closed his eyes. His breath condensed in a thin stream as a long exhale left his lips. He looked as if the air was literally flowing out of him, like a balloon that would end up crumpled and shriveled at my feet.

"Fucking Pete Dwyer," he said quietly. It was not the reaction of an innocent man.

I leaned over and tried to stretch, telling myself I needed to ease some of the stiffness out of that hamstring, but really finding a reason to turn away. When I bent over and flattened my back, a rush of cold air sneaked under my jacket, found the moisture between my shoulder blades, and sent a sick shiver through my bones. Once I started shaking, I couldn't stop.

"What did he say about me?"

"That you were one of Lenny's guys. That you were the one who delivered the cash from Crescent Security in New Jersey to Lenny in Boston."

"That little pisshead." He smacked one of the metal benches hard with his fist, sending a loud, vibrating *bong* through the entire section of bleachers and, apparently, his arm. *"Goddammit."* He grabbed his wrist, whirled around, took a few steps away and came right back. "You've got to let me explain this, Shanahan." It was more a plea than a statement.

I looped the towel around my neck, packed my gear, and zipped the bag.

"You can't just walk away without—I can't believe

this." The words spilled out as he paced in a crazy loop, stopping and starting, shaking out his wounded wrist. "*Fucking asshole* Dwyer. Ask me anything, just stay here and let me explain."

"I can't." My voice cracked. I could barely talk and I could feel myself shutting down, sector by sector.

"When, then? When can I explain this to you? Shanahan—" He grabbed my arm, panicked fingers digging through a jacket, a sweatshirt, and a layer of long underwear. He was probably holding tighter than he realized. I looked down at his shoes, black loafers covered with a light dusting of orange track sand. Athletic fairy dust. If only it could make this go away.

"What's locker thirty-nine?"

He loosened his grip, and when I looked into his eyes, I knew that he was going to break my heart. His hands fell to his sides as he turned to watch another liftoff. I watched him.

"Thirty-nine is Lenny's lucky number. He hit in Vegas one time, or maybe it was Atlantic City. I can't remember. Roulette or something. I guess he won big." His voice was steady, but he looked as if it hurt to keep his eyes open. My own eyes were burning as I watched him turn even farther away. "It's the airport locker where I made the drops. We had two keys so I'd put the envelope in there and he'd have someone pick it up."

A heaviness, a dreariness settled like a dull pain into my chest. I hadn't realized until that moment how much I had wanted this not to be true, how much hope I'd been holding out. I didn't want to let it go. I blamed him for making me let it go.

"Goddamn you. God*damn* you, Dan. All of this talk about honesty and integrity and honoring Ellen's memory. Going through the closed door. It's all bullshit. You're one of those guys behind the closed door."

He stood with his head down, taking whatever I had

to dish out. If I'd wanted to shoot him, I don't think he would have objected. "Did Ellen know?" I asked.

"I—I never told her."

"Is that why she didn't tell you what she was doing? She thought you might tell Lenny?" My body had cooled down, but I was hot and getting hotter, fueled by a growing rage, the kind I hadn't felt in a long time. "Like you told him about the snitch."

His eyes grew wide. "I didn't tell him about Johnny. I swear I didn't."

I gaped at him as he chattered on, not believing that he didn't realize what he'd just said.

". . . And I never betrayed Ellen. I told her the truth. And everything I've told you has been the truth."

"How did you know it was John?"

"What?" As I stared at him, his confusion slowly gave way to panic as he figured it out, too. "Somebody from the ramp told me. I don't even remember who it was."

"I don't believe you, Dan." I picked up my gym bag and slung it over my shoulder. "You're one of them . . . and I never saw it coming. Shame on me."

"What he's talking about, that stuff happened a long time ago. It had nothing to do with Ellen. It has nothing to do with you."

"How can you say that? I believed you. I trusted you and you lied to me."

"How? How did I lie?"

"By letting me believe you were someone you're not."

"I'm not even smart enough to be someone I'm not. Jesus *Christ*. I was gonna tell you—would you *stop,* please."

He reached for my arm, but this time I pulled away. We stood at the gate of the airport track facing each other, both breathing hard. The cars were blasting by just a few yards from where we were standing, and the noxious fumes were starting to make me sick. Something was making me sick, and I thought if I didn't get away from him, I was going to pass out. I stepped closer so I didn't have to yell over the road noise.

"The person I thought you were, Dan, I really liked that guy. Now I wish I'd never met you."

He stepped back, and we stared at each other for another trembling moment. The expression on his face moved with stunning speed from guilt to anger to sadness and finally to something that I could only describe as pure pain, like a big open wound. I could see that I had hurt him. It didn't make me feel any better.

Instead of walking up to the traffic light, I waited for an opening and made a limping dash across the four-lane road. I could still hear the blaring horns when I got to my room and slammed the door behind me. I took off my sweaty clothes layer by layer and left them in a damp pile on the floor. After my shower—history's longest hot shower—I went to the window to close the curtains, looked down, and saw him still there, sitting alone in the bleachers, hunched against the wind like an old man. I don't know how long he stayed there. I closed the curtains and never looked again.

Chapter Thirty-five

I answered the phone without taking the cool, wet washcloth from my eyes.

"Lenny's going ballistic." Molly's voice broke through the dreamy haze between awake and asleep. "He says he hasn't seen you in two days and wants me to find out if you're ever coming back to work again."

"What did you tell him?"

"That you had an appointment downtown."

"Who am I meeting with?"

"One of our big freight forwarders. Are you going to make it in at all today, or should I make up something else?"

"Make up something else."

"He's not going to like it. You've already got him muttering to himself."

"What time is it?"

"They don't have clocks in that hotel?"

"Molly . . ."

"It's almost noon. You want to tell me what's going on?"

"Not really. Any messages?"

She was quiet, deciding if she was going to be put off that easily. She must have calculated her odds of success from the sound of my voice and found them to be not in her favor.

"Matt Levesque called. He wants you to call him back. And Johnny McTavish called."

"What did he say?"

"That he was returning your call."

"Did he leave a number?"

"Are you kidding? He wouldn't even leave his name, but I knew it was him."

"All right. Call me here if anything else comes up."

"Are you sure you're—"

"I'm fine, Molly."

"Suit yourself."

She hung up in a huff. I flipped the cloth to the cool side and drifted back into my half sleep.

I thought about letting the phone ring this time, but the hotel had no voice mail, just one overburdened desk clerk that might never get around to taking a message.

"Hello."

"Someone knows."

It was Matt. I'd been dozing long enough that the washcloth was dry and stiff. I pushed it off and covered my aching eyes with my hand. "Who knows what?"

"I got nailed. My boss called me in this morning. She wanted to know why I requested that pre-purchase agreement file from archives, and I couldn't exactly say it was for any project I'm working on now."

"How'd she know?"

"She didn't share that with me."

Dan was the only person who knew I had been talking to Matt and why. I tried not to think about that. "What did you tell her?"

"I told her the truth, that you called and asked me as a personal favor to pull the files. You didn't think I was going to throw myself in front of that train for you, did you?"

"I didn't ask you to lie for me. Did you say anything about Ellen?"

"She didn't ask and I didn't tell. But she did rip me a new asshole for not keeping her informed of a request from outside the department. I think that satisfied her for the time being."

"I'm sorry, Matt. I didn't intend for you to get into trouble. It's not worth it." I swung my feet to the floor, but couldn't find the energy to move from the edge of the bed. So that's where I sat, my head in my free hand. "None of this was worth it."

"I detect a note of despair, of profound disappointment, perhaps a hint of cynicism . . . definitely bitterness—"

"I'm not bitter," I snapped rather bitterly. "I'm just done. This was never my fight to begin with. And now it's over."

According to the clock-radio, it was 1:27 in the afternoon, but the room was still dark, almost all natural light blacked out by those mausoleum hotel draperies. Very disorienting. I went to the bathroom to check the damages in the mirror. My eyes were bloodshot from crying, the bags underneath disturbingly pronounced, and my hair, which had been wet from the shower when I'd gone to bed, had dried into a free-form fright wig.

"Am I talking to myself here?"

"I'm sorry, Matt. Did you say something?"

He let out an exasperated sigh. "I said, when the files never showed up from archives, I started thinking about who else might have kept a copy of the pre-purchase adjustment schedule. And then it hit me—our outside accounting firm keeps copies of everything. So I called a guy who worked with us on the deal, one of the baby bean counters they had in here and he had it on disk. Pulled it right up. He was so proud of himself. Probably figures there's a promotion in it. What would that make him? A senior bean counter?"

"This is the schedule Ellen created? The one she was looking for?"

" 'Majestic Airlines Proposed Acquisition of Nor'easter Airlines. Pre-purchase Adjustments for the Twelve-Month Period August 1994 through July 1995.' I've got it right here in front of me. There's a list of vendors with the date and amounts paid. But if you don't want to hear about it, that's fine. It just seemed important to you at the time, which is why I went out on a limb for you, but don't let that influence your decision in any way. Don't worry about any possible damage to my career, and just forget the fact that I was sneaky enough to find—"

"Matt."

"What?"

"Be quiet."

"Okay."

I was trying to decide whether the soft pounding in my head was a headache or the faint heartbeat of a curiosity that refused to die. Across the room, a sliver of bright light shone through where the curtains almost met. The telephone cord was just long enough for me to walk over there. The drapes felt nubby when I ran my finger along the edges, and I wondered if I would see Dan if I opened them. The thought of him still sitting in the bleachers with his head down made me sad. Angry. No, sad.

"You're still there, right, because I don't have all day to work on this."

"I'm thinking," I said.

I could hang up. I could refuse to learn whatever it was he was dying to tell me. I could skate through the rest of my time in Boston, letting Big Pete run the place, doing what Lenny wanted, never questioning his motives, never knowing what really happened to Ellen, or what was in that package. I'd probably even get promoted. I'd become the first female vice president for Majestic Airlines in the field—my dream come true.

And it would never feel right. Never.

I pulled the curtains back and let the afternoon light come in. "Read me the list."

"Now you're talking." Matt began to read, ticking vendors off the list so quickly at first, I had to slow him down. We'd gone through about twenty names, and he was getting bored and speeding up again, when I heard it.

"Stop. Back up and read me that last one."

"Cavenaugh Leasing?"

"That one just after that."

"Crescent Consulting."

"Crescent Consulting? Not Security?"

"Believe it or not, I can read."

"Majestic made payments to Crescent Consulting? Is that what that means?"

"Yep."

"*Before* the merger?"

"That's what this says."

"How much?"

Pages shuffled at his end while I looked around for my briefcase. Where the hell had I dropped it? The room wasn't that big.

"Roughly three quarters of a million bucks over eight months."

"Three quarters of a *million*?" My heart thumped an exclamation point. "That's it. That's got to be it."

"Got to be what?"

The corner of my briefcase peeked out from under the bedspread. I dropped to my knees, opened the case, and found the file on Crescent inside. With the phone wedged between my shoulder and ear, I began digging, looking for Molly's computer printout. "What was the timing of the payments, Matt?"

"Three installments—two hundred thousand in October '94, two hundred more in December of that year, and three hundred in July of '95."

I sat on the floor, leaned back against the bed, and flipped through the printout until I found what I needed. Molly had said that the IBG contract vote had ruined everyone's Thanksgiving. I'd made a note of the specific date—November 20, 1994. So, a payment in October, the contract vote in November, and a payment in December. Merry Christmas, Lenny.

"When did the Majestic-Nor'easter deal close?"

"July 21, 1995."

And one big incentive bonus the next year when the deal closed.

"Are you going to tell me what this Crescent Consulting is?"

"I told you before. It's that local vendor used by Nor'easter in Boston in the early nineties, allegedly for background checks and other odd jobs. It turns out that Crescent Security is also Lenny Caseaux. I suspect Crescent Consulting is, too."

"Can't be. It's a conflict of interest to be the vendor providing services to the company you work for."

"He didn't provide any services."

It took him a nanosecond to work through the logic. "No way."

"Way."

"That's embezzling."

"Yes, indeed." I flipped the printout closed and got to my feet so I could pace. "When Lenny Caseaux was the GM in Boston, he stole over two hundred grand from Nor'easter by paying fake invoices to this Crescent Security company. It was nickel-and-dime stuff— it took him five years—and it didn't seem like enough to buy a union contract. But seven hundred thousand in ten months would be plenty."

"Buy a contract? You lost me."

"Lenny paid Big Pete to make sure Nor'easter's IBG contract proposal failed."

"Who's Big—"

"Pete Dwyer," I said. "He runs the union up here."

"Lenny bought the contract—"

"—to make the merger happen." I paced around the bed and back again. "That's exactly what I'm saying."

"And then got Majestic to pay for it." Matt was getting into it now. "Brilliant. The guy's a genius."

"A genius? I think you're missing the bigger picture here."

"Okay, so he's an evil genius. I never would have guessed that Lenny Caseaux had the brains to pull off something like this and not get caught. Contract fraud, election tampering—you're talking federales here. The FBI. Probably the Securities and Exchange Commission since it impacted the value of the company. Definitely fertile ground for shareholder lawsuits. No wonder everyone wants to keep this buried. And he got away with it."

"That's the part I don't get. I can understand how he could approve payments to himself at Nor'easter, although why the auditors didn't catch it, I'll never know."

"From a financial controls standpoint, Nor'easter was a nightmare. That part would have been easy. The genius of the plan was getting Majestic to fund the payoffs."

"How could he have done that? He didn't work for Majestic at the time, and he couldn't approve those payments himself."

"You said that Crescent was a security company." I could hear Matt sucking on his pen as he talked, something he always did when he was into heavy thinking.

"A fake security company."

"Lenny could have set up Crescent as a provider of consulting services to the deal. As part of due diligence, they could have been hired to review training programs, check compliance, test checkpoints, stuff like that. With a deal like this, you can do just about anything. You've got consulting fees all over the place, and it just becomes part of the negotiation as to who's going to pay for what. He probably got an agreement that Crescent could bill Majestic instead of Nor'easter. It even makes sense because Nor'easter was short on cash at the time. And the fact that it was a pre-purchase adjustment makes it that much easier to hide. There's no budget, and two hundred grand a pop wouldn't really stick out compared to the other charges on this list." He snorted. "You should see the attorneys' fees."

"So Lenny and the other Nor'easter investors who wanted to cash out of the airline business anyway figured out a way to get Majestic to pay the kickbacks which ultimately insured that Majestic would buy their company—at a profit. And Lenny apparently set it up."

"I told you, pure genius," he said.

"I still don't get how he could even get Crescent considered as a vendor. As you said, someone would have to negotiate that."

"That's easy. Lenny Caseaux sat on the negotiating team for Nor'easter."

"He did?"

"Yeah, I thought you knew that. That's where I met him."

"Did Ellen know him back then?"

"We all knew him. He's not exactly shy. And he was always hanging around Ellen."

I thought about what Molly had said about how Ellen might have responded to Lenny, to someone who showed interest in her. "Did they seem . . . did they know each other well?"

"Who?"

"Lenny and Ellen."

"They spent a lot of time together, which is why it makes sense that she's the inside person."

"Ellen?" The spiral phone cord caught on the frame at the foot of the bed and nearly sent the phone flying.

"As you pointed out, Lenny needed someone on the team to approve his invoices and not ask questions. Lenny Caseaux and Ellen Shepard spent so much time together people started thinking they had a thing going on. So it works like this: Lenny-who-is-Crescent sends her the invoices and she approves them. Majestic cuts a check to Crescent and the paperwork goes to file. Lenny buys the contract, the deal goes through, and he and his pals cash in. Ellen gets her promotion to a job for which she has not a single qualification. And there you have it. Makes perfect sense."

"Do you have any proof at all for what you're saying, or is it all just conjecture?"

"What do you think happened to the original of Ellen's pre-purchase agreement schedule, the one that was in archives?"

"I have a feeling you're going to tell me."

"Ellen swiped it."

"What are you talking about?"

"After she called me and I told her where she could find the files, she flew to Denver, went out to the archives warehouse, and took it."

"How do you know this?"

"When the archivist couldn't find the file, I took a ride out there just to make sure he knew what to look for. When my secretary made the request, all she'd given him was a reference number. When I described to him the schedule that I wanted and told him that it was in the merger files, he told me that Ellen had been there in person. In the flesh."

"Does he know her?"

"He doesn't get that many visitors, and he remembered her red hair. It reminded him of his sister. She asked him to show her where the merger files were. Who else could it have been? Something must have happened to make her think that it was going to come out and she needed to hide the evidence."

"Something like what?"

"I don't know. You found out about it, didn't you? Maybe someone else up there knew about it."

"Lots of people up here seem to know about this," I said, "but no one talks. It's like the Irish Mafia."

"Maybe someone threatened to talk. Whatever . . ."

I thought about the mysterious Angelo and whatever he knew and the fact that Ellen had fired him. I thought about Dickie Flynn and his deathbed confession. I slid down to the floor, where I could get back into my briefcase. "When was this trip to archives?" If Ellen had been in Denver, it would likely be on her list of secret travel destinations.

"He said it was the first day he was back at work after the holidays."

The last trip she'd taken had been to Denver— United on December 29. It was right there on the calendar. She went out and back in the same day. Eight hours of flying and only three hours on the ground in Denver. You'd have to have a singular purpose in mind to do that. I felt so disappointed. Betrayed, even. "You didn't even know her," is what Bill had said to me, and he'd been right. And the package, maybe we couldn't find the package because she'd destroyed it. "What about the hard copies of the invoices, the signatures?"

"Gone, too, although no one in Accounting remembers seeing her there."

"I just can't believe this about her. Can you, Matt? You knew her. Can you really see Ellen doing something like that?"

"I think I have a way to find out for sure. What if I can find out who signed the Crescent invoices?"

"Then you would be very clever, indeed. I thought there were no copies around."

"We had this admin support person on the task force, Hazel. She was viciously organized. It was scary. And she worked with Ellen a lot."

"Did you know her?"

"She loved me. I used to bring her lattes in the morning just to stay in her good graces. I figure I'll buy her another double-tall for old time's sake and find out what she's got. I doubt if she'd have copies of the invoices, though. The best she might have is some kind of record of who signed. That sounds like something she'd do. If Ellen signed them, then we'd know for sure."

I pulled myself up and wandered back to the window. "When do you think you might know something?"

"I've already got a call in to Hazel. As soon as I get something one way or the other, I'll call you." There was a slight pause. I'd run out of things to say and was just waiting for him to run out of steam. "You haven't commented on my theory, Alex. It's pretty amazing, don't you think, how all the pieces fit, and especially how I figured it all out?"

"Very elegant, Matt. It's a very elegant theory."

After I hung up, I stared down at the empty bleachers. Dan was long gone, and so was the blue sky. The overcast sky was so intense in its bland whiteness, it hurt my eyes. I was tempted to close the curtains, but I didn't. If I was going to work, I needed light.

Most of Ellen's things were in and on top of her personal mementos box, which was back in the corner of the room. All in one motion I hoisted it onto the bed. Several items slipped off the top and fanned out over the sheets like a deck of cards. Pick a card, any card. I slipped a file from the middle of the stack, one that I'd already read twice. Armed with a bottle of water from the mini bar, I settled in on the bed and began to read it again. The next time I looked up, it was after five o'clock.

I picked up the phone and dialed the office. There was no reason to think Molly would still be at work, but as the phone rang and rang, I was hoping. Please, please, please, please, please pick up. Finally she did.

"Molly, did you ever get that password for the officers' calendars?"

Chapter Thirty-six

When my eyes adjusted to the low light, I saw two people kneeling in prayer—a Delta flight attendant in the last pew to the left, and Dan in the first pew on the right. With his head bowed, he was on his knees below a statue of the Virgin Mary.

I stood in the back and surveyed the windowless chapel. A single spotlight shone on a heavy wooden cross over the raised altar. The only other light came from rows of offertory candles along the walls. The design of the church was slick and modern, but the smell was ancient—of old incense and burning candles, oil and ashes. I hadn't been inside a Catholic church for over fifteen years, not since my father's funeral, but I still recognized that smell. This was a place where people brought their sins.

When I arrived at Dan's pew, I genuflected and made the sign of the cross. He saw me, crossed himself, and slid back in the pew, propping both feet up on the kneeler. Instead of his usual bouncing and fidgeting, he was still. "You're Catholic?" he asked, his voice barely above a whisper.

"Not anymore."

"Why not?"

I looked at the gleaming white marble altar, hard and unforgiving. "The whole deal is presided over by aging, celibate white men whose job it is to tell you how to live a clean and pure life in a dirty and complicated world. It doesn't make any sense to me, and I don't need help feeling guilty. What about you?"

"My kid's always asking me if I go, so I do. Besides, it's the only place on the field where it's quiet enough for me to think." His voice was so low that only the two of us could hear.

"What are you thinking about?"

"My grandmother. She raised me." He tipped his head back and stared up at the ceiling. "She used to tell me that men were put on the earth to take care of women."

"That's quaint."

"She was a tiny Italian woman, but she was a pistol. Nobody messed with her. 'Husbands are supposed to take care of their wives, and fathers are supposed to take care of their children,' she'd say, 'and that's the only way it works.' "

"Do you believe that?"

"I believed it all my life. And now my wife has left me, my little girl sees me twice a month if I'm lucky, Ellen is dead, and you hate my guts." He rubbed his eyes and focused on the offertory candles burning at the bare ceramic feet of the Virgin Mary. Most of the candles were lit, evidence that there were still people who believed. "I don't think my grandmother would be proud of me." His voice trailed off, and all I could hear was the sound of the flight attendant in back saying her rosary, the beads tapping lightly against the wooden pew. "Ellen knew," he said.

"What?"

"Vic Venora told her about me, about locker thirty-nine. That was the last conversation I had with her. She did the same thing you did, she stormed off. Only that was the last time I ever saw her. Alive anyway." He stared into the flames of the offertory candles and for a moment seemed transfixed by them, by the light of other people's prayers. "I can't stop thinking that if she hadn't found out or if I'd told her myself, she could have trusted me. She wouldn't have tried to do this thing on her own. I could have helped her. But I never got a chance to explain it to her."

And just like that, it all fell into place. His obsessive pursuit, his endless rationalizing, his reckless disregard for himself: it was all driven by the most powerful and relentless of all impulses—guilt. "Explain it to me, Dan. I'd like to understand."

He stared down at his shoes, his face heavy and his eyes unseeing. He began slowly. "I was twenty-eight years old, still working as a ramper in Newark. I'd been married five years and was still living in my father-in-law's house. I was working my ass off every day, and every night I was taking classes, trying to get into management. One day Stanley calls. Stanley Taub. You know him?"

"He used to be the GM in Newark for Nor'easter."

"Right. He didn't know me from a hole in the wall, but he calls me to his office and tells me he's got a shift supervisor job open on the ramp. Asks me, do I want it? I couldn't fu—I mean, I couldn't believe it. I thought he was kidding. Then he says there might be a few things I'd have to do that I might not like. I tell him I'll clean toilets if I have to. I'll wash his car. I was going to make some decent money for the first time in my life, so I said, fine, sign me up."

Even now he couldn't hide a hint of the excitement he must have felt. "Stanley wasn't talking about cleaning toilets, was he?"

He shook his head. "At first he'd ask me to do stupid shit, like drive him into the city and drop him off so he wouldn't have to park. Then he started telling me without really telling me to stay out of certain areas on certain shifts. 'I don't think you need to be down in cargo tonight,' he'd say, 'I've got it covered.'"

"And you stayed away?"

"I didn't know I had a choice. I thought the deal was to do what he said or go back to slinging bags, and there was no way I was gonna do that. The baby was already two years old, and if I had to kill myself, I was getting us our own apartment. I did what I was told."

"Where did Lenny come in?"

His head hung so low, he was almost talking into his shirt. "Lenny needed someone to run these envelopes up to Boston from Jersey, and Stanley recommended me."

I stared down at my hands in my lap. "Envelopes full of cash?"

"Swear to God, Shanahan, I never looked. My instructions were to fly to Boston and leave the envelope in locker thirty-nine at the Nor'easter terminal, so that's what I would do, then turn around and go back home. I never knew who picked it up. I never heard of Crescent Security. I never even knew what the envelope was for. Didn't want to."

I believed him. Not knowing or wanting to know would have been inconceivable to me, but it was as much a part of his character as loyalty to his boss. "How much money did you make for all this?"

He put his hands beside him on the pew, rocked forward, and stared down at his shoes so that I couldn't see his face. "I got paid extra overtime without working it. It came in my paycheck."

That couldn't have been much, and it was so much like him to sell out at a price that was far too low. "Why did you stop?"

"Michelle." He tilted his head, looked at me, and couldn't suppress the smile. "She was so beautiful, so perfect. One day she looked up at me with those big innocent eyes, and I saw myself the way she might see me and I got scared. I started feeling like I didn't deserve her and that God was going to punish me, take her away from me. I decided I would never again do anything that wouldn't make my kid proud, and I never took another dime."

"Lenny couldn't have been too pleased."

"He told me I'd never get promoted as long as he was drawing breath, but what else was he gonna do? Fire me for not stealing anymore?"

"You were in Boston by then?"

"Yeah. You know, the whole time I was in the union working the ramp, everyone down there was sticking it to the company in every way they could. Every day I had a chance to do it, too, and I never did. I put on a shift supervisor's uniform and I find out management's stealing more than anyone and I'm thinking, If everyone's sticking it to the company, who is the company?"

He sat back with his shoulders slumped and his hands folded in his lap, looking as if he'd taken a pretty good beating from the world, and I realized that in his mind he had never lied to me. He never could have. Everything he was, everything he wanted to be, was right there on his face. If I had known him when he was scamming, I would have known he was scamming, the same way I knew now that he was telling the truth.

"Did you tell Big Pete about John McTavish?"

"On my grandmother's eyes, I did not tell him."

"Do you know how he found out?"

"No, but I've been thinking about it, and I remember now how I found out. Victor Venora. He made a point of tracking me down to tell me."

"That could have been Big Pete making sure that you knew. The real question is, How did those guys find out?"

He looked all around the chapel and then back at me. "Why did you call me?"

"Because I calmed down. I got a little perspective,

and I decided I was a jerk for believing Big Pete and not giving you a chance to explain."

"Thank you." he said, his voice hoarse, ragged.

"My pleasure . . . and there's more. I've spent the past five hours going through every piece of mail, every document, everything I have that belonged to Ellen, and I think I've figured some things out. I need to tell you about it."

"I'm on my way to meet Angelo. Come with me and we'll talk on the way."

Chapter Thirty-seven

"Can you believe this shit?" Dan guided the car into the bumper-to-bumper flow of Route 1A. "We're never going to make it. Angelo's gonna bolt before we get up there."

The exit to the Sumner Tunnel, the short way into town, was closed to all but taxi cabs and buses. It was a traffic-control measure that usually happened at the airport this time of night on Fridays. A trooper stood in the road with the lights of his blue-on-blue State of Massachusetts patrol car flashing and rain dripping from the bill of his cap. Using a flashlight, he'd funnel reluctant drivers onto the dreaded detour route. And there was no more reluctant driver than Dan at that moment.

"God*dammit.*" He banged the steering wheel, then banged it again for good measure.

"Calm down. There's nothing we can do about this. Where are we going?"

"Angie's worried about being seen with us. He's got us going way the hell out to some dive in Medford or Medfield or some goddamned place." He leaned forward and wiped the fog off the window with the sleeve of his jacket. When he had cleared a hole big enough, he craned his neck and peered up into the sky. "I don't like the way it looks out there."

I made my own porthole. All I could see were

sheets of rain falling on us from out of a pitch-black sky. "This is supposed to turn to snow later."

"I know. What's the big discovery?"

This wasn't exactly the venue I had in mind for breaking the news, but it would have to do. I turned in my seat so that I could face him. "My friend Matt called earlier today."

"Finance guy Matt?"

"He found a copy of the schedule of pre-purchase adjustments, the one Ellen was looking for."

As I explained about the seven hundred thousand dollars and the three payments and Crescent and everything but the part about Ellen being involved, he was riding the brakes, inching into the traffic, and I was mainly talking to the back of his head. "You're not listening to me."

"I am listening," he insisted. "There were three big payments from Nor'easter to Crescent, which is really Lenny, and he used the money to buy the contract. That's your big news?"

"The payments to buy the contract came from Majestic, not Nor'easter. *That's* the big news, Dan. Lenny—or someone—figured out a way to get Majestic to pay for the whole thing. But to make it work, he needed a partner on the inside at Majestic, someone on the task force to approve his fake invoices to Crescent." I took a deep breath. "It could have been Ellen."

He hit the brakes abruptly, and we both slammed against the seat belts.

"Son of a *bitch*." For a split second I thought he was yelling at me, but his anger was directed at the driver of a panel truck who was maneuvering to merge from behind us. Dan deftly cut him off. "Who's saying that about her?"

"Matt." I shifted around in my seat. My jeans were

starting to feel tight. "And me, Dan. I think it's possible that she was involved."

"This is a joke, right?" He glared at the driver of the truck in the rearview mirror. "I can understand that fucking pisshead finance guy thinking something that stupid. What is he, like twelve years old? But you, Shanahan, what is that? You're mad at me so Ellen's dirty, too?"

"Ellen and Lenny worked on the merger together. They were on different sides of the negotiation, but apparently they became close. That project lasted eight months."

He was stiff-necked, gripping the steering wheel and staring straight ahead. "That doesn't prove anything, for chrissakes."

"I've been working on this all afternoon, going over and over every detail. I went through it all again—the box we brought down from her house, her letters, her files, her documents. I watched that dating video about a dozen times, and I went through a whole pile of her mail that had been forwarded to the airport—"

"What did you expect to find?"

"Some kind of a clue as to her motives. Why she was involved in all this."

"She was involved because that cocksucker Dickie Flynn got her involved when he sent her that package."

"I think she was involved before she got that package. Think about it. She could have turned that package over to the feds, or Corporate Security. She didn't tell anyone what she was doing. She was sneaking around on other airlines. And I found something in her files. She requested and received extraordinary signature authority while she was on the task force."

"So what?"

"Under her normal authority, she couldn't have

signed those Crescent invoices. They were too big. She made special arrangements so that she could."

"Can't you just believe that she wouldn't have done something like that?"

"But she did. I found the request and the approval in her files."

"I'm talking about the whole scam. I'm telling you she wasn't that kind of person."

I leaned back against the passenger door. "Dan—"

"I say she was clean, that she was trying to do the right thing, and you won't take my word on that. So what it comes down to is, you don't believe me. You don't trust me." He ran a nervous hand through his hair and stared through the wet windshield into the red blur of taillights. The combativeness in his voice had gone. He sounded almost plaintive. "You don't trust me."

The only sounds in the car were the blasting heater and the sluicing of the wet windshield wipers, steady as a metronome. I turned around to face front and wished like hell that we weren't stuck in traffic, that we could put some distance between us and this place we were in.

"Listen to what I've found, then you can decide for yourself. Six days before she died, Ellen made a trip to Denver. I don't know if you remember her list of secret trips, but it was on there. It was the last destination."

He didn't respond, but I knew he remembered.

"She flew out and back the same day, and it looks as if it was a special trip to visit the archives. The archivist remembers her. She asked to see the pre-purchase adjustment schedule. When Matt went looking for the same documents a few days ago, they were gone. The original invoices with the signatures are also missing."

"That doesn't mean she took them."

"Come on, Dan—"

"Or *if* she took them, and I'm not saying she did, she took them to build the case against Lenny. That's what we've been saying all along. She took them to keep them safe."

"Then where are they? Where is the evidence?"

"We'll find it."

"Think about this. If she was on the inside working the scam with Lenny, then her signature would be on those invoices. Destroying them would be one way to cover up her own involvement."

"Give me one good reason why she would be involved in something like this."

"She was sleeping with Lenny."

He swung his entire upper body around to face me. If we'd been going any faster than four miles an hour, we might have swerved off the road into a ditch. "Bullshit, Shanahan, bullshit. I told you before that's crap."

"Molly pulled up Lenny's travel schedule from the past eighteen months. When we checked it against Ellen's list, ten of the fifteen cities matched. Ten. And one of the five that didn't was the last trip to Denver. She was in the same city with him ten different times. In secret."

His head canted to one side, slowly, almost like a door opening. The traffic was picking up and spreading out, and he had to pay more attention to the road. Maybe that explained why he didn't say another word for almost three miles—a long, slow three miles.

He finally broke his silence. "Was Lenny in Boston the night she died?"

"There's no record that he flew into Boston," I said, "but I think he was here. He could have driven."

"Why do you think that?"

I reached into my back pocket, pulled out an envelope, and opened it up. "I found this letter in her mail. It just came this week."

"What is it?"

I pulled it from the envelope. It was too dark to read, but I didn't have to. "This is a letter from a place called Maitre d' Express. It's a dinner-delivery service."

"Like Domino's Pizza?"

"No. They only do the delivery part. You can order from lots of different restaurants around town, and they bring it to your house. Inside is a credit card receipt and a letter saying that Ellen still has to pay for her last order even though she never took delivery."

"What does that have to do with anything?"

"It was for the night she died."

He looked over at me but didn't say a word.

"The receipt was for one hundred fifteen dollars. Twenty-five was for the delivery from Boston to Marblehead. That leaves ninety dollars, which even by Boston standards is a lot for one meal. So I called Maitre d' Express and they had a record of the order in their computer. One appetizer, two salads, and two entrees from Hamersley's. At eight o'clock she called and cancelled, but it was too late. The order had already been made up, so she was charged anyway."

Shadows moved in and out of the car with the steady flow of headlights streaming toward us. I watched his face. He was working his jaw, but I saw no other sign that he was listening.

"Here's what I think happened that day. Ellen spoke to Lenny on the phone sometime during the morning. I don't know what was going on between them, but he must have talked her into seeing him that night at her house. Before she left work, she cancelled her trainer's appointment for that night at the gym, but according to her running log, she went run-

ning that afternoon along the Charles, so she wanted
to get a workout in, but didn't want to keep the appointment that night. She got home around four and
called this place to order dinner for the evening."

"And when Lenny showed up he killed her."

"One thing's for sure. Whoever killed her knew her.
He had access to the house, probably a key, and the
code for the security system. Or she let him in. No
forced entry. He knew about her mother, knew
enough about her and her life to make the murder
look like a plausible suicide."

"Why would he kill her?"

"Could be that Dickie's package triggered something. Maybe there was some kind of blow-up between
the two of them and they stopped trusting each other.
Maybe she was accumulating the evidence to use
against him. It's clear that Ellen had the evidence, not
Lenny, and he's still looking for it, he and his pals
the Dwyers."

At the end of our exit ramp, he took a right turn that
put us on a poorly lit spur. I looked out the window at
an industrial area of aluminum-sided warehouses and
vast parking lots filled with eighteen-wheelers backed
up to raised concrete loading docks. It was lonely and
cold and desolate.

"The thing I don't get," I said, "is why she cancelled
the dinner. What happened to her between four in the
afternoon when she ordered and eight o'clock when
she cancelled?"

He had nothing to say to that. Neither one of us
said another word for the rest of the drive out.

Angelo DiBiasi's white stubble crept down the soft
roll of flab at his throat. His worn cotton T-shirt covered a narrow chest, which ballooned into a big, hanging gut that kept him from pushing in close to the
table. With one eye almost shut, he cocked the other

at me as he spoke to Dan. "Why'd you go and bring her for?"

"Don't start with me, Angie. I told you I might bring her."

"And I told you not to—"

"Which just goes to show you're not in charge here. You're the one who's sitting at home on your butt with no job, and she's the one who can bring you back, so be nice."

Dan's tone had an urgent edge, as though he was running out of time and patience, even though we'd just arrived. We were at a fluorescent island of a truck stop by the side of the highway. It had stools at a long counter and ashtrays on every wobbly table.

When Angelo looked at me again, it was with eyes that were puffy and red-ringed, the kind you get from lying awake at night. Or crying. Or both. I offered him my hand across our sticky Formica table and introduced myself. "I'm sorry about your wife, and I hope we can work something out."

He switched his cigarette to his other hand and returned the gesture. His fingers were long and thin in my hand, the only part of him that seemed delicate.

"Let's get this over with." He let go and turned back to Dan. "I don't want to be seen with the two of youse." He took a quick tobacco hit, then moistened his lips with the tip of his tongue. "You bring something in writing describes this deal?"

"We don't have a deal yet," Dan said, "which is why we're talking."

"That's not what you told my wife. Why'd you have to go and call her anyway? You got no right calling and bothering her with my business." His chest puffed out and his back stiffened, and he looked like an old rooster as he shook his head full of white hair. "What you did, a man should never do to another man."

Dan stirred his coffee. "I'm sorry I had to bother

Theresa, but since she's the one who's sick, I thought she had the right to know there was a way for you to get your job back. You didn't tell her." He lifted the cup to his lips, had another thought, and put it back down without drinking. "And besides, you've got a strange idea of what's right. She starts chemo in two weeks and you're out boosting TV sets, getting yourself fired and losing your medical benefits."

"I was taking that TV home for her," he sputtered, "so she'd have it to watch when—" He stopped abruptly and turned toward the window. It was a big picture window that looked out over the parking lot, where snowflakes were beginning to drift down into the rain puddles. His cigarette was wedged tightly between his thumb and index finger. We sat in silence and watched as he smoked it all the way down to the filter. As soon as he stubbed out the butt, he started a new one. "Tell me again," he said wearily. "what you want and what you got."

Dan put both elbows on the table. "I don't know what it is you know, Angie, but my boss went to a lot of trouble to try to talk to you before she died, so I've got to think it's big. You give me what she was looking for, and we'll bring you back to work. No termination, no hearings or arbitration, none of that shit. You just come back tomorrow like you never left."

"You're talking about the boss killed herself, right. Not this one." He nodded in my direction without looking at me, and I couldn't tell if he was genuinely confused or yanking Dan's chain.

"I'm talking about Ellen Shepard."

"How am I supposed to know what she wanted? I never even met her."

"Don't waste my fucking time, Angie. I'm not in the mood."

Angelo sat back and kicked one leg out, stretching

as if he had a sore knee. "Why should I tell you anything? I can get the same deal from Big Pete without being no snitch."

"If Big Pete's going to bring you back, it means he's doing it through Lenny, and if Lenny wants to bring you back, he has to wait until after arbitration. Those are the rules, Angie, and who knows how long a hearing might take? Yours probably won't take much longer than what?" Dan checked with me. "Six months?"

"I once had a guy who waited a whole year," I offered helpfully.

"I'll take a little time off." Angelo glanced nervously from Dan to me and back. "Now's a good time anyway."

"Right," said Dan, "and at the end of your 'vacation,' maybe you're at work with full back pay. Then again, maybe you wait six months and never come back. Hard to say what happens with an arbitration panel. But let's say you do get back. Do you know what's waiting for you here?"

Angelo stared, his breathing growing shallow between drags.

"Me."

He'd been close to the edge from the beginning, and now I saw perspiration forming on his upper lip.

"If you come back off Lenny's deal, Angie, I'm going to make you my own personal rehabilitation project. I'm going to see to it that you never have time to think about stealing again because you'll be working your ass off."

Dan edged closer, pushing the ashtray out of the way. Angelo's eyes shifted back and forth, trying not to focus on Dan but unable to look anywhere else.

"I'll sit guys down to make sure you've got work to do, Angie. You won't have a second to yourself, and if you try to steal from me again, I'm gonna catch you and that's going to be it. You'll be out on your ass for good."

"That's harassment."

"Nothing in the contract says I can't make you do your job."

"Jesus fucking Christ, Danny." He stubbed out his butt, jamming so hard, stale ashes spilled onto the table. "I don't got enough problems without you threatening me all over the place?" He lowered his head, squeezed his eyes shut, and massaged his temples with the heels of his hands, turning his entire face crimson in the process. Between the cigarettes, the sick wife, pending unemployment, and Dan's pressure, I feared for the guy's vascular health.

"Angelo," I said, "here's another way to look at it. Your wife starts chemotherapy in two weeks."

He nodded, eyes still shut.

"Take our deal and your benefits will be restored tomorrow. Take Lenny's deal and you're going to have to sit out for six months, maybe longer, with no benefits and no guarantees. How are you going to pay the bills in the meantime?" His hands slipped around to cover his eyes. "Do you want your wife worrying about that when she's trying to get well? Your wife's peace of mind means a lot to you, I can tell. Tell us what you know, come back to work, and give her that peace of mind. It would be worth more to her than a TV."

He looked at me through bloodshot eyes. "Full back pay?"

"Yes."

"All my benefits, including flight bennies?"

"Of course."

He slumped back in his chair and studied the ceiling as he wiped his nose with the back of his hand. When he finally sat forward, Dan and I leaned in, too. In that moment before he began, as we all stared at each other, I knew that this was as close as we'd been to the truth—any truth—about Ellen Shepard's death, and I could barely hold still. I watched Angelo's face and everything seemed to slip into slow motion as he opened his mouth and said, "I want a better deal."

"A better *deal*?" I couldn't believe I'd heard right.

"I want to retire today, but I want the last two years of my salary and full benefits, including my pension."

"Are you out of your fucking mind?" Dan spoke for both of us.

"You got me in a position where I got no choices, Danny. I got forty-one years in, and I ain't walking away with nothing."

"You got yourself in this trick bag and you got some balls trying to use it to jack us up."

"Listen to what I'm saying to you." He looked around the diner and lowered his voice. "That lady boss of yours, the other one, she was right. I do know something. And if she knew it, too, that's why she's dead. So I'm askin' you, if they killed her, how long do you think I'd last down there on the ramp?"

Dan and I exchanged a glance. No one else was in the diner with us except the kid who was working the counter and doing his homework. I could hear the squeaking of his highlight pen as he marked his textbook. A prickly wave danced up the back of my neck and crawled underneath my hair. "Angelo." My heart was pounding in my throat, and I was surprised that my voice didn't waver. "Do you know that Ellen was murdered, that she didn't kill herself? Do you *know* this?"

He nodded. "I know too much for my own good."

"You *miserable motherfucker*. All this time you didn't say any—"

I laid my hand on Dan's arm. "Tell us what you know, Angelo, and I'll get you whatever you want." I looked into his eyes and I knew, no matter what Big

Pete had promised him, that he was scared, that he loved his wife, and he wanted to get this over with. Even so, he held out as long as he could, until the corner of his mouth began to quiver. "There's two parts to this story," he said finally. "There's who killed her, and there's why. I'll give you the who tonight. You get me my deal and I'll give you the rest."

Dan pulled away from me and sat back, arms crossed tightly across his chest. I nodded to Angelo and he began.

"Big Pete, Little Pete, and Lenny—used to be Dickie, too, before he kicked the bucket—they was all involved in this thing happened here a few years back, and it turned out that she somehow knew this secret and was gonna blow the whistle."

"What secret?" I asked. "Was it the IBG vote?"

"I ain't sayin' what it had to do with until I get my deal, but it wasn't that. That was nothing. What I will tell you, certain people weren't where they said they were the night when she got killed."

The prickly feeling came back, only this time I felt it across my whole body.

"It so happens that night I was down at the employee parking lot taking care of some personal business. While I was there, Little Pete comes flying up in that big truck his pop bought for him. He's coming back to work in the middle of his shift, which was stranger than hell because once he's gone he never comes back."

"What time?" I asked.

"Around midnight."

"Was he drunk?" asked Dan.

"He'd had a few, but I've seen him a lot worse. I gave him a ride up to the line so he could find Big Pete. On the way up, he was jumpy, like he needed a drink. He couldn't stop yapping about how big changes was coming because of him and everything was going to get back to normal."

"What did you take that to mean?" My throat was tightening.

"Nothing. The kid's always spoutin' off about something. But he kept pushing, so I asked him, does he know this on account of his pop telling him? Because everybody knows that's the only way the kid ever knows anything is it comes from his pop, right? I tell him this and it pisses him off. He says his pop didn't know nothing about it, that he and Lenny had a scam going." Angelo lowered his eyes and blew out a long stream of smoke that scattered the wisps of ashes off the table. "Finally, he couldn't keep it in no more and he just comes right out and says it. The dumbfuck bastard sits right in my tug and tells me he just killed the lady boss."

Dan's fist slammed down on the table, dumping over Angelo's coffee cup. Angelo bounced back and out of the chair. I shot straight up. My chair flew back and tipped over as the hot liquid spread across the tabletop. Dan was the only one who didn't react. He sat there frozen, his arm still flat against the table, his fist squeezed so tight it was shaking. Hot coffee soaked the sleeve of his cotton shirt. I looked at him and he looked back. "Son of a bitch," he said. "That fucking son of a bitch killed her. I knew it."

I pulled a wad of napkins from the chrome napkin holder and dropped them into the spilled liquid. I lifted Dan's arm out of the mess and handed him a wad. Eventually, we settled back into our seats and I asked Angelo, "What else did he say?"

"I told him he was full of shit. To prove it." He glanced nervously at Dan. "He showed me the key to her house."

"Where did he get the key?" I asked.

"Lenny gave it to him."

The table was covered with wet, sepia-colored mounds that looked like sand dunes and smelled like stale French roast. The smell of cold coffee was making me sick, and I could barely put two thoughts together, but I tried. Ellen must have set up the date to meet Lenny at the house. Lenny gave the key and the security code to Little Pete and sent him in his place. So they both killed her. "Does anyone else know what happened that night?"

"No. Big Pete made sure of that after he found out. He was so mad, I thought he was going to kill that kid. He had me drive Little Pete home."

"So Big Pete knows everything."

"Absolutely."

"What about the package?" I asked.

"What package?"

"Dickie Flynn's package in the ceiling."

"I don't know nothing about no package."

"Tell us, Angelo," I asked, "why they had to kill her."

He shook his head.

"Will you tell the police?"

"I ain't saying dick to no cops, and I ain't telling you no more." He stood up and slipped his jacket on. Then he leaned over the table and lowered his voice. "Get me my deal and I'll give you what you need. It's time it all come out, anyway."

The windshield wipers in Dan's car were fighting a losing battle with the blowing snow. The car shuddered against another strong blast of wind. We were idling in the parking lot of the diner, waiting for the heat to kick in. Both of us were staring straight ahead. After a while I noticed that the window was fogged and we couldn't see anything. I tried to block out everything but the facts, because everything but the facts scared me to death.

"It's pretty strange," I said, blowing on my fingers, "that Angelo was willing to tell us that Ellen was murdered, that Lenny set it up, and that Little Pete did it. But he won't tell us why."

"He thinks he's got more leverage on the why. It's how he thinks he's going to get his deal."

"That's what I'm saying. He's telling us without telling us that the motive for Ellen's murder is bigger than the murder itself. What do you think it is?"

"I don't know and I don't give a fuck." Dan wasn't wearing his gloves, and his hands looked like bones wrapped around the steering wheel. "I'm going to kill Little Pete. And when I'm done with him, I'm going after that other prick Lenny. I'm going to wrap my hands around his fucking pencil neck just like—"

"We have to go to the police, Dan."

"Are you deaf? Angie just said he wouldn't talk to the police."

"They'll make him talk. That's what they do. I don't want the two of us to be the only ones who know what he said."

"The police already gave up on this, remember?" He put the car in reverse, wedged his arm behind my seat, and twisted to look behind him. He screeched backward, stopped quickly, and slid on the quickly icing concrete.

"Where do you want me to drop you off?" he asked, glowering at me through the dark.

"Drop me *off*?"

"You can do what you want. I'm going to the airport."

"Wait." I grabbed his arm, trying to think fast as he was about to put the car in gear and set in motion something that could only end badly. "I'll make a deal with you. I won't call the police until we find Dickie's package if you promise to stay clear of Little Pete."

"You don't think there is a package anymore, remember?"

"I don't know if there is or not, but let's keep looking."

He stared straight ahead, grinding his teeth and tapping one finger on the wheel. "I already looked everywhere I could think of for that package."

"We haven't really looked at the airport."

"It's not there."

"We haven't looked. You want to make sure that Lenny gets nailed for this, don't you? If there's evidence against Lenny, it's in the package."

He tapped a few more times, started to nod slowly, then put the car in gear and swung out onto the highway.

"Deal," he said, just before he hit the gas.

Chapter Thirty-eight

Dan was sitting with his legs crossed on the top of my desk, fidgeting with a ruler. He looked as if he were in a life raft on a sea of papers. In a final spasm of manic frustration, we'd taken Ellen's neatly labeled files and binders and dumped them all onto the floor—and found nothing. With no place else to look, we'd gone over every inch of that massive desk, thinking the package might be concealed in some secret compartment. That idea had turned out to be as flaky as it sounded.

"I still don't know why you thought it would be here," he said for the fifth time. "She never kept anything important at the airport. I keep trying to tell you that."

"It was worth a shot," I replied for the fifth time, "before we schlepped all the way up to Marblehead again."

I was sitting on the floor in the corner in a zombie-like trance. I was so tired, my brain was beginning to seize up like an engine running without oil. I couldn't remember the last time I'd eaten, and worst of all, the heat had kicked into high gear again and the temperature in the office was approaching critical. But I knew that if I let myself feel any of that, I'd never move from that spot, and I had to get Dan away from the airport. I had no idea if either of the Dwyers was on shift, but I didn't want to take any chances.

I checked my watch. Almost nine o'clock. "If we're going up to the house tonight, we'd better get moving."

A cell phone twittered and we locked eyes.

"Don't look at me," he said. "I don't carry one of those damn things." He jumped down from the desk, and I crawled over to the mound of papers, the apparent source of the ringing.

"Here it is." He pulled my backpack from under one of the piles and handed it over. I dug out my phone and punched up the call.

"I found you."

The sound of Bill's voice was like a rush of cool air in that arid desert of an office. The minute I heard it, I felt the muscles in my shoulders release and the tension flow out. In so many ways, he was exactly what I needed right then. "Can you hold on?"

"Is this a bad time?"

"No. Just give me a second." I covered the phone with my hand. "Dan, I'm sorry, I need to take this call."

He was scratching the top of his head with the ruler. It took him a moment, but he caught on. "Which means get the hell out of here." The ruler clattered onto the desk as he headed out the door and closed it behind him.

From the sound of the background noise, Bill was in his car. "I am so glad you called. Where are you?"

"I'm back in Colorado. What are you doing up there? Lenny's hysterical."

I started to move in a tight figure eight around the piles on the floor. "Did he call you?"

"Yes, he did, which means he's truly desperate because he never calls, even when he should. And who is this guy Angelo?"

I froze. "He mentioned Angelo?"

"He said you were trying to do an end-around and

offer Angelo a deal without telling him. Lenny wants
to approach the IBG International and make his own
deal to bring him back to work. Should I let him?"

"*No*. Absolutely not. Jesus." I paced a little faster
and my shoulder muscles started to bunch again. Angelo must have told Lenny that he'd talked with us,
but why on earth—maybe to play both ends against
the middle. "Bill, whatever you do, don't let Lenny
make that deal. If anything, Angelo needs to be protected from Lenny. Protected from himself, too, it
sounds like."

"Tell me who he is and why any of this is
significant."

"I told you about Angelo. He's the ramper that
Ellen fired before she died. Dan and I met with him
tonight, and he told us that Lenny had Ellen killed."

"He told you *what*?"

"Little Pete killed her, but Lenny gave him the key
to her house. Angelo actually saw it."

"Saw the murder?"

"No, the *key*." I was talking too fast, frustrated that
he wasn't keeping up. "The night of the murder Little
Pete came back to the airport and showed Angelo the
key he used to get into Ellen's house, to get in the
house and kill her."

"Where are you right now?"

"At the airport. *Are you listening to me?*"

"Alex, you have to get out of there. If any of this
is true—"

"I need one more day, and I need you to approve
my deal for Angelo. He told us who killed her, but
he wouldn't tell us why. I need to know why—"

"*You* need to know?"

"Yes, I need to know." I kicked one of the piles of
paper on the floor. "It has something to do with that
package from Dickie Flynn and I think we can find
the package if we have a little more time. And if we

find the package, we get Lenny." Assuming there still was a package.

When I slowed down enough to notice, all I could hear was the sound of his breathing. And then I couldn't even hear that. "Bill, are you there?"

"Listen to me carefully," he said, his voice calm and steady. "Don't think about what you're going to say next. Just shut up and listen."

I stared up at the old yellow tiles in the ceiling. I couldn't believe how wound up I was—and how annoyed. I wanted him to be in a frenzy, too, to support my frenzied-ness. But he was so rational he was making me feel like a raving madwoman. I was losing perspective, which is exactly what he was about to tell me and exactly what I didn't want to hear. "I'm listening."

"If what you're saying is true—"

"It's all true, I know it—"

"I asked you to listen to me."

"I'm sorry. It's just . . . you sound as if you don't believe me."

"It doesn't matter what I believe. That's what I'm trying to make you see. If Lenny knows that Angelo talked to you, then it's not up to me how much time you have." He paused to let that sink in. "Do you understand now?"

I wiped the perspiration out of my eyes with the short sleeve of my T-shirt. He was right. If Lenny knew that Angelo had talked to us, then the Petes knew and that could not be a good thing for any of us— especially Angelo.

"I'm bringing in the FBI," he said, "and I'm sending Corporate Security out. Tom Gutekunst will be on the red-eye tonight. He can be in Boston first thing tomorrow morning."

"Angelo's not going to talk to Corporate Security or anyone else. Don't you . . ." I paused for a moment to get the shrillness under control. He was right; I was wrong. He was being reasonable, and I was being stubborn to the point of petulance. But I couldn't let it go. "Don't you want to know what Angelo knows, which is why Ellen was killed?"

Big sigh. "What about Fallacaro? What if he goes with Gutekunst tomorrow?"

"If it's too dangerous for me, it is for Dan, too."

"Maybe so. But I'm not in love with Dan Fallacaro."

"I'm not going to bail out and leave Dan to finish this—" What did he just say? I switched the phone to the other ear. Maybe I wasn't hearing right. "What did you say?"

"I said that I'm in love with you, Alex."

My knees almost gave way.

"I am hopelessly . . ."

My hands trembled.

" . . . desperately . . ."

Tears welled up in my eyes.

". . . pathetically in love with you."

I had to reach around, find the edge of the desk and lean back. He'd never even said that he loved me—needed me, wanted me, but never that he loved me, much less desperately loved me, and even though I'd been aching to hear it, I'd never asked him to say it because I was afraid of what I might hear.

"I don't want to lose you again. I don't want a life without you in it."

I tried to keep my thoughts from racing. I dropped my head all the way back and let his words roll over me. He was in love with me. And I couldn't stop smiling.

"I'm out here in Denver," he went on, "completely helpless while you're running around in Boston with some people who are apparently quite dangerous. All I want is for you to exercise some good judgment. Is that so much to ask?" The background noise was gone, and I knew that his car had stopped. Without the interference he sounded closer, as if he were there with me, whispering in my ear. "If you're worried about Fallacaro, then tell him to leave, too. But whether he goes or not, I want you out, Alex. I want you safe." He let out another long sigh. "Now I have to go. I'm late for a dinner, and I've been sitting outside the restaurant for twenty minutes."

"There's so much more to this that I have to tell you." But at the moment my head happened to be in the clouds and I couldn't remember what it was.

"Tell me tonight. I'll call you. Right now I have people waiting for me inside. But I'm not going to hang up until you give me your word. Will you go home tonight and wait for help?"

I would jump off a cliff for him right now. "Yes, I'll go home."

"Good."

"But how about this? When Tom shows up tomorrow, I'll give him everything we've found out, but I'm going with him to talk to Angelo. And we have to go back up to Marblehead to look for that package."

"What about tonight?"

"I'll take Dan and we'll go home. Just don't let Lenny bring Angelo back."

The line began to pop and crackle, then grew into a steady stream of static, and I lost him for a moment. "Bill?"

"I heard you," he said, cutting in and out, "and I'm losing my battery. I'll call you later tonight, on the *hotel* phone."

"I'll be there. Bill . . ." He didn't answer. "Are you there?" Nothing. "I love you, too," I said softly, but the connection was gone.

Dan was in his office with his feet up on the desk. He had the computer keyboard in his lap, and he was scanning the monitor.

"What are you doing?"

"Checking the work schedule for tonight."

"You're looking for Little Pete."

"I just think it's a good idea to know where he is."

"And is he working?"

"Not according to the schedule posted yesterday."

I breathed a silent sigh of relief. "I'm sorry about kicking you out."

"I understand. You women all have your secrets."

"You should talk."

He allowed a little touché smile. "Can we get the hell out of here," he moaned, "before I melt? It's a long way up to Marblehead."

"I'm ready, but we're not going to Marblehead. I've got some things to tell you."

"Hey," he yelled as I headed back to my office. "what's all over your butt?"

"Excuse me?"

"You've been sitting in something. Your ass is all white."

I twisted one way and then the other, trying to see behind me. Sure enough, there was something that looked like chalk dust all over my jeans. "I don't know." I tried to dust it off and got it all over my sweaty hands. "I think it's from that corner over by the window where I was sitting. There's been a pile of this stuff on the floor since the day I got here. It doesn't say much for our cleaning crews."

"I can't take you anywhere, Shanahan. You're a mess."

I went back to my office and loaded up my back-pack. While I waited for Dan, I went to the corner to investigate the strange white residue on the floor, the stuff that had reminded me of rat poison on my first day in the station. I crouched down and rubbed a bit of it between my fingers. It felt grainier and heavier than chalk dust. There was no obvious source at the base of the wall or around the window. I stood up, wiped my hands on my jeans, and was starting to go when I saw more of it on top of my two-drawer file cabinet. My backpack hit the ground with a thud as I stood and stared straight up at the ceiling. It wasn't chalk dust.

"Dan." He didn't answer. *"Dan,"* I yelled, climbing up on the cabinet, "Come in here."

"What?" he yelled back. "I'm coming."

He walked in just as I was pulling a brown envelope out through the space where the corner tile had been. More of the white stuff had fallen when I moved the tile. Acoustic tile shavings were in my eyes and stuck to the damp skin on my face. I had to blink several times before I could look down and see him standing next to the cabinet. I presented him with Dickie Flynn's package.

"You guys always said the ceiling was the best place to hide things."

Chapter Thirty-nine

The TV powered up with its distinctive electronic snap, and a blast of full-volume static boomed from the set. The scratchy noise felt like sandpaper scraping across raw nerves.

"God Al*migh*ty." Dan scrambled .for the volume control, punched the wrong button, and turned the static to blaring canned-sitcom laughter. Laughter, especially fake, felt obscene in the fragile silence and made our situation that much more surreal. He found the volume and turned it down as I fumbled with shaking hands to get the cassette out of the envelope.

"Where's the fucking remote?"

"Are you sure Delta's not going to mind us being in here?"

"I told you, we have a deal. I loan them a B767 towbar when they need it, and I get to use their VCR whenever I want."

I put the tape into the slot—tried to, anyway—cramming it in a few times before I realized one was already in there. Every step seemed to take forever as I found the button to eject, pulled the cassette out, and put ours in. Dan found the remote, killed the light, and moved in next to me in front of the screen. His shoulder was warm against mine as we leaned back against the conference table, and I was glad that whatever we were about to see, I wasn't going to see it alone.

I took a few deep breaths, trying to stop shaking. It didn't work.

He aimed the remote at the screen. "Ready?" Without waiting for an answer, he hit Play.

Within seconds, the picture changed from the high, bright colors of situation comedy to the grainy black-and-white cast of a surveillance video. The date and time were marked in the lower right-hand corner, and the rest of the screen was filled with the image of a small aircraft parked in the rain on a concrete slab. It was a commuter, so there was no jetbridge, just a prop plane parked at a gate. I looked at the markings on the tail. A wave of recognition began as a tightening of my scalp when I realized that I also recognized the gate. The date—check the date again. The tight, tingling feeling spread from the top of my skull straight down my back and grabbed hold, like a fist around my backbone. It was March 15, 1995, at 19:12:20. The Ides of March.

Without taking his eyes from the screen, Dan found the Pause button. We stared, as frozen as the image before us, and I could hear in his breathing, I could feel in his stiffening posture, that he was thinking what I was, that it couldn't be, please don't let it be—

"The Beechcraft," he whispered.

The Beechcraft, he'd said, not *a* Beechcraft. I looked at him, grasping for reassurance, hoping not to see my worst fears in his face. But the odd TV glow turned his skin into gray parchment and made deep hollows of his eyes. Under a day's growth of dark stubble, he looked stunned.

"Are you sure? Is that . . ." I tried to swallow the lump in my throat. "Check the tail number."

He didn't check. He didn't have to check. We both knew what we were looking at. It was one of Dickie Flynn's surveillance tapes of the ramp, the one from March 15, 1995. That was the night that Flight 1704 crashed outside Baltimore. This was the Beechcraft that had gone down, and this was our ramp it was parked on. It was less than three hours before the fatal landing, and I had no doubt that when he raised the remote and hit Play, we were going to see things we weren't supposed to see. We were going to find out the things that Ellen knew, and maybe understand why she was dead.

I turned back to the screen, eyes wide, neck rigid, and stared straight ahead. A feeling of dread filled the room—Dan's or mine or both, I couldn't tell. It was growing, filling the small space and, like that heat in my office, pressing back on me and making it hard to draw a breath. I wondered if Dan could feel it, too, but I couldn't look at him. I was glued to the screen, afraid to keep looking, but afraid to look away.

He held up the remote, but before he restarted the tape, I felt him pull himself up, square his shoulders, and center his weight, like a soldier girding for battle. He hit Play and the rain began to fall again.

The rain was falling hard on the evening of March 15, 1995, hard enough that I could see the drops bouncing off the wet concrete. During the first minute or two of the tape, that's all we saw, the Beechcraft sitting in a downpour. Occasionally, a ramper would walk through the shot, or a tug would cut through the narrow passage between the airplane and the terminal, which they weren't supposed to do.

A fuel truck pulled into the frame. Dan had been still, but when the truck stopped just behind the left wing, he started shifting his weight back and forth from one foot to the other.

"That's Billy Newman," he said as the driver climbed out and went to the back of his truck.

"Who's he?"

"A fueler."

"Does it mean something?"

"I don't know, boss. He's just another guy out there."

Not knowing exactly what we were looking for, everything meant something—or nothing. We had to watch every movement, every motion closely, and when Billy Newman disappeared behind his truck for an inordinately long period of time, we were both drawn a little closer to the screen. But when he reappeared, all he did was go about the business of fueling the aircraft. He hooked up on one side and stood in the rain with his hood pulled over his head. When the first tank was full, he went around and started on the other side.

"This is killing me." Dan pointed the remote and fired. "I'm going to fast-forward until something happens."

"Are you sure? We don't even know what we're looking for."

"If we miss something, we can start it over. Besides, I have a feeling we'll know it when we see it."

The tape whirred as the cockpit crew came out, stowed their gear, and boarded. Then the passengers appeared, most carrying umbrellas and forming a line to the boarding stairs. I tried to be dispassionate, to look with a coldly analytical eye for anything unusual in the high-speed procession. But in this moment captured on this tape, these people were about to die. I knew it and they didn't, and I thought maybe I should look away, lower my eyes and—who was I kidding? I was like any other wide-eyed, slack-jawed, rubbernecking ghoul. I felt ashamed and I felt dirty. At the faster speed, their movements were hyper and manic, almost comical, and I heard echoes of that canned sitcom laughter. We should slow this down, I thought. We're hurrying these people along when what they need at this moment is more time.

"*Wait,* stop it there."

"I see it." Dan was already pausing and reversing.

"Goddammit." His gentle shifting from foot to foot accelerated to jittery rocking as he searched the tape, first going too far back. He hit the Rewind button, accidentally going still further back, then had to fast-forward again. I watched the seconds on the time stamp, each tick up and down winding the tension a little tighter.

Finally we were in normal speed. A tug towing a cart full of bags and cargo pulled into the frame. The vehicle, moving too fast for the conditions, skidded to a stop at the tail of the Beechcraft. I held my breath. The driver stepped out into the rain, stumbled, and nearly fell to the wet concrete. Dan saved him momentarily by stopping the tape.

"Oh, my God." I'd been staring at the screen so intently, my eyes were dried out and my vision was starting to blur. But there was no mistaking the identity of this man—his size, his build, the span of his wide shoulders. It was Little Pete, and Little Pete was drunk.

Dan was squeezing the remote with one hand. The other was on top of his head, as if to keep it from flying off. "That fucking moron," he said in a voice that was so quiet, it was scary.

"Did you know he worked this trip?"

"I didn't know he was in this kind of shape. No one did."

His hand slipped from the top of his head, brushing my forearm in the process. I almost didn't feel it. The pieces were beginning to fit together, each one falling into place with a dull, brutal thud that felt like a punch to the solar plexus. "Someone knew, Dan. Someone knew." A terrible feeling of panic began to take hold of me. But I had to stay focused. "Let's keep going."

He restarted the tape, and Little Pete continued his grotesque dance, reaching back for the steering wheel to keep from going down. He stayed that way for a few seconds, swaying as if the ground was a storm-tossed sea. And then, God help us, he began loading the aircraft.

My stomach tightened into a hard lump as I watched him lift a dog in its carrier out of the cart, stagger to the aircraft, and slide it through the aft cargo door, stopping to poke his fingers through the cage before pushing the carrier all the way in. I couldn't tell if he was teasing the animal or trying in some sloppy, sentimental, drunken way to give comfort.

In contrast to the passengers' movements, Little Pete's in normal speed were slow and dreary and indifferent, but knowing what had come later that night, every single thing he did was painfully riveting. Pete followed the dog with the bags, stopping occasionally to pull a scrap of paper from his pocket and make a notation.

Dan shook his head. "I can't believe he's actually keeping a load plan."

"It doesn't look to me like he's following any kind of a plan. He's stuffing the load wherever he can make it fit."

"You're right, but he is keeping track. See there." Little Pete pulled out the scrap again and made some adjustment with his pencil. He finished by trying to fit two boxes in the forward compartment. It didn't take long before he gave that up and shoved them in the back with the dog. "He didn't load anything forward," said Dan, "Did you see that? All the weight he put onboard is in the back."

"It was out of balance," I said, feeling the air go out of me as another piece thudded into place. Little Pete had been drunk the night of the fight with Terry McTavish and reversed the load on a jet, which is more or less what he'd done here. "Little Pete loaded it wrong, and the flight crew got blamed."

We watched him close the cargo compartments, almost slipping again at the rear door. He disappeared into the cab of his tug, then popped out with his glow-in-the-dark wands. Appearing remarkably composed, he stood in front of the aircraft, in front of the captain, and guided the airplane out of the frame.

Little Pete walked back into camera range and stowed his wands.

Dan and I stood for a long time staring at the screen after he'd driven away. Neither one of us made a move to turn off the tape, even though there was nothing left to see but rain falling on a bare concrete slab.

Eventually, I felt the insistent aching in the middle of my back and realized I'd been standing stiff enough to crack. Dan had started moving around. He looked as if he was in fast-forward mode himself, pacing around the table and talking to himself. "That son of a bitch. That cocksucking, motherfucking, degenerate scumbag. He was drunk. He fucked up the load. He caused the crash. That's what this has all been about."

I found the light switch and flipped it on, but not having the energy to pace, I leaned back against the closed door as much for support as to ease my sore back. "How did the captain get the plane off the ground?"

"What do you mean?"

"If the load was out of balance enough to bring the plane down, how could he have gotten it off the ground? He would have been tail-heavy."

He answered without ever breaking stride. "It doesn't take that much on a Beechcraft to move the center of gravity. It's a small airplane. A couple hundred pounds in the wrong place would do it. He could have been able to take off but not land. That's possible."

"I can't believe it."

"Why not? They use flaps on landing but not take-off. Plus, the fuel tanks are forward, so if the tanks were full, they could have compensated—"

"No. I'm saying I can't believe anyone would be that negligent, that stupid. How could they let him work like that? Even his father—especially his father."

"C'mon, Shanahan, you know these people. And how stupid are they if they covered it up and got away with it?"

"Yeah, how did they do that?" I dropped down into one of the chairs that ringed the conference table. Spread out in front of me was the stack of papers and documents that had spilled out of Dickie's envelope along with the tape. "The whole thing was caught on a surveillance video, Little Pete is clearly drunk, and yet the true story has never come out. The pilots took the fall for what he did. Obviously, the tape never came out, but still—"

"Lenny had to be part of it," he said. "He was the GM. There's no way this thing gets covered up and he doesn't know about it."

"No doubt. Little Pete Dwyer didn't fool anyone on his own." I traced the edge of the conference table, following the line with my thumb, avoiding eye contact. "And if Lenny was involved, Dan, I think we have to consider that Ellen was, too, at least in the cover-up. There's plenty of motive for murder here all the way around."

His response was instantaneous. "You will never, ever convince me that Ellen Shepard was part of this."

"Maybe she got sucked in. Once you've committed contract fraud, once you've gone that far, if something like this happens, you have to cover it up just to protect yourself. You keep getting in deeper even if you don't want to."

"Buying off a contract is one thing, but twenty-one people died here."

"And if the true cause had ever come out, there

would have been no deal. You know that. You would have had investigations and lawsuits all over the place. Nor'easter would have been grounded, maybe even had their certificate yanked. What started out as contract fraud to make the deal happen ended up being a cover-up to make sure it didn't blow up."

He stood across the room from me on the other side of the table with his feet shoulder-width and his arms crossed. The look on his face was as closed as his stance. "Ellen didn't know about this."

He was so confident, so sure that even if he hadn't known everything about Ellen, he had known the important things. He simply refused to believe the worst about his friend. I rested my head against the high back of the chair and stared at the TV screen. The surveillance tape was still running. Neither one of us had made a move to turn it off. I envied Dan his certainty, and I wished so much that I had known Ellen. That I didn't have to draw my conclusions about her from what she hung on her walls, or what was left on her kitchen counter, or the look in her eyes in that dating video when she said she didn't want to be alone anymore. The rain continued to fall on the concrete on March 15, 1995. It was falling harder, and no matter what the facts said about Ellen, I wanted Dan to be right. I didn't want her to have known about this.

"Let's look at it from a different angle. Ellen knew nothing about the crash—the true cause of the crash—until she got to Boston. Dickie sent her this package, she saw the tape and realized that Lenny had used the money they'd stolen—"

He opened his mouth to object again, but I kept going. "Used the money for something besides the contract payoff. She got angry or scared, and that's why she took the evidence. When she figured out what he'd gotten her into, she panicked."

He stared at me for a long time, and I couldn't tell

what he was thinking. But he must have been considering the theory, and he must have decided he could live with it. "She got to the evidence first," he said, picking up the thread, "she threatened to go public, and they killed her for it." He tapped his lips with the tip of his index finger. "Now all we have to do is prove it."

"That's not our job."

He turned away in frustration, then circled back and motioned to the TV screen. "Aren't you even curious about how they did this? That pisshead Dwyer kid took that Beechcraft down and is still out working the ramp loading airplanes. He's working tomorrow. What if, God forbid, something happened and we knew about this and didn't do anything?"

"We can take him out of service. Or assign him to the stock room."

"Boss, I don't want this guy anywhere near one of my airplanes."

Having seen what I'd just seen, it was hard to argue with that sentiment. With both palms flat on the surface, he leaned across the table. "Shanahan," he said, looking me directly in the eye, "I need to finish this tonight."

His tie had disappeared long ago, his shirttail was out, and I noticed for the first time how thin he'd become, too thin for his suit pants. His face was drawn, his forehead lined with every sleepless night he'd spent thinking about why Ellen had died and, more painful than that, what his role in her death might have been. I had a feeling that watching that videotape had taken more out of him than he could have admitted, and it occurred to me that he might have been leaning on that table because he was too worn out to stand up. No matter what I had promised Bill, there was no way Dan was going home tonight. With the answer right there in front of us on the table, he didn't have enough left to wait it out until tomorrow. It had to be finished tonight.

I checked my watch. Tom Gutekunst from Corporate Security would be in at six o'clock in the morning. We had almost eight hours. I reached out for a stack of papers.

"Sit down before you fall down," I said, handing him half, "and start with these."

Chapter Forty

Every once in a while I'd look up to see Dan's lips moving as he read through the papers in his lap.

I was still plowing through the first document I'd picked up. It was officially known as the National Transportation Safety Board Aircraft Accident Report for Nor'easter Airlines, Inc., Flight 1704, Beech Aircraft Corporation 1900C, Baltimore, Maryland, March 15, 1995. It looked like aircraft accident reports look—standard formats, factual, statistical—and I was having a hard time with it. I had just seen the people who had boarded that flight, human beings that were here reduced to tables and charts and codes. The loss of their lives and the loss of equipment were treated not dissimilarly with everything measured, weighed, counted, and set down on a page in black-and-white.

I flipped back to the beginning and started again, reading the same words I'd read twice already, looking for the highlights this time and trying to retain at least some of the information.

On March 15, 1995, a Beech 1900C which was operating as NOR 1704 crashed on final approach to Baltimore. Seventeen passengers, the captain, and the first officer were all killed. The dog being transported in the kennel in the aft cargo compartment had survived.

In the section marked PERSONNEL INFORMATION, I found out that the captain had been forty-one years old. He'd flown with Nor'easter for seven years and worked as an instructor/check pilot for this type of aircraft. Fellow crew members described him as "diligent, well trained, and precise." The first officer was thirty-six. His position with Nor'easter was his first regional airline job, but he'd been flying for eight years. It was an experienced crew.

A few pages over and a couple of paragraphs down was the section marked HISTORY OF THE FLIGHT. On the day of the accident, the captain arrived at the airport in Baltimore at 1300 for a 1400 check-in. No one who saw him that afternoon reported anything unusual about his behavior. That day he and his first officer flew a round trip from Baltimore to Syracuse with a scheduled stopover in Boston each way. They flew two more round trips between Baltimore and Boston that afternoon and evening. Flight 1704 was the last scheduled for the day. They'd never made it home.

On that final leg, the flight was delayed in Boston due to bad weather, and didn't take off until 2015, ninety minutes after the scheduled departure time. Weather at the time of departure was heavy rain, low clouds, and poor visibility.

At 2149, the Baltimore tower cleared NOR 1704 to descend to and maintain 6,000 feet.

At 2156, NOR 1704 contacted the tower and requested the current Baltimore weather. It was thirty-seven degrees, low broken clouds, winds out of the northwest at ten knots.

At 2157, NOR 1704 was cleared for landing.

Ground witnesses who saw the aircraft on the short final approach to the runway said its wings began to rock back and forth. The aircraft went nose up, then into a steep bank and roll. The right wing contacted the ground first. Its forward momentum caused it to cartwheel, breaking into pieces and scattering wreckage over a quarter mile. The accident occurred during the hours of darkness. Part but not all of the fuselage burned. The aircraft was destroyed. No survivors.

I stared at the page until I thought I heard Dan say something, but when I looked up, he was still sitting exactly as I'd seen him before, with his feet on the table, one hand on the reports and the other on the armrest propping his head up. Behind him on the TV screen, the tape was still running. I found the remote control and turned it off.

"What's the matter?" he asked.

"Nothing." If I'd not said anything at all, I'm not sure he would have noticed. He was talking to me, but completely absorbed in what he was reading.

One of the appendices in my report was a map of the wreckage, a computer-generated diagram that showed the major pieces, of which there were many, and where they had landed relative to each other and the airport. I turned to the back and looked at it again, studying it more closely this time. I was trying to remember what this crash had looked like. I was searching for the image, that signature shot that is so visceral, so horrible, or so poignant that it gets burned into our collective consciousness and becomes shorthand for this and only this tragedy. Workers in hip waders and diving gear slogging through swamps with gas masks and long poles. A flotilla of boats out on gray seas with grim-faced men dragging parts of people and machinery out of the water. Scorched mountaintops and flaming oceans and fields of snow fouled by oil and soot. Tail sections with logos intact, absurdly colorful amid the twisted, blackened ruins. I tried to remember 1704, but when I closed my eyes, all I could see was that patch of empty concrete. It was so quiet in the room I could almost hear the rain.

"Holy shit, boss." Dan's feet dropped to the floor, jarring me back to the present. "Holy *shit*."

His raised eyebrows and excited smile told me he'd hit pay dirt. "Tell me."

"You're not going to believe what this is. You've got the official version there of what happened that night"—he nodded to my report—"but I've got the real story." He held up a ratty pile of dog-eared, hand-written pages he'd been reading. It was stapled in the corner, but just barely. "This is Dickie Flynn's confession."

"Confession?" The word alone, freighted with all that Catholic significance, brought a shudder of anticipation. What sins were we about to hear?

"Everything that happened that night in order—bing, bing, bing. And see that? Dickie wrote it himself and signed it." He turned to the last page and held it up just long enough for me to see the scrawled signature of one Richard Walter Flynn. "According to this, Dickie was here that night and right in the middle of everything."

I set my report to the side. "How did they do it?"

"I'll show you. What did the investigators say was the official cause?"

"Pilot error. They say the pilot miscalculated the center of gravity, that it could have been as much as eleven inches aft of the aft limit, which significantly screwed up the weight and balance."

"In other words, he was tail heavy."

"Too much weight in the back," I said. "He lost control when the flaps were lowered for landing."

"Fucking Little Pete. Goddamn him." He was up now and searching for something. I assumed it was the remote and tossed it to him. Almost in one motion he caught it and started the tape rewinding. "Okay, let's walk through it. The captain is responsible for calculating the center of gravity, right?"

"Right."

"But he's got to have all the inputs to do the calculation. He needs passenger weight, fuel load, and the load plan for cargo—weights and positions."

"Yeah, yeah," I said, anxious for the punch line. "Standard stuff."

Dan raised one finger, signaling for patience, and I got the impression he was walking through it out loud to try to understand it himself. "In Boston, the Operations agent is responsible for collecting all the inputs on a worksheet. On this worksheet he converts gallons of fuel to pounds, applies average weights for passengers and carry-ons. Cargo weights are pretty much a pass-through from the ramper who loaded the plane. He radios the results to the crew and they do their thing. At the end of every day, the worksheets go into the station files."

A sharp click signaled the end of the rewind. He started the tape, and Billy Newman reappeared and fueled the Beechcraft again, this time in fast-motion. Dan switched to normal speed as the fueler walked toward the camera. "Here's Billy coming into Operations to turn in his numbers for the fuel load."

The next time he stopped the tape was after the last passenger had boarded. The ticket agent who had worked the flight closed up the airplane and approached the camera just as Billy had. "Here's the gate agent coming to turn in the passenger count."

Now we were back up to the point where Little Pete came flying into the picture, skidding recklessly up to the aircraft. He let it fast-forward through the loading. Before he stopped it again, I understood. "He never came into Operations."

"Bingo. He doesn't have a radio, and if he'd given them directly to the crew we would have seen."

"How do you know he didn't have a radio?"

"Dickie said."

"Okay, but he updated his own plan," I said. "We saw him."

Dan had his head down, checking the facts in Dickie's chronology. "Little Pete changed the load, updated his numbers, and never told anyone."

I tried to follow how this would have worked. We were supposed to have safeguards in place for this sort of screw-up. "First of all, Kevin Corrigan is a good operations agent. Without the ramp's input, he would have had a great big hole in his worksheet. He never would have let that happen, and even if he had, the crew couldn't have calculated the center of gravity without the cargo load. They wouldn't have even taken off."

"I agree with you. Kevin is a good ops man. It's too bad he wasn't working that night."

"Who was working?"

"Kevin was back in Ireland at his brother's wedding. It was Dickie."

I sat forward in my chair and concentrated hard. Between the heat and everything else that had gone on tonight, I was feeling addle-brained. "Are you saying that Dickie Flynn, *ramp manager* Dickie Flynn was working as an operations agent the night of the crash?"

Dan was nodding. "Yes. He was a manager then, but he started out as an ops agent and he used to cover Kevin's shift now and then when he couldn't find anyone else to do it. That's what he was doing here that night"—he tapped the confession with two fingers—"and that's why he knew so much. He worked the trip, he and Little Pete."

"Dickie," I said, "was in a position to cover for Little Pete."

He nodded. "Now you're getting it."

"But Dickie still had to give the captain a number. Did he just make it up?"

"As near as I can tell, Little Pete called a preliminary load plan to Dickie over the phone before he ever left the ready room to work the trip. They're not supposed to do that, but sometimes they do because the loads never change on these little airplanes. Little Pete was drunk, which we just saw, and didn't load the airplane according to the plan. He put all the weight in the tail. He marked the changes on his own load sheet, probably intending to call it in. Then he disappeared."

"And no one ever got the updated numbers."

"According to Dickie, the storm was getting worse, the captain wanted to go, he couldn't find Little Pete, so he gave him the numbers he had, figuring Little Pete would have told him if he'd changed anything."

"Which meant the pilot's calculation didn't match the actual load, and it was enough of a difference to take the plane down. Jesus." I rested my forehead in the heels of my hands and considered the unusual confluence of events that had taken place that night. It's always that way with a plane crash. There are so many backups to the backups to the fail-safe systems and procedures that it always takes not just one but an unusual chain of strange events to bring one down. I looked up at Dan, who was sitting back in his chair as if it was a recliner. We were through with show-and-tell. Once again, the image left on the screen was that bare apron in the rain. "Why wouldn't the investigators figure this out?"

"No black boxes, for one thing. An aircraft either has to have been registered after October 1991, I think it is, or have more than twenty seats to require boxes. This one didn't qualify."

"I saw that in the NTSB report. No boxes and no surveillance tape because Dickie took it. The crew was dead. That means the only people left who knew what really happened were Dickie and Little Pete."

"They weren't the only ones who knew. When Dickie heard that the plane had gone down, he figured out what happened. He got scared and wanted to change the worksheet to cover his own ass. To make it look like the captain's mistake, he needed to know what the real load was. But nobody could find Little Pete or his plan. This is where our buddy Angie comes in."

"Angelo?"

"Big Pete called him at home that night after the accident and got him out to look for Little Pete. Angelo found him up in a bar in Chelsea and, get this, the knucklehead still had this right where he'd left the damn thing—in his pocket." He'd pulled a piece of paper from his stack and held it up. "This is Little Pete's load plan, that thing he kept pulling out of his pocket."

"Let me see that." It was a wrinkled, computer-generated load plan with one corner torn off, and it was a mess. Almost every position had been marked through or overwritten. "You've got to hand it to Dickie, he kept a thorough record."

Dan took the plan back. "Angelo stashed the kid somewhere and ran this copy back over to the airport. Dickie dummied up a second worksheet, gave a copy to Big Pete, who got it to Little Pete. Twelve hours later, the kid had sobered up, everyone was telling the same story to the investigators, and it looked like the fight crew made the mistake. Case closed."

"Until," I added, "Dickie decided he didn't want to go to his grave with the souls of twenty-one people on his conscience. No wonder he spent the rest of his life getting drunk. Does he talk about Lenny in there?"

"Oh, yeah." He smiled a killer smile. "Lenny was

right there from the beginning. He came out that
night, and according to Dickie, he and Angelo went
on the Crescent Security payroll—at least for one
big payday."

"That's what the pay stub in Ellen's file was all
about. The ten grand, that was Dickie's portion of the
hush money. Ten thousand bucks out of a total seven
hundred thousand-dollar payoff. Not a very high price
to sell your soul."

"Dickie always did get the short end of the stick."

We sat for a moment in silence with the papers and
documents scattered all around us. All the pieces had
come together in the worst possible way, and I felt the
weight of all we had found out in that room. I felt
crushed by the enormity of the thing—of all that had
happened and all that was going to happen.

Finally, Dan roused himself to stand up and go over
to the television. He was going to pop out the cassette,
but I stopped him. "I want to watch it one more
time."

He turned to look at me. "Why? Are you looking
for something?"

"The passengers' faces." I needed to see them
again, to see them as individuals—as men and women,
children, mothers, fathers, husbands, wives. I didn't
want them to be fused together into an entity that I
knew only as "the twenty-one people killed in the
crash of flight 1704."

Without a word, Dan qued through the tape and
found the beginning of the boarding process. This time
as we watched in normal speed, I made sure to look
at each one as they passed by in the rain and climbed
the boarding stairs.

Seeing their images on tape reminded me of Ellen's
video, of how I had felt when I'd heard her voice,
when I'd seen her smile, saw doubt on her face and
frustration and determination—all the things that

make us who we are. Seeing her that way had made real to me someone I'd never met. It had created a void in my life for someone I'd never even known.

As I stared at the screen, I thought about the surviving family and friends of these victims, what it was going to do to them to see the people they had loved, still loved, in their final moments, and the silent black-and-white image started to blur again.

Chapter Forty-one

Dan stared at my computer monitor. "Who's H. Jergensen?" he asked.

"I don't know." I was trying to wrangle the papers on the floor in my office into one pile so that Molly wouldn't have a heart attack when she arrived for work on Monday. The heat had finally stopped pouring in, and our offices were now merely sweltering as opposed to life-threatening. "Why?"

"Because you've got an e-mail message from him and it's urgent."

"What's in the subject line?"

"Matt Levesque."

Matt . . . H. Jergensen . . . H . . . *Hazel.* "Hazel. Is it Hazel Jergensen?" I raced over and almost lifted him bodily out of the way so that I could sit at the keyboard. "Move, move, move."

"All right. Jesus Christ. What is it?"

"It's the invoices to Crescent, finally. Or at least a reasonable facsimile." I sat down and clicked into the Majestic electronic mailroom to find the message. "Hazel Jergensen worked for Ellen on the task force and, according to Finance Guy, kept records of everything. He thought she might have a record of who signed the invoices to Crescent. Dammit." I was talking as fast as I could, typing as fast as I could, and missing keys. "We're going to find out once and for all if Ellen was in on this, at least the embezzlement part." After multiple tries I found the message, double-clicked, and waited for it to come up.

Dan hadn't responded, and when I turned to find him, he was as far away from the computer as he could be and still be in the office. "Don't you want to know?"

"To be honest," he said, "I've already found out more than I ever wanted to know."

"What if it wasn't her? We don't know for sure, Dan. This will tell us."

The CPU seemed to labor endlessly, whirring and clicking as I watched the blinking cursor on the screen. The wool fabric on my chair was making the hollows at the backs of my knees sweat right through my jeans. When the message finally appeared, it was in pieces. "Here it comes."

Half a note from Hazel appeared first, saying simply that Matt had asked her to . . . the rest of the message came up . . . forward the information. I punched up the attachment. The first section included titles and column headings—vendors, amounts paid, check numbers, and in the far right-hand column "Approved by:" I tried to stay calm, but it was tough. If it was all here, Hazel had sent us exactly what we needed.

"C'mon, c'mon, c'mon," Dan coaxed. I hadn't even noticed, but he was now leaning over my chair, breathing over my shoulder as the report began to appear.

The screen changed hues as the last of the data popped up. The spreadsheet was so big, we could see only the first few columns.

I scrolled down through the A's. There were lots of B's. Lawyers, accountants, auditors, consultants—advisers of every stripe. At one point I got frustrated and went too fast, and we ended up in the H's. Finally I found it. My heart did a little tap dance from just seeing it there. Crescent Consulting—big as life.

I took a deep breath and heard Dan do the same. "Are you ready?" I asked him.

"As I'll ever be. Go ahead."

I shifted the view so that we could see the whole spreadsheet. When we saw the signature, we both sat back at the same time, me in my chair and Dan against the desk. I thought I heard him deflating back there. Or maybe that was me. I scrolled down until we'd seen all of the Crescent entries.

Ellen had signed every one.

I felt sad. That was the best way to say it. Disappointed and sad. Dan had drifted away again. "Dan, I'm sorry. But isn't it better to know than not to know?"

He turned around, started to say something, and his beeper went off. Before he could respond, mine went off and they beeped together, making for an eerie, syncopated stereo alarm.

"Operations," I said, silencing the tone on mine.

"Both of us," he said quietly. "It must be something big."

"Yeah, Kevin . . . uh-huh . . . in my office . . ." Dan held the phone to his ear. "No, I've had the phones rolled over . . . What? When?" He hesitated, glancing at me. "I'll get in touch with her. Okay, I'll be right down."

"We haven't dispatched an aircraft in over an hour," he said after he'd hung up. "We've got one on every gate, at least two on the ground trying to get in, more on the way, and visibility is for shit. Kevin says everything just stopped."

"Weather?"

"It's not the weather."

Even in the overheated, overcharged atmosphere I felt a deep, deep chill as he dashed into his office.

I followed him. "Then what is it?"

"All the rampers have disappeared." He snatched a hand-held radio from the charger. "Kevin can't find anyone."

There was a current running through Dan. I could feel it. The high-voltage kind that's always marked dangerous. His engines were revving. I took a wild guess. "Are the Dwyers on shift?"

"Little Pete is. He must have swapped with someone."

I clamped onto his right elbow, afraid that he might be out the door and into the operation before I knew he was gone. "What are you planning to do?"

"I'm going to see if I can get some airplanes off the ground."

"Don't bullshit me. You're going down there to find Little Pete."

"I'm not going down there to find Little Pete, but if that cocksucker happens to be around, I won't walk away from him."

"There's something not right here, Dan. An entire shift doesn't just disappear. Someone's trying to get us down there. Don't be stupid."

"No one ever accused me of being smart."

He was standing still. He wasn't doing anything but looking at me, yet I could still feel his momentum pulling us both toward the door. I was panicked that if I let go, he was going to slip away, and this time I'd never see him again.

"Let me go, boss."

I looked at him closely. He was tired, disheveled, unshaven—and completely still. I'd never seen him so still, and I knew I had no chance of stopping him. I let go, but only to reach for the second radio still nested in the charger. Before I had it clipped in place, the door to the concourse opened and slammed shut. We stared at each other. "Dickie's package," I said.

"What did you do with it?" he whispered.

"Did I have it last?"

The footsteps were approaching, albeit slowly.

I bolted next door to my office and found the envelope on the desk, right where I'd left it. We'd never replaced the ceiling tile, and as Dan jumped onto the file cabinet, I handed the package up to him. The footsteps grew louder, but the pace was downright leisurely, out of place in an airport operation, especially in this one on this night. I thought I even heard . . . yes, he was whistling. Hurry, Dan, hurry *up*. As he maneuvered the tile back into place, he ducked and I flinched as something fell from the opening, bounced off the side of his shoe, and landed on the floor. I could see it back there between the wall and the cabinet. It was a small, plastic object, clear plastic.

Dan jumped down with a thud. "What the hell was that?"

"I don't know." It was just beyond my reach, and as I stretched for it, I had to turn my head flat to the wall and couldn't see what it was. I could almost reach it with my fingertips. It was so close . . . so close . . . *got it.*

"Yoo-hoo."

I didn't have time to look at it, but I could feel what it was by its shape, and I knew immediately that we had found the missing cassette tape from Ellen's answering machine. I didn't even have time to stuff it into my pocket. I closed my fist around it, put my hands behind my back, and turned around to see Lenny coming through the reception area straight toward us.

"Anybody home?"

He was looking sharp tonight in camel-colored slacks pleated at his narrow waist, an ivory shirt, and what appeared to be a very fine matching camel sweater. A pullover. He stood in the doorway leaning against the jamb, as calm as I was frazzled. "And what

a stroke of good fortune to find the both of you together like this. I can't believe my luck."

We must have looked totally caught in the act. I
was standing stiffly in front of my desk with both
hands behind my back. Dan was behind the desk, and
I hoped to hell he'd stay back there. It was only a
few hours ago he'd been talking about tearing Lenny's
throat out with his bare hands. I swallowed hard,
leaned back awkwardly against the desk edge, and
reached for a calm voice. "It's kind of late in the day
for you, isn't it, Lenny? Especially on a Friday."

He stared at us for a long time, looking from my
face to Dan's and back again. He was sneaky enough
to recognize sneaky when he saw it. "Is it?" He
slipped a pack of gum out of his pocket and offered
me a piece.

"No, thanks." He didn't offer any to Dan.

"In light of the disaster that is unfolding outside in
your operation at this very moment, I would say if it's
too late for anyone, that would be you. I must say,
I've never seen passengers quite as angry as the ones
out on your concourse at this very moment." The
Louisiana drawl was extra-thick and creamy tonight,
almost dripping. "What's keeping you all so busy in
here tonight?"

"We were just on our way out," I said, casually
stuffing my hands into the front pockets of my jeans,
depositing the tiny cassette there.

"Good," he said, strolling into my office, taking his
time, letting his gaze linger here and there. My heart
sank when it lingered a little longer on the file cabinet,
on the sprinkling of acoustic tile scrapings that were
still there, probably because they still had Dan's foot-
prints in them. He didn't go so far as to look up at
the ceiling, but he knew. Dammit. He'd worked in
Boston a long time. He knew.

I glanced back at Dan. "Maybe one of us should

stay in here and monitor the phone," I said. That was a stretch, but the best I could come up with under the circumstances. I was mainly trying to get Dan's reaction, and I did.

"You can stay if you want," he said quickly, "but I'm going downstairs."

That was my choice. Stay with the tape and let Dan go take on Little Pete by himself, or go with him and leave the tape for Lenny to find.

Lenny was delighted. "Come on back in here when you all have got things under control."

"If it's as bad as you say out there," I said, "we could use your help."

"I was on my way to offer my assistance, but since you're both here, I'm very comfortable leaving things in your capable hands. Especially with Mr. Fallacaro here, one of the best operating men around. Isn't that right, Danny boy?"

I could almost taste the tension as something passed silently between them, something I could see but could not understand. What I knew was that these two men hated each other. It was for all kinds of reasons, but mostly for the secrets they knew about each other. I slipped around to the side of the desk so that I could be closer to Dan.

"I know what you did," Dan said to Lenny.

Lenny chewed his gum and smiled. "Don't know what you'd be referring to, Danny boy, but whatever it is, wouldn't you have to include yourself? In for a penny, in for a pound, my friend. And how is sweet Michelle? How is she going to like visiting her daddy in a federal penitentiary?"

Dan almost came over the desk. It took all my strength to stay in front of him as he screamed over my shoulder and jabbed his finger at Lenny. "You ever say my daughter's name again, cocksucker, I'm going to kill you. I'm going to rip your balls off and shove them down your lying throat, you filthy bastard."

Not surprisingly, Lenny was moving back and not forward. He stayed clear as I maneuvered Dan out the door and into the corridor. When he couldn't get past me to get to Lenny, he pounded the wall. "I *hate* that motherfucker."

"Stay out here, Dan."

"He's going to find it."

"Be quiet."

He lowered his already hoarse voice. "He's going to get the video and we won't have anything."

"There's nothing we can do. It's a surveillance video taped on company-owned surveillance equipment. It belongs to the company. Everything in there is company property. We'll think of something else. Don't come back in."

I went back to get our jackets. I also wanted my backpack, which still had my cell phone in it. Lenny, looking smug, was lounging in my doorway. "You all better skedaddle," he said, winking at me, "while you still have an operation left to save."

I was dripping wet again, but in the whole melee Lenny had never even broken a sweat. I guess reptiles don't sweat.

"And by the way," he said, easing into my desk chair, "when you get downstairs to the ramp, say hello to Angelo for me."

Chapter Forty-two

With the environmental-control system in the terminal gone haywire and all the moist, overheating bodies crammed together, the atmosphere was suffocating. The odor of sweating scalps and ripe underarms hung in the air like a damp mist. The angry determination on Dan's face made me nervous.

"We're looking for Angelo, right? Nobody else."

His distracted nod gave me no confidence. "I'll take the north end to the firehouse," he said, zipping his jacket, "and you take the south. And let me know what you find out in Operations."

He pulled on his gloves. Made for skiing, they were heavy-duty, but to me they looked like boxing gloves. He was so pumped up by the encounter with Lenny, I knew that no matter what I said, he was a heat-seeking missile headed straight for Little Pete. And there was no way he was going to win that fight.

"Stay in radio contact with me," I said into his ear, then pulled back so that I could see his eyes. "Please, Dan."

He could do no better than a grim-faced nod, and I watched him disappear into the crush of angry passengers. He'd been walking away from me like that since the day we'd met.

If the departing crowd that first night of my arrival had been hostile, these people were homicidal. My destination was Operations, but I couldn't take one step without someone stopping me to ask something I didn't know. Or to yell at me.

The quickest way to move was around the crowd. I worked my way over to the windows and what I saw there, rather what I couldn't see, stopped me cold. A DC-10, a very large aircraft, was parked just outside the window at the gate, but it was snowing and blowing so hard, it was barely visible. With my hands cupped around my eyes to block out the overhead light and my nose pushed up against the window, I could see more. Ground equipment was scattered everywhere, the bellies of the aircraft were open, and the cabin was lit, making for a ghostly line of blurry portholes that disappeared into the blowing snow. But as far as I could tell, the ramp was deserted. I couldn't find a single soul moving down there.

I felt a shove from behind and a sharp elbow to the kidney that flattened me up against the glass. I whipped around, but it was just a passenger who had himself been pushed. Someone else grabbed my arm and I jerked it back.

"Miss Shanahan." It was an agent, but it took a moment for me to register that it was JoAnn. She'd been working the night I'd arrived, and here she was again in the middle of another disaster, this one even worse. "I heard you were over here," she said, quickly. "I've got about a hundred people wanting to talk to the manager. Will you help us?"

The scene, I swore, was getting more chaotic as I stood there. The noise level was rising with the tension, and her dark eyes pleaded for me to take charge again. And I wanted to. I wished more than anything that straightening out the operation was the biggest thing I had to worry about tonight. When I didn't respond immediately, the look on her face turned from desperate hope to cold cynicism. When I took off my Majestic badge and slipped it into the pocket of my jeans, she started to walk away.

"Wait a second." I put my hand on her shoulder. "Lenny Caseaux is in my office right now. Call him and ask him to come down. If he won't, start queuing up passengers to go see him in the administration offices. All right?"

As the idea sank in, she nodded with a sly smile. She could have fun with that one. More power to her.

The chaos upstairs had been almost unbearable, but the silence downstairs was worse. Somewhere at the far end of the long, deserted corridor, a door not properly latched slammed open and shut, and as I passed by open doorways and empty offices, I could hear the storm outside, the wind bellowing and the grit and debris raining against the windows.

Kevin was as beleaguered and overwhelmed as I'd ever seen him.

"Why did you send everyone home?" he asked without even looking up.

"What?"

His curly hair was limp from repeated comb-throughs with nervous fingers, and when he did make eye contact, he could barely focus on me. "Tell me what's going on, Kevin."

I waited as he answered a radio call from the irate captain on Gate forty-three who demanded to know the same thing. Kevin calmed him down the best he could, telling him to sit tight.

"The assignment crew chief came in half an hour ago," he said, turning back to me, "to drop off his radio. He said he had authority from you to send everyone home immediately. He said you declared a weather emergency."

"I didn't do that, Kevin. It had to be Lenny." He answered the radio again, this time responding to

JoAnn. I wanted to grab the mike from his hand and make him pay attention to me. Instead, I went to the closed-circuit TV monitors and checked every screen, but there was nothing to see in the near-whiteout conditions. By the time he'd finished his call, I'd projected all kinds of horrible scenes onto the white screens, and my temples were pounding with more possibilities.

"When's the last time you saw Little Pete?" I blurted.

"Little Pete was in here earlier," he said. "He was looking for Angelo, and that's another thing—"

"Angelo's still on the field?" He looked at me as if my eyes had popped out of my head, which they might have.

"He called about an hour ago from the mail dock. Why the devil did no one think to mention to me that Angelo was coming back?"

"Angelo has a radio, then."

"No. They were all out when he got here. He called on the phone, and I told him to go home. He said he'd just gotten here and he was staying. It's probably a good night for him to raid the freight house."

"Did you tell Little Pete where he was?"

"Of course I did. He's a crew chief. He was looking for a crew."

My hand went automatically to my radio. "Dan Fallacaro from Alex Shanahan, do you read me? *Dan*, do you read?"

"He was looking for you, too."

"Who, Dan?

"No, Danny called in about twenty-five minutes ago. Little Pete was looking for you."

I felt cold, frigid, as if the wall had disappeared and the storm had come inside, inside my body. "What—what did he say?"

"Danny? He said not to use the radios, that Little Pete has one, whatever the hell that means." The desk unit cackled with the angry voice of another captain. Kevin reached for the microphone to respond. Before he could, the captain spewed out a stream of expletives that would have made Dan blush. This time I did grab the microphone, told the captain to can it, then turned the radio off. Kevin stared at me, aghast.

"What did Little Pete say about me?"

"He said that he knew you were on the field and that he wanted to discuss his grievance with you. A few grievances, I think he said. And what do you think you're doing turning that radio down?"

I tried to stay calm by using the perspiration glinting off his high forehead as a focal point. "This is not going to make any sense, Kevin, but I need you to do something for me and it has to be right now and I don't have time for questions. Just listen."

His eyes drifted over to the now silent radio. "Are you sure you know what you're doing?"

"Get your phone book out. I need you to make some calls for me."

"Dan Fallacaro from Alex Shanahan, do you read me?" The ready room was abandoned, just as the locker room had been. A desktop radio in the crew chiefs' office was on, blasting my calls, feeding back the heavy strain that was turning my voice hoarse. I knew Little Pete might be listening, but I needed to know how Dan knew that Little Pete had a radio.

"Dan, please respond. Over."

"This is McTavish to Shanahan. Do you read?"

"John McTavish? Is that you?" I suddenly felt a little better. John's solid presence had that effect on me, and I hoped that he was close by. "Where are you?"

"I just came up from Freight and I'm down at Gate Forty-five with my crew." I could barely hear him over the wind. "We're trying to get this 'ten out of here. What the hell is going on?"

"Have you seen Dan?"

"He's—"

The whine of an engine drowned him out completely.

"Say again, John. I didn't hear you."

"My brother saw Danny heading toward the bag room."

"Inbound or outbound?"

"Outbound, I think. Terry says he was in a hurry. You want me to find him for you?"

I stood at the window looking out and trying to decide. "John, I need you to find Angelo."

I waited and got back nothing but static.

"Do you copy, John?"

"What about this airplane?"

"Forget about it. Take your crew and when you find him, don't let him out of your sight. Do you understand?"

"If that's what you want. McTavish out."

I went back through the locker room and swapped my lightweight jacket for a company-issued winter coat. Bulky and long, it enveloped me in the pungent odor of the owner's exertion. I put my cell phone and my beeper into the pockets, and my radio, too. I wasn't going to be able to hear it anyway. Then I zipped up, found the nearest door, and stepped outside.

All I could do for the first few seconds was huddle facing the building with my back to the wind. The cold went right through all my layers. I might as well have been standing there in a bathing suit. When I turned into the wind, a brutal blast blew my hood back, and I was sure that my hair had frozen in that instant. But I couldn't feel a thing because even though I was wearing gloves, my fingers were already numb. I could barely make them work to pull the hood back up, and then I had to keep one hand out to hold it in place. My eyes were watering. Ground equipment was everywhere. Vehicles were parked as if each driver had screeched to a halt and leapt out. Some of the bag carts sprouted wings when the wind lifted their plastic curtains out and up. It wouldn't have been surprising to see one of them take off.

I followed the most direct path to the bag room straight across the ramp and past the commuter gate, the same gate that Dan and I had seen on the videotape. When was that? I'd lost all sense of time. Another Beechcraft was parked there, and I wondered why no one had taxied it to a more sheltered spot. We'd be lucky if it was still in one piece tomorrow.

What was normally a two-minute walk seemed to take forever as I put my head down and trudged into wind. I stopped now and then to look around for Dan and to make sure I was still alone out there. Someone could have been right behind me and I wouldn't have heard him.

Stepping into the outbound bag room and out of the shrieking wind brought relative calm and deep silence. I stood inside the doorway, searching for my radio and trying to get some feeling back.

"Kevin, come in. Kevin Corrigan, come in please." It was hard to talk with frozen lips.

Bags were everywhere—on the piers, on the floor around the piers, and at the ends where they'd dumped off into huge, uneven piles that clogged the driveway all the way to the ramp-side wall. The bag belt had apparently run for a while before someone had figured out the crew had abandoned ship.

"This is Kevin. Go ahead."

"Do you have an update?"

"Partial."

"Call me on my cell phone."

"Roger."

It took seconds for him to call. "The troopers are busy," he said.

"Busy?"

"Everyone's occupied at the moment by an aircraft excursion."

"Whose?"

"TWA had one slide off the runway, so there's a bunch of them down there. Apparently the roads coming in and out of this place are a nightmare, so all the rest of them are on traffic control."

"Traffic control? Did you tell them what's going on?"

"I told them, but it's a pretty wild story, you have to admit."

I pushed a clump of half-frozen hair out of my eyes and would have gone to Plan B if I'd had one. I'd been counting on help from the troopers.

"They said they'd respond as soon as they could break a unit away. I'll keep calling them."

"What about Big Pete?"

"His wife doesn't know where he is, but she says he's got a beeper. She doesn't have the number, but Victor does, if you can believe that. I'm waiting for Vic to call me back."

"You haven't heard from anyone, have you?"

"Does Lenny count? He's upstairs hyperventilating. He sounds like he's going to have a heart attack."

"Good. Nothing from Dan?"

"No, but Johnny Mac called for you. Did you hear?"

"What did he say?"

"He talked to Terry and he says you should go to the other bag room—inbound."

"Goddammit." I was in the wrong bag room. I hung up, put up my hood, and went back out into the storm.

* * *

The door to the inbound bag room was a heavy steel slab, but it might as well have been balsa wood the way it whipsawed back and forth in the storm. I found the brick doorstop and used it. I wasn't sure that it would hold, but it was dark in there and dim light from the ramp was better than no light at all.

The heavy air trapped within the four concrete walls had smelled of plaster and paint and turpentine when I'd met Big Pete there. As I stepped through the doorway and around the drop cloth, the same one that had blocked my way last night, I couldn't smell anything. Hoping not to go any farther, I cleared away the anxiety that had lumped in my throat and called out, "Dan?"

The only response was the swishing of the tarps as the wind pushed in through the open door behind me.

To turn on the lights I had to find the fuse box, the one Big Pete had showed me. I wasn't sure I could remember where it was. I was sure that it was farther in than I wanted to go. I called again for Dan and listened. Nothing.

Damn.

I pushed the hood off my head—the better to sense someone coming at me from the side—then took a few edgy steps. I tried to feel left and right with my hands, but my fingers were numb from the cold. I used my palms to guide me, brushing them along the heavy drop cloths as I moved, trying to visualize the narrow corridor that they made. I could almost feel the darkness thickening around me as I moved deeper into the silence.

"*Dan,* are you *in* here?"

I leaned forward trying to hear, took a step, and landed on something slick. My heart thumped into my throat and stayed there as my foot skated out from under me. I made an awkward, spine-twisting grab for something, *anything* to keep me from going down, and for the longest moment I hung backward over the cement, clinging to a tarp that couldn't possibly hold my dead weight. Adrenaline kicked in as I pulled myself upright, driving my heartbeat into a wild, demented rhythm that made me dizzy. I leaned over, hands on my knees, and took a breath. Then I took another, and another, breathing deeply until the stars in front of my eyes had faded.

Even bent over with my head that much closer to the cement, it was too dark to see what I'd slipped on. But I had a sinking, sickening feeling that I already knew. I held on to the tarp as I slid my foot back and forth, trying to feel what it could be. I wanted to believe that it was oil or grease or some strange lubricant that only felt like blood, but the rational part of me wouldn't go for it.

I pushed aside the tarp I'd been squeezing, angling for some light. The second I moved it, it gave way from whatever had anchored it to the high ceiling. I slipped out of the way—barely—as it crashed into a heap. Everything in me said to bolt, but I was transfixed because without the tarp to block it, a slant of light had fallen across my feet. The light was dim, but enough to show that it wasn't a pool at all that I was standing in, but a thick stream that flowed along the floor under the drop cloths—a thick stream with a deep red hue.

This time my breath couldn't make it out of my chest. I kept sucking in air, fighting for oxygen, but nothing came out. I started creeping back, moving until I was backed up flat against a wall. There was so much blood. I stared at it, and all I could feel was a miserable, stinging pain in the tips of my fingers. They were starting to thaw out.

I reached down for my radio, held it close to my lips, and pressed the button, squeezing until I thought the housing would crack. "Dan Fallacaro, come in please." My tongue was too big and my mouth felt as if it were coated with chalk. "Dan, are you out there?"

Static.

I tipped my head back against the wall. This was the wall where Big Pete had found the fuse box, right? It *had* to be the same wall. If it wasn't, what else was I going to do? Slowly, I began to feel my way toward the place where I thought the box was. Once my knuckles scraped against the box's open door, it wasn't hard to find the heavy switches behind it. The first one I flipped turned on the overheads.

I closed my eyes, waited for them to adjust to the light, and opened them again. All around me were the blue tarps. I couldn't see farther than four feet in any direction. The dark stream at my feet had turned to vivid red. It was coming from the direction of the bag belt. I turned myself that way, pushed aside the first tarp, and made myself move as far as the next. The motion was slow and forced, jerky and detached because I was afraid—terrified—to go forward.

"Dan, if you're out there, please respond." My breath vaporized as I tried the radio again. The static seemed to go right through me. I was coming apart inside. My eyes burned as I pulled aside the next plastic curtain. I thought about Michelle.

"Please, Dan, *please.*"

I wondered what she looked like, if she had his green eyes. I called again, I think I did, as I approached the last curtain, and tears were coming because I knew he wasn't going to answer. I lowered my head and squeezed my eyes shut. I hadn't prayed to God in fifteen years, and I pictured him in his heaven laughing at me as I tried to now.

O my God, I am heartily sorry for having offended Thee . . .

I opened my eyes. My white running shoes were smeared with blood. My head was pounding, about to explode. The longer I stood there, the harder it was going to be.

. . . and I detest all of my sins because of thy just punishment . . .

I put my hand on the edge of the drop cloth. It felt cold and gritty.

. . . but most of all because I have offended Thee, my God . . .

I moved it aside slowly. My eyes focused on the scene in front of me and I had to turn away. And then I started to cry.

. . . who art all-good and deserving of all my love.

It wasn't Dan.

I covered my eyes with both hands and wept. It wasn't him. Crying made my head hurt more and sobbing made it harder to breathe and I was boiling in that giant coat so I unzipped and let it slide down to the floor like the weight that had just slipped off my shoulders. The cool air that brushed against my damp skin felt like—*tasted* like—relief and I tried to pull it in in long, deep breaths. It wasn't him.

It was someone in a Majestic uniform. When the spasms stopped, I turned back to the gruesome sight. He was stomach down on the bag belt with his arms draped over either side. His left hand was in front of me, twisted back against the ground, palm up, and I felt some of the weight return because this man had long, slender fingers, fingers that I remembered from the coffee shop, ones that I had held in my own hand just a few hours ago. It was Angelo. I looked for his face, and when I saw it, bile came up the back of my throat, my stomach lurched in a dry heave, and I had to look away again. No wonder there was so much blood. His head was crushed, smashed between the belt and defective safety door that had dropped like a guillotine and cracked open his skull.

I felt it before I heard it. The pressure in the room

shifted. The tarps snapped around me. The door slammed shut. By the time the hollow boom had finished caroming off the bare walls, I was on my knees, crouched, listening. The sound of the storm was gone. The tarps were still. It was perfectly quiet, and if I was really lucky, the door had slammed shut all by itself.

I crouched lower, trying to listen with my whole body. And then I heard him coming, not by the sound of his footsteps, but by the sound of his fingers sliding along the tarps. I tried not to panic even though I could barely move. Better to look around for a way out.

There was a door, the door to the terminal, and it wasn't that far away. If I moved now, I could get there before he cleared the last drop cloth. But I had to go . . . *now*. I lunged out of the crouch, covering the distance to the door faster than I would have thought possible. I slammed my shoulder into the door—and it didn't move. It *had* to open. This door was not supposed to lock from this side. It was fire code. I pushed again and then again, but it was solid. I was trapped.

The sound of brushing fingers had stopped. He'd heard me. I imagined his head cocked just like mine, the two of us mirror images reacting to each other. Maybe I could make it to my radio and call for help. Maybe I should hide. Maybe—

"God*dammit*, who the hell is in here?"

If the door hadn't been there to catch me, I would have sunk all the way to the floor. My legs turned wobbly and all my bones seemed to dissolve as the tension flowed out. I closed my eyes and called out. "Dan?"

"Boss?"

I pushed toward him, and when I saw him I couldn't keep from wrapping my arms around his neck. Even though he was wet from the storm and ice covered his jacket, all I felt was his warm, living, breathing, completely intact body. He held me until I was ready to let go; then I stepped back so I could see his face. He looked so bewildered it made me laugh. "I thought you were dead."

"I'm not dead."

"Clearly. Where have you been?"

"Out looking for you. I found Angie and, Jesus, I nearly puked all over the place, and then I put my radio down somewhere and I couldn't remember where I'd left it—"

"We have to get out of here." I pushed him toward the door.

"Why?"

"Because the door to the terminal is jammed and I think Little Pete did it and there's no other way out. Come on, come on, let's go."

He didn't budge. *"Dan . . ."*

"You can't go out there like that. Don't you have a coat?"

He was right. I went back for the coat, trying not to look at the body as I slipped it on. When we were both bundled up, we stood at the door preparing to go back out to the ramp and meet the storm's fury.

"Ready?" His voice was muted by the thick muffler twisted around his neck.

I pushed in close behind him and gave him a nudge. He leaned into the door, and the second it was open, the wind seemed to catch it and pull it out of his hands. The blast of air that hit me was so cold, it burned my eyes shut and I was blind. I heard a loud crack, my head snapped back, and I fell backward, landing hard on my tailbone. Something landed on my chest and stayed there, something heavy enough to crush the air out of my lungs. I couldn't breathe. I couldn't see. The bag room was spinning. I tried to throw off the weight.

"Jesus fucking Christ. Jesus Christ—"

The weight on my chest was Dan. He was on top of me trying to get up, and I was trying to get out from under him. My forehead was throbbing, the coat felt like a straitjacket, and I couldn't think straight. I couldn't think at all. The door slammed and it was quiet. Dan rolled off and I sat up. When my vision finally cleared, my brain unscrambled, and the fog lifted, I was staring up, way up, into the face of Little Pete Dwyer.

"You people," he said, shaking his head, "you goddamned people. You just couldn't leave it alone."

Chapter Forty-three

Dan made it to his feet before I did, then reached down and offered his hand to help me up. If he'd been a few inches shorter, he would have broken my nose when our heads collided. As it was, he'd cracked me pretty good in the forehead. I reached up and touched the throbbing, tender welt that was forming there.

Little Pete was like a mountain in front of the door. Dan was a foot and a half shorter and gave up at least fifty pounds to the guy, but that didn't faze him. "Get the fuck out of the way," he demanded.

The bigger man glanced down. "What are you gonna do if I don't? Write me up? Put a letter in my personnel file?"

He sounded calm, bemused even, but the scar above his eye was fresh and angry. He'd just come in from a raging storm, and I found it very disturbing that he wasn't wearing a coat. All he had on was his winter uniform over a T-shirt. The long sleeves were rolled up, the better to display those club-like forearms. He wasn't shivering. I didn't see any goose bumps. Whatever was burning inside him tonight seemed to be keeping him plenty warm—but it was making me shiver.

Dan made a sudden move toward the door. Little Pete raised one arm, putting his fingers on Dan's chest and stopping him cold. "Take a step back," he warned with a quiet resolve that I would have expected from his father but not from him. "Take a step back," he said, more slowly this time, "and give me your radio."

"Go fuck yourself, Junior."

I felt a warning tremor inside as Little Pete moved out of the doorway, pushing Dan in front of him. As he did, he turned slightly and my tremors escalated to a full-blown temblor. He had a gun. It was black and flat and stuffed down into the back of his pants. The handle was smooth, and though it looked very large to me, the weapon seemed like a toy against the broad expanse of his back.

"He doesn't have a radio," I said quickly, shifting to auto-rational. "Take mine." I fumbled the heavy unit from my pocket and offered it to him.

Little Pete was still staring at Dan. "I know he had a radio. I heard him using it."

"It's lost in here somewhere. We don't know where it is." I pushed my radio toward him again. "Here's mine."

When he turned to face me squarely, I saw the dark stains on the front of his shirt—dark and wet. While I was staring at the blood, Angelo's blood, he took the radio from my hand and, with what seemed like a casual flick of the wrist, sent it rocketing across the room and exploding against the only cement wall that wasn't blocked by plastic. I stared at the ruined pieces on the ground, and then I was staring at the red stains on my own shoes. We both had Angelo's blood on us.

Dan's taunting broke the silence. "Big fucking man you are, you jerkoff. You killed a *radio*. Old men, women, and radios. What's next? Puppies and kittens?"

I watched one of Little Pete's big hands curl into a fist and flex. Curl and flex. I'd heard all about this guy's towering temper, and I wondered how it showed itself. Did he do a long, slow boil and then explode?

Or did it come in a blinding flash, an uncontrollable, indiscriminate blast that leveled everything in its path? I wished I knew what to expect from him.

"Cell phone," he said to me, still flexing and curling.

"What?"

He moved in close and leaned over me, close enough that I could smell his sweat, that I could feel his whispered breath like lighter fluid on my skin; it was worse than if he had touched me. "Don't make me say everything twice," he said, "I hate that."

I wanted to put both hands on his chest and shove him away. But I could feel something from him that was as strong as the stench of blood, tobacco, and alcohol. I looked again at the stains drying on his shirt. I looked into his eyes and saw the same dead-calm resolve that I had heard in his voice. This was a man who had nothing more to lose—and knew it.

I did what he asked.

"Good girl," he said as I handed over my flip phone. He admired the small device. "That's a nice one." Slipping it into his back pocket, he turned his attention to Dan. "Take off your jacket."

Dan, of course, didn't move, didn't even blink. Pete reached his hand up, and Dan slapped it away. I could feel drops of perspiration rolling down the underside of my arm as I watched the two men size each other up like a couple of junkyard dogs. Pete reached up again, quicker this time, and came away with one end of the muffler that was wrapped around Dan's neck.

It happened so fast.

"God, *don't*—" was all I could get out as I rushed toward Little Pete. He easily held me back with one arm as he used the other to jerk the muffler taut over Dan's head, lifting him almost completely off the ground. Dan's hands flew to his throat and he started to choke.

"Stay away," Pete barked at me, "or I'll break his neck."

I felt paralyzed. An image of Ellen flashed, Ellen hanging by the neck. It scared me so much, I stopped breathing, just as Dan must have. Little Pete was holding him up with one hand, flexing the long length of sinew and muscle that was his forearm. He was pumped up, turned on by his own physical dominance. But Dan looked as if he was dying. His face was blue, his eyes bulged, and he made a horrible, gasping sound.

"Let him down," I begged, "please, let him down."

He started to unwind the makeshift noose, one leisurely twist at a time. When Dan was free, he went to his knees, grabbing his throat with both hands.

Little Pete took the muffler and draped it around his own neck. "I can help you get that jacket off, too," he said, grinning, "but I might have to break your arms to do it."

I had no doubt that he would.

Dan was still bent and gasping, and I wondered if there was enough air in the room for both of us. I put my hand on his back. He looked up at me, his face red and eyes watering.

"Do what he says, Dan."

He struggled to his feet, and I helped him slip the jacket off. Little Pete stepped in, raised Dan's arms over his head, and gave him a thorough pat-down. Then he took the jacket from me.

"Where do you get one like that?" he asked as he searched the pockets. "You get it around here?"

"What?" I had no idea what he was asking about.

He shot me a warning glare. "I told you about making me ask twice about things."

"I'm sorry, I don't—"

"The phone. That little cell you got. Where'd you get it?"

"Denver," I said, struggling to stay in tune with whatever he was talking about. "I bought it in Denver before I came out here."

"What kind of range has it got?"

My jaw tightened. My legs were shaking so much, my knees were almost knocking. I didn't know the answer and I didn't know if that would upset him and I didn't know if I should make something up and—

"They don't let you have cell phones in prison, asshole." Dan had recovered his voice, just in time.

Having found nothing but a wallet, keys, and spare change in Dan's jacket, Little Pete dropped it on the floor, pulled a pack of cigarettes from his shirt pocket and, just as his father had last night, rolled a cigarette slowly between his thumb and forefinger before lighting up. He started to move as he smoked, brushing his shoulder along one of the tarps as he paced back and forth. I had a feeling he was trying to figure out what to do next. I wished Big Pete were here to tell him. God knows what he'd come up with on his own.

I unzipped my jacket. Had to. Even though it was cold in the bag room, I was so hot I was going to faint. Dan had both hands clamped against the back of his neck. With his head dropped back, I could see the long red striations beneath the collar of his shirt.

"Are you all right?" I asked him, keeping an eye on Little Pete.

He stared straight down at the floor, looking disgusted, ashamed even, and I remembered what his grandmother had drilled into him, that men were put on this earth to take care of women.

"Dan, he's bigger than both of us put together, he's been drinking, he has a gun, and I don't think he cares if he lives or dies tonight. Do you really think it's a good idea to provoke him?"

Still he didn't reply.

"The goal is to survive," I said. "If you don't care

about yourself, do it for me. I don't want to be left alone with him." I looked into his eyes and didn't look away until he nodded.

Little Pete had his own radio clipped to his belt, and every once in a while it would report. He'd cock his ear and listen and check his watch. At one point I heard Kevin calling for me. We all did. It seemed to remind Little Pete that we weren't in a vacuum. After one last deep drag on the cigarette, he dropped it to the cement and stepped on it.

"You two quit your whispering over there," he said, checking his watch again. What was he waiting for?

"Go that way." He pointed toward the tarp-lined passageway, the one that led to the back where Angelo lay. I went first, then Dan. Pete followed. When I got to the opening around the bag belt, it was hard for me even to look at the corpse. Not Little Pete.

"Stand over there where I can watch the two of you, and don't do nothing stupid."

We moved to where he was pointing, to his left, and stood with our backs to the wall. We weren't far from the door to the terminal, the one he'd already blocked somehow.

He walked to the bag belt and bowed his head for a moment of reverential silence over the man he'd just murdered. "Fuckin' Angie," he said, his voice filled with moist emotion. Then he slipped one foot under Angelo's knee and, careful not to disturb anything, launched himself over the belt, over the body, and into the center of the racetrack. He went straight to the far side of the loop and came back with a box, one that rattled. He climbed back over and set the box on a painter's bucket. It was Myers's Rum, a whole case, probably up from the Caribbean duty free and most certainly swiped from some unsuspecting tourist. And it had already been opened. Just what this situation needed—booze.

"Compliments of Angie," he said as he uncorked one of the distinctive, flask-shaped bottles. Then he raised a toast to his victim. "Here's to you, old man." He tipped his head back, closed his eyes, and took a long pull. When he finished, he wiped the back of his hand across his mouth and addressed the corpse again. "You shoulda kept your big, rat-bastard mouth shut."

Dan could contain himself no longer. "What," he sneered, "it's *Angie's* fault you had to smash his skull in?"

"No, it ain't his fault." Little Pete whipped around and pointed the flask at Dan, and I cringed to think that it could just as easily be a gun as a bottle of rum. "It's your fault."

"*My* fault?"

"You're the one who called Theresa. You can't even handle the situation man to man. You gotta go and get his wife involved." Pete took another quick hit from the bottle. "He's laying there dead because of you."

"You are the biggest dumbfuck—"

"Hey," I said, mostly to Dan, "can we just calm down, please?"

Little Pete was smug. "He's just pissed off that I'm in charge tonight, that I'm the one calling the shots. Ain't that right, Danny boy?"

"The fact that you're still breathing pisses me off."

Little Pete laughed. "How about you?" he asked me. "Do you want to see me dead, too? Everybody else does."

"I don't want any of us to be dead, including you."

He nodded, smiling faintly. "She's smarter than you, Danny boy. She's smart enough to be scared of me. You should be scared of me, too."

"Why should I—"

"We're both scared of you," I said, cutting Dan off. "And you are in charge tonight. We both see that."

Little Pete narrowed his eyes, suspicious perhaps that someone actually agreed with him. "Let me ask you a question," he said, speaking to me now as if we were old friends. "Don't you think that a man's got a right to protect his name?"

"What name?" Dan snapped. "Dickhead?"

"I'm not talking to you." He turned back to me. "See, that's how I look at this whole thing. It's like self-defense. She knew what was going to happen if she didn't mind her own business. Once she was gonna do what she was gonna do, I didn't have any choice—but she did."

My jaw was trembling and my eyes were burning as I listened to him casually mention that he had killed Ellen. It was horrifying, and more so to hear his justification and to know that he believed it. This man was capable of anything.

"She made the choice herself," he said, "so she did kill herself. The bitch was warned."

It seemed important to him that I believe him, important that someone be on his side, and I'd decided that's what I would do. What I didn't count on was Dan's reaction. When he started toward Little Pete, I grabbed him. The muscle in his forearm was hard as bone.

"What do you think is going to happen here tonight, Pete?" I was talking just to talk, not saying anything, trying to stay in front of Dan and buy us some time.

"You think he even knows? Like this murdering bastard's got some kind of a plan. His pop's not around to do his thinking—"

"Shut the fuck up, asshole."

Yes, Dan, shut the fuck up. Little Pete was drinking more and thinking less. I could hear it in his loosening voice, see it in his dulled reactions, and every time he turned, the gun was there. Dan wasn't much better. His skin was drawn so tight, I thought I could see the muscles underneath, and he was literally vibrating with the effort to stand still. "You are such a worthless piece of crap," he yelled. "Nothing is ever your fault."

"Dan, *stop.*" I was panicked because I knew he wouldn't. I knew exactly what was going to happen and I had no way to stop it.

"It's *my* fault you had to kill Angie. It's *Ellen's* fault you had to kill her. Let me ask you something. Whose fault was it that you killed those twenty-one people in the Beechcraft?"

I was almost afraid to look at Little Pete. He was standing perfectly still next to Angelo's body, about eight feet away from us. His long arms hung awkwardly at his sides. A quick lunge would have put him at Dan's throat in an instant. For a second I thought that's exactly what he would do, as he seemed to fight back the urge, squeezing the bottle in his hand instead. He squeezed it until it shook. I noticed that it was empty. When he noticed, he turned and walked to his rum stash, pretending he'd been headed over there anyway. He slipped the empty back in, pulled out another bottle, and uncorked it. "That was Dickie's fault," he said after slamming a third of the bottle back like Gatorade.

Dan threw up his arms. "Of *course,* it was Dickie's fault."

Little Pete turned. "The tape's going to show that. It's going to show that I didn't do it."

"How do you figure that?" I asked him, trying to keep him engaged.

"I gave Dickie the right load." Again he was trying hard to convince me—or himself. "He had the right numbers. He fucked it up when he gave them to the captain. It's all on the tape, which is why he had to hide it." Bottle in hand, he paced in a circle around his makeshift bar. "We never get what we need around here. Never enough manpower, equipment that's for shit, and then when something goes wrong, blame . . . blame the union." He was ticking off the points, but in a mechanical way, groping for something he used to know, was supposed to know. "Blame the union. I had . . . I had to try three tugs that night before I found one that worked. That's right. It took me an hour to find wands, I never did find a goddamn radio, and the tug that I did find was out of gas."

"Yeah, that's a good excuse. The simplest goddamn job in the world and you screw it up. You have to be the stupidest fucking moron on the face of the earth."

"I *gave* him the right numbers, and he never radioed them to the captain."

Dan pressed him. "How did you give him the numbers? You just said you couldn't find a radio that night. And you never went into Operations."

Little Pete turned away and stood with his back to us, sucking down rum. The gun never looked more menacing. "You management fucks," he said quietly. "It was Dickie. It was Dickie, it was Dickie, it was fuckin' *Dickie Flynn.*" He lowered his head and took a few deep breaths, and when he turned to face us, his eyes were dead. He seemed to have come to a decision. He never looked at Dan, and I had the terrifying feeling that Dan did not exist for him anymore. He touched the radio and checked his watch again. "Fuck this shit," he said as he reached around for the gun. "Let's go."

"Wait." I blurted it out, then just kept talking. "You never saw the tape, did you, Pete? You never would have. And you can't remember, right? All you know is what your father told you to say." I looked at him, at his face, and tried to understand what he was thinking. "You're waiting for Lenny. That's the plan. Lenny's supposed to find the tape and bring it to you. That's why you keep checking your watch, right?"

"It's all going to come out," he said, "after all these years."

"Listen to me. The tape will not vindicate you. And the other stuff that's with it will prove that Lenny was part of it. If he finds that package, he will destroy it."

He shook his head.

"He has to," I said. "Think this through, Pete. Lenny's not going to incriminate himself."

He rubbed his forehead with a hand that was shaking, the same hand that had reached for the gun and never made it.

"We can take you to it. The tape," I said. "We found it tonight and we hid it, and if you hurry up you can get to it before Lenny does."

He stared at me and I tried to look trustworthy, so sincere he couldn't question my motives. I felt that he wanted to believe me, that he wanted to believe that someone was telling him the truth. He began to nod, and for the moment I could breathe again. Barely. At least if we could get outside, we had a chance. We could lose him in the storm, maybe, or the troopers might show up. We had a chance.

Dan was behind me. I turned to look at him, and he looked back in a way that gave me a sliver of confidence that he would calm down, too.

"Do you drink?" Pete asked, rummaging through the box of rum.

Neither one of us responded until he turned to look at me.

"Do I *drink*?" I was stunned by the question, but more so by the fact that he was about to uncork his third bottle. I figured he was going to offer me some, which I took as a good sign. "Yes, I drink."

"I hate a woman who drinks. She was drunk that night," he said, bleary-eyed and talking almost to himself. "She smelled like alcohol. I hate a bitch who drinks." He took the bottle out and stuffed it into his

pocket. When he looked at Dan, he was not so bleary-
eyed, and when I saw the smile I knew before he said
anything that it was all over. "How did she smell when
you found her?"

Dan was past me before I had any chance of stopping him. I saw Little Pete's arm swing around toward
the gun.

"Nooooo!" I lunged for his arm, but he whipped
around and smashed me in the head with his elbow.
Everything flashed white and the bag room tipped like
a big, rolling ship. I went all the way to the floor. I
saw Dan rush Little Pete—he seemed to be moving
very slowly. He went for his knees and Little Pete
went down, they both did, falling backward into the
open box of rum. The entire case crashed to the ground,
rum spilled out onto the floor, and some of the bottles
that didn't break shot across the concrete like
hockey pucks.

I tried to get up. Everything was going too fast. The
two men stayed down for what seemed like a matter
of seconds. Dan had landed on top, but then he was
on the ground on his back. Little Pete had tossed him
aside like a newspaper. Dan came back. Little Pete
shoved him again, and this time he bounced off the
wall and cracked his shoulder.

Little Pete was reaching to his back, and the thought
that any second the gun was going to come out broke
through the cotton in my head. But then he fell to his
hands and knees, crawling around on the floor. He'd
lost it. He'd lost his gun.

My hand found one of the bottles on the floor and
I grabbed it. Little Pete was still scrambling for the
gun, not paying attention to me.

When he saw me coming, he ducked his head and
put his shoulder down. It took both hands to hook
him around the neck and keep from flipping over his
back. I had to drop the bottle. He reared back like a

grizzly bear trying to throw me off, but I held on and found the muffler that was still draped around his neck. I grabbed it, closed my eyes, and squeezed as tight as I could. He gripped my hands and tried to pry me loose. My face was pressed against the back of his head, and the smell of him was in my nose, in my mouth, my head—the sweat and the rum and whatever he put on his hair to make it spike. And blood. He smelled like the blood that was on his shirt. I held on. He tried to shake me off and couldn't. He reached back and tried to pull me forward over his head, and I felt his big, grubby hands groping my back, trying to grab hold. I wrapped my legs around his waist. Then he tried to stand up. I knew once he was up on those powerful legs, he would win.

I heard an ear-splitting yell, felt a brutal jolt, and then all three of us were tumbling through one of the tarps and into a wall. The tarp came down over us like some kind of a jungle trap. In the dark, arms and legs went flying everywhere, nobody landing any punches, nobody having any room.

The tarp came off and we broke apart.

I was on my butt, palms flat to the floor, my back against the wall. My jacket was gone and everything in my body felt broken or ripped. Dan was doubled over holding his gut, coughing up blood and trying to breathe. Little Pete was disappearing behind one of the tarps on his hands and knees, and I knew he would find the gun. I looked up at the wall over my head, then pushed myself up, crawling up by my shoulder blades. My legs didn't want to hold me, and when I made it to the fuse box I couldn't see the switches—something was in my eyes—but I could feel them. I flipped every one. If it was on, I turned it off; if it was off, I turned it on. The lights went out and the room went totally, blessedly dark. I wanted to sink back down to the floor and curl up into a ball on my side.

And then the alarm sounded—three long blasts like the dive signal on a submarine. Yellow-tinted warning lights in the ceiling flashed, making a weird strobe-like effect. A familiar rumble started, stopped, then started again as the bag belt tried to engage, then turned into a train wreck of calamitous noises—high-pitched whining and grinding gears and screeching metal. Angelo's body was mucking up the bag belt works.

I wiped my eyes and looked for Dan. When I got to where he'd been, he was gone.

Under the clanking and grinding, I heard them. The sound of their scuffling was disorienting, suffocating under the flashing lights, and I felt as if something was about to fall on me or into me and I'd never see it coming. I ripped down the tarp that was in my way. As I stumbled toward the two men, I ripped them all down, leaving a trail of plastic dunes in my wake. When I pulled down the last one, I saw Little Pete straightening up and stepping back. It looked like an old black-and-white movie, herky-jerky in the flickering light. Even the grinding belt went silent as he raised his arm and pointed the gun at Dan. But Dan was looking at me.

The shot was so loud, like an explosion. I drove into Little Pete from behind, buckling his knees. He fell over backward on top of me, and some part of me saw Dan go down.

Then I was moving, slipping, stumbling toward the ramp, toward help. It was a straight shot to the door with the tarps down. Just as my hand hit the knob, he was right there. He grabbed my ankle and I fell through the door, onto the ramp and into the storm. My chin hit the hardpacked ice and snow, jarring every tooth in my head. The door had slammed open, bounced against the wall, and slapped back against my elbow, but I couldn't feel it. All I could feel was his grip, like an iron manacle as he tried to pull me back in. I clamped onto the doorjamb with both hands as he gave my leg a vicious yank, lifting me off the ground and nearly ripping both shoulders from their sockets. It was harder and harder to hold on with fingers that were cold and numb. I was slipping, gasping, the door was flapping, and right in front of my nose was the brick . . . *the brick.* The doorstop brick was *there.* Rough and hard and heavy and within my reach. But I had to let go of the doorjamb . . . only one chance to do it right . . . try to pull myself forward . . . aching arms, then let go . . .

He pulled me inside, but when I rolled onto my back, I had the brick in my hands. I aimed for the top of his skull, but it was so heavy I couldn't wield it fast enough and he had time to flinch. I got him on the side of the head, yet it was enough that he let go and stumbled back and I was up and running. Cold air and wet snow blasted me. I was slipping, barely staying on my feet, moving across the ramp. I turned to look and he was coming, god*damn* him, he was coming with the gun in his hand, mouth open, screaming. But I couldn't hear above the roaring.

The Beechcraft was still there. When he raised the gun, I ran to the far side, putting the aircraft between us. I stayed behind the wing, well back of the engines because—*because they were running.* This airplane was going to move. I leaned down to peer under the belly, to find where he was. He was crouched on the other side, one hand down on the ramp for balance, staring back at me. For a split second we watched each other. The wind was still blowing, the snow was coming down, the noise was deafening, and he was just staring at me.

Then I saw a light, two headlamps and flashing lights coming toward us. I broke forward toward the nose but slipped and fell. From the ground, I saw that he was standing, saw his legs as he circled toward the

front of the aircraft. I tried to get up and fell again—
this time, I thought, for good because he was rounding
the nose cone, coming straight at me.

Behind me the engines revved. The aircraft was
about to roll. Every instinct pushed me away, out of its
path, but I made myself go backward, crawl on sore
elbows, back toward the engine and under the wing.
Just as Little Pete cleared the nose cone, the faint
whine of a siren began to break through. He heard
it, too, because as he came toward me, he smiled
and shook his head as if to say, "Too late." He
stopped. He raised the gun. The aircraft began to
move, and all I could think was that it was so loud I
wasn't even going to hear the sound of the shot that
would kill me.

I rolled into a ball on my side and covered my ears
as the captain made a sharp right turn to taxi out. I
saw Little Pete's boots as he tried to step aside. He
had no time to scream. As the right wing passed over
me, I closed my eyes, but even with my hands over
my ears, I could still hear the sickening thump of a
propeller interrupted.

And then it was quiet. Everything stopped except
the falling snow. It had stopped blowing. The captain
killed the engines, and the noise vacuum was filled by
the sound of the sirens. For the longest time I didn't
move. I just lay there listening. When I opened my
eyes, they wouldn't focus. And they hurt. My elbows
hurt, and my legs and my back and the side of my
head.

I squinted down past my knees and saw a fireman
leaning over something, reaching down to something
toward the nose of the Beech. The second fireman to
arrive looked down and turned away, gloved hand at
his mouth. I turned on my back as someone arrived
with a blanket and helped me sit up. The captain appeared, hatless in the snow. He bent over the body,

looking where they were looking, put both hands on his head.

A fireman was asking me questions. Was I hurt? Could I walk? Did I need help? What happened? I watched his hand coming toward me and mumbled something that might not have been coherent. He helped me to my feet and wrapped the blanket around me. I was shivering and I couldn't stop. My chin stung, and blood was running down the outside of my throat and maybe the inside because I could taste it. I smelled like rum. He tried to help me over to his rig, but I pulled him instead toward the bag room, dragging him with me and yelling for someone to call the EMTs. The whole jagged scene began to replay in my mind, especially the part where the lights went out and the gun went off and I remembered, didn't want to remember, but I remembered seeing Dan fall. I put my hands over my eyes. I was trying to sort it out, and when I looked up, he was there. He was standing in the doorway, gripping the doorjamb, one arm limp at his side.

The fireman went for a stretcher. When I got close enough, Dan tilted his head back and looked at me through the blood running into his eyes. "Did you kill that cocksucker?"

"The Beechcraft killed him."

"Good."

I put his arm around my neck, but I wasn't too stable myself. "Did he shoot you?"

"I don't think so."

"Your shoulder is bleeding. Let's wait for a stretcher."

"Fuck no. I want to make sure that motherfucker is dead."

"He's very dead, Dan. Take my word for it."

The EMTs arrived and took us both to the truck. They were from the firehouse on the field, and Dan knew all of them, called them by name. He refused to go to the hospital, not unless they insisted, which they did.

Someone was pushing through the circle of fire-fighters and EMTs orbiting around the body. I heard the noise and looked out. They tried to block him, but nothing was going to stop Big Pete from getting to his son. He sank to his knees, leaned over, and tried to pull Little Pete into his arms. When they wouldn't let him, he dropped his head back, opened his mouth, and let out a long, terrible scream that in the snow and dying wind sounded otherworldly, not even human. He did it again. And again. Then he was silent, motionless, bent over the body. Someone put a hand on his shoulder. He reached down to touch his son one last time, then stood on shaky legs. He searched the crowd that had formed, searched and searched. When he found me, he didn't move and neither did I as we stared at each other. I didn't hear the people yelling, machinery moving, and sirens blasting. I felt the snow on my face as he wiped the tears from his. I pulled the blanket around me, trying to stop shaking and watched as they led him away. He looked small and old and not so scary anymore. Not at all in control.

I couldn't stop the shaking. I smelled like rum and I couldn't stop shaking.

The coarse blanket scratched the back of my neck as I adjusted it around my shoulders. I had passed the first hours of the morning in the company of Massachusetts state troopers—and this blanket, the one the firefighter had given me on the ramp. Without thinking, I'd walked out wearing it, which turned out to be a good thing since it was now covering the blood stains on my shirt.

Last night's events had thrown the operation out of

whack, to say the least, and our concourse had the feel
of leftovers, of all the ugly business left unfinished. It
was still dark in the predawn hours, and the overhead
fluorescents seemed to throw an unusually harsh light.
Dunkin' Donuts napkins and pieces of the *Boston
Herald* were everywhere. A few passengers with no
place better to go were sacked out on the floor. Some
were stuffed into the unyielding chairs in the departure
lounges, chairs that weren't comfortable for sitting, never
mind sleeping. One of our gate agents must have taken
pity on these poor souls. Some of them were draped
with those deep purple swatches of polyester that
passed for blankets onboard our aircraft.

I still had lingering shivers, violent aftershocks that
came over me, mostly when I thought about how
things could have turned out last night. And my nose
wouldn't stop running. Reaching into my pocket for a
tissue, I felt something flat and hard. The instant I
touched it, I remembered what it was—the tiny cassette that had fallen from the ceiling of my office. I
stood in the middle of the concourse cradling it in
the palm of my hand, the missing tape from Ellen's
answering machine. I stared at it. A clear plastic case
with two miniature reels and a length of skinny black
tape. That's all it was. It could wait. I started to stuff
it back into my pocket. True, there would be no way
to listen to it at my hotel—no answering machine—
and if I left now it might have to wait for a while.
Even if I wanted to listen to it, I'd have to go back
to my office yet again, and I didn't want to do that. I
didn't want to have to stare again at the gaping hole
in the ceiling through which Lenny had apparently
pulled Dickie Flynn's package of evidence. I looked
at the tape. It was such a little tape. How important
could it be? What more could we possibly need to
know about the dirty business that Ellen had involved

herself—and me—in? Could I even stand another revelation?

I closed my hand around the cassette and started walking, slowly at first, then faster, and the faster I walked the angrier I felt. Pretty soon I was fuming, cursing the name of everyone who had made my recent life such a hell on earth. As far as I was concerned, being sliced up by a propeller was too good a fate for Little Pete Dwyer. And Big Pete, he deserved to lose his son that way for being such a cold, arrogant prick. And goddamned Lenny, the sleazy bastard, I hoped he rotted in jail for everything he'd done and maybe some stuff he hadn't. Even the thought of Dan made me simmer, just the idea that he had almost gotten himself killed right in front of me. All I wanted was a hot shower, hot food, and cool sheets. Every last cell in my body was screaming for it. But no. I had to reach into my pocket and pull out the last detail. The world's biggest question mark. The mother of all loose ends. God damn Ellen, too, for making this mess to begin with, and for leaving it here for me to deal with. I stood in the doorway of my office and wondered why couldn't she just leave me alone.

Chapter Forty-four

The sun was coming up. It slanted through the venetian blinds in much the same way it had on the day I'd first walked into this office. The same bright ribbons of light lay across the old desk. Molly's answering machine sat atop the glass slab, in the center of the carved Nor'easter logo. The logo reminded me of what Molly had said that first day about why the desk had been hidden in Boston. "No one would ever look for anything good here," she'd said. I pressed the Play Message button and listened one more time to Ellen's final gift from beyond the grave. Molly was right. There was nothing good here.

I should go, I kept thinking. I should get up and take this tape to the proper authorities. But all I did was sit and stare and watch the sun come up. I couldn't seem to do much else.

The computer monitor flickered. Another report was up. I turned and looked, squinting at the bright screen to keep the characters from fuzzing together. When I saw what it said—same as the last one—the dull pain behind my right eye surged again, this time through the center of my skull. I pushed at it with the heel of my hand, but the throbbing wasn't going to stop unless my heart stopped beating. I punched Print Screen and slumped back in my chair.

"It's good to see you in one piece."

The voice, unmistakable, came from the doorway

behind me. I hadn't heard him come in, but that's how
Bill Scanlon always came into and out of my life—
without warning and on his terms. I swiveled around
to see him, too tired to be startled, too numb to have
felt his presence.

He leaned against the doorjamb with his leather
briefcase in one hand and that familiar blue cashmere
coat in the other. His suit hung perfectly from his lean
frame, a deep charcoal gray that brought out the fine
strains of silver in this thick black hair. Impeccable,
as always.

When I didn't answer, he stepped quietly into the
office and put his coat and briefcase on the floor and
closed the door. "Are you all right?"

I wasn't all right, might never be again. The look
on my face must have told him as much because he
started to come to me. More than anything I wanted
him to. I wanted to put my face against his chest and
feel the steady comfort of his breathing, to feel strong
arms against my back, keeping me from flying to
pieces. But before he could round the desk, I shook
my head and nodded toward the windows. Someone
might see. He stopped, but his eyes seemed to be asking, "Are you sure?" When I nodded again, he moved
to the chair across from mine and sat down. "Tell
me," he said, "I want every detail."

I couldn't find my voice. Instead, when he sat, I
stood. Rising from my chair, my spine creaked and
my muscles ached. Moving across the floor, I felt like
a bent old woman that had lived too long. I felt him
watching me as I stared out between the wide slats of
the blinds, and I knew that he would sit quietly and
wait for me, wait as long as I wanted.

The snow that had been so cruel last night was brilliant this morning. Lit by the early morning sun, it was
a glistening carpet that rolled from the far side of the
runways all the way down to the bay. Beneath my

window, rampers were filtering back to start the first shift, and the scene was beginning to look normal again. The only reminder of last night was the sweet, sticky odor that kept drifting up from the dried rum stains on my shirt. That and the answering machine on my desk.

"It would be easier if you tell me what you already know," I said finally, without turning around. If I didn't have to look into his eyes, I could function at least marginally.

"Actually, I already know quite a lot. I was on the phone all night from the airplane. I know that this Pete Dwyer person, the son, he killed a man, the one you were trying to meet with. Angelo, right?"

"Yes."

"Then he tried to kill you and Fallacaro. There was an altercation of some kind and he ended up hanging from a propeller. He's dead and you're a hero. Is that about the sum of it?"

It was hard to get the words out, hard to keep from crying. "Keep going."

I heard him stirring behind me, pictured him crossing his legs and leaning forward, elbows on the arms of the chair and hands clasped in front of him. He would be uncomfortable not asking all the questions, not directing the flow of the conversation. He didn't like not being in charge.

"Lenny is in custody," he went on, "for reasons I can't figure out. There seems to be some indication that you were right, that this Little Pete did kill Ellen, but there's still no evidence to prove it and we don't know why he would do such a thing. As it turns out, with him gone, we might never know."

The tears started to come, flowing down the tracks worn into my face from a night filled with crying. I put my head down and covered my eyes with my hand. When I heard him stand, my breath caught in my throat. When I heard him move toward me, I told myself to step aside, to move away, to get out of reach before it was too late. But I felt so exposed. I felt as if my very skin had been stripped away and that even the air hurt where it touched me. I needed comfort so badly, and I knew that if I didn't turn from him *right now,* I might never turn away. Still, I didn't move. Couldn't. But I said the one thing I knew would make him stop. "The police have the package." Then I closed my eyes and waited.

My computer hummed quietly on my desk. A shout came up from the ramp, a man's voice muffled by the heavy glass window. Bill said nothing. I wiped my eyes and turned to face him. "Lenny tried to destroy the evidence," I said. "He had it. He took it down to the ramp last night and tried to burn it in a trash barrel."

His face was perfectly calm, placid even. When I tried to swallow, the front of my throat stuck to the back and it was hard to keep going. But I did. "The storm was so bad that he couldn't get it to burn. One of my crew chiefs caught him."

The thought of John McTavish with his big hand around Lenny's wrist while his brother Terry pried the envelope loose gave me one tiny moment of satisfaction in an ocean of pain.

"They saved the evidence, Bill. The confession, the video—the police have it all."

There was the slightest hesitation before a smile spread across his face. "That's great," he said. "So there *was* a package. You were right about that, too." He probably would have fooled someone else. But I heard the forced enthusiasm, felt him straining under the veneer of graciousness. I knew with a certainty that was like a knife through my heart that the warm regard in his brown eyes, focused so intently on me right now, was false. He started moving casually away, tracing the edge of the desk with his index finger as he backed toward the window. "What was in this rescued package?"

"Don't make me tell you what you already know."

He smiled uncertainly. "I don't know what you mean."

I went to my credenza, where the schedules I had printed were lying in the tray. I lifted the first one out, laid it on the desk, and pushed it across the glass-top surface, a distance that seemed like miles. "That's your travel schedule for the past twelve months." He looked down and read it, then looked at me as if to say, "So what?"

I placed a second sheet next to the first, the list of Ellen's secret destinations, and tried to still the shuddering in my chest. "This is Ellen's. You were in the same city with her fifteen times out of a possible fifteen different occasions." I pulled the wrinkled page from my back pocket and smoothed it on the desk. Spots appeared like raindrops as my tears fell onto the page, bleeding into the paper, smearing the black ink as I read Ellen's note one more time.

. . . I feel myself going under again, and the only thing that keeps my head above water is the motion of reaching up for him. And I can't let go. Because when I'm with him, I exist. Without him, I'm afraid I'll disappear. Disappear to a place where God can't save me and I can't save myself.

I laid it on the desk in front of him. "She wrote that about you."

He never looked at the second schedule. He never looked at Ellen's note. He looked at me. He fixed his gaze on me and wouldn't let go. "What are you trying to say, Alex?"

"I don't have to say anything, Bill." I reached across the desk to the answering machine and started the tape.

The voices had the hollow, tinny quality of a cheap answering machine, but there was no mistaking Ellen's voice with that light Southern accent, still so unexpected to me. The tape was queued up right where I'd left it, at the point where Ellen was talking, her words tumbling out in a torrent of anguish and pain.

"Crescent Consulting. I know you remember this. We paid them hundreds of thousands of dollars. I signed the invoices. Crescent Con—"

"Crescent Consulting. I get it." Bill's voice was a stark contrast—calm, rational, a little irritated underneath the clicking and popping of the static. He must have been in his car. *"What about it?"*

"It was a sham. Nothing more than a bank account that Lenny used for kickbacks. You knew about this, Bill. You had to have known."

"Let's not talk about this right now. I'm on a cell phone."

"We're talking about this now." She sounded panicked, almost hysterical. *"Don't you dare hang up on me."*

"All right, all right. Why would you say something like that?"

"Because of the special signature authority. All that garbage about how much you trusted me. You set me up. The only reason you had me request a higher limit was so that you wouldn't have to sign those invoices. Every single invoice from Crescent you forwarded to me. Every one. You knew, Bill"—she was fighting back tears—*"and I can't believe you did this to me."*

Finally, she couldn't hold on anymore, and her voice dissolved into sobs, mighty, rolling sobs. As soon as one stopped, another one started, and I knew that they had come from someplace deep because when I had cried with her this morning the first time I'd heard this tape, the pain had come out of my whole body, through every part of me. It sounded like—felt like— a thousand years' worth of holding in.

When she'd cried herself out, there was silence, and then Bill's voice, gentle and soothing. *"I thought it was better if you didn't know."*

"Do you think anyone is going to believe that I didn't know?"

"Ellen, you didn't do anything wrong. I'm the one who screwed up, and I'll protect you."

"Tell me what you did. Tell me what you've gotten me involved in."

"Back when we were working on the Nor'easter deal, Lenny came to me with this idea that we wouldn't have to wait for the vote . . . that he had some way of buying off the IBG—"

"He didn't just buy the contract vote, Bill. He used the money to cover up this crash, this—the real cause of an aircraft accident, for God's sake. We gave him that money, Majestic did, you and me, and my name is all over—" She stopped as if she still couldn't believe the words that were coming out of her mouth. *"That Nor'easter Beechcraft that went down in 1995 . . . I've got this surveillance tape, this . . . these documents that Dickie Flynn had put away in the ceiling. It wasn't the pilots. It wasn't their fault. It was Little Pete Dwyer, and Dickie Flynn, and Lenny—"*

"Do you have this package?"

"It's right here in my hands, and I don't . . . I think I need to take it to someone. I can't—Oh, God, Bill, don't ask me—"

"No, you're right, we need to get it to the right people. Let me just think for a minute."

"Tell me . . . one thing," Ellen said, pleading. *"Tell me that you didn't know about this crash, that it was only this IBG contract business that you knew about."*

He didn't hesitate. *"I knew absolutely nothing about it. I swear to you. And if Lenny did what you're saying he did, I'll have his ass."*

"Thank God, Bill. Thank God."

"We have to take this package forward. All I'm going to ask is that you hold off for a day or so until I can get out there. I want to sit down with you. I want . . . it's important to me that I get a chance to explain it to you. I want you to understand. And I want you to help me figure out what to do, Ellen. We can get through this together."

There was no response.

"Ellen, listen to me. Don't think about what you're going to say to me next. Just listen. Are you listening?"

I was listening, and my knees felt weak, knowing what was coming next.

"I am in love with you, Ellen. I am hopelessly, desperately, pathetically in love with you, and I don't want to live my life without you in it. I'm not going to let anything happen to you, Ellen. Don't you know that?"

I turned off the tape.

My hands started to shake and tears streamed down my face. I had listened to that bit of tape over and over. There was nothing on that tape that I hadn't already heard. But listening to it with him, watching his face as he listened to himself deceiving Ellen, using the same line on her that he had used on me, was almost more than I could bear. Any expression, any reaction at all from him might have given me at least a seed of doubt, if that's what I'd wanted. But when he looked up at me, his face was stone. When he looked at me, I felt him measuring my resolve, wondering what it would take to get me to back down, and calculating his risk if I wouldn't. That was the moment when I knew that it was true—that it *could* be true. All of it.

"It was you," I said, backing away, taking one step, then another until I was up against the opposite wall, as far away from him as I could be in the cramped office. "You were Lenny's partner on the inside, not Ellen. You were the one who stole the money, and you used her to shield yourself, you bastard." The words came pouring out, searing the back of my throat and making my eyes burn. "You knew about the crash from the beginning. You knew that she would eventually figure it out, and you knew that she would take that evidence forward. You were the one who had Ellen killed, not Lenny. It was you."

His only reaction was to look down and touch Ellen's note, brushing his fingertips across her words, thinking, perhaps, that he could make them disappear. A tiny smile formed on his lips. "Ellen always did have a flair for the dramatic."

I felt my body begin to collapse in on itself, felt the four walls disappear and the world drop away until it was just the two of us standing in a barren wasteland, barren as far as I could see. And I knew that I was looking at the life that I'd made for myself, and when I looked again, I was alone, desperately alone.

He walked over to the window and stood with his hands deep in his pockets, rocking up and down on the balls of his feet. "That must have been some storm last night. It had mostly blown itself out by the time we landed."

I watched him, stared at the side of his face as he squinted into the bright sun.

"Have you seen the video?" he asked, in a tone that can only be described as jaunty.

"Last night," I whispered, leaning against the wall for support. "I saw it last night."

"I've never seen it. I imagine that it is quite extraordinary. I suppose I'll see it now. Everyone will, won't they?"

When he turned toward me, the light was coming from behind him and I couldn't see his face, but his manner was as smooth as ever and I knew that he was grinning. I could hear it in his voice. His tone wasn't flippant exactly, just light, and very, very confident.

It pissed me off.

"Why do you suppose she left it here that night?"

"Maybe she got smart and decided she didn't trust you after all."

"I have some ideas about that video," he said, "Would you like to hear them?"

"No." I pushed myself away from the wall and slowly made my way back to my desk. When I got there, I leaned over it, using both arms to support myself.

"What did you tell the authorities?" he asked quietly.

"I told them what I knew at the time."

"Which was what?"

"That on the night of March 15, 1995, Little Pete Dwyer worked Flight 1704 under the influence of alcohol, and his negligence caused that plane to go down. I told them that the incident had been recorded on a surveillance tape from beginning to end and that, as a part of a cover-up, Dickie Flynn, Big Pete Dwyer, and Lenny Caseaux stole that tape and altered official company documents. I told them that it was my belief that Dickie and another man, Angelo DiBiasi, were paid ten thousand dollars each to keep quiet about what they knew. I told them that Lenny Caseaux would have done anything to keep the sale of Nor'easter on track so that he could cash out his stock and become a rich man."

I stopped for a breath, but my lungs wouldn't fill. He was closer now and I could see his face, could almost see the wheels turning as he listened, sifting the facts, and pulling out what he needed.

"What else?"

"I told them that the money for these payoffs and others was embezzled from Majestic Airlines, that Lenny had an accomplice working inside, and that that person was Ellen Shepard."

I paused again as I remembered talking to the

troopers just hours ago, how sure I had been about
Ellen, how wrong I had been.

"She threatened Lenny with exposure," I said, my
voice fading, "and he had her killed. Little Pete killed
her." I sat down in my chair, suddenly exhausted.
"That's what I told them."

"This is why Lenny is in custody."

"Lenny is in custody because his name is all over
Dickie Flynn's package of evidence, along with both
Dwyers, Dickie himself, and Angelo." The late Angelo. Another pang of guilt. The thought of him lying
on that bag belt came back to me, and I knew that
he was dead, too, because of Bill, that Bill had tipped
Lenny off with information that I had given him, just
as he must have told him about John McTavish. I'd
told him enough that he'd figured out that John was
the source. I'd blamed Dan, but I had been the leak.

"Did they believe you?"

"Why wouldn't they? I was very convincing."

"I'm sure you were. Is that all you're going to tell
them?"

I plucked his travel schedule off the desk and held
it up. "Are you asking me if I am going to tell them
that it was not Lenny who arranged Ellen's murder?
That you were the one she was expecting the night
that she died? That you sent Little Pete in your place
to murder her?"

His neck stiffened. "I never even met this Little
Pete character."

"Of course not. That would be stupid, and we know
that you're not stupid." I dropped the page back on
the desk. "That's what Lenny was there for, to do all
the dirty work. You gave him your key to Ellen's
house. You gave him the security code, and you made
sure that Ellen would be home that night waiting for
you. Then you booked yourself on a flight to Europe
and waited for news that she was dead."

"It sounds rather elegant," he mused, "when you put it all together like that, clearly thought out."

"You're saying it wasn't?"

He regarded me with a wistful smile, looking disappointed that I might think ill of him. "Do you know how much the stock price has appreciated since I started running this airline? Three hundred and fifty percent. Three *hundred* and fifty percent, and it was the Nor'easter deal that put us over the top. That deal was the last missing piece, and do you want to know the irony?"

He slipped onto the corner of the desk and rested there, half standing, half sitting. He picked up a dish of paper clips and seemed to find it fascinating. "All this business here in Boston, none of it made any difference. Looking back, the Nor'easter deal was going to happen anyway. Lenny takes credit for the contract failing, but it's my bet the thing would have sunk under its own weight anyway. It was all for nothing." He took one of the clips out and studied it, turning it over in his hand.

He dropped the clip into the bowl, put the bowl on the desk, and went back to the window, where he stood with his arms crossed. "A strange thing happens when you operate for any length of time at this level and particularly if you achieve any measure of success, which I have. You start to feel that you can't do anything wrong, that whatever you do is right just because you want to do it." He turned slightly. "Silly, isn't it? And extravagantly arrogant. But you need to be to get where I am." He waited a beat, then came back to the desk and stood across from me. "I convinced myself that I was the only one who could save this company. And Nor'easter. At one time it wasn't clear that the contract would fail, and I thought it best not to risk it. What was a couple of hundred thousand dollars against all the jobs I saved? The tremendous wealth I created?"

"What about Ellen?"

He sniffed and with studied nonchalance glanced down and straightened the crease in his slacks. "You never plan for people to get hurt. That's one of the variables you can't predict. But things get . . . distorted. Once you're in, you're in. When a problem comes up, the only question that matters is, can you think your way around it? Are you smart enough?" He shrugged. "Ellen was a problem. She was going to be, anyway."

I stared at him. His tone was absolutely flat. We could have been analyzing a business deal gone bad.

"It's unfortunate," he said, "but Ellen was pulled into this whole affair by that drunken bastard Dickie Flynn, the self-serving son of a bitch." He looked at me and laughed as if he were relating a funny story that he was sure I would find amusing also. "Can you imagine saving that tape the way he did, then dumping it on poor Ellen? And Lenny, trying to cover up a damn plane crash with all those nitwits involved. The thing was flawed right from the beginning."

"You would have been smarter about it, no doubt."

"I never would have tried to cover up negligence. They told me after the fact, after it was too late, but in that situation you have to go public in a big way because there are too many people involved. And the risk if you're exposed is too great. You have to deal with it head-on, diffuse the risk, take away all the leverage. That's why this videocassette is so powerful for us. Do you see?"

"No."

"That video will be run over and over on every newscast, every news magazine, every cheap tabloid reality program. You can't buy that kind of exposure. So you ask yourself, how do you use that? You make an immediate disclosure, at which point you announce a very well-thought-out program of complete coopera-

tion with the authorities, comprehensive safety reviews, and enhanced operating procedures. You prove
to everyone that the people responsible have been
dealt with, sternly, and—this is very important—you
meet with the families of the victims face-to-face. In
fact, you'd like to do that before you go public. And
every time you open your mouth to talk about it, you
tie the *crash* to Nor'easter and the *response* to Majestic. Pretty soon all people will remember is Majestic's
great response." He smiled again. "Most people, Alex,
are waiting to be told what to think."

"You already have a plan."

"I always have a plan."

"And where am I in this plan?"

"Don't you know?" He looked at me with those
hotter-than-the-sun eyes beneath those long, lush eyelashes. Then he began to move around to my side of
the desk. I stood up, backed away, and kept going
until I felt the wall again against my shoulder blades.

"Don't I know what? That you are *hope*lessly, *des*-
perately, *pathe*tically in love with me?"

He seemed to be floating toward me, moving without walking, immune to the natural forces that teth-
ered the rest of us to this earth. I could have moved
away, but there was really no place to go. He was
going to keep coming until he'd had a chance to play
his final hand.

"I told you what I thought you needed to hear,
that's all. I should have told you the truth."

The smell of rum surrounded me like a seedy cloud,
but as he moved toward me, ever so slowly, his scent
was stronger.

"What is the truth?"

"We're good together. That's the only truth there
is, Alex, the only one that matters." He was very close
now, and I could feel his whisper as much as I could
hear it. "You wanted me the other night as much as

I wanted you, and nothing that's happened since has changed that. I want you right now. I want you so bad I can taste it. And you want me, too."

I needed to be angry, and I was. I needed to hate him, and I did. But I could also feel his breath in my hair. I could feel the heat through his clean cotton shirt, feel the flush beneath my own clothes. I could hear his breathing grow shallow, more ragged as he got closer.

"As far as the police are concerned," he said, "what you told them is exactly the way it happened. Lenny paid the kickbacks on the contract with money he and Ellen stole, he took even more money to cover up the crash, Ellen was so remorseful that she killed herself, and I'm the guy who can make the whole thing make sense. All you have to do is give me that little tape."

"What about Lenny? He knows everything."

"Lenny's not going to discuss his role or anyone else's in an alleged murder. There's still no proof that she didn't kill herself. Besides, he's going to need lawyers, and I can get him the best. Lenny will be all right. But to really make this work, I need you."

He leaned in closer, and now there wasn't much that separated us except for the smell of the rum. My back arched against just the idea of his hands on me, his long, graceful fingers touching me in ways that no one ever had before or since. No matter what else was happening, no matter what he had done or what I might do, there was something between us and it was never going away. And there was truth in that connection, if only in that its existence could not be denied. Maybe he was right. Maybe that was the only truth when you got right down to it, and maybe it was foolish to try to fight it. Maybe that's what Ellen had tried to say in her note, that life without that connection was no life at all.

I think of how my life would be without him, and the thought of letting go scares me to death.

He bent his head down as if to nuzzle my neck. He didn't touch me, but still I felt the rush of blood through my veins, a powerful surge fueled by a heart beating so wildly, it threatened to lift me off the floor. I tried to breathe, but when I did, I breathed him in. I closed my eyes, fighting for control, and tried to remember the rest of the passage, hoping for some kind of a message from Ellen, some kind of safety in her words.

When I think about life without him, she'd said . . . *my lungs fill up with something cold and heavy, and I feel myself going under and . . .* and what? *And the only thing that keeps my head above water is the motion of reaching up for him . . . without him I'll disappear to a place where God can't save me and I . . . can't . . . save . . . myself.*

I opened my eyes and scanned the room, searching for the note. I wanted to see it, to see that it was still there. It was on the desk where I'd left it. I can't save myself is what she'd said. "But she could."

"What?"

I hadn't even realized I'd said it out loud. "She could have saved herself."

When I looked at him, he was wearing that smile, the one that changed him, the one that changed me. "Ellen didn't need you, she didn't need Dan, and she didn't need God to save her. She could have saved herself. All she needed was to know that, and she wouldn't have disappeared. You couldn't have made her disappear if she'd known that, if she'd felt it. She couldn't feel it."

He stared down into my face and I stared back.

"But I do."

He took a step away and then another, and I watched him back off, fascinated by what I was seeing—finally seeing. It was a reverse metamorphosis. The smile disappeared, and then the charm, the

smooth self-confidence, the easy authority, all began
to fall away. He was like a butterfly wrapping himself
back into a cocoon, turning from awe-inspiring and
breathtaking to small and tight and ugly. Ugly but, I
knew, authentic.

By the time I'd completely exhaled, he was across
the room, around the desk, and sitting in my chair.
When he spoke again, even his voice sounded different. "You should give me the tape," he said, but with
no inflection, conserving energy, saving the charade
for some fool who would still buy it. He tapped the
answering machine with one finger. "There's nothing
on here to incriminate me beyond that silly contract
business, and I can make even that questionable. Why
put yourself through it?"

I was still catching my breath, but I was breathing.
I was taking in buckets of air, filling my lungs, feeling
the oxygen flowing through me. I felt lighter, almost
buoyant. I felt as if I could fly. "Put *myself* through
it?"

"I know you've thought about the consequences of
making accusations against me, "The Man Who Saved
the Airline Business." The hint of a smile appeared.
"Who's going to believe you, a lonely woman with no
life beyond her career who slept with the boss and
couldn't take it when she got dumped? And, of course,
one of the most effective defenses is to attack the
accuser—that would be you—and the victim, Ellen."
He was sitting up straight now, gears grinding, getting
into it. "Ellen had plenty of secrets, some you don't
even know about. My defense team will dig them up.
My PR team will get them out there. What about you,
Alex? Is there anything about you that you wouldn't
like to see in the left-hand column of the *Wall Street
Journal*? Because that's where this will all be played
out. My team is going to set upon you like a pack of
wild dogs. It won't be pleasant."

He looked at me expectantly, but I wasn't biting. I was too worn out and besides, there was nothing personal in this. He didn't really hate me, any more than he had loved me. The curveball I'd just thrown him was nothing more than a twist in the road, another detour, and he was having fun with it.

"The best opportunities come from disaster," I said.

"What?"

"That's what you told me once."

He smiled openly, genuinely. "That's right. That's exactly right. I think this just might qualify as a disaster. Certainly for you it does." He stood up, stretched, and meandered to the other side of the desk. "I'll have to resign, which is inconvenient. But there's always a demand for people like me. Hell"—he reached down for his coat and briefcase—"depending on how all this plays out, it might make me more marketable. It depends on how we spin it. Now that I think about it, you have more to lose than I do."

"You can't take anything else away from me, Bill."

"What about your job? I know you. You'd be lost without it. You love this business, this company—"

"No, I loved you. And I quit."

I'd said it so fast, I wasn't sure the words had actually come out, so I said it again slowly this time and tried to feel it. "I quit, Bill. I resign, effective immediately." It felt good. It felt right.

He stared at me as I rounded the desk and reclaimed my seat, the one he'd just vacated. It was still warm. I flipped open the trapdoor on the answering machine and made sure the tape was still in there. He laughed. "You thought I took it? Where's the challenge in that?"

"Just checking," I said.

He put one arm through his coat, then the other, then paused to straighten his tie as if he were about to go onstage. Maybe he was. To him, all the world was his stage. "So you'll be available to come and work for me again. That's nice to know. It's tough to find good people."

"No one's going to work for you. You're going to go to jail."

"I'm not going to jail. When you're dealing with the legal system, the smartest one wins. I'm smarter than they are, and I still think there's a possibility you won't turn in that tape. I'm not counting on it, of course, I'm just working the probability into the equation. I'm liking my chances better and better."

"I don't think you're getting out of this one, Bill. I don't care how smart you are, or how good your lawyers are. But if by chance you do, it won't be because of me."

He turned to go, opened the door and stopped. "It's good to hear you say that you loved me. I'm not sure that you ever did."

"Love you?"

"No, say it." He smiled. "I know that you loved me."

I leaned back in my chair and watched him walk away, through the reception area and out the door. Then I listened to his footsteps as he made his way down the corridor. Ellen's note was still on the desk. I pulled it in front of me and read it again.

. . . *I think about my life before him, about the work that filled my days and the ghosts that walked the night with me, and I feel myself going under and the only thing that keeps my head above water is the motion of reaching up for him. And I can't let go.*

You should have let go, Ellen. I wish you had let go.

I put the note in one pocket and the tape in the other. Bill was wrong about me in one respect. I was going to turn this tape in. But he was right about me, too, as he had been so many times before. I had loved him.

But I had also let go.

If you enjoyed Lynne Heitman's HARD LAND-ING, get ready for another thrilling read! DARK SIDE OF DAWN established Merline Lovelace as a premier author of romantic suspense, heightening anticipation for her next book, AFTER MIDNIGHT. Don't miss it!

Lieutenant Colonel Jessica Blackwell never imagined she would return to Valparaiso, Florida, the town her mother fled from in disgrace when Jess was a girl. But given the biggest opportunity of her career, Jessica decides she can put the past behind her. When Sheriff Steve Morgan shows up on her doorstep in the middle of the night, however, and starts asking hard questions, she realizes that the past has a way of catching up—with a vengeance.

Enjoy this special preview of
After Midnight—
a Signet paperback coming in Fall 2001.

Nothing good ever came out of the night.

Jessica Blackwell had accepted that grim truth long ago. As a consequence, she'd learned to function at peak performance on three or four hours of sleep snatched at random times in odd places. She'd also learned the danger of opening her door to strangers after midnight, even when they flashed a badge. Particularly when they flashed a badge.

Eyes cold, palms suddenly damp, Jess stared at the nickel-plated star nestled in its black leather case.

"Lieutenant Colonel Blackwell?"

She wrenched her gaze from the shield to the man behind it.

He topped her by five or six inches, which didn't happen often. At five eight, Jess usually looked most men in the eye. Tipping her chin, she forced herself to return his casually assessing gaze.

"Yes."

"I'm Steve Paxton, Walton County Sheriff. I'd like to talk to you."

Common sense made her cautious. Experience made her wary. "What about?"

"An incident that happened a few hours ago. Mind if I come in?"

The outer door muffled his north Florida drawl, but the politely disguised demand came through with cold clarity. Whispers of another night, another such demand crawled along Jess's nerves.

Her every instinct screamed at her to slam the inside door and shut out the darkness. Shut out the rustle of the breeze combing through the palmettos. Shut out this unfamiliar, unwanted figure in worn jeans, a white shirt, and a black baseball cap.

The discipline gained with sixteen years as an officer in the United States Air Force stood Jess in good stead. Her hand didn't so much as tremble when she reached out and unlocked the storm door. Metal hinges that had already fallen victim to the rust caused by humid August days and muggy nights creaked as they opened.

"Sorry to bother you so late."

The cap came off, revealing tawny, sun-streaked hair. Dispassionately, Jess took note of broad shoulders, a square chin, a nose flattened at the bridge, as though it had connected with a fist or two in the past. His skin was dark oak, and his eyes a clear, startling aquamarine, as stunning as the vast, changeable bay only a few dozen yards from her front door. Jess supposed most women would consider the man sexy as hell. She might have, too, if he weren't the sheriff of Walton County.

"This could have waited until tomorrow," he said with an apologetic smile, "but I saw your lights on and decided to stop. Hope I didn't disturb you?"

"No, I was just unpacking a few boxes."

His glance roamed the front room of her rented condo. Stacked cartons took up one whole wall. Wrapping material littered the parquet floors.

"Looks like you still have a ways to go."

"Yes, I do."

Ordinarily, she would have had her home in order by now.

With seven moves in sixteen years, Jess had mastered the fine art of organizing her nest within a few days of reporting to a new assignment. This move was different. She'd arrived at Eglin, the sprawling base that ate up a good chunk of the Florida panhandle, almost three weeks ago and had yet to get her things sorted out. A good part of that she could blame on her new job. With only a few weeks' notice, she'd packed up, driven across the country from California, and taken the helm of the largest supply squadron in the Air Force. The fact that her predecessor had been relieved of command and charged with criminal neglect following a massive fuel spill that had blackened almost a hundred miles of Florida coast had certainly added tension to the move.

The challenges of her new command thrilled Jess and consumed her daylight hours. It was the long stretches between dusk and dawn that took their toll. The tightly closed plantation shutters gracing the windows kept the night outside where it belonged, but Jess had slept even less than usual since moving into this airy, spacious condo overlooking Choctawahatchee Bay.

Folding her arms across a faded orange T-shirt proclaiming the Fifth Annual Lompoc Run for the Cure, Jess gave him a look of polite inquiry. "What can I do for you, Sheriff?"

"I need to know if you called or received a call from Don Clark earlier this evening."

"The realtor who leased me this condo? No, I didn't. Why?"

"Don's wife found him dead a few hours ago."

Jess didn't blink, didn't move so much as a muscle. Her racing mind had conjured up a dozen possible reasons behind the sheriff's visit, but death wasn't one of them. It came like a punch to the gut.

"How did he die?" she asked, keeping her voice carefully neutral.

"We'll have to wait for the ME to make the official determination, but it looks like an apparent suicide. He hooked a garden hose to his Buick's exhaust pipe and sucked gas."

"And his wife found him?"

"Yes."

Jess wouldn't wish that brutal shock on anyone. "How awful for her," she murmured, "but I don't understand why you would think I talked to her husband earlier this evening. Or what difference it would make if I had."

"Well, it's like this." Paxton toyed with the baseball cap, circling it around and around in his big hands. "Carolyn Clark said Don developed a bad case of the jitters these past few weeks. Acted real nervous. At times seemed almost depressed. He wouldn't tell his wife what was bothering him. She thought it might have had something to do with the business."

Jess lifted her shoulders. "I don't know anything about his business. Or about Don Clark, for that matter."

"My information is that he found you this place."

"He did. When I found out I was coming to Eglin, I got the E-mail address of his realty office from an ad he'd placed in the *Air Force Times.*"

"When was that?"

"A little over a month ago. Clark E-mailed me pictures of various properties, including this condo. He sent me the lease, which I printed out, signed, and sent back to him."

Paxton nodded, but his glance had dropped to her hands. Jess realized she was rubbing an old burn on her thumb and index finger. Hunching her shoulders, she slid her palms into the front pockets of her cutoffs.

The sheriff brought his gaze back to hers with a leisurely sweep that took in her bare legs, braless state, and total lack of anything approaching makeup. Jess couldn't decide if the glint in those unnerving, incredible eyes belonged to the man, the cop, or both.

"So you never spoke to Don Clark personally?"

"I stopped by his office to pick up the keys when I drove into town. He had them waiting. We went over the terms of the lease, and I left. That's the one and only time I've ever had a conversation with the man. Now suppose you answer my question, Sheriff. Why did you ask if I'd called or received a call from Clark?"

"Because Carolyn heard her husband say your name on the phone."

Jess's skin prickled. "My name?"

"Your name, Ms. Blackwell."

He rolled the *Mz.* out Southern style, slow, courteous, but Jess's heart was pounding too hard and too fast to appreciate the local flavoring.

"A little over an hour later, she found her husband slumped over the steering wheel of his Buick."

Five seconds ticked by, ten. Jess's nerves were screaming when the sheriff broke the small silence.

"As far as we know, your name was the last thing Don Clark said before he killed himself. You have any idea why, Ms. Blackwell?"

"No." She looked him square in the eye. "Do you?"